150 Pounds

ALSO BY KATE ROCKLAND

Falling Is Like This

150 Pounds

Kate Rockland

THOMAS DUNNE BOOKS   ST. MARTIN'S PRESS

NEW YORK

This book is dedicated to my husband, Joe,
who loves me at any weight.

————————————

THOMAS DUNNE BOOKS.
An imprint of St. Martin's Press.

150 POUNDS. Copyright © 2011 by Kate Rockland. All rights reserved. Printed in the United States of America. For information, address St. Martin's Press, 175 Fifth Avenue, New York, N.Y. 10010.

www.thomasdunnebooks.com
www.stmartins.com

Library of Congress Cataloging-in-Publication Data

Rockland, Kate.
    150 pounds / Kate Rockland. — 1st ed.
        p. cm.
    "Thomas Dunne books"
    ISBN 978-0-312-57601-1 (hardcover)
    1. Chick lit.   I. Title.   II. Title: One hundred fifty pounds.
    PS3618.O35446A615 2012
    813'.6—dc23

                                                    2011033819

First Edition: January 2012

10 9 8 7 6 5 4 3 2 1

Shoshana and Alexis

December

CHICAGO

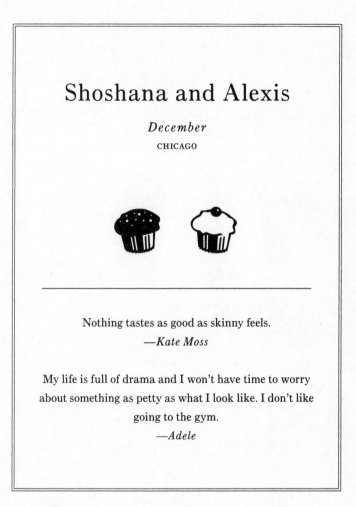

Nothing tastes as good as skinny feels.
—*Kate Moss*

My life is full of drama and I won't have time to worry about something as petty as what I look like. I don't like going to the gym.
—*Adele*

IN PERSON, OPRAH HAD THE CLEAREST SKIN SHOSHANA had ever seen. Her eyes were a dark liquid brown (the same shade as her own!) and her smile was a flash of diamonds. She analyzed Oprah's body unknowingly; thinking about the female form was what she did for a living. Shoshana was astounded at the recent tabloid headlines that called Oprah "fat" and "hefty." The reality was she was at least four dress sizes smaller than Shoshana, and looked more like a curvaceous aunt who wanted to hold everyone to her bosom than someone with a serious weight problem. *Fucking media,* she thought.

Sitting backstage in *The Oprah Winfrey Show*'s green room on the West Side of Chicago, sipping a paper cup full of mint tea, Shoshana let out a deep sigh. It was a cliché to state that Hollywood, and by extension American culture, was shallow and held ridiculous standards for female beauty, but as she watched the American icon on the monitor, five minutes away from being on national television, the truth hit home.

She looked down at her own body and imagined her stats being shouted into the microphone at a boxing match: *And in this corner, weighing in at two hundred and fifteen pounds, standing five-foot-seven, with bouncy, achy, size-EE breasts . . . Shoshana Weiner!* And the crowd goes wild.

She ran a trembling hand over her midsection, smoothing down the cute purple polka-dot dress she had paired with silver leggings and the purple headband with a sparkly sequin bow (a splurge at J. Crew!). She was a sucker for any accessory and loved loud, wild patterns. (She liked to think her personality was so outrageous, the rest of her might as well match.)

Her own touch calmed her quaking nerves. Her body was solid, strong. She was proud of her large breasts, small waist, and curvy butt. All of the walking she'd been doing lately was giving her toned calves. She was willing to bet that was one place people never looked: her calves. They were too busy checking out her gigantic boobs, probably. Her "Twins of Doom," as she referred to them on her blog.

Shoshana was nervous about being on television, her round face shown to millions of people. She threw back a sip of the tea like a tequila shot.

"First time on TV?"

A middle-aged, tall, and slender black man approached her holding a clipboard and wearing headphones. He'd had his eyebrows waxed, and smiled with the whitest teeth Shoshana had ever seen. He had three squiggly waves shaved into the left side of his head. His expression was kind, and she wondered if he was sent in to relax her, like the opening act in a comedy show. There were only three guests today, including her. The first was Kirstie Alley, who was seated on Oprah's yellow couch in a plum-colored long dress, one leg crossed over the other. The theme of today's show was women and their views on weight; Kirstie was laughing, her bleached-blond head of hair thrown back, wide pink lipsticked mouth open as she told a funny story about dating younger men in their twenties.

A smooth voice tickled her ear: "This might feel cold," the stagehand told Shoshana in a gentle voice, his hands comfortably slipping down the back of her dress, attaching some kind of black box with a wire to her thick waist.

"Just remember, talk regularly when you're up there; this baby mike will make you sound perfectly clear to the audience." He sounded affectionate about his microphone, as if he were proud of what it could accomplish. Shoshana appreciated people who took pleasure in their jobs, who felt pride in their work. In Hoboken, New Jersey, where she lived, she liked talking to the garbage man who picked up the trash on her street and learning from him the different fabulous items people threw away. Once, he told her, he'd found an engagement ring that fell out of a Raisin Bran cereal box.

"Oh . . . okay. Thank you." She pushed some thick flyaway locks of hair out of her eyes and set down her tea on a nearby high table. It was whisked away a second later by another stagehand, this one blond and petite. It was as if the woman had been trained to anticipate Shoshana's every move.

"Don't be nervous, honey. A lot of our guests whisper their secrets to Oprah," the male stagehand said, his dark eyes twinkling. He squeezed her arm and she smiled at him. Hey! It was working. He was definitely making her feel calmer. *Palm tree waving in the wind on a tropical island, palm tree waving in the wind on a tropical island.* Her sister Emily had suggested earlier at lunch that she project a calm image behind her eyelids when she felt nervous.

Suddenly her phone rang. The sounds of Lucinda Williams's "Are You Alright?" filled the room, causing the other guest to stare at her. The call was from Shoshana's mother, and she'd programmed her phone with this ring because her mother was always calling Shoshana and asking if she was all right.

"Mom!" she hissed. "What are you doing calling me *now*? I'm about to go on."

"Honey, I know that. That's why Em and I are calling. We snuck into the bathroom when Kirstie went on stage. She's looking good, isn't she? The woman is over sixty, you know."

"I thought she looked just as pretty when she was a chunker."

She heard a little chuckle come from the stagehand, but he quickly covered his mouth to hide it.

"Are people allowed to talk on the phone in here? Isn't there some rule against it?" The other guest was standing nearby, with her arms crossed against her bird-thin chest. Shoshana saw the stagehand offer her a chocolate-chip cookie from the goodies on the table. The woman declined it by shaking her head so hard Shoshana feared it might slip right off her neck.

"Mom, I have to go. Just have that bottle of scotch ready for when I totally make an ass out of myself."

"Shoshana Jane Weiner! That is why your sister and I called you. We wanted to let you know what a talented, beautiful, and smart woman you are. You're going to knock their socks off out there. Just remember how many girls at home are watching and looking up to you. This one's for the Fatties."

Her mother always knew how to make her feel better.

"I love you, sis!" her sister yelled in the background. "Knock 'em dead!" Emily worked in a tattoo shop on the Lower East Side, had pink-and-black-striped hair, and (at last count) thirteen pierced holes in her body. She'd even had her belly button done, which impressed Shoshana to no end because Emily was a big girl like herself and didn't exactly have washboard abs. Emily was also her best friend and lifelong confidante.

Shoshana had never told her this, but Emily was the reason she'd started the *Fat and Fabulous* blog. At 315 pounds, she'd had shit shoveled at her by people her entire life. Elementary school, high school, neighbors, cousins . . . everyone seemed to think they were the first one to mention that maybe, they didn't mean to pry, just worried about her health, of course, don't take this the wrong way . . . but did Emily know she could stand to lose a couple of pounds? Sure, Emily was tough as nails and as a child would beat the living daylights out of anyone who teased her about her weight, but Shoshana couldn't help feeling overprotective of her. Kids could be so mean. Shoshana remembered Emily being poked with a pencil in the third grade by Steven Myers, because, he said, "She probably can't feel it." Emily subsequently was suspended for two weeks, after breaking the pencil in half and stabbing Steven in the arm with it. (It had left a scar, which he still showed them. It was ironic because Emily would later date him briefly in high school, and soon grow bored and dump him.)

Shoshana watched her younger sister try every diet under the moon and stars. At one point she'd gotten down to 125 pounds, but it was the toxic result from a liquid diet that caused her to faint at work and have bright blue, Avatar-like poop. Then there was Atkins, which called for drinking straight whiskey, to avoid the calories in beer. After one particular night of too much fun in a West Village cowgirl bar, Shoshana rode with her sister to the emergency room to have her stomach pumped. In the end, the result was always the same: Emily put the weight back on, then hit a downward spiral of depression as a result of the shame and guilt.

This finally led Shoshana to start *Fat and Fabulous,* a blog that began as a simple battle cry and went on to pick up millions of loyal readers. Its popularity was the reason she was here today—Oprah's producer had called two weeks ago to ask Shoshana to speak about the experiences she'd faced as a larger woman, as well as what her readers had gone through. Shoshana called her fans "Fatties," affectionately, of course.

Her mother, Pam, had also been on yo-yo diets her entire life, starting in her teens when her bell-bottoms began getting more and more snug. She was the heaviest now since Shoshana's father died several years ago, and she was a compulsive overeater. Today, her weight hovered close to three hundred pounds. Because Shoshana was always the smallest Weiner girl, her mother and sister tried to protect her from becoming large. She'd still been skinny up until she hit puberty at fourteen; Pam and Emily would dive at her if she opened the freezer on a quest for Häagen-Dazs, emitting that sloweddown, Hollywood freeze-frame "Nooooooooo . . ." when she'd select ice cream from the freezer.

Pam felt her own fat reflected poorly on who she was as a person—that she was weak somehow. Shoshana remembered one frigidly cold day last winter when her mother discovered she'd gained too much weight to fit into her winter jacket; and yet she refused to buy a new one. Shoshana and Emily had tried everything in their power to get her a new coat, even getting her a gift certificate from Bloomingdale's for Hanukkah. Only Pam used the money to buy matching purses for her daughters.

They brought home catalogs from the few plus-size stores that existed. "So let me get this straight. You are going to freeze instead of buy a larger coat?" Shoshana had asked her mother, who only shook her head, the glitter of tears in her eyes. "Pick out something for yourself, girls. I don't deserve to buy any new clothing until I lose this weight." It was such a vicious cycle, because she never would lose it, and instead went around town with an open jacket, freezing. It broke Shoshana's heart. She knitted Pam four scarves last winter, trying to keep her warm.

After starting *Fat and Fabulous*, Shoshana grew closer to her mother and sister than ever before—it was like she'd given them permission to open up about being big. She wrote a memorable post about the coat aversion and received hundreds of positive e-mails from her readers. One posted a similar story on the comments page; she'd felt too humiliated about being heavy to buy maternity clothing when she was pregnant. "I thought obese women didn't deserve to wear them. I'm already fat, and being pregnant didn't allow me to feel that glow that other expecting mothers do. Besides, you could barely tell I was pregnant anyway, because of my weight problem."

Shoshana *ached* for this reader—unable to celebrate one of life's greatest moments with fun, feminine maternity clothes. It was what kept Shoshana going, women just like her sister, like her mother. They deserved to love themselves. They deserved to have people not look at them like criminals because they were big. They might be Fatties, like her, but they were also Fabulous!

Shoshana stole a quick glance at the other guest; her blond head was bent as she pored over carefully typed notes. Shoshana sighed. She'd planned on just winging it.

"Three minutes!" the stagehand said, holding up three fingers and muttering quickly into his headpiece.

Shoshana squared her broad shoulders. Lifted her chin. Opened her purse and ran a swipe of pink gloss over her lips for the thousandth time. She was sure she single-handedly kept the lip-gloss economy running. Buying a small, sparkly tube or a lovely round glass jar with beautiful packaging was a cure-all to any bad day. Some people did drugs. She had a twenty-bucks-a-week pucker-spoiling habit, which she figured was better than a heroin addiction. Or gambling. Or even smoking cigarettes.

"One minute."

For luck, she stuffed into her mouth a Hershey's Kiss, which had been sitting in her pocket since she'd left the hotel, and ignored the glares she received for this small act from the other guest. A woman should have a piece of chocolate every day. It made life so much *richer*. Besides, doctors say it's good for your heart. At least the dark chocolate kind. But she'd just had milk chocolate. Oh, what the hell. Shoshana figured one day they'd come out with a study saying *every* kind of chocolate was good for you. She might as well not pass it up now, just in case.

"All right girls, it's time!" The female stagehand smiled at both women. "You'll both be wonderful!"

"Thank you!" Shoshana said. She wasn't sure why she was whispering like she was in temple. Oprah gave off a bit of a holy aura, perhaps. "I'm nervous!" she admitted to the other guest, who, not responding, set down her notes and brushed past, knocking into Shoshana slightly in her determined walk. Shoshana frowned, following her. She'd read the girl's blog and knew her subject matter to be slightly militant in its message, but she didn't know she would be the same way in person . . . *Palm tree waving in the wind on a tropical island, palm tree waving in the wind on a tropical island.*

The sound of the woman's stilettos echoed in the hallway. Shoshana sometimes wore heels, but only on special occasions. Like . . . that time her landlady died and she went to her funeral. Six years ago. Okay, so maybe she really didn't ever wear heels. But why did she need two plastic contraptions on her feet, designed to make her already-aching back hurt even more and push her Twins of Doom forward until she toppled head over heels? With her tiny, size-five feet, wearing heels would be like foot binding.

When she heard her name called, she immediately stood still, unable to walk another foot. She was frozen to the spot, the high-decibel sound of two hundred women clapping at once washing over her, a shower of noise. Since she'd started her blog five years ago after graduating from college, she'd never imagined it would take her to this moment. It had been just for fun, a lark, while she looked for her first job. Then it *became* her first job. Her only job.

"Oh, my god, are you having a panic attack or something? Maybe a sugar rush from all that saturated fat you consumed in the green room? Let's *go*."

Shoshana realized the skinny girl was screaming at her, which broke her daze. "Oh, don't get your size-zero panties in a bunch," she shot back, rolling her eyes and strutting past her, entering the soundstage first. She hadn't gotten this far in life to be bullied by the prom queen. The prom queen could go fuck herself.

The floor was marked with taped arrows, and Shoshana followed them, the soft fabric of her dress swishing between her thighs. And—oh, my goodness! Suddenly there was Oprah, like a mirage in the desert. She prayed to the no-trip gods as she climbed several steps onto the stage and took a seat on a yellow couch next to Oprah's brown leather chair. Shoshana immediately reached for the mug of water on the table in front of her. It was pure instinct; if there was food or beverage of any kind in her peripheral vision, she'd make a beeline for it. Having something to consume always felt soothing.

While bending toward the beverage Shoshana remembered millions of women were watching her at home, and she'd just given them a shot of her ample bosom. *Great.* She made a mental note to keep the girls in check, and fought the urge to apply more gloss. The tube was tucked into the right cup of her bra, along with the Hershey's Kiss wrapper.

"Please welcome to the show Shoshana Weiner and Alexis Allbright."

Tentative clapping now. The audience wasn't sure yet how it felt about its guests. A sea of faces, mostly female. Some black, white, shades of brown. They wore red sweaters, shiny white pearls, and print dresses. They crossed their legs and folded their hands, pleased to not be waiting outside in the cold anymore. Some fiddled with jewelry. Others placed their pocketbooks beneath their seats and whispered excitedly to their friends and sisters seated nearby.

Oprah shifted her body toward one of the three cameras. Shoshana, having no clue which one to look at, stared at Oprah. She was mesmerizing. She seemed to sparkle everywhere, from her light blue eye shadow down to her expensive-looking peep-toe pumps. She looked like someone's fairy godmother.

Oprah started her opening monologue: "Alexis and Shoshana have the two most popular blogs on the Web today that cover women's weight issues. Next to my own, of course."

A light scattering of laughter.

"With millions of hits a day, and a slew of advertisers and press hanging on their every post, these rising stars are two young women to watch. As Americans continue to obsess over celebrities and their ever-changing bodies, and contradictory studies seem to emerge daily from scientists debating health concerns in regards to weight, I thought we could have an open and real discussion about how women feel about their bodies today, as Alexis and Shoshana have completely opposite viewpoints. All I ask of my audience is that you listen to both sides before drawing any conclusions. I have to admit to you, you know my history and relationship with weight has been *well* documented by this show *and* the paparazzi, whether I like it or not . . ."

Strong laughter.

"So for someone like me, whose weight has gone up and down, this issue hits particularly close to home. I am not going to lie, this is a very sensitive show for me."

Shoshana nodded her head. She hoped she looked encouraging. Her co-guest scanned the audience, making a visual connection with each member. Oprah turned toward Shoshana then, and it was like the sun shining on the side of her face, her smile was *that* warm.

"We'll start with Shoshana. Now, is it true you refused a high-paying speaking engagement at a boutique in Manhattan because the store did not carry over a size ten? My producers tell me that story got picked up by many different newspapers across the country and a podcast as well."

Deep breath. "Yes, that's true, Oprah. I don't mean any ill will toward the store, which actually had lovely clothes, but I asked them why they wanted me to speak about my blog to their customers if they didn't carry my dress size."

"I see. Well, that's certainly understandable. Have you been asked to talk elsewhere since?"

"No, but if you know anyone who needs a motivational speaker, I could really use the money."

The audience laughed. "You go, girl," someone called out. Oprah changed the direction of the conversation.

"And how do you feel about blogs about women's weight being called the 'Fat-O-Sphere'?" Her melodic voice floated through the room, caressing the cheeks of her audience, relaxing her guests, except for Alexis, who looked like a cobra poised for the strike. Shoshana noticed her hair was so perfectly sleek it looked like a blond helmet. Shoshana's long mane looked better when she didn't brush it, thicker and more voluminous.

Shoshana decided to match Alexis's body language, leaning toward Oprah and crossing her legs at the ankles. She wanted to be taken seriously.

"Oprah, first of all let me say thank you so much for having me on your show. Today's show is not only about weight, but also about women's feelings, which matter more to me than anything else in the world."

She got some applause then, which encouraged her. Her voice grew stronger.

"The Fat-O-Sphere is a title journalists, including myself, have given to a group of blogs that have exploded over the Internet in the last five years. They grew out of a worldwide frustration at the way women's bodies are viewed as objects to be criticized in the mass media. We are taking back the word 'fat,' if you will."

"So you've got this blog, and you call it *Fat and Fabulous*?" Oprah asked. "Does that mean that you condone unhealthy eating habits?"

"I'm so glad you asked that. Not at all. I have a new columnist, Dr. Amanda Weber, who is a nutritionist with Columbia Hospital, and she posts once a week with healthy, yummy recipes that are great sources of nutrients and vitamins and calcium for women of all sizes." She spread her hands, gesturing to make her point. Her mother, Pam, always joked Shoshana had inherited this trait from an Italian grandmother on her father's side. "Now, when I say 'fat,' what I really mean is healthy at any size, which is my motto."

She glanced quickly at her mother and sister in the front row, who were nodding their heads. Emily gave her a fist pump.

"And what about this campaign to ban Girl Scout cookies by Ms. Allbright here?" Oprah asked, shifting gears now to include Alexis.

Shocked inhalation from the audience.

Shoshana shook her head. "I feel the most sad about this, because as a child, being in the Girl Scouts was such an empowering experience. It was girl power! Selling cookies gives the sense of entrepreneurship and business skills at a very young age."

"I'm going to let Alexis respond, too," Oprah said. "Let's open the floor to Alexis Allbright, a writer living in New York City, who runs *Skinny Chick*, a blog about her life in New York and her dietary habits."

Alexis's blue eyes gleamed. Unlike Shoshana, she lived for debate. Her parents had fought her entire life, her father was a trial lawyer, and she had once thought she wanted to be a lawyer herself.

"Oprah, let me first echo Shoshana's words that I am also grateful to be on your show. I've watched it since I was a little girl, and I think both Shoshana and I can agree that you have done wonders for women's self-esteem. Now let's start out with the facts. Thirty to forty percent of today's children are projected to develop diet-related diabetes in their lifetimes, and the National Action Against Obesity called once again this year for a boycott of Girl Scout cookies. My question for Shoshana is, if you think the Girl Scouts should be allowed to continue to sell items to neighbors for 'self-esteem,' why don't they use a healthy product, like vitamins, energy bars, or protein powder? Why does it have to be cookies, which are filled with fat, artificial flavoring, and empty calories?"

Shoshana smiled. This was an easy one. A softball. "I think children are supposed to eat cookies, first of all. It's almost like a right of passage. Cookies are delicious. Protein powder is not." She leaned back on the couch and reached for her mug, taking a hurried sip of water. She felt satisfied she'd given just the right answer. *Score one for the Fatties,* she thought.

The audience burst into laughter, some women on the right back section standing up and clapping. The cameraman panned across the front row, where many people were nodding enthusiastically. For Shoshana, the room began to take on a soft glow.

"I'd like to introduce a message I came up with myself, which I've titled 'secondhand obesity,'" Alexis said a little too loudly, to try and wrest the attention back to herself. She tipped her head, and her stylish, straw-blond hair swished along her jawline. She wore a sleek black suit jacket with matching pencil skirt. Her blouse was gray silk, and very low-cut, exposing a bony chest. She had small earlobes with tiny gold Celtic knot earrings that endeared her to Shoshana somehow.

"Please tell us what that is," Oprah said. "It sounds horrible!" Her tone was jocular, but Alexis nodded vigorously, ignoring the laughter of the audience.

"It *is* horrible!" she said. "If you're overweight you are already very sick. Gravely sick. Ask any doctor and they'll say you are putting yourself at risk for heart disease and death. Shoshana is spreading a dangerous message."

At that, Oprah shook her head slightly. Alexis realized she'd gone overboard and quickly backtracked and tried less dramatic wording.

"Secondhand obesity is a fat lifestyle and fat body passed down from parent to child. Fat parents make fat children; it's as simple as that. If your father hands you a lollipop, or, as I like to call them, death sticks . . ."

Shoshana snorted, and then covered her mouth with her hand to stop the rude noise. Alexis pretended she hadn't heard.

". . . to calm you down after a fall on the sidewalk, that's secondhand obesity. If dinner at your house consists of macaroni and cheese and chocolate pudding and cornbread and stuffing, then you'll give the same dangerous foods to your own children when you become a parent. It's a terrible cycle, and with my blog, *Skinny Chick,* and that's a trademarked name, people, I'm trying to help Americans make healthy eating choices."

Silence in the studio. The mechanical sounds of cameras lifting into the air, turning on their axes.

"I have to admit, I really love macaroni and cheese," Shoshana began. "Oh, my god, on a cold winter night, your roommates are out, you climb onto the couch and put on a chick flick, preferably one with Matthew McConaughey shirtless, pour a glass of wine, and dig into a bowl of creamy mac 'n' cheese . . . That's my version of heaven, and I can't imagine denying myself a pleasure like that."

Oprah laughed along with her audience. "Girl, I can't tell you how many times I've done that, too," she said. She turned to Alexis. "Is that really so bad, to enjoy macaroni and cheese? My trainer says everything is fine in moderation."

"I do admit to eating it in college like the next girl, but the average box of macaroni and cheese is chock-full of preservatives, dehydrated cheese powder, and dyes. Look, my blog is not just about looking great in a bikini, although I certainly give you a ton of advice from trainers and chefs for that! Accepting yourself mentally as obese might help your self-esteem, but I can assure you it will not help your chance of living into a ripe old age. I know my message isn't as soft or cuddly as *Fat and Fabulous,* but I am very concerned with the things I heard Shoshana say today, and I'd like to show a slideshow I videotaped while walking down Sixth Avenue in Manhattan yesterday afternoon."

"Sure, queue the videotape, Bryan," Oprah said to a stagehand just to Shoshana's left.

A hush fell over the audience and stage as the same screen that had been previously displaying pictures of Kirstie's weight changes over the years now lit up behind Oprah. Images flashed on the screen of heavy people walking around Manhattan, shot from the neck down, their flabby arms waving down cabs, underwear lines showing through their sausage-tight stretch pants, holding the hands of their chubby youngsters. Shoshana felt her heart constrict. Any of these women in the video could have been her, going about her daily routine. She hated these Fattie videos constantly shown on the news to depict the American fat problem as an epidemic comparable to the plague. Come on! Anyone looks like crap when they're headless.

She also felt angry that these people had been violated, but from the expressions on everyone's faces in the audience it was clear they felt quite the opposite. Americans are drastically overweight as a whole, and there was a lot of truth in what Alexis was saying. Action had to be taken. As the images continued to light up the stage, the audience grew rapt. Probably the millions watching on their couches at home, too. Shoshana imagined a stay-at-home mother in Kansas City reaching inside a Fritos bag, her hand suddenly freezing before the chip made its way to her guilty mouth. She looked over at Oprah, who was watching the video carefully, her face the epitome of openness, not showing where her opinion lay but everything about the firm set of her mouth proclaiming: *I am presenting both sides! I am avidly listening to both of my guests and letting my audience figure out how they feel for themselves.*

Shoshana was suddenly struck by how good Oprah was at her job, not being judgmental in the slightest. She felt the odd sensation of jealousy course through her. Sometimes it was exhausting being the face of a cause. The truth, the real, down-and-dirty truth, was that Alexis, horrid witch that she was, *did* present some good ideas and arguments. Shoshana really was an easygoing person at heart, and unable to be militant for her cause. Sure, she'd devoted her life and career to helping big girls like herself feel better about the way they looked in a size-fourteen halter top, but she didn't always feel up to the task of being *the* leader of Fat Nation, when really there were so many different types of fat that sometimes it was really unfair that she had to include all of them under her belt, almost like a president being ashamed of Florida, or parents not *really* loving all their children equally.

Some people weren't just fat, they were obese, and when Shoshana received their e-mails full of self-hatred and lines about wanting to hang themselves with a rope or throw up their lunches, she had to meet extreme *head-on* with extreme, so she assured them they were beautiful. With 91 percent of all college-aged women admitting to dieting, and anorexia causing more deaths per year than any other mental illness, *something* had to be done. She'd picked up the expression "God doesn't make junk" from a priest who lived next door to her mother, and she quoted Father O'Reilly from time to time to her readers. She felt the expression covered everyone, and gave great comfort.

And yet sometimes . . . sometimes when the door to her bedroom was closed or she was in the shower, alone, she could relax enough to be honest with herself. The fact was that she exercised daily. And, although she ate a lot, and didn't deprive herself of some of her favorite desserts and junk food, she also tried very hard to have a balanced diet, with servings of wheat, fruits, proteins, and vegetables. She power-walked every week with her sassy friend Nancy. She swam every Sunday, twenty laps, at Stevens University. She drank lots of water throughout the day. Why should she have to include people who stuffed their faces night and day with McDonald's and Breyers, and then expected her to cover their butts in her general argument of loving one's self?

The answer was that if she didn't stick up for the heaviest women, clinically obese women, if she didn't tell them they were not pieces of shit, people like Alexis Allbright would make not only the five-hundred-pound people want to slit their wrists, but the two-hundred-pound people feel they had no place in society, either. It was all or nothing and she was most certainly all in, but sometimes being the leader of a movement was not all fun and games. Sometimes she wanted to lie down and throw up her feet and read a junky novel, skip writing her daily blog, and buy a frickin' Lean Cuisine for dinner once a week at Shop Rite without worrying that she might run into someone she knew who would snatch it out of her hands, hold it over their head as evidence, and shout, *You see? Shoshana Weiner is a fake! She's a phony! She's watching what she eats. She's just like them!*

But then she would sit down to watch mindless television, and be dumbstruck by shows like *Bridalplasty,* where brides-to-be, who should be reveling in being themselves (after all, why did the guys propose to them in the first place if not because they liked their looks?), instead are so filled with self-hate that they're getting lipo at twenty-five and having their noses broken and stitched back together to win a free wedding.

Shoshana blinked. She realized she was in Chicago. Onstage. With Oprah.

"We've seen Alexis's video. I'd like to open up the floor to my audience to find out what they think," Oprah said, turning her body. She had on a beautiful blue and green glass bead necklace that shone under the bright lights whenever she moved.

A young black woman with a buzzed head, dark blue pencil skirt, pretty ruffled white blouse, and squarish jaw stood at a microphone in the aisle. "I am a surgeon and have three young children. I am also a single parent and have a hard enough time being home for my kids. If I want to give them a Twinkie for dessert sometimes, is that really so wrong?"

The audience clapped in encouragement.

"What's your name?" Alexis asked.

"It's Liza," the woman responded, looking slightly surprised she'd been asked.

"Would you give your child a cigarette, Liza?" Alexis asked calmly.

Someone gasped. Shoshana looked around, only to realize it had been her.

But Alexis wasn't finished.

"How about heroin? Of course you wouldn't. But you'd give them a Twinkie. I find it sad that Americans give their children candy as a reward. What about a fresh, sweet carton of raspberries? How about a quarter, to put in their piggy bank?"

"Isn't that philosophy a little strict?" Oprah asked, raising her perfectly plucked eyebrows.

But Alexis was on a roll. There was a gleam in her eyes. "Obesity is killing us, and the prime suspect is junk food. Now, if you're asking me to set a killer loose in your home, fine. But I'm not going to stop until our taxes cease going to fund obese patient care, and people stop dying from premature diabetes and heart disease. I will not relent, even a little bit. I feel it is my duty to keep people healthy, and therefore, allowing secondhand obesity for kids is a no-no on my blog."

"I don't know about you, but this conversation is really making me want to go eat a Twinkie," Shoshana said dryly.

Rainfalls of laughter from every row.

She continued. Funny was her strong point. It always had been. In school, Shoshana was friends with every single group, from the jocks to the skaters to the cheerleaders. If she could make a person laugh, that person wouldn't judge her for her size. Wouldn't call her mean names behind her back. Would see her as a person, a funny person.

"I mean, how many times did the girl say 'Twinkie'?" Shoshana continued. "You'd think they were paying her for subliminal advertising or something."

More laughter, filling the room, bouncing off the walls. Oprah was smiling and nodding, encouraging her.

"Look. When I see Blake Lively, Nicole Richie, and Paris Hilton in magazines in designer gowns with their rib bones literally sticking out the sides, it breaks my heart, because I know for every picture in a magazine there is a young, easily influenced girl looking at it and just reaching puberty, starting to have emotions, and feelings toward her developing body. And I know, just as you do, that seeing those so-called 'glamorous' images truly can alter a young girl's perspective. Suddenly her curvy thighs and full breasts aren't so beautiful and exciting anymore. She wants rid of them. She wants to look like the celebrities in the fancy dresses and the models selling sexy products like perfume and clothing and sunglasses the kids at school are wearing. It's not a flaky concept. I assure you, it's a split-second look at those pictures and then down at her own body, an instant that can alter her belief system. Now she hates the way she looks. She idolizes these girls, and will do anything to look like them. Including starvation and jeopardizing her health. How many of us have to die of anorexia before we say enough is enough?"

Strong clapping that filled the room.

Alexis waited until the noise dimmed down. "You are leaving out the medical details of what goes into making a person overweight. There are many studies that say how much fatter Americans are becoming every year."

"And you are leaving out the fact that some people are born big-boned, and can't help being big," Shoshana shot back. "How do you think reading your blog makes those people feel? They can listen to your advice to work out 'just thirty minutes a day' or try one of your fad diets, and they'll still be larger than you find appropriate. It's not their fault, and yet you continue to place blame over their heads. What do you think reading *Skinny Chick* does to their self-esteem?"

Alexis said something, but it got lost in the clapping, and she waited again until it started to die down. Oprah smiled at her audience, pumping her arms slightly for people to reel it back in, to remember that she had another guest on the stage who should have the platform again, even if her message was the unpopular one.

"Shoshana is leaving out a very important detail," Alexis said quietly yet deliberately, like a great director building tension for an explosive scene. "One that she purposefully keeps from the readers of *Fat and Fabulous.*"

Anticipation hung in the air like a spider's web.

I do? Shoshana thought. *I am?* Suddenly her stomach dropped. Oh, no. Surely she wasn't going to go *there*. No one would be that cruel.

"Her father died of a heart attack," Alexis said in a syrupy, faux-concerned voice. "Four years ago. He was only forty-nine. He was mowing his front yard and simply dropped dead right there. It was a preventable tragedy."

The smell of freshly cut grass. Emily playing Billy Idol's "Dancing with Myself" in the living room. She'd just applied lotion on her hands, and when she raised them to her mouth the smell of vanilla was overwhelming.

A hush had come over the room.

"At the time of his death he was over three hundred fifty pounds," Alexis finished quietly.

Her father lying in the sharp green grass, right hand still clutching the mower's handle. Sweat stains on his gray Rutgers T-shirt. Cicadas humming all around her. His brown cigar, still lit, lying next to him. His wide face, the one she loved so much, seen hovering over her when she was in her crib, grimacing when she hit him on the thumb with a hammer when she was five, breaking into a smile from the stands at her high school basketball game, was now still and beet-red around his beard.

Shoshana finally looked up, into Alexis's ice-blue eyes. How could someone with eyes that beautiful be so awful? So this was the face of evil, she thought. She was unable to speak. It felt like a hand, perhaps a very skinny and pale one like Alexis's, was wrapped around her throat. If she opened her mouth to speak she'd burst into tears. Her vision blurred as she desperately fought off crying.

Alexis saw her opponent weakened and rattled off her final statistics to drive home her point. "According to the Centers for

Disease Control and Prevention, one-third of America's children are overweight and seventeen percent of teenagers are clinically obese. That's more than three times the rate of a generation ago. Did you know there is a link between cancer and obesity? The American Cancer Society claims one hundred thousand lives lost to obesity-related cancer a year."

Someone booed her, but she ignored it, continuing with her facts: "There's a great book out there called *The Fattening of America*. Its authors cite that over the past three decades, only *decades,* American obesity rates have more than doubled. It accounts for ninety-three billion dollars in health bills a year. So you can boo me all you want. The numbers speak for themselves."

"Are you okay, honey?" Oprah asked Shoshana. "I could see that might not have been something you were ready to talk about on national television."

She'd done CPR on him, and how odd it had been to put her mouth on top of her own father's gummy white lips. She'd put one hand over the other, pumping on his huge chest she'd pressed her face against so many times as a child when he'd give her a bear hug. One of his eyes was half open and it terrified her, like a monster in a horror movie. She'd dripped tears on his face, finally screaming, "Help!" over and over again until her mother ran outside, the screen door flapping and slamming behind her. She had been in the middle of baking a cherry pie and had flour on her hands and an apron which scattered like confetti as she ran toward her husband and daughter. "Oh, Bill!" she'd screamed.

"Yes, I'm fine, thank you." She'd finally found her voice. She tried to conjure up her calming image. *Palm tree waving in the wind . . .* Oh, to hell with it. God! Why was she such a wimp? She wished she had something on Alexis, something to trip her up and expose her. But she had nothing, nada, zilch. She wasn't really much of an arguer anyway, had always hated fighting and avoided it at all costs. Combine that with her nervousness about being on TV and she was lucky she'd managed to get out two words up here.

Oprah was a professional and knew when it was time to wrap

things up. "We're going to go to commercial. When we get back we'll have our resident personal financial consultant, the wonderful Suze Orman, back to help us curb those shopping sprees." She leaned forward toward her audience, a twinkle in her eye. "I'm going to hide my checkbook under my seat, just in case she tells me I've been spending too much. I suggest you do the same! We'll be right back!"

The cameras panned away. Alexis turned toward Oprah. "I've always wanted to know what happens when you go to commercial," she said, as if nothing were odd, as if she hadn't just struck a blow to Shoshana.

Oprah smiled at both her guests. "Thank you for coming on the show, ladies, my assistant will see you back to your families." It had been a good segment, having these two bloggers on. Her producer had suggested it, and she'd been glad to implement both the popularity of weight blogs and women's issues at the same time. She'd thought Alexis had been the perfect villain and Shoshana the hero. Shows didn't always work out this smoothly, but today had. Oprah had known the information about the girl's father, she had excellent researchers on her staff, but she'd chosen not to use it, and wasn't sure how she felt about Alexis doing so. On the one hand it created tension, which always makes for good TV, but she wished Alexis hadn't brought up Shoshana's father's death; it obviously had been devastating for her. She'd clammed up ever since. And clamming up made for very bad TV.

A woman wearing black jeans, a blue button-down shirt, and a Yankees baseball cap approached the stage. A large black apronlike belt was strapped around her middle, and she began touching up Oprah's makeup, quickly taking out brushes and an eyelash curler. "How's your niece doing?" Oprah asked the woman. Shoshana and Alexis didn't get a chance to hear the specifics of how this particular child was feeling as the same skinny guy with the clipboard and headphones who had been with them in the green room was now offering his hand to both girls, and Shoshana accepted, feeling the soft material of the couch beneath her palms as she stood up.

Emily and her mother were waiting in the green room. They

arranged happy looks on their faces for Shoshana's benefit. When they saw their daughter and sister walk down the hall, they squealed and ran to her, covering her with kisses.

"You were amazing!" Emily yelled, hugging Shoshana so hard she nearly fell over. Shoshana put her face in her sister's neck and inhaled her original scent of patchouli oil and strawberry bubble gum. Emily's eyes flashed as Shoshana realized she was glaring at Alexis, who was retrieving her purse from a small locker. She sat down on a couch and changed into much higher heels.

"You should be ashamed of yourself," Emily spat from across the tiny room. "You obviously have some serious mental issues."

"Em, shush," her mother said, embarrassed. She hated conflict, like Shoshana. But Emily hadn't traveled around the world as a roadie for the Dropkick Murphys or tattooed half of Manhattan to let some horrible woman show her big sister up on TV.

"Rumor has it my sister's blog has twice the readers yours does," she spat at Alexis, who was still struggling with the strap of her flashy Miu Miu pumps. She had a Hello Kitty Band-Aid wrapped around her heel.

"Close," Alexis said calmly. "She has five million, I have three. And I read her blog every day. I'm a big fan of her writing, it's smart and witty."

Emily was momentarily silenced. "Well, whatever," she said finally. "That was still a dirty move to bring up our father. Obviously you don't have any family values or else you would never have mentioned his death just to prove a point."

Shoshana and her mother were both beet-red by now. They held Emily by each arm and tried to escort her out of the room, so they could get back to the Four Seasons and rest before their flight back to New Jersey in the morning.

Alexis walked right up to Emily and looked her in the eye. "I'm sorry you feel that way, but I felt it pertinent to mention that although fun to read, your sister runs a dangerous blog that suggests unhealthy ways for young women to live. Accepting yourself as fat is an unhealthy notion. I did not bring up your dad to upset any of you, but because it was important information for Shoshana's readers to know, and she doesn't ever talk about it on *Fat and Fabulous*."

Emily, Shoshana, and her mother stared at this tiny, thin woman with that fashionable clothing and sad face. Shoshana held on to her mother and sister, her hemp purse held tight against her frame. She felt a white-hot rage, and, being a good-natured, friendly girl, it was hard for her to tell anyone off. She finally came up with a comeback, but her voice shook: "I feel sorry for you, really. You seem very unhappy."

Alexis opened her mouth, her expression pained, and held out her arm as if to ask them to hear her out, but the three Weiner women turned and sashayed out of Oprah's studio, arms entwined, hips swinging. They signed out with security, thanked everyone on set, and were whisked into a limo parked directly outside. The driver had a menorah stuck with suction cups to his dashboard, which made Shoshana smile. She watched the city fly by outside her window, people walking through gray slush, clutching shopping bags, their faces flushed red with the cold. Stores had holiday lights strung throughout, giving the streets a cheery glow. Hanukkah had passed last week, and Christmas was just around the corner. She had to remember to buy gifts for her roommates. Maybe before her flight in the morning.

As the doorman greeted her and her family, Shoshana realized suddenly that she was exhausted. "Being a superstar is tiring," she said once they'd passed the ornate lobby in a flash of sound and faces, taken the elevator to their room, and flopped onto the gigantic feather bed. It was late, and outside her window were star-shaped ice crystals. A soft powder of snow had fallen, bathing the room in a periwinkle light. There was laughter on the sidewalk, someone ringing a bell for holiday collections, the honking of the street bus.

Emily jumped into bed beside her, and their mother wearily sat down in the middle of both daughters.

"Let's order ridiculously expensive lobsters off the room service menu and watch cheesy porn," Emily squealed.

"Emily, don't be crass," Pam said, getting up and changing into pretty pink flowery pajamas. "Besides, I don't want to put it on the hotel room's bill; I know Oprah is paying for it."

"Mom, she's like a zillionaire," Emily said, rolling her eyes. "Besides, her assistant told me to when we were backstage. I believe her exact words were, 'Live it up in Chicago!'"

"And lest we forget, it's not every day we get to stay in the Four Seasons," Shoshana said, pinching Emily on her large behind. In retaliation, her sister slapped at her hand.

Pam saw she was up against a losing battle. "Well, all right, but *just* the dinner, girls. Not the, er . . . other thing." Pam and her husband had dutifully saved all their earnings, socking money away for their girls' educations. She rarely spent money, and *never* on herself. When her husband had been alive he'd take her to dinner for their anniversary and she'd feel so guilty about the cost of the food she would debate between three possible menu items for nearly fifteen minutes while the waiter stood there patiently. Bob used to tease her that her autobiography would someday be titled *I Should Have Had the Fish*. She smiled now, remembering.

Emily was working the sleek white phone by the bedside. "I'll have three lobsters, two bottles of Dom Pérignon, and a bowl of chocolate-covered strawberries," she trilled.

"Emily Anne!" her mother hissed, mortified.

Shoshana laughed and leaned back against the plush bedding. She reached into her pink laptop case and pulled out her computer, plumping up some pillows behind her back and pressing the power switch. One of her many girlfriends, Nancy, was updating posts on her blog while she was away. Shoshana had written about a recent *New York Times* story about how stored fat could help safeguard against certain diseases, and she wanted to check if she'd gotten a lot of responses. She watched her mother and sister bicker over whether to watch *Eclipse* or *The Switch*. After a few minutes the bellhop came with the food on a silver tray, and left after Emily flirted with him, turning his cheeks pink.

Shoshana scrolled through the message boards on *Fat and Fab-*

ulous. The usual, from *Skinny Chick* readers, who thought Shoshana was spreading a "dangerous message," but for the most part the results were overwhelmingly positive. She even saw that a doctor, a man from a hospital in Boston with the screen name "Dr. Bill," had posted that he thought the article should be republished in a medical journal he ran. Having more positive comments than negative always made for a good day. She thought briefly of Alexis, who was probably on a flight home now or maybe alone in her hotel room eating carrot sticks, and whether she suffered from the same torture of reading through her message boards daily and being besieged with negative posts. The girl struck Shoshana as the cliché tragic case, the popular girl with a hidden resentment for other women and who therefore hid behind her eat-healthy blog to spew hatred for anyone different. But what she couldn't shake was the feeling that Alexis hated *herself* more than anyone else.

She was interrupted in her thoughts by a flying pillow that bounced off her head. "Come on, Shoshana, can't you turn that thing off for one fucking day?" Emily yelled, as she drank champagne straight from the bottle.

"Language!" Pam exclaimed.

"Sorry, Mom."

"But I agree with your sister, Shosh. Let's have some girl time. You've done enough today to raise women's spirits."

"Okay, you both are right. I'll sign off. Looks like a lot of readers are going to watch the *Oprah* segment in the morning; I just hope they don't think I was a total douche."

"What's a douche?" Pam asked.

"It's a feminine hygiene product," Emily responded dryly.

"Emily! I know that," Pam said, exasperated. "Your sister was using it in a different context."

Shoshana giggled.

"Anyway, sis, you were fabulous," Emily said.

"Fat and Fabulous," Pam chimed in, giving her oldest daughter a pinch on the cheek.

Sandwiched between her mother and sister, eating lobster off a plate with a gold ring around it, Shoshana still could not shake her thoughts about Alexis. She may have beat her in the argument on *Oprah,* but wherever she was tonight, she couldn't be as happy as Shoshana felt right now with her mother and sister, her two best friends in the world.

Alexis

January

NEW YORK

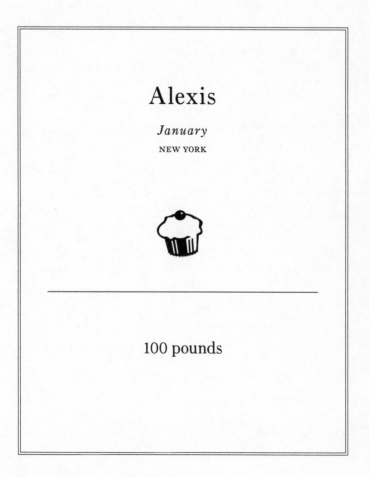

100 pounds

Skinny Chick

First Annual Wedding Gown Challenge

Did you know that studies show more than 50 percent of women lie on their wedding day? No, ladies, I'm not talking about that "promise to be faithful" vow. Women weigh in for the walk down the aisle with no expectation of maintaining that number year after year. After the dress has been preserved, the flowers have wilted, and the day-to-day functions of marriage present themselves . . . well, some of us are straying.

This is why *Skinny Chick* is starting a national Wedding Gown Challenge: Can you try on your wedding dress one year later, and see if it still fits? How about five? Ten?

We've all heard of bridal boot camps. But I ask, are these one- or two-week fitness jolts really necessary? Shouldn't we instead make healthy and smart food choices all the days of our lives? According to the *New England Journal of Medicine*, gaining a mere ten to twenty pounds after age eighteen increases your chance of premature death by 15 percent. So no, that baby weight really isn't cute. Neither is blaming age, or Father Time. The way to combat obesity is to not get fat in the first place.

Portion control, the Allbright thirty-minute exercise plan which I blogged about last week and can be found in the "Archives" section . . . that's how you'll keep the weight off. Starving one's self into an unhealthy weight for your wedding day doesn't make happy brides, or put a dent in America's obesity epidemic. The wedding challenge means not only dealing with dirty socks on the floor, the stress of children, and balancing a household budget, but entering marriage at a healthy weight and *staying* that healthy weight for a lifetime. And to that I say, "I do."

AT FOUR-THIRTY MONDAY MORNING, ALEXIS'S ALARM clock sprang awake to the sound of her roommate Billy's very loud and mechanically recorded voice: "Aleeeexiiis, it's me, Billy. You are sleeping, but it's time to wakey-wakey. I know you want to lie around in bed for another two hours, but you know who lies in bed, don't you?"

"Fat girls," Alexis murmured, half asleep. Laid across her throbbing eyelids was a pink eye cover filled with frozen gel; she'd had two appletinis last night and felt sluggish. But at only fifteen calories a pop she'd been able to enjoy them sans guilt, somewhat. She and Billy had gone to Eastern Bloc in the Village (where Billy worked part-time) and then hopped in a cab with two sailors who were in town for Fleet Week, and made their way home to Nineteenth Street, where they lived above the Container Store.

"Fat girls!" Billy screeched, his gleeful voice filling her bedroom and bouncing off the walls, which were dark with the last gasp of night, save for the yellow slant of streetlamp cutting diagonally across the dark wall next to her queen-sized modern bed.

She fumbled around for the snooze button, then remembered she'd purposely bought the only alarm clock without that feature. She tried reaching under her headboard for the plug, only to let out a long sigh. It was solar-powered. Alexis wrestled her alarm clock on a daily basis. Oh, but Billy's nasally voice was still assaulting her.

"If you want to keep that fabulous figure, it's time to get out of bed and head to the gym. Only . . ."

Alexis mouthed the words along with Billy, her face once again smushed against her pillow.

". . . don't wake *my* pretty ass up!"

It always made her smile, that last part. It was true. Billy didn't get home from Eastern Bloc most nights until the sun was rising. They'd become best friends their freshman year at Columbia and been inseparable ever since, living together since graduation five years ago.

Fumbling around in the dark, she found her five-pound weights and strapped them around both ankles, the loud *zip* of Velcro sounding violent in the stillness of the morning. She'd done the best she could to give her bedroom character and neat, modern sleekness on a writer's salary: large black-and-white posters with Hitchcock movie stills (she and Billy loved his movies) took up three of the four walls. She'd painted her radiator a pretty white color. A large, chunky white chandelier she'd bought on super sale at ABC Carpet hung over her bed. The strands of crystals woven through its arms would sometimes break off, and Alexis would find one on her pillow, shining like a diamond. She had a dark gray shag rug that she vacuumed daily, and a small, sleek IKEA desk over by her window at which she wrote, tiny clear Lucite bins holding her assorted paper clips and pens. Her room was spotless and organized.

She felt her calf muscles working under the weights as she shuffled to the bathroom, yawning, and turned on the small light over the shower and plucked her pink Dora the Explorer toothbrush out of the glass. As a joke, Billy bought Dora for her and a blue Diego brush for himself.

Princess Pinkerton, the gray-and-white-striped cat Billy had found in the back alley of his bar and brought home last December wrapped in his brown Marc Jacobs leather bomber jacket, was squatting and shitting in the large potted jade tree just inside the bathroom, next to the toilet.

"Get out of there!" Alexis hissed. The cat was perched on the edge of the pot. Alexis and Billy were trying to break her of this habit. Billy even recently put in a call to a cat behaviorist in Portland, Oregon, who suggested they fly her out for a group therapy session with other neurotic cats, something they obviously couldn't afford on bartender and blogger salaries.

"But it's the *cat* whisperer, Alexis," Billy had protested. "He's going to be the next big reality pet star. And Princess Pinkerton could be famous!"

She'd shaken her head. Sometimes Billy's optimism could be overwhelming. Alexis might be a pessimist, but she liked to think of herself as a realist.

She finished brushing her teeth, and shuffled into the kitchen to find a man standing in her kitchen.

"Can I help you?" she asked.

He jumped about a mile. Naked from the waist up, he wore blue boxers with oversized white polka dots. He was drinking a glass of water, some of which he'd spilled onto his chiseled chest. And yes, a dark blue inked tattoo of an anchor was on his sculpted, muscular bicep. Alexis squinted at him; he looked familiar. And wow, didn't Billy have all the luck, getting laid by a guy this hot. She could pour maple syrup on him and eat him for breakfast. If only it didn't have so many calories.

She realized she'd spoken her thoughts.

"Er, thanks," he said, looking embarrassed.

"Oh! I didn't realize I said that out loud," she said. "Rough night and all that. Well, if you'll excuse me, I have to make my breakfast."

"Sure, of course. Go right ahead." The sailor moved over an inch.

Right. He was one of the sailors they'd been drinking with the night before. Fancy meeting him in her kitchen. Her stomach growled. Alexis grabbed a banana from the hammered-metal fruit bowl next to the sink and diced it exactly seven times. She always sliced it seven times. Then she poured herself a glass of nonfat milk, holding up her fist to measure the amount. Last, she walked over to her purse, which was thrown over the back of a kitchen chair, opened it, took out her iPhone, and tapped the app that helped her track her daily caloric intake.

"You got some kind of OCD or something?" the sailor asked, watching her.

Alexis sighed. She'd been explaining her dietary restrictions and careful eating habits since she'd formed the Healthy Vikings in her small, private Catholic school. She'd been the president, of course. It had three members, girls on Alexis's cheerleading squad who were too scared of her to turn her down when she set about recruiting. She'd been popular in an eerie way—passing judgments that cut too close to the bone to be ignored, splitting up couples she thought shouldn't be dating in the first place with nasty gossip. Alexis was popular in school because her father donated a million dollars so it could be one of the first in Greenwich, Connecticut, to give each kid his or her own laptop, and because she was a member of nearly every club the school offered. It was simply better to be with her than against her, like the Mob. She was a hard worker and excelled in every subject equally.

When one teacher, an Arkansas transplant and sweet young woman, grew worried that Alexis might indeed be quite lonely during freshman year despite all her extracurricular activities, she called a meeting with Alexis's parents and presented her case. Her father's response? "I donated money to this school to be called out of court for *this*? Every kid gets sad sometimes. It builds character. Talking about feelings is a bunch of new age horseshit, if you don't mind my saying so."

He'd spun on his Gucci loafer and left, her mother looking out the window with a pained expression, wanting to be anywhere else, wearing ridiculous white driving gloves. Alexis's older brother (by exactly three years to the day, they shared a birthday) Mark caught wind of the whole ordeal, and wrestled Alexis into a headlock in the school's hallway as he walked to football practice the next afternoon. He'd be dead the following year, killed by a roadside bomb in Iraq, but she didn't know that yet. That day he looked very much alive as a hive of activity buzzed around him: student council signs swinging from nearby lockers, the squeaking of their sneakers as they walked, classroom doors opening and students pouring out in waves, the dimple in his right cheek creasing as he smiled down at her, the shouting of jokes and insults by his teammates as they ran ahead of him, football helmets cradled in strong, muscular young arms like soldiers with rifles. She could smell his brand of deodorant and the peanut butter energy bar he'd just devoured.

"Hey, little sis."

"Hi, Mark."

"You're not too old for a noogie, right? Say the magic words and I'll let you go."

She giggled, punching him lightly in the stomach as he let go of his grip around her head and put his arm around her shoulders instead.

"Goonies say, never die!" They both loved The Goonies. *Sloth was Mark's favorite character.*

She felt something knotted within her simply . . . relax. He had that effect on her, as he did on everyone else, too. "You know I love you, don't you?" he said quietly into her ear, so as not to allow people walking by to witness any of their private exchange.

Her eyes welled up, but she looked away toward a nearby green locker that had the initials KG + JG *scratched on it. She didn't know them. "Yes," she'd whispered back.*

And that had been the end of that.

But now she was late for the gym. Her phone emitted a sharp *bleet*, as Alexis quickly downed the glass of milk like a shot. She had another app that reminded her when she was running behind for her workout. Out of the corner of her eye she saw a blur of motion as sailor boy reached out and helped himself to a slice of her banana.

Alexis sucked in air and let out a small scream.

Sailor boy's arm dropped to his side, the banana still mashed into his cheek, making him look like a chipmunk.

Billy came rushing out of his bedroom. "What is it? What's the matter?" He glanced at the clock on the stove. "It's five-oh-four. Why aren't you at the gym?" Billy was Korean, had black spiky hair and smooth, caramel-colored skin. His eyes were large and black, framed by beautifully long lashes that were his best feature (which he'd tell everyone who would listen). He was the same height as Alexis, five-foot-two.

Two eyes peered out of the darkness from Billy's room at Alexis. She realized it was the other sailor from last night. Tom, or Tim. Or maybe it was Tony? She couldn't remember.

"Sailor boy over here thought it might be okay to take one of my banana slices," Alexis said.

Polka-dot Boxers Sailor let out an embarrassed chuckle. Alexis realized he sounded embarrassed for *her*. The nerve.

"What's with your roommate?" he asked Billy. "She got a stick up her ass or something? I ate a slice of banana, and she screamed like I was stabbing her in the eye."

Billy strode slowly but meaningfully over to him. He came up to the sailor's nipple.

Pause.

He reached up and slapped him across the face.

The sailor stood there, his hand on his cheek, wearing a shocked expression. Alexis heard Billy's other boy toy scurry back into the shadows, quickly slamming the door. The sound of the lock being turned echoed across the tiles in the kitchenette.

"What the fuck was that for?" Polka-dot Boxers Sailor asked.

"I'm going to explain something to you, so open up your big dumb waterlogged ears," Billy said, hands on his narrow hips. "Do you have any idea who you just took a slice of banana from? Whose breakfast you so cavalierly interrupted? Motherfucker, this is Alexis Allbright. Editor in chief of *Skinny Chick*. Queen of Chelsea. Bitch of all bitches."

"The blog?" the sailor asked, lifting his thick eyebrows at this news.

"*The blog*," Billy replied.

"Oh, my god," he said, putting a hand up to his reddening cheek. "I read your blog, like, every single day. I fucking worship you. I used to be a fat kid when I was younger." He pointed to his washboard abs. "Really."

Alexis smiled the wafer-thin smile she reserved for people she didn't like.

"That interview you did with Anna Wintour I read like five hundred times on my laptop when we were stationed off the coast of Mexico. It got me through the lonely nights."

"Glad I can do my part for my country," Alexis said. She was starting to calm down.

"*Now* do you understand why taking her banana slice was so disrespectful?" Billy asked, his tone that of a preschool teacher speaking to a very small child. "Girlfriend isn't going to eat anything for another five hours, as you know from her blog. And when she *does* eat, it will be a meal consisting of fewer calories than you have brain cells. And she has to now go work out. While the rest of the world sleeps in their lazy little beds."

The sailor was tripping over himself to apologize. Alexis let him off the hook with a wave of her French-manicured hand. She never got anything other than a "Frenchie," as she called them. Her mother had always said color on fingernails looked vulgar.

"Don't worry about it, honey," she told him. "If you can say *Skinny Chick*'s motto to me, all is forgiven."

The sailor grinned. Now he was on familiar ground. "A few calories a day keep the spandex away," he sang.

"Good boy," Billy said, patting him on the butt like a dog. The sailor went skipping off to the bathroom, glowing as if he'd just met Angelina Jolie.

Suddenly a second door opened and a dark mane of hair appeared. Alexis and Billy both sucked in their breath at the same time. "All right out 'ere?" a voice called spookily in an indeterminate accent. It seemed to warble, or echo somehow, like a ghost wailing inside a haunted house.

"Er . . . everything's fine. Sorry we woke you," Billy whispered.

Their third roommate was the only person on the entire planet who truly scared the shit out of both of them. Not having any friends, they'd had to rent out the third bedroom in their apartment when Alexis quit law school to start her blog. Billy was between bartending jobs at the time, and they needed the money. God knows, she'd rather take in Hannibal Lecter before going to her father for money, after he'd told her she was "dead to me" when she dropped out.

So when Vanya answered their Craigslist ad, and had the deposit ready, they'd accepted her on the spot.

Her profession was unknown, and they'd never really gotten an actual look at her face after several years of cohabitation. Only brief flashes of light green eyes, nearly yellow like a cat's. Her hair was down to her waist and Wonder-Woman black, with a blue sheen. Her skin was a translucent white and she spent most of her days in her room (like a vampire!) playing the kind of weird music with bells sounding and cymbals pinging one heard in a spa. Billy had a theory she was a dominatrix, as she seemed to work only at night, and often wore thigh-high patent-leather boots. She'd once left a book out on the living room table, and Billy and Alexis had pounced on it. The title? *Wicca Today: 15 Curses for the Modern Witch*. Billy had emitted a little scream and dropped it on the floor like a hot pan. Later, Alexis saw him carefully place it back on the table, precisely as it had been left. His hand had been shaking.

This morning was only the second or third time they'd heard her speak. Billy shrank closer to Alexis. Vanya had a mix of accents; one couldn't be sure if she was Irish, Scottish, or Transylvanian.

"Just a little disagreement," Alexis said. "Sorry we woke you up."

Billy made a small choking sound. Alexis *never* apologized.

"Being hot and skinny means never having to say you're sorry," she often said.

Vanya retreated back into her room (Alexis could swear she saw her feet not actually touch the floor), its walls painted such a dark purple it was cavelike, the reflection of a mirror on the ceiling casting a silver light onto the crack under her door. Only, her door didn't shut, not really. It seemed to *suck* closed, like a force field swirled around her space and it was retreating back into itself.

Billy wiped his forehead with the gold sleeve of his Louis Vuitton pajamas. "She scares me," he said. Then, as he turned to Alexis, they both started giggling uncontrollably, holding their sides and then each other. Billy was the only man Alexis felt comfortable with touching her regularly. She occasionally slept with men (some married, some not) in five-star hotel rooms, but if they called her or tried to contact her afterward she always told them to lose her number.

She and Billy were so close it was as though they were married. Dating someone seriously would feel like an intrusion on their friendship; whoever it was would be an outsider. He wouldn't get their seven-year buildup of jokes and familiarity. They'd both dated but never seriously. Most people who found out about how close they were usually recognized their friendship for what it was: needy and strange. They vacationed together, applied self-tanner to each other's bodies, and even took baths in their humongous clawfoot bathtub the rich old lady who owned the apartment before them left when she died, their feet hanging over the tub's lip on either end.

Billy handled the recruitment of advertisers for *Skinny Chick,* serving drinks to people in the entertainment industry who wanted to promote their new movie or album on the blog. "I'll go and get my gay," Alexis would say, when advertisers called wanting to speak to someone about the site. Billy worked three jobs: he helped run *Skinny Chick,* bartended, and worked as a fashion consultant for *Vogue.* He styled the models for photo shoots, lugging items from his own collection (he had a twenty-seven-inch waist, and sometimes the models wore his clothes unawares), or he'd borrow a credit card from *Vogue* and go shopping for the shoot, with specific outfits in mind. Billy was a genius when it came to dressing women, and even though freelance budgets at many magazines were dwindling, they always found the dough to hire him. Before she met Billy, Alexis dressed provocatively, wearing very short dresses and thigh-high boots. She cringed now, remembering. Her mother had never really helped steer her in any direction with fashion; Bunny wore tennis skirts and tops around the house, which was ironic because she hadn't picked up a racquet since she peered down the neck of a bottle of vodka years ago and never looked back up. Billy helped give Alexis a more streamlined, polished, adult look. She still was allowed the occasional short dress, but the label had to be Stella McCartney, not Bebe.

Though Alexis founded *Skinny Chick,* Billy came across as much more warm in business meetings and over the phone. Clients were scared of Alexis. Men and women alike. She weighed one hundred pounds soaking wet. She wore five-inch heels, everywhere she went, even to the supermarket. Her blond hair was dyed so heavily it was nearly white, and pulled into such a short bob it gave her young face a severe look. Once, when she looked into the carriage of a neighbor's new infant, the baby had instantly scrunched up its soft face and burst into tears, the mother embarrassed and shushing it.

But now Billy was ready to go back to sleep. Or at least to bed. "I was having the strangest dream," he told Alexis.

Alexis glared at him.

"I know, I know, you have to go work out," he said, rolling his dark, beautiful eyes. "Just listen. So I'm nestled there between my two sailors, and I'm dreaming that I go on Craigslist, because you know how I have that obsession where I look at crap people are selling in our neighborhood?"

"Of course."

"So I go on there, and lo and behold, there is my signed poster of Liza Minnelli from *Flora the Red Menace,* you know, the one I waited for three hours in January outside the auction in Midtown and caught a deadly strain of pneumonia to get?"

He'd caught a cold, and it had been a mild one.

"On sale for fifty dollars. *My* Liza poster!"

"You are *such* a gay stereotype," Alexis said drolly.

"I know, shut up. So! I keep scrolling down, and ooo, there's a lovely TAG watch for a hundred bucks, and I look closer, notice the scuffing on the band . . ."

"Let me guess, it's your watch," Alexis said, rolling her eyes.

"Yes! Yes! All my shit is being sold online. It was like some crazy *Groundhog Day* situation."

"Only you weren't living the same day over and over again."

"Maybe not exactly the same. But isn't that weird? I'm *totally* calling Jasmine."

Jasmine was Billy's psychic, who charged seventy-five dollars an hour.

"I put a lock on your cell so it won't dial her."

"I'll call from the house phone."

"I shut it off. It cost too much, anyway."

"Damn you, Alexis! You skinny, heartless bitch. Don't I feed you diet pills when you go up a pound every Thanksgiving? And put grapes in the freezer and call it dessert? And pretend to be your husband when married guys you banged call the house? And for what? So you can come between me and the only woman I've ever loved?"

Alexis sighed and threw on her pink cashmere cardigan that hung on the back of the door. She tossed her keys in her purse and put her hand on her hip. "*I'm* the only woman you've ever loved."

"Other than Nana Kay." Nana Kay was Billy's mother's mother, who came over from Korea ten years ago. As both his parents disowned him because of his sexual orientation, Alexis and Billy both adored Nana Kay. Billy once lived with her for several years. She was four-foot-ten and had an apartment in an assisted living facility in the Bronx, where they visited her from time to time.

Alexis loved her overstuffed apartment, the shelves in her living room crammed with books, which reminded her of Penny Oliver, a girl from grade school whose adult teeth grew in before her baby teeth fell out. Shameless, she'd open her mouth and grin widely for anyone who asked, looking like Jaws with double sets of teeth.

Nana Kay cooked traditional Korean food and they'd drink her homemade wine until deep into the night, playing old records and dancing. She still applied whore-red lipstick every morning, and at eighty-two, she was Alexis's hero. Well, second hero. The other was MeMe Roth, of course.

"Right. Other than Nana Kay. And don't you forget it. Now make me proud and go enjoy your man meat."

Billy pretended to pant like a dog, which made them both laugh. She tried to stop laughing when she got to the elevator. Once, when she was five, her mother said it caused wrinkles, and she'd never forgotten the tip. Alexis thought about her parents and sighed. She'd never felt particularly close to either of them, and the last three years that had gone by with no communication hadn't helped. Mark's death had caused a rip in their family that could never be repaired. Bunny, who'd had a small drinking problem when he was alive, was now a certified drunk. Dad dealt with his grief by burying himself in work at his bustling, successful Greenwich law firm where he was a partner.

Dad had met Billy only once while briefly in New York for work. Alexis had called him, initiating the get-together. "The only time I have is if you come with me to a Giants game with clients," he'd said. So she did, dragging Billy along for support. She sat there, while her father made cracks about her blog and asked when she was going to "get some damn sense and go back to the law."

Billy, sensing her unease, had pointed to the field in front of them. Halftime was ending, and the team was trotting back onto the field in a blur of blue and white. "All those tight pants! It's like we're at the ballet," he'd whispered, making her giggle.

Now, standing in her hallway, Alexis pressed the elevator button with one perfectly manicured finger and listened to the sounds of its cables rising up to meet her, like the building's innards slowly waking the same time as the city. At the end of the hallway a large window showed the sun peeking over a few jagged buildings, which caused her to squint, so she dug in her purse and put on her Chanel sunglasses Billy had stolen from the time he'd dressed all the actresses on *As the World Turns*. They were white and very wide and slimmed her face, which was a perfect circle, and therefore always gave her grief. She'd inherited her father's looks along with his stubbornness; Mark took after their mother, with their heart-shaped faces and easy dispositions. Having a circle for a face is cute when you're a baby. But when the rest of you is slim and streamlined, it adds five pounds in photographs. At least it did in Alexis's mind.

"I have a Christina Ricci face," she would complain to Billy.

"I know, darling," he'd say. "But your ass is so skinny, I don't think you can lose another pound. I'd have to put you on ano watch."

Her phone beeped again. She stepped onto the elevator and pressed a button to silence it. It was 5:10 in the morning. "I know, I know," she muttered out loud in the silence of the hall. "I'm late. I should be at the gym by now." She worked out at the very elite Soho Gym, which was co-owned by several celebrities. It cost $500 a month and she barely was able to pay her rent because of it, but her membership was absolutely essential. Her weight hardly ever altered more than a pound or two other than that scary week last year when she'd found herself weighing 110 and had to go on a quick liquid diet that had left her with terrible diarrhea (Billy joked they'd need to air out the apartment with large fans), but lately her personal trainer Sarah was helping sculpt her arms and give her already-flat stomach definition.

Walking along Sixth Avenue, Alexis kept up a constant stream of thoughts in her head. As a writer, she was a natural people-watcher. Unsurprisingly, she picked apart mainly women.

She's fifteen pounds overweight, she shouldn't be wearing horizontal stripes with those wide hips, she could use a good lip wax, what was that woman thinking wearing leggings with that ass, if you're not pregnant don't wear an Empire-waist dress, if I ever get that overweight please take me into the pasture and kindly put a bullet in my brain. It was a habit she had, like some people don't step on cracks or always turn right when lost. When women passed her on the street she instantly judged them. Height, weight, whether they were prettier than her, highlights real or fake, how many times they'd gone under the knife . . . It never failed to leave her with an anxious feeling, and she knew she'd feel better if she could only stop comparing herself to every New York woman, but it was a hard habit to break. It was just who she was.

Entering the gym, she waved to Carlos, who worked the front desk of her gym. He doubled as a yoga teacher, and he was always inviting her to his class, but Alexis knew yoga was for lazy people who didn't want a real workout.

"Namaste," he teased her as she swiped her card.

"Whatever," she replied.

Alexis passed the room where she sometimes took spin class, then walked by the personal training room, currently occupied by the resident kickboxing expert, Leona. She was Hispanic and had long, curly black hair she put in two buns on the top of her head and a killer bod. Some gyms touted a mix of people trying to get into shape and those already in it; what Alexis liked about Soho Gym was that everyone was already gorgeous, like Leona. She didn't have to do crunches on the mat next to any fat, sweaty slobs wearing T-shirts with the sleeves cut off, advertising mechanic shops. Soho Gym was a place where people wore makeup on the elliptical machines.

Alexis, who had worked out with Leona last winter when Sarah went on her honeymoon in Alaska, waved. In turn, she looked up from demonstrating jabs to a short, pale, fleshy banker-type guy on the punching bag and winked.

Alexis strode into the women's locker room and stripped off her cardigan. Inside her specially-assigned locker was a brush. She ran it quickly through her hair, then slipped on a slim black workout headband. She went over to the scale and stripped off her clothing, then climbed on. It was chilly in the room, and she shivered. She congratulated herself inwardly: the needle wavered between ninety-nine and one hundred. She'd lost a pound, perhaps from all the stress of going on *Oprah* last month. She hadn't been nervous onstage because she knew she was in the right with her message of health, that awful fat girl Shoshana was *completely* in the wrong, but she had been on edge in the weeks leading up to the show.

To prepare for *Oprah*, Billy bought her books on speaking in public. He decided she needed a voice coach, designated himself, and made her walk around the living room with books on her head for posture. "This feels like something out of the fifties," she'd complained. "Like etiquette class." Billy told her to shut her trap and pay attention, and she had to admit that doing ridiculous voice exercises with him like gargling with salt water to relax the throat had somehow ended up relaxing her, in the end. She'd clearly been the victor in the *Oprah* debate.

If Billy was her only friend, her personal trainer, Sarah, was someone she admired greatly and respected. She *would* consider Sarah a friend, as they'd been working out together several years now, but since she paid her extravagant amounts of money she wasn't sure if that constituted an actual friendship.

Sarah was forty but looked not a day over twenty-five. She was tall, svelte, Puerto Rican, and rumored to have once picked Carlos up over her head and bench-pressed him. (Carlos weighed in at 190, all muscle.) She had coffee-colored skin, and huge green eyes with long black lashes. She worked out three hours a day and had one of the tightest bodies Alexis had ever seen. She was married to an oncologist at NYU Medical Center. Alexis worshipped Sarah and they'd had many discussions about the epidemic of obesity in America. Sarah was very concerned with fast-food chains in New York City, and she led a large protest with *Skinny Chick* readers when a McDonald's opened next door to the gym. They'd made the six o'clock news. Since then, Sarah wrote a monthly column with exercise tips for Alexis, which always received a lot of attention and hits.

Alexis would come across Sarah in the gym doing crunches

hanging upside down from a bar like a bat, or spotting women in the weight room. Today she was sitting on a spin bike and reading a magazine when Alexis found her. She peeked at the cover and saw *Parents* written across it. *Weird,* Alexis thought. *All of the cooler magazines like* Vogue *and* Nylon *must be taken already.*

"I'm ready to be tortured!" Alexis joked, admiring Sarah's very toned brown biceps. Sarah had a unique program in which she worked out alongside Alexis, pushing both of them to achieve the optimal workout. People in the gym were used to seeing both women balanced on large balls, their stomach muscles clenched, as they slowly did bicep curls.

"Hey, it's Skinny Chick!" Sarah said, grinning. "Carlos and I were just rehashing how great you were on *Oprah*. We laughed our asses off when that other blogger tried defending eating junk food. I seriously think she had some warped ideas about nutrition."

"I know!" Alexis said, plopping down on an exercise bike next to Sarah. Maybe this was her new program, to slowly warm up on a bike before the punishing and grueling workout that most days she jumped right into. "I kept thinking about people dying from heart disease, who have to get their legs chopped off from diabetes, and here this girl is saying it's okay to indulge. I just felt I had to carry the right message, even if it's not what people want to hear." She felt valiant and brave talking about her mission with *Skinny Chick*. It always gave her that rush, which studying the law had lacked. She didn't see how taking people for every cent they had when going through the worst time in their lives (her father's firm dealt with high-profile divorce cases) was helping humanity in any way.

"Well, you're not doing this to be popular," Sarah said. "Don't worry, people will eventually come around to our way of thinking, once they start having relatives and loved ones whose weight problem impacts their daily way of life."

"Right!" Alexis chirped, pedaling her feet around and around. Her sneakers looked bright against the purple of the sky's sunrise. The gym had floor-to-ceiling windows all around, and she could see some people rushing off to work, coffees clutched in their hands, talking on their cell phones, wrapping scarves around their necks as they hit New York's pavement.

Sarah smiled. "Ready for torture hour?"

"Always. Are we going to warm up here on the bikes?"

Sarah's face changed, and Alexis's heart dropped. Something was different. Alexis didn't *do* different. "What is it?"

Sarah gave a little nervous laugh and that scared Alexis even further. This woman pulled truck tires across the room with a single rope and could do five hundred sit-ups without getting out of breath.

"You're not going to another gym, are you?" Alexis asked. She put her arm on Sarah's, only to realize it was the first time the two women had touched, other than when Sarah spotted her in the weight room. "Because seriously, I love this place, but if you leave I would *totally* follow you to your new place of employment."

"Oh, no, I'm not leaving, honey," Sarah said. "Don't worry!" She put her magazine down on the floor between them, then placed her hands on either side of the bike and pedaled faster, her knees high as she pumped her feet. "I seem to have gotten knocked up, is all. Can you believe it? In my old age?" She smiled ruefully but Alexis could tell she was somehow . . . happy.

What the hell?

"But I thought you hated kids," Alexis stammered, remembering a conversation they'd had years ago about not walking past the gym's day-care center for fear of germs. She jabbed at the bike's control screen, not making eye contact.

Sarah laughed. "I do! I can't stand them. They cry and whine and poop their pants. My body is going to get so big, and it will take twice as long at my age to get it back to where it was. Trust me, this was not planned. I've been training for the Ironman for the past six months!"

"Is Aldo excited?" Alexis asked slowly. She was so surprised, her voice was almost a whisper. In the years she'd been working out with Sarah, this was something she'd never considered. That she would be left high and dry by her trainer, whom she paid exorbitant amounts of money to, money she barely had.

Sarah turned to her, taking one of her hands in her own, which surprised Alexis yet again. Neither woman was very touchy-feely. "He is so fucking thrilled it's not even funny." Her face broke out into a smile. She had dimples on both cheeks. "He keeps running around the apartment shouting that he can't believe he knocked me up at forty. You know Latin men. So proud of their dicks."

Alexis swallowed. "Well, if you're happy, then I'm happy for you, Sarah." She mustered up a small smile. "Congratulations!"

"Thank you, Alexis. And don't worry. I'm not going to work out alongside you as much, but we can continue our appointments. I'll be more like a traditional trainer; a coach. I'm only three months along, and I plan on working up until I deliver, you know me."

"Yeah, you're tough," Alexis told her lightly, but inside she felt utter panic. Her life was going to change. Sarah was her mentor—she didn't want to work out with anyone else. She wasn't a particularly social person, and couldn't see meeting with another trainer, male or female. Oh, *why* did people have to grow up and get married and have fucking babies? All this did was ruin things. Babies were financial burdens, they caused friction between husband and wife, and they were bottomless money pits.

Alexis thrived on routine. From the time her alarm sounded while the sky was still dark to when she closed her laptop at five o'clock in the evening, every day was exactly the same. That's how she liked it. She was disciplined and a hard worker. She had no patience for anyone who didn't have the same values. How could Sarah, who had worked so hard for so many years to build her business, gathering a clientele and reputation as a kick-ass trainer, give it all up for a baby? How could someone so much like herself be looking at Alexis now with starry eyes, a red flush of excitement across her cheeks? How could she have gotten herself *pregnant*? Surely by forty a woman had control over her reproduction! A baby would ruin everything.

After their two-hour workout ended, Alexis again congratulated Sarah, and confirmed their Wednesday appointment.

"I have a doctor's appointment that morning, but I could do ten?" Sarah asked casually.

Alexis's hand flew to her cheek. She felt like the sailor Billy had smacked. She'd seen Sarah three times a week for three years straight, always Monday, Wednesday, Friday, always at five-thirty in the morning. Neither woman had missed a day, and now this thing, this *parasite,* was screwing up her entire world. Once, Alexis had all four wisdom teeth pulled on a Tuesday afternoon, and was working out the following morning, high as a kite on Percocet.

Seeing her client clearly distressed, Sarah quickly said, "You can write the blog later in the day, right?"

"No, not really," Alexis said. She stopped pedaling. "I write from nine to three every day, Monday through Friday. It's not as easy for me to change my schedule as you might think." Just thinking about *Skinny Chick* made her want to rush home to see what the reaction in the blogosphere was to her wedding-day post. If only her readers knew how far away from getting a ring on her finger (or wanting one) Alexis was. It amused her—who was she to dole out wedding advice?

Sarah sighed. "Well, I guess I could change my appointment to another day, but this doctor is really famous and hard to get a time slot with . . ."

"Great!" Alexis said brightly. "So I'll see you Wednesday as usual."

She ignored the widening of Sarah's eyes and walked to the locker room. Alexis knew she was being awful but was unable to stop herself. This happened all the time, the overwhelming need to get what she wanted, the thrill of prevailing, and then the crash-and-burn feeling of recognizing there was a reason she had only one friend in the whole world, no boyfriend, no family she was close to: she was unbearable.

And yet, that line that most people wouldn't cross, Alexis always did. She'd played softball in high school, a fact that amused Billy. (He'd once tried on her old uniform, prancing around their apartment. It had fit him better than it had her.) She'd been skilled as pitcher, one of the best in her town, and her mojo was fucking with the head of each batter. Alexis got a reputation for changing up her speed more times than any other pitcher in the league. She enjoyed watching her opponents squirm. She loved winning. That feeling never dissipated.

She knew Sarah was loyal to her and the closest thing to a female friend she had, and yet . . . she still wanted her to provide the same service, which was to be her trainer three times a week, at the scheduled time. Why should *her* routine have to get screwed up just because Sarah couldn't remember to take her birth control pill?

As she flung her workout bra and shorts on the organic bamboo bench beside the shower and stepped under the water, she suddenly heard loud, heaving noises and looked around for their source, only to realize they were coming from *her*, that she, Alexis Allbright, was crying, for fuck's sake. Because her personal trainer was pregnant. She laughed as she lathered her hair with the Aveda shampoo provided by the gym. She scrubbed so hard her scalp would be bright red the next day. How ridiculous! This was a happy time for Sarah, she'd been her loyal trainer for years, never canceled a single appointment, had kept Alexis in fabulous shape . . . but Alexis knew that if Sarah was trying to change her regular appointment today, it wouldn't be the last time. For the next six months things would change a lot, and Alexis didn't like change. She was successful exactly because of her strict adherence to her schedule.

Her readers logged on to *Skinny Chick* as soon as they got into work, and she didn't get up to three million clicks a day without being über-disciplined. She stood under the scalding water until her shoulders were fire-engine red, turned off the faucet, and dried off.

On her way to the exit, she saw a bright yellow laminated sign perched on the front check-in desk. She walked over to have a closer look. "Looking good, baby, looking good," Carlos called out to her.

"Thanks, Carlos!" She picked up the poster. "What's this event?"

"Oh, that's actually going to be pretty dope. Sarah and I are both going. A chef, Noah Cohen, is going to give a simple, healthy cooking lesson. He worked at a few New York establishments, Nobu, Gramercy Tavern. In his bio it says he's from Colorado and makes a mean chili."

Alexis fingered the poster, looking at the photo of Noah. He was tall, with coffee-colored skin, and the picture highlighted his soft bed of dark brown curls with sunny blond tips. His sleeves were rolled up and thick, sculpted muscle peeked through, a vein bulging in his arm like the *David* statue. His eyes were his best feature, a brown like melting chocolate, and mischievous, like he would be the first guy at a party to do a keg stand. His ears stuck out slightly from the sides of his head and this tiny imperfection made him seem even more personable. He had a shadow of a beard across his square chin and mouth, a hint of goatee. He had a dimple in his right cheek. He reminded Alexis of the skater guys from high school who would annoy her by performing noisy, messy tricks outside the window while she was studying in the library.

Alexis found herself hoping his blond highlights were natural, as she didn't find men who dyed their hair very masculine, and then wondered why she cared what this particular man did with his hair. In the picture, he was wearing a traditional white chef's attire, open at the throat and showing a gold Jewish star peeking through. He had large hands and a huge grin that stretched across his whole face, like Mick Jagger's. She wondered how he could be both black and Jewish (he must be, with the last name Cohen?), then remembered Sammy Davis, Jr., was black. And Jewish. And *why* on earth was she standing here trying to figure out this man's heritage when she had a column to write?

Carlos took the flyer out of Alexis's hands slowly. "Ha! You've got the hots for him already! This guy is a lady-killer. Like, thirty women have already signed up for this class. It's the most we've ever gotten for one of our special cooking series. I think he looks like one of those Calvin Klein models that have that billboard on Canal, you know, the ones in their underpants that everyone gets all worked up about?"

She rolled her eyes. "I do not have the hots for him, I don't even know him," Alexis said, putting on her coat. "If he has good ideas about nutrition I could use him on the blog, that's all." *Really! Carlos was so immature sometimes.*

"Sure, sure. Well, it will be good to see you there," Carlos said. "It's next month, so you might want to sign up now because there's only two spots left."

"No problem. I'll just pay now," Alexis said. "How much is it?"

"Fifty bucks," Carlos said.

Alexis swallowed. She only had a hundred dollars left in her bank account. She was due checks from advertisers on *Skinny Chick,* but so far they were behind on payment. Since the recession, checks were arriving in the mail slower and slower. She made a note on her iPhone to call around to her various advertisers when she got home, and signed up for the course. Since it was related to her blog, she could probably write it off come tax season.

"Can you take a check?" she asked Carlos, who was greeting people as they hustled in, carrying gym bags and flashing IDs at him.

"For you, doll? Anything."

Alexis reached into her Chanel bag she had on loan for five more days from the Web site *Beg, Borrow, Steal.* She carefully wrote out the check, dating it for a week from now, when she'd hopefully have more dough, hoping Carlos wouldn't notice. He didn't.

"See you in class," he sang after her, as she pushed through the revolving front door of the gym.

"Namaste," she called back jokingly, her head spinning with Sarah's news and the fact that she'd just signed up for her first cooking class ever, and one she really couldn't afford. But really, all she could think about was Noah's deep, warm brown eyes. She suddenly had to meet him. She was filled with excitement about a total stranger. What did that say about her?

The day was definitely not going as scheduled.

Shoshana

February

HOBOKEN, NEW JERSEY

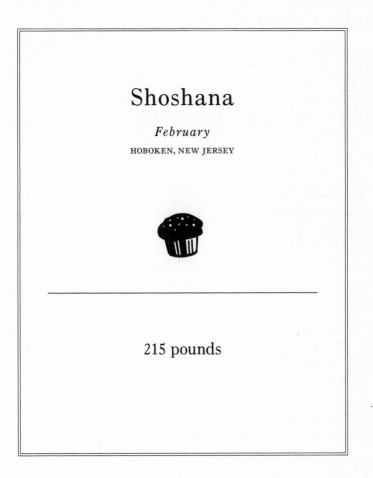

215 pounds

Fat and Fabulous

PEDICURE BEFORE FOOD

Okay, so I know my job is to talk about food, and how important it is to eat it. And believe me, I eat frickin' plenty. But if someone threatened me with an imminent Indian burn on my arm unless I chose between pedicures and food, I'd starve. May we discuss? Oh, how do I describe the warm flow of love that moves up from my toes to my heart while my feet are being scrubbed, washed, lavished with lotion, and pampered? We all like to pretend to be queen for a day (at least I do) and sitting there on that pedicure chair, well, one might just mistake me for royalty atop my golden plastic throne.

For those thirty minutes of heaven, it doesn't matter that I wear a size sixteen. Sure, I'm in public, but it's a different kind of public in the nail salon. It's all women, and believe me, no one is looking at how wide my ass is or how big my boobs are (and you all know from reading this column that they're gigantic!) when there's free issues of *Us Weekly* to pore over and important decisions to make such as how hot one likes their water temperature or choosing between Bikini Strap pink or Meet Me at Sunset red. I pick crazy colors: purples, hot pinks, blues, and greens. Because when you're fat with a capital *F* you stand out anyway, so who cares if you have wild toes?

I used to not like myself very much, and you all have heard about my struggles with depression. For so long in my teens and early twenties I denied myself the pleasures of getting a pedi because I thought, *Shoshana, you are so fat you don't deserve this. That's for other girls, skinnier girls.* Well, today I'm taking a stand. Or a seat, if you will. What you weigh does not determine your quality of life. If you want to have happy feet, you get happy feet!

This theory works for bigger pleasures as well. Can't fit into Theory jeans? So what? You still can take that vacation, drink that fine wine, buy that second home. Hedonism rules! So what if you're Fat? It's the good *F*-word. Say it loud and say it proud. Now close that laptop and go out there and get a pedicure!

XO,

Shosh

SHOSHANA'S ALARM CLOCK WENT OFF EARLY THURSDAY afternoon. In response, she chucked a pink ballet flat at it that had mysteriously ended up on the pillow next to her head. One of a set she'd bought just last week at Target, it was part of her attempt to look more grown-up, because she had to meet with advertisers in the city later in the week, and because of her look, which she liked to describe as "Stevie Nicks meets a fairy in the woods." The shoe bounced off the alarm, hitting the button for the radio, and the sounds of Adele came streaming out.

"I love you, Adele, but shut up!" Shoshana yelled. "It's the break of dawn!"

"It's noon," Andrea said, laughter in her voice, as she came into Shoshana's room and plunked her petite body down on the bed. "You are *so* not a morning person, Shosh; it's hilarious."

"In another part of the world it's much earlier," Shoshana moaned.

"I brought you a cup of coffee," Andrea said. The mug read DON'T ANNOY THE WRITER. SHE MAY PUT YOU IN A BOOK AND KILL YOU. It was a present from Shoshana's father, who had salvaged it at a yard sale. (Her parents were suckers for a good yard sale. They'd been tickled with delight when they learned such an event held in Hoboken was called a "gate sale," given the lack of yards in the city.)

"Okay, now I'm suspicious," Shoshana said. She sat up in bed and took a sip. She licked her lips. "Suspicious, but now in ecstasy."

"Can't I just be a good friend and bring you a cup of joe to be nice?" Andrea asked, fluttering her eyelashes.

"No, you cannot. Give it up."

Andrea was one of four women Shoshana lived with on Bloomfield Street, on the second floor of a five-story walk-up, above Empire Coffee. Luckily, they all equally prayed to the caffeine gods in the morning, so their four-bedroom apartment (Andrea and another roommate, Karen, shared) was in the perfect location. Shoshana woke daily to the faint vibrations of beans being ground.

Andrea had jet-black curls, and large, almond-colored eyes. She was Puerto Rican and Dominican, and she'd been Shoshana's roommate during their freshman year at Princeton. She'd strolled in and said, "Hi, I'm Andrea. I'm here so Princeton can fulfill its affirmative action quota." They'd been friends ever since, along with the three other girls, all Princeton grads now trying to push and shove their way into success in New York during bad economic times. Andrea really wanted to be an actress, and took the PATH into Manhattan and went on auditions some mornings, other times on Saturdays. She'd been in a deodorant commercial three months ago where she had to apply the deodorant fifty-seven times, and she'd been eaten alive by mosquitoes later that evening at a cookout, finally giving her a real excuse for calling out of work.

"Do you remember when I told you that someday, and that day may never come, I'll have to call on you to do a favor for me?" Andrea was asking. She moved closer to Shoshana, snuggling into her back.

"Are you seriously quoting *The Godfather* to me?"

On the wall near her bed was a framed photograph of Lane Bryant, the dress manufacturer. It had gotten knocked askew. (They'd had a few friends over the night before and there'd been an impromptu dance-off in her room.) Shoshana reached out and straightened the picture with her toe. Bryant was the first person to make plus-size clothing on a national scale, with the idea that larger women came in three body types: all-over stout, flat-busted stout, and full-busted stout. Shoshana was definitely in the full-busted stout category.

"Okay, you caught me. I do need to ask you for a favor. Frankie says it's okay, don't you, Frankie?"

Frank Sinatra, the one-eyed, long-haired mini-dachshund-slash-Chihuahua-slash-unknown mix Shoshana had adopted three years ago, right after her father died, was sprawled out on the pillow next to Andrea's head. He wore a doggie T-shirt with a tiny picture of Janis Joplin stretched across its front. Hearing his name, he let out what might have been a groan of pleasure as she stroked his lumpy-shaped head. He was very famous in the Church Square Park dog run, and around town, as Hobokenites loved that he was named for one of their own. (He also had a wardrobe to rival *The Real Housewives of New Jersey*.) The real Frank Sinatra (or shall we say the furless one) had once lived on Monroe Street, just a few blocks away. Shoshana named him after Old Blue Eyes because of an incident on the day she took him home from the animal shelter in Jersey City. After stepping off the light rail, she took him for his first walk about town. The dog was not content to pee anywhere near her apartment, so a frustrated Shoshana walked toward the back of Hoboken, away from the water, to Monroe, and wandered around. Well, wouldn't you know that as she rounded the corner of Fourth, her tiny little ugly dog wagged his hairless tail and quivered all over like one of those metal detectors on the beach coming into contact with gold. She heard the sound of his tiny toenails scraping against the ground, and when he finally lifted his leg and let out a stream of yellow pee, she looked down and gasped: he was peeing directly on a giant gold star, marking the plot where Sinatra was born! And thus, a tiny runt of a dog was given the macho name.

"God, this dog is ugly," Andrea said in a singsong voice. Sinatra licked her nose, not upset over the insult. "But he sure is a sweetie pie."

"You're not ugly, are you, son?" Shoshana asked Sinatra, who promptly licked her across her mouth.

"Gross!" Andrea exclaimed. "You shouldn't let him lick you like that. Dogs carry different germs than us."

"They do not," Shoshana said. She laughed. "There aren't special dog species germs."

He was the ugliest dog Shoshana had ever seen when she visited the shelter, but she fell in love with him immediately. She knew all about being judged on appearance. He weighed four pounds (on a good day) and had a long, mostly furless skinny body with black and white spots, like a cow. Where he did have fur was around his face and ears, like an old man. He had an unexplainable missing left eye, which was grown over with luminescent, pale pink skin like the inside of a shell, and a tongue that didn't set right in his jaw and therefore stuck absurdly out the side through his teeth. Shoshana suspected he'd been abused at one point, given his injuries.

"Why's his eye like that?" a child in the park with chocolate on his face once asked her, as she was out walking.

"He's a pirate," Shoshana answered, smiling when the kid's jaw dropped open.

Sinatra was the love of her life and she didn't go anywhere without him in one of her large, unfashionable bags made from recycled material, his face sticking out, his crooked tongue flapping against his cheek as the wind swept his face and whipped his fur back, making him look like a bat.

"I'm actually glad you woke me up," Shoshana said. She took off the pink eye cover that she wore to sleep and placed it on her white Shabby Chic for Target bedside table.

She'd been having the strangest dream, that Victoria Beckham, Lindsay Lohan, and Paris Hilton were all holding hands and dancing in the moonlight on her mother's back deck in Summit, and it seemed only natural that their little bit of skin left would slip right off and their skeletons would gleam, their jawbones creaking into eerie, see-through grins, as they joined hands and danced, bones clacking, wind whistling through their rib cages.

Andrea had started bouncing on the bed.

"I really do hope I throw up on you," Shoshana said, throwing a pink, lace-trimmed pillow at her friend, which bounced off her head. She had a pillow problem. Something about them just filled her with happiness. Her favorites were crocheted ones with silly sayings, like STRESSED SPELLED BACKWARDS IS DESSERTS, or CON-SERVE WATER, DRINK MARGARITAS.

"I wish you would, girl," Andrea said. "It would make my case for calling in sick a little more believable." She worked as a cocktail waitress at the W Hotel in Hoboken down by the water and hated it.

"You're not seriously calling in sick *again*, are you? Andrea, you are going to totally get fired and you need this job! We've got the rent bill coming up in six days." Shoshana had always been the most responsible of her group of girlfriends; maybe it had something to do with being the firstborn. She was the mama bear. Friends flocked to her for advice, to borrow five bucks, or to help them learn how to knit. She was never judgmental in any way.

Andrea stopped jumping and threw her arms around Shoshana. "I know, I know!" she said, sighing. "But I seriously can't go to work tonight. For one, it's snowing. And two, I have a date." Sinatra had a momentary freak-out, barking like crazy and jumping in little leaps around Andrea, who still hadn't forgiven him for taking a poop inside her favorite fake Chanel purse last month.

"Yo, your dog is a spaz," Andrea said, watching him warily.

Shoshana sat up. She was wearing a gray Yankees T-shirt, size extra-large. Her breasts felt heavy on her chest. Her long auburn hair stuck out in all directions from her face. "I'm not going to do you any favors if you insult my furry son." She walked over to the window, raised her pink shade with a frilly white tassel, and blinked. "It's snowing?"

"Yup! Since early this morning, lazy bones." They stood shoulder to shoulder and surveyed the street. The snow covered everything: telephone poles, cars, sidewalk.

"Okay, forget I asked. I'm going to need my sunglasses just to get out of this bed." She groaned. Then, noticing the big grin on Andrea's face, she asked, "So you have, like, a *date* date? With whom?"

"Shosh, you are the only person I know who says 'whom' correctly in a sentence."

"Grammar is rad, what can I say?"

They both sat back down into the bed.

Andrea excitedly got into a cross-legged position. Shoshana did the same, and their knees touched, making a figure eight on the bed. "All I can think about is this guy! It's nuts. I think I might be falling in love. Seriously." Andrea said she was falling in love with someone new approximately once a month.

"Tell me all about him." Shoshana put on a fake deep fatherly voice. "I'd like to meet the young man, find out what his intentions are."

Andrea giggled. "He's actually kind of, um . . . young for me. I met him at work. He's parking cars while he finishes school."

"Oh, my god, is he in high school?"

"No! You pervert." Both girls giggled hysterically. Shoshana was used to this; she started most mornings with one of her roommates ensconced in her bed, giving her the latest gossip, filling her in on their lives. It was only natural in a house with five women. "He's a junior at Stevens, he's majoring in, like, bioengineering or something. I don't know what it means, but it sounds really smart. He's twenty. I think he wants to design weapons, like Robert Downey, Jr., in *Iron Man*."

"Well, that only makes you six years older. That's not bad. And besides, men date younger women all the time! The only downside is he'll have to wait around outside when we go to the bar. We can tie him up to a lamppost next to Sinatra."

They both giggled.

"Yipes, I didn't think of that." Andrea shrugged. "I'll wait it out. He's only got six more months until his birthday."

Shoshana giggled. "Right on, sister. Rob that cradle!"

"Besides, he has a six-pack! How many guys our age have six-packs?"

"How did you see his stomach? I thought he parks cars at work. Wouldn't he be wearing a uniform?"

"Um, well, we kind of did it already in the coat-check room. So this is sort of our first *official* date."

"Ah, I see. Well, sometimes you have to find out if he's good in the sack before you do the whole calling-in-sick-to-work bit for a guy. What's his name?"

Andrea turned red. "Marty. I know, I know. It's a really dorky name, but it was his father's and he's kind of stuck with it."

"I think it's a perfectly nice name," Shoshana said. "Besides, he's got to be better than your last boyfriend, who had a hole in his car near the pedals so he could throw his weed out in case he got pulled over. What was his name? Jeff?"

"I think so. Oh, my god, remember? I used to think how crazy it was that I could see the road rushing by while he drove. It felt like I'd roll right through and end up flattened on 287." Andrea shook her head.

Shoshana petted Sinatra, who was sprawled on her lap on his back, his tiny paws in the air, his spotted baby belly puffed out.

"Soooooo . . . are you going to call Asshole Boss Man or not?"

"Of course I am," Shoshana said. "So what will it be this week . . . still the Lyme disease? Or have you a migraine?" She rubbed her eyes, her auburn hair framing her face like a lion's mane.

"You look like the exorcist," Andrea told her.

Sinatra saw something outside the window he didn't approve of. Possibly a stray cat; Hoboken was full of them.

"Do you want my help or not? Sinatra, *please* stop barking. We all know you're very tough and masculine and scary." His high-pitched barking coming from a pint-sized throat was definitely *not* helping her slight hangover from the wine she'd consumed last night. She wasn't a big drinker, but she loved to have a good time and try different types of reds from the Tuscany region. She and Andrea would sip out of the pretty, stemless glasses their roommate Jane got as an engagement present for her upcoming summer wedding, and make up wine reviews such as, "This merlot has a distinct flavor of tree bark."

Andrea sat behind her, braiding her hair. Shoshana had beautiful, stunning hair. A cross between brown, red, and spun gold, she'd not cut it since middle school and it looked prettiest up in a messy ponytail, as it was naturally wavy and tendrils would fall throughout her day and loop around her face like a mermaid's. She rarely wore it down, but would from time to time take it out of its rubber band, letting it swing down her broad back nearly to her waist. Her skin was luminescent, a smooth white, causing people to state that most annoying of all idioms, "You have such a pretty face!" as if having a pretty face meant she held some kind of responsibility to be thin, as if she were throwing away a genetic gift.

"I was thinking chicken pox," Andrea said.

"Andrea, no one over the age of five gets chicken pox. Asshole Boss Man will never believe you!"

Andrea chewed this over.

Shoshana suspected Andrea had ADD and therefore waitressing was the worst possible job for her friend, but she'd never say so, as it wasn't encouraging. Andrea had to wear a black miniskirt that was so short she couldn't bend over to put people's drinks on their table, placing them in their hands instead.

"Okay, okay," Andrea said finally. "The Lyme disease, then. Web MD says four weeks after the initial red rash I'd start developing flulike symptoms, so maybe you can tell Asshole Boss Man that I'm throwing up and feverish?"

"You looked up symptoms on a health Web site to obtain more information so your made-up disease would sound more believable?"

Andrea nodded. "Of course," she said, like it was the most normal behavior in the world.

"Okay, that's just sick," Shoshana said, laughing. She started gathering up empty wineglasses and a bottle friends had strewn around her room.

"What are you blogging about today?" Andrea asked, changing the subject, her dark eyes wide. One of Shoshana's biggest supporters, she often read and helped edit her posts before they went live. She'd once written a very popular story for *Fat and Fabulous* about Latin men and how they appreciated the rounder booty. And how she appreciated them appreciating it.

"I just posted a column on how pedicures are the friend of the Fat," Shoshana said. "The concept was that even if people are making me feel like shit about being a big girl, I can go get a pedicure and the sun comes out and birds chirp and a rainbow suddenly fills the sky."

"I know what you mean!" Andrea said. "I love pedis. I'd give up sex before I'd give them up. I'd give up *orgasms* for pedicures."

Shoshana laughed. She had a loud, infectious boom of a laugh, which filled the room and bounced off the walls. "Liar."

"Hee, hee. You got me there. Now you have to call Asshole Boss Man."

"Okay, okay," Shoshana said, shifting over and feeling around on the ground for her purse. "Can we just call him ABM from now on? Saying the whole word takes too long. What's his real name, anyway?"

"No idea. I almost called him Asshole Boss Man to his *face* the other day, it was crazy-town. That's the trouble with changing waitressing jobs every month; your bosses' ugly faces start to blend together." Andrea's jobs were short-lived, mainly because she was known to tell off customers if they got on her bad side, not to mention her unreliability when it came to showing up for her shifts.

Shoshana finally found her purse under the bed and lifted it up.

"Ew, what is that bag *made* out of?" Andrea asked, pinching shut her nose.

"Um . . . it's hemp. Why?"

"It smells funny." Andrea was on a mission to rid Shoshana of her hippie attachments. She'd once thrown Shoshana's Birkenstocks down the garbage chute in college.

"Do you want me calling or not? Because I have a life."

"Okay, we both know that's a lie, but I do need the favor. Pretty please? I'll bring you breakfast in bed."

"Done."

Andrea scurried off to pop a bagel into the toaster. The toaster had been another one of Jane's engagement presents her roommates apprehended for general use. In addition to the wineglasses and toaster, they'd recently held a romantic-yet-ironic Taco Bell dinner with candles from Tiffany's (a present from Jane's grandmother), eaten Triscuit crackers with Cheese Whiz on a Bloomingdale's silver platter while watching a Giants game, and taken long, luxurious showers, then wrapped themselves in Jane's new fluffy Bloomingdale's towels. "Grown-up stuff," they'd whisper reverently, excited to finally have nice things, even if it didn't *exactly* belong to them.

Jane's fiancé, Andrew, did something mysterious for a hedge fund and made a crapload of money—neither he nor Jane cared if everyone used their stuff. As she could never get a straight answer about what he did for a living, Shoshana liked to start the rumor that Andrew was probably running a Ponzi scheme, which Jane would then laugh nervously at, also in the dark as to what her fiancé did.

Shoshana rooted around in her hemp purse, which she could admit *did* smell a tad like dirt, and found the cheap cell phone that had come with her phone plan. It had a *Fat and Fabulous* sticker with pink lettering on the back of it.

As she flipped open the phone it rang, playing Sheryl Crow's "Leaving Las Vegas." It was the ringtone she'd programmed for her lawyer friend Greg, who loved to fly to Vegas on a whim (he could afford it) and play blackjack, often taking his girlfriend of the week with him. Shoshana and Greg dated during their freshman and sophomore years at Summit High, realized they had very little interest in ever seeing each other naked again, and remained close friends ever since. Greg was handsome albeit short, about five-foot-seven, with soft, receding brown hair he wore cut close to his head. He had a large, hooked nose, olive-toned skin, and a sculpted body from all the time he spent in the gym. His intelligent hazel eyes were his best feature. He came from a wealthy, old-Jersey family and had nice Jewish good looks. Shoshana had practically lived at his house in high school. She loved Greg's

mother Shirley, a real wiseass who often said she would trade Greg
for Shoshana as her child any day.

"I think my mom likes you better than me," Greg would complain.

"Of course she does," Shoshana said. "I visit her more."

"The problem with her liking you so much is she acts rude to all
the girlfriends I bring over to meet her."

"Well, what can I say? You can't top perfection," Shoshana would
say, running her hands over her plump body, her eyes twinkling.

The fact that Greg was short didn't put off the models he dated.

Shoshana's mother, Pam, once said her youngest daughter was
good at "collecting people," and it was true. She always stayed
friends with ex-boyfriends, much to the astonishment of her roommates, whose relationships ended with the occasional restraining
order or car-egging.

"Hey, Greg."

"Hey, Shosh."

She smiled. He sounded hungover also.

Andrea wrung her hands and left the room, shooting annoyed
looks at Shoshana.

"How's it hanging?" he asked.

"Oh, you know, shriveled and a little to the left as always.
Sounds like you have the Irish flu." She leaned over and turned on
her iPod. Strains of Feist began to play.

"A little. How's the crazy henhouse?"

"Gregory, just because I live with four other women doesn't mean
it's a henhouse, you misogynist pig." His mother called him Gregory,
and Shoshana did as well, because she knew it annoyed him.

"Well, how's it anyways?"

"Crazy."

They both laughed.

"I hear you're listening to your usual vagina music," Greg said
scornfully.

"Okay, seriously? I've been telling you this for ten years. Just
because I only listen to female musicians doesn't mean it's vagina

music," Shoshana said. "And please don't say 'vagina.' It just sounds weird coming out of your mouth. Sorry I don't like frickin' watered-down nineties rock." She imitated his voice. "Oh, I'm Greg Hirsch. Excuse me while I turn the ladies on with Three Doors Down."

Greg laughed. "I prefer Spin Doctors."

"Of course you do. So enough chitchat. How was the date?"

As a lawyer in the district attorney's office in Trenton, he often dated other lawyers, and went out last night with an attorney who worked on child custody disputes. That was all Shoshana knew about her, but she was eager to learn more. "By the way, points for not dating another model. Those girls were sweet, but I'm glad you're starting to broaden your horizons."

"Well . . . it went okay, I guess. But I don't think I'd see her again."

Shoshana sighed. Greg was ridiculously picky when it came to women. She still couldn't believe they'd once dated, as they'd been so ill matched romantically and physically. (She was at her heaviest in high school, at nearly three hundred pounds.) Greg was the only short guy Shoshana had ever gone out with. Her dream boyfriend would look like a cross between Keanu Reeves and Zac Efron, and be strong enough to pick her up and swing her around.

"What was the problem with her, exactly? Wait. First things first. Tell me where you ate," Shoshana asked.

Greg smiled from his bed in the Shipyard, an upscale lifestyle building built in uptown Hoboken along the waterfront with stunning views of the Manhattan skyline. His building had a doorman, elevator, pool, and workout center. Shoshana made fun of him for living in what she called "Yuppie Paradise," but at the same time would force Greg to hand over his pool pass to her when the mood struck. He joked that he was "roughing it" when he walked the nine blocks downtown to Shoshana's prewar walk-up.

When he took women out, which was pretty much every night, Shoshana needed to know what restaurant he ate in and what they ordered for dinner—food was always on her mind. Just one of the many things about her that amused him. He appreciated her friendship and held her opinion above his buddies'—she always told it like it is.

"We went to Strip House in the city," he said.

"Oh, my god, I think I just came," Shoshana said. "Keep going." Andrea came back into the room, shot Shoshana an odd look, and walked back out.

Greg laughed. "We started with sides of buttered spinach and potatoes, and then we both had the ribeye."

Shoshana was a vegetarian (she thought it was mean to eat something that had dreams), but she appreciated a finely made meal when she heard about one.

"And did she eat?" she asked.

She always asked him this, weeding out dates that ordered only salads and picked nervously at them. She didn't care how thin the women were that he took out, but they had to have a healthy appetite if they were to earn Shoshana's approval.

"She ate everything on her plate. Oh! And she licked the knife at the end," he said.

"Promising! And for dessert?"

"I told her I was stuffed, so she went ahead and ordered a chocolate mousse for herself and finished it off solo."

"I love her already!" Shoshana squealed. "When is the second date? Wait, I know. We'll do it here! We'll throw a party, you can bring her, and then I can meet her all casual-like."

"Okay, but don't get your hopes up. There were a few red flags."

Shoshana got out of bed and started searching around her room for her towel and the new Malin+Goetz facewash she'd recently emptied the last of her checking account out to buy.

"What red flags? I swear if you say one of her toes was longer than the big toe, or that she had lettuce stuck between her front teeth, I am hanging up the phone."

"Would you just listen? After dinner we went back to her place."

"This is getting good. Get to the juicy parts."

Andrea came back into the room for the third time and held

her palms up, mouthing, *Did you call my work yet?* She placed a plate with a bagel and cream cheese on Shoshana's bedside table on top of a pile of beach read novels. Shoshana shook her head and shooed her away, slamming the door. She heard a sharp kick sound from the other side.

"So she opens a bottle of red wine—"

"I love red wine!" Shoshana interrupted.

Greg laughed. "You love any kind of wine, as long as it has alcohol in it. Would you let me finish?"

"Sorry. Please continue," she said. She opened her door and walked in her pretty Hanes plus-size pink cotton bra and underwear past Andrea, ignored her glare, opened the door to the bathroom, and sat down on the toilet. "By the way, I'm peeing while I'm talking to you."

"Of course you are," Greg said. "Okay, so *anyway,* we're making out on her bed—"

"Greg, no one says *making out* anymore. That's so dorky." Greg sometimes was too serious and lawyerish. Shoshana saw it as her duty to shake him up. She went to wipe and discovered there was no toilet paper. Again.

"Agh!" she shouted. "Is it really that hard to refill the toilet paper? How many times is a girl expected to drip-dry?"

"Gross," Greg said.

"Aggie used it all up for a sculpture," Karen said calmly from inside the shower two feet from where Shoshana was peeing.

Shoshana screamed. "Karen, I didn't know you were in there! What the hell are you doing?" She dropped the phone from her ear and fished around on the floor for it, Greg's voice calling out, "Hello? Hello?"

Karen stepped out. "Just drying myself off. You're the one who came barging in here to pee, lady, without checking the shower to see if there was anyone in it."

Shoshana giggled. "And do you check the shower every single time you come in the bathroom?"

Karen wrapped the towel around herself. She was tall, five-

eleven, and in her second year of Columbia Law School. She had
short wavy brown hair, bright green eyes, and played volleyball at
Chelsea Piers on a competitive women's team throughout the year.
At Princeton, she and Shoshana would often work out at the gym
together, Karen cheering Shoshana on. Despite being a large girl,
Shoshana loved working out at the gym (if only to stare at the cute
butts of the boys in the weight room).

"What kind of sculpture is she making that she needs toilet paper?" Shoshana asked, doing a little shake sitting down. "Hold your
horses," she bellowed to Greg, who was emitting loud, annoyed sighs.

"I don't know. Last week she'd stolen my Kashi cereal to sculpt
with. I made her give me five bucks for it."

Their roommate Aggie, short for Agatha (named for a very
dead grandmother on her mother's side), was a sculptor. She often
used various odd things from around the apartment in her work.
One time she'd asked Shoshana for three tampons and made
dreadlocks out of them for a self-portrait and displayed it at PS1 in
Queens. She was always late on the rent, but the rest of the girls
forgave her out of love. Once, Aggie paid rent in change, all $400
of it. Shoshana had to drive her to their landlord's office on Adams
Street, Aggie hauling into the backseat large zip-lock bags filled
with quarters and dimes.

"Do you want to hear the story or not?" Greg shouted, his voice
sounding small and tinny through the phone.

Shoshana rolled her eyes at Karen and mouthed, *Gregory,* to
her as Karen slipped gracefully out of the room to continue getting ready for class.

"I do, I do," Shoshana reassured Greg. She did one last shimmy,
kicked off her undergarments, and hung them on the back of the
door. She felt an immediate pinch in her back as her breasts swung
forward. Her bra looked like a parachute next to her roommate
Karen's size-34A bras, all hanging on a nearby hook to dry after
she'd washed them in the sink. She turned on the water.

"Shosh, are you still there?" Greg's voice came through to her
on the phone.

"Yes, Greg! Did your fragile ego take a blow because I wasn't paying attention to you for five seconds?"

He laughed. "It did, actually."

She rolled her eyes.

"So we're starting to kind of dry-hump on her bed—"

"Wait, *what*? You said you were only kissing! You have to fill in the good parts!"

"Shoshana, I'm hanging up the phone. I am not telling you about the sex! You're supposed to be giving me advice!"

"Was there sex? Greg, you whore!"

Silence on the other end.

Shoshana groaned. "Fine. Be that way. I'm listening."

"Anyway, we're doing whatever, and lo and behold, in her closet are a whole row of her little expensive jeans, all carefully hung on hangers with little clips."

"What size were they?" She always liked to know what size clothing people wore.

"I don't know, maybe six? Eight? Anyway, don't you find it pretentious?"

"What, that she wears a size eight? Certainly not. She's my new hero, what with the licking of the knife and ordering dessert and all that. I can't wait to meet her."

"No!" he said, laughing. "I mean that she hangs up her jeans. I mean, who does that? I feel like it's a talisman of bad things to come."

"Okay, Greg, seriously, you're not Harry Potter. Don't say 'talisman.' It will turn girls off."

"Whatever. All I'm saying is that I feel like most nice, normal American girls fold their jeans and put them in a *dresser*. Anyone who hangs up their jeans probably votes for Nader and litters."

Shoshana stuck her tongue out at the phone.

"See? This is exactly why we broke up. You are so crazy! You go out with this girl once, and you're coming up with all these wild assumptions about her. Go out with her again. Let her pick the restaurant. Stop nitpicking every girl you go out with. You're such a mathlete." Greg had been on the math team in high school, and she'd never let him live it down.

"You know you loved my mathematic self," Greg teased. "That's how I got you to sleep with me in the first place."

"More like I was fifteen and desperate to lose my virginity. Besides, you served up that 'mystery punch' at your parents' house," Shoshana said, examining her toes. "I would have slept with anyone after drinking that. I sincerely hope you've come up with better tactics to get laid since then." She needed a pedicure badly. One big toe's pink polish was chipped.

Greg chortled. "That's right! I forgot about that. I think it was rum, cranberry juice, and a ground-up lemon peel. I'd just seen *Cocktail* and wanted to be Tom Cruise."

After a few more parting insults, Shoshana hung up with Greg, only after wrestling out a promise he would go on a second date and bring her home a slice of cake from their dessert. With her love life in the crapper, she had to rely on friends' dates to bring her home goodies. She made a mental note to work harder on finding a boyfriend.

Shoshana stepped into the shower, letting the steam run over her face to open her pores before exfoliating. She felt weightless under the water. She thought about her friendship with Greg as she rooted through the various bottles of shampoos belonging to her roommates and found her brand, which claimed to use water from a spring in Alaska but was probably actually from the Gowanus Canal.

She thought again about her lack of a love life and realized she hadn't had sex in over six months, which was depressing. She wanted a boyfriend, but not badly enough to sleep with random people. She had a JDate account Andrea had signed her up for without asking. And put up a picture of Denise Richards. From a still in *Wild Things*. Topless. Needless to say, Shoshana had gotten a lot of e-mails to go through and delete.

The truth was, she was having so much fun with her friends that, although she wanted love and romance, it didn't feel all that important. She was twenty-six years old, saw her mother and sister daily, lived with four crazy women, and had a wide network of not just friends, but *best* friends.

Shoshana knew eventually she'd meet someone great, but she wasn't going out every night to the bars to find Mr. Big. She often wondered if there was something wrong with her; it seemed every other woman she knew had been suckered into the *Sex and the City* mentality: that their lives revolved around meeting a man, settling down in a fabulous apartment, and having adorable babies. She was happy with her life, something she knew people like Alexis Allbright had a hard time wrapping their malnourished brains around. She'd always had this mystical, tingling sensation that she was somehow . . . destined to do something interesting and different. That she had a *life purpose*. It was this glittery future that would swim into her thoughts, when she least expected it. A gut feeling told her this destiny did not have to include a man.

Lately all her dates had been failures, but she wasn't giving up hope just yet. Aggie had taken an attractive picture of her last week to replace the Denise Richards one. She stood on a chair, claiming Shoshana's face looked less wide when shot from up above. Shoshana had worn her favorite three-quarter-length pink plaid dress, outlandishly large diamond hoop earrings down to her shoulders, a matching pink and white plaid scarf in her auburn hair, and red lip gloss. Everyone agreed she'd taken a great photo.

If nothing else, JDate provided good material for *Fat and Fabulous*.

The first guy had been pretty bland, like eating a rice cracker. Date number two had told her that her feet looked beautiful in her open-toe gold sandals and she'd gone home happy, thinking she'd call the guy again, until Greg said he probably had a foot fetish.

The third, last week, was with a man named Asher, a graduate student at Rutgers, who was in the middle of getting his Ph.D. in American Studies.

The first thing she noticed about him when she met him at a small Italian restaurant in the West Village was that his right eye blinked continuously, open and shut, like a traffic light. She later remembered lights that blink meant "caution," which she should have paid attention to. He had a flat haircut, like an early Paul McCartney but not nearly as handsome, and when he stood up to shake her hand he was very, very short. Shorter than Greg.

She'd tried to make the most of it. You never knew when Prince Charming might come galloping into your life, perhaps even disguised in wrinkled chinos with too many pockets that looked like they'd been purchased around when the first episode of *Melrose Place* aired.

"You look just like your picture," she'd told him, to break the ice. She'd read somewhere it was a common compliment for on-line daters.

"And you look . . . similar," he said, taking in her 215 pounds. And she'd put her long hair into a bun and everything for this troll of a man. Hmph.

"So, tell me about your Ph.D. program," she said, after ordering blueberry pancakes and a mimosa. The booth squeaked when he moved and Shoshana had to stifle a laugh. It sounded kind of like a fart.

He glanced furtively around the restaurant. "Do you think any-one's listening?" he asked.

Shoshana bit her lip. "What?" Did he mean listening to the fart?

"What about those two men over there? Probably FBI, right?"

She turned to look at two overweight truckers in flannel shirts, their pockets protruding with Marlboro reds.

"Definitely not listening." She started texting "SOS" to Andrea underneath the table. Maybe she'd get lucky and her roommate would take the PATH into the city and pick her up with an ex-cuse; Andrea was well practiced at coming up with date-escape strategies.

He grabbed the back of her neck and pulled her close to his face. He messed up her bun. His breath smelled like raccoon poop.

"I'm writing the history of the New Jersey Devil." He leaned back in the booth, looking extremely satisfied with himself.

"Okay, next time, no talky, no closey," Shoshana said, as two steaming plates of food were placed before them. She patted her hair back into place.

"Sorry. I just have to keep things hidden from the government. They want to sabotage my dissertation."

Shoshana burst out laughing. "I think the government has more important things to do than worry about the Jersey Devil. Besides, it's just an urban legend. You know it's not real, right?" She took a bite of her meal and closed her eyes in ecstasy. Delicious! He started to speak and she cracked one eye open, wishing he would stop.

He glared at her. "You know, you sound just like my mother. The Devil is real. I've been following his tracks in the Meadowlands for the last six years."

She stared at him. "Well, everyone needs a hobby," she said at last.

He leaned back in the booth, looking her over head to toe. It appeared he was switching gears.

"Just so you know, I'm totally into you. My mother was a large woman, and I've been attracted to fat girls ever since. You have a lovely pear shape."

Okay, that was the final straw. Shoshana put down her fork. Gave her food a longing look. It really was a shame to waste it. She gathered up her purse, came around to Asher's side of the table, and leaned over to whisper in his ear.

"Have you ever actually *looked* at a pear?" she said. "It starts thin, then it gets fat, and it never gets thin again. It's not a cute fruit."

And with that she threw her auburn hair over her shoulder and walked to the train.

As she stepped out of the shower, she realized she'd forgotten to tell Greg about the date from hell, so she called him back while she towel-dried her hair, which fell in damp waves down her back. She called Greg approximately seventeen times a day.

"Forgot to tell you something," she said when he answered.

"I was just about to go into the office, you caught me. I realized I forgot to ask you how JDate was going." Greg was reading her mind as usual.

"You work too hard. Well, since you asked . . . after the Jersey Devil, the boring guy who doesn't drink because he doesn't like feeling out of control and still lives with his mom, and foot-fetish man, I *did* get a very nice note just last week from a nose, ear, and throat doctor who lives on the Upper East Side."

"So? What's the problem?"

"Um . . . okay, promise you won't laugh?"

"I promise."

"His last name is Lowcock. First name John, last name Lowcock."

"Like Lokok? Sounds Asian."

"No, spelled like it sounds. Low and then . . . you know."

"Oh, that's fabulous. You have to go out with this guy. In fact, maybe I could come along just to shake his hand."

"Greg! You're not helping," Shoshana said, giggling. She walked back to her room, where Andrea was perched on her bed reading a trashy celebrity magazine.

"What's so funny?" she asked.

"Tell Andrea hi," Greg said through the phone. Shoshana did the explaining and the greeting. Greg was over often and friendly with all her roommates except Aggie, who'd once stolen his golf-ball money clip and cemented it into a sculpture of an erect penis. It had been the tip and he'd never forgiven her.

"Greg says hi."

"Hello, Gregory."

"But what if we meet, fall in love, get married, and then my name becomes Shoshana Lowcock?" Shoshana wailed.

"Junior high must have been hell for this guy," Andrea said, shaking her head.

"If that were my name I'd totally own it," Greg said, his voice full of mirth. "Hell, yes. My name is Lowcock. Then I'd scratch the bottom of my pants leg meaningfully."

"Greg!" Andrea and Shoshana both squealed. Andrea was leaning on Shoshana's shoulder, listening in.

"Okay, Greg, you perv, I have to go. Andrea's making me call in sick for her."

"Again?"

"Yup. Okay, see you later."

Shoshana knew Andrea's boss's phone number by heart and called, gave the excuse quickly (she was a terrible liar, so she spoke fast), and hung up.

"I'm going back to bed," Andrea said. "Come get me if Steven Spielberg calls and wants me to audition for his latest movie."

First things first. Shoshana decided to forfeit getting a pedicure in town in favor of doing it herself; that way she could take care of business without leaving the comfort of her bed. She did everything from her bed. Once, when she'd broken her big toe playing soccer in a town league she belonged to, she'd hosted an entire dinner party from the confines of her bed. Friends had sat cross-legged around her, drinking wine and chattering. Spilling potato chips on her sheets.

She painted her toenails, scrunching up the little rubber clingers that held her small, rosy toes apart. She had tiny delicate pink nails, which she carefully painted blue, her foot propped up on a white pillow on her bed stitched with lettering: BETWEEN TWO EVILS I ALWAYS PICK THE ONE I HAVEN'T TRIED YET. It had been a present from her mom, for her twenty-fifth birthday, who knew Shoshana adored Mae West quotes. And pillows, of course.

Shoshana regularly wrote *Fat and Fabulous* from home. She'd been a homebody all her life. She felt grateful to have been sprung free by the recession from her horrid office clerical job at an allergist's office in Jersey City. (Who wanted to listen to people sneeze all day?) On days she didn't sleep in, she'd wake around nine-thirty, stretch, throw off her large candy-cane pink-and-white-striped duvet, and glide her tiny feet into white fur slippers with small heels on the bottoms that always made her feel like a movie star. After breakfast she wrote a first draft of her daily column, checked in with various writers, read the message boards, and scanned the headlines for any news about weight issues.

In the early afternoon she often went for a power walk with her wealthy friend Nancy, who lived uptown in the Hudson Tea Building, near Greg's building. Nancy had Kanye West and Eli Manning for neighbors. She owned a vintage clothing boutique in town and dated a local cop, Anthony Morelli, off and on, and Shoshana was now well versed in the fiery passions of the Italian man.

Both women were fat and fabulous; thus they shared a mutual hatred for jogging. Jogging is not a friend of the Fat. All that pain surely cannot be worth the cardio benefit. The last time Shoshana had tried to jog, her boobs had fallen out of her bra three times in broad daylight. So they power-walked. Or at least they walked kind of fast. When they weren't gossiping.

Shoshana's favorite part of the walk was the end, when they stopped off for a glass of wine, and Nancy, knowing everyone in town, would fill Shoshana in on the latest dirt.

After her walk and after attaining a suitable wine buzz, she'd go home, shower, pick out a dress from her closet, and see who felt like getting takeout dinner. (She adored dresses, never wore pants unless they were stretch leggings, and *abhorred* shorts.) She'd often thought of posting on her hatred of shorts and pants, but knew what the result would be: hundreds of hate e-mails from her readers:

Dear Shoshana:
The whole point of Fabulously Fat is to empower round women. How dare you write about how fat girls shouldn't wear shorts. All you are doing is perpetuating anxieties that we already feel about our bodies, instead of doing your job, which is to make us feel comfortable in our skin.

She had to be extremely careful when using a self-deprecating tone. As the Face of Fat, she had to be persistently positive, which could get tiring. When she slipped, the e-mails piled up in her in-box fast and furious. One reader, a fellow blogger named Ashley from Idaho, claimed Shoshana had no right calling herself fat at 215 pounds. As Ashley weighed somewhere around 300, she felt anyone with smaller numbers on the scale was merely "chubby" and didn't have enough credibility to be in the Fat-O-Sphere.

Shoshana had written Ashley back:

Dear Ashley,
I'm delighted you read Fat and Fabulous. *I can assure you I am fat.*
Statistically, I am obese. When I walk onto a bus, or sit down on the
subway, people glare at me, like I'm supposed to apologize just for
living and breathing the same air as them. Like I should say, Sorry I
exist, people. *So I hope you'll trust me to continue to be the voice of*
the Fattie, and hopefully you will keep enjoying the blog.

She felt sometimes as if she were a campaigning politician, futilely attempting to please everyone. But her readers meant the world to her, so she tried to stay above conflict as much as possible.

Another snafu occurred when she wrote a seemingly bland post about her favorite snack, hummus and wheat crackers. Shoshana received hundreds of e-mails stating it sounded suspiciously like she was advertising a diet.

The irony was *Fat and Fabulous* was just the opposite. There were rules: Her readers were not allowed to post anything regarding diets in any form. Not even if they'd found one that helped them lose weight. This had been a controversial decision, but she, along with other colleagues who ran blogs for big girls, such as *The Rotund* and *Manolo for the Big Girl*, refused to allow any talk of diets on their message boards and did not post diet stories. The motivation behind her starting *Fat and Fabulous* was to empower women, not suggest ways for them to starve.

She also did not allow diet advertisements on her blog—tricky, given how much money they offered to shell out. Shoshana refused; what with five million insecure readers looking for answers and salvation, they were sitting ducks for the diet industry. But Shoshana wasn't going to help them; any diet her mom and sister tried over the years had left them feeling ill, or they'd gained all the weight back (sometimes double the pounds!). The industry was a sham, and it made Shoshana angry that it was so profitable. There were big bucks in making women feel like shit.

Finding herself alone again in her room, Shoshana realized she was still hungry and padded downstairs for a snack. Their small kitchen was cheerily painted a bright robin's-egg-blue, and strung from the ceiling were colored holiday lights that Karen had duct-taped to hang in waves, which gave a warm glow to the cheap white cabinets. Aggie was cooking on the stove, using a big wooden spoon to stir a suspicious-looking substance bubbling in a black pot that looked like a cauldron.

"Whatcha got cookin'?" Shoshana asked her nervously. "And what did you do with all the toilet paper in the house?" Aggie liked to "experiment" with various foods. She'd often mix together two recipes into one, swapping ingredients. She had a small vegetable garden growing on the fire escape that she slaved over and would integrate the spare rusty-brown carrot or ill-looking parsley bunch into her meals.

Aggie turned to Shoshana. She had bright red hair, dreadlocked and tied up on top of her head in a messy knot, and white skin with old pockmark scarring from adolescent acne. She was tiny and elf-ish, five-foot-nothin', huge blue eyes, and a scattering of freckles across the bridge of her nose. She worked as a barista downstairs at Empire Coffee to supplement her nonexistent income of being a sculptor.

"I'm sorry about the toilet paper, Shosh! I totally used it in this work yesterday and then forgot to buy more. I'm going to the A&P for pickles in a little while, so I'll pick some up."

Shoshana wisely decided not to ask what the pickles were for. They were either part of a cooking experiment, or to be stuck into a sculpture. Either way, she wanted no part of it.

"I'm cooking herbs for life longevity. Want some?"

"Er, no, thanks. I'll risk the shorter life."

"Up to you," she said cheerfully, shaking her dreadlocks. "By the way, you were great on *Oprah*! They showed a rerun of the episode with you from two months ago."

"Thanks! Did you watch the whole thing?" Shoshana, surprised, sat down at one of their wooden chairs Aggie had salvaged from the street on garbage night. Aggie wasn't exactly technologically advanced, and had held a protest in their living room against buying a flat-screen TV last month, calling it "consumer garbage." Eventually she'd settled down, put away her sign, and sat on the couch watching *Glee* with the rest of her roommates. They were used to Aggie, and loved her dearly, but there was no denying the girl was *odd*. The only child of two hippie parents, she'd lived on a commune in Ohio until breaking free and running away at eighteen. The director had believed eternal salvation meant wearing tinfoil hats when out in the sun and that eventually they would all get onto a spaceship and live on another planet if they prayed hard enough for it. Aggie still couldn't walk by a box of foil in the grocery store without shuddering. Shoshana was still a little hazy on the details when it came to Aggie's time on the commune.

"I watched it through the window of someone's apartment on Grand Street this morning," Aggie said guiltily, sticking into her mouth one of her dreadlocks, which had curled down from the bun, and sucking on it. She'd attached little silver bells, and they jingled when she turned her head.

"Wait a minute—you stood outside someone's apartment? How did you not freeze? It's the middle of the winter."

"I dunno. I was looking around on the ground for pinecones for one of my sculptures and when I looked up, I saw the most beautiful sight; it was you, and you were on the *television*! This family had the show on, and the mom was feeding her baby at the kitchen table, not even watching *Oprah,* even though she had it on, which don't you kind of hate it when people turn on the TV but don't watch it, just, like, for background noise? It's such a waste of electricity."

"Um . . . Aggie? Can you kind of get to the point? Because I have work to do."

"Oh! Right. So anyway, I gathered up about twelve pinecones in my canvas bag and then just stood there and watched you. It was kind of hard to hear through the glass . . ."

"I can imagine," Shoshana said sarcastically, but Aggie didn't pick up on it.

"But toward the end that Alexis person started shouting nice and loud and then I could hear just fine. The mom didn't even see me, but I had an excuse all cooked up in case they did, that I was looking for my earring in the bushes. And by the way, Alexis was totally demonic! Her aura is totally *off*. You looked beautiful up there. Oh! And you sounded really smart when you were talking about your blog and facts about big women's health. I was impressed."

"You could see her aura through the TV, now, could you?"

"Of course I could," she said, like it was the most obvious thing in the world. "It's a sickly green color, a very worrisome shade of moss. Pea soup. It means her chi is waaaaaaay messed up. Anyway, enough about her. I was so proud that I knew you, and you looked so beautiful and knowledgeable up there onstage!"

Shoshana was touched. Aggie's head was always so up in the clouds. Up until now, she wasn't sure Aggie actually knew about what she did for a living. "Thanks, Aggie," she said, hugging her.

Shoshana quickly pulled away, retching. "Ugh! What's that smell?"

"Must be the herbs, then," Aggie said defensively.

"It smells like dead monkey!"

"Well, then, I'll be sure not to offer you any," Aggie sniffed, turning her tiny elfin back to Shoshana. Aggie seemed impervious to cold, never wore a jacket, and had on a thin white cotton dress that had a big circle cut out in the back, through which her two shoulder blades pressed together like moth wings. You could see her tiny pink nipples through the front of the dress.

"I'm sorry, Aggie, you know I love you," Shoshana said, planting a kiss on her friend's cheek. Aggie, never one to hold a grudge, beamed at Shoshana before continuing to stir her pot.

Shoshana grabbed two slices of whole-wheat bread, a jar of peanut butter, and an orange. She threw it all on a plate and headed upstairs to her bedroom and shut the door. She loved living with four women, but sometimes she had to hide.

Climbing into her bed, she could hear the shouts of a teacher outside, leading a line of children across the street. "Hold hands with your buddy! Walk between the white lines!"

Shoshana walked over to her window to wipe condensation off the glass and felt the cold wet on her palm. Tiny light flakes of snow danced down from the sky, only to disappear once they hit pavement. Mothers walked side by side, pushing strollers like a brigade. There's a joke in Hoboken that you never see a child out of a stroller. And that there is a baby boom here, with a three-child limit: once the third baby pops out you grow tired of living sardinelike in a two-bedroom for three thousand a month; it's time to venture forth to that foreign land we call the suburbs. Families move a few exits down the Turnpike and expand to Montclair, Jersey City, Madison, and Summit. Shoshana planned on sticking it out in Hoboken for as long as she possibly could. Should she get married, children would have to simply live stacked one on top of the other. She would not move to the burbs no matter what.

She heard a car door slam and two small, hunched old ladies clutching triangle-shaped plastic purses emerged from their car and peered up at a tall sign in front of their car. "Can we park here?" Shoshana heard one of them ask a passerby, her wrinkled face creased further in confusion. The man crossed his arms and read the sign slowly.

"Can I park here?" is a refrain heard everywhere in Mile Square City. On the right side of every street is a white sign with green lettering. That means you can stick your car there for four hours. If you should miraculously find an empty spot on the *left* side, well, that is a different story. The left side has a *green* sign with *white* lettering, and you need a resident sticker on your car that you give up your firstborn child to attain. On top of this, you must also be aware that there is street cleaning every day from nine to eleven. And if you can follow all that, the streets where the cleaning takes place switch daily. All this makes for a very pedestrian-friendly city, but confusing parking situations. Hobokenites constantly look for assurance from strangers walking by that they are reading the sign system correctly, and they're not about to have the parking police come by with their little handheld computers that spit fifty-dollar tickets out like sticks of gum. If you are in line at the dry cleaner's, the bakery, or the library, it is not uncommon to get a debilitating neck strain from craning your head toward the window, carefully keeping tabs on your double-parked car.

But you wouldn't have your flashers on, oh, no, sir, not if you're a local. Flashers signal weakness; a bleeding deer leaving a trail through the woods. Only a novice puts on the flashers in Hoboken, and that's who gets saddled with the dreaded white ticket slipped beneath the windshield wiper. If you're from Hoboken, you simply double-park for as long as you want. Double-parking, sans flashers, is a way of life here.

Shoshana left the window and helped Sinatra hop up on the bed. She plumped up her many pillows, forming a chair of sorts she could lean against. She moved a larger-sized one to her lap, so her computer's heat (when it was thinking, it emitted a hot blast) wouldn't scald her. She called her Web site manager, who lived in Park Slope and updated her blog daily, implemented advertisements, and kept things running smoothly. They spoke briefly, and agreed to touch base the following week to talk about a redesign of the entire blog. She peeled her orange and bit into one half-moon section, feeling the sugary burst of juice on her tongue.

She logged on to *Fat and Fabulous* and began reading the morning's message boards. A lot of positive feedback was still streaming in from the *Oprah* show as well as several sympathetic e-mails. Her favorite was from Erin of Austin, Texas:

Dear Shoshana,

I never knew your father passed away, I totally understand why you'd want to keep that private and I just wanted to offer you my condolences. At first I was surprised that you kept something a secret, since you usually tell your readers every detail of your private life. Fat and Fabulous *has done amazing things for my self-esteem. I am a librarian at an all-girls prep school and I weigh 300 pounds. I feel like your blog helps me open discussions between the high-school-age girls at my school so they can love their bodies just the way they are. Anyway, I appreciate everything you've done for me in*

*my life and wanted to reach out and say how sorry I am about your
father's passing.*

Her phone rang. Shoshana sighed. She wished she were one of
those dedicated writers who could shut off her phone so as not to be
disturbed. She'd once read an interview with a novelist who would
cuff her leg to her desk chair in order to force herself to work. Sometimes Shoshana thought writers made up things to sound interesting. *I mean, how did that woman pee for goodness' sake?*

She heard her mother's voice and was immediately enveloped
in a warm calm.

"Hi, Mom," she said.

"Honey, did you know they're showing another repeat of the
Oprah show today?"

Her throat tightened. "Oh. I didn't know that, no."

"Well, do you want to drive here and we'll watch it together?
Your sister is home, she got that lovely new assistant to watch the
store and she doesn't have anyone to draw pictures on today."

Shoshana smiled. Her mother always called tattooing "drawing
pictures." She didn't seem to grasp the concept of the needle pen-
etrating skin.

"I can't, Mom, I just woke up and I have to do some work on the
blog. I literally haven't done anything yet today, and I have to check
in with all my writers and see when the heck they're going to turn
in their work."

"Your sister and I will be watching the show again. Emily wants
to see if she can spot herself in the audience, of course."

She was half listening to her mother, and half drifting into her
wave of thought. Shoshana felt something shift within her. The
Oprah experience still bothered her.

"Are you proud of me, Mom?" she asked quietly. She stuck a
pink fingernail on the down arrow and scrolled through several
more posts on her message board. There were a lot of women very
angry with Alexis Allbright. One had superimposed red devil

horns and a tail onto a picture of her, taken from an appearance she'd made on *The View* last year.

"Well, I *was* proud of you until I saw this kid on *Ellen* who is a five-year-old piano prodigy who they say is better now than Beethoven in his prime."

"Mom!"

Pam laughed. "Of course I'm proud of you, what kind of question is that?"

"I don't know. I've been kind of bummed out since *Oprah*. Alexis had way more health facts to throw at me than I did. I feel like I came off kind of silly."

"Shoshana, if you think for one second I give . . . well, I give an *owl's behind* about what Alexis Allbright says or thinks, you've got another thing coming."

Shoshana had to smile at the expression. Pam wasn't much of a curser.

"Dear, no one cares about boring statistics but doctors. Your posts are funny and smart and witty. You make people feel good about themselves again, and that is a skill. Your father and I have always been proud of you, and if he were here today he'd give you a big hug. Now, promise me you'll come over later after you do some work. Emily is shouting that she'll make spinach lasagna for dinner, your favorite. And you know she's not always willing to eat your vegetarian stuff. It sometimes has an odd . . . taste. You can bring Sinatra. I've bought him a new chew toy."

Her mother called Sinatra her hairy grandson and doted on him. He could do no wrong in her eyes, even when he dug up her azaleas and peed all over the backyard, leaving little white circles where the grass withered and finally died.

"Okay, okay. I'll drive home after I do some work. Love you, Mom."

"Love you, too. And keep your chin up!" There was a click as her mother hung up her old white phone, which had hung in their kitchen as long as Shoshana could remember. Its ring was cranky, a hammer hitting a bell. Her parents had bought it at a flea market when they were dating, and Pam refused to get rid of it.

Shoshana read through more message boards, made a few notes for tomorrow's column, and closed her laptop. She heard Karen and her long, volleyball-champ legs walking down the stairs on her way to law school and the creaking sounds of the metal gate swinging behind her as she left for the train. Andrea's light snoring came through the wall next door. Well, good. She worked a lot of nights and Shoshana knew she was tired. Plus, she had to get her beauty rest before her big date. She hoped this guy was a good one; some of Andrea's past beaus were doing hard time in the clink.

It was one o'clock and time to call Nancy.

"Is this Fancy Nancy?" she asked, when her friend picked up the phone.

"In the flesh," she said, in her low growl of a voice. She had a thick Jersey accent that sounded just like Kathleen Turner in *Serial Mom.*

"Ready for our walk? It's pretty cold out, but I feel like I need to do something healthy after the few glasses of wine I had last night. I think my insides are made out of grapes now."

"Meet you at Dunkin's?"

"Word."

They disconnected. Shoshana put on her pink XXL sweatsuit, brushed her long hair into a high ponytail, slipped on shoes, and set out, dragging a protesting Sinatra along with her. He was a high-maintenance dog and didn't like being out in any weather below fifty degrees, but Shoshana knew he'd like it once the cold air hit his tongue. She dressed him in an army fatigue jacket with a fur-trim hood.

As she passed an old-style Italian club (one of several still scattered throughout this mile-square town) she caught a flash of soccer on a television bolted into the wood-panel wall, an overwhelming smell of cigar smoke (the no-smoking-inside ban had come and gone here, like a fad), and glimpsed old men clustered around the entrance. They patted their breast pockets for their next cigar, spoke in rapid Italian (oh, what were they *saying* she wanted to know), and slapped one another on the back, telling stories. They wore tweed jackets, skinny gray ties with bright red designs on them, high-waisted pants with cuffs on the bottoms, and suspenders Shoshana imagined she could have walked past the club any decade of the last century and the men would look exactly as they did now. There were never any women in sight.

She had a library book to return, so she walked down Fourth. The snow had let up and there was a light dusting on the ground. The sun peeked through clouds, casting the town in a grayish yellow light. Kids were having a snowball fight in Church Square Park and Shoshana scooted out of the way of an incoming missile. Because of the snow the colors were crisp: the bricks on the top of Our Lady of Grace Church shone bright red against its surroundings. *On the Waterfront* was filmed here, and the church looked even more beautiful in color than in the black-and-white film. She pictured Brando sauntering in, a cigarette dangling from his mouth.

As they neared the dog park Sinatra let out a high-pitched yelp and his furless body wiggled with excitement. Last fall she took knitting lessons with Aggie at Patricia's Yarns up the street, and beneath his jacket Sinatra was decked out in a very festive blue and white sweater: Giants colors. There was a fenced-in park for big dogs, and a neighboring one set up for small dogs, but Sinatra didn't know his puny size and preferred to gallop and chase tennis balls with Great Danes and pit bulls, for reasons Shoshana would never understand. She thought it might go back to his kennel days. When she adopted him, he was being nursed by a very large pit bull, much to the amazement of the shelter's staff, but now that she knew Sinatra's bewitching charms, she could easily see why the pit bull had chosen to mother him. Thus, Sinatra loved oversized dogs, and didn't mind being occasionally stepped on or having his butt sniffed by dogs big enough to eat him for lunch.

"See, aren't you glad you came outside?" she cooed to him, as she opened the gate to the park. She waved to a few regulars, and sat down on a bench to finish the latest beach read she'd bought last week because it made her feel warm. After a couple of minutes she looked up to see Sinatra riding on the back of a German shepherd. "Five-minute warning!" she called to him, like the mother of a preschooler. And sure enough, soon Sinatra seemed to sense it was time to go see Aunt Nancy, and he came trotting over.

White snow on the branches of the trees reflected off the library's windows as she walked. It was hard to imagine the ashen boughs ever holding succulent green leaves again. She dropped off her library book in the metal box outside the building instead of going inside; it was so cold out that if she warmed up slightly she'd want to head right back home and get back into bed.

As she walked uptown, a snowplow with orange circling lights made beeping noises as a cop helped direct traffic around it. Over her sweatshirt Shoshana was wearing a black down jacket that went to her knees and had an attractive cinched metal belt that she felt gave her a waist. It came with a fake fur hood that matched Sinatra's, and she now gathered it over her head for warmth. It framed the scene in an oval shape in front of her: the mailwoman pushing her mail cart with red mittens, two skinny Hispanic teenage girls wearing Day-Glo high-tops and skin-tight jeans pressed against one another, popping gum and giggling as they walked, a harried-looking mother pushing twin boys in an expensive-looking double stroller with a plastic awning down in front of them to keep the warmth in, a group of loud, laughing men walking to a late lunch, a father walking with his daughter balanced on his shoulders, her cheeks rosy from the cold. The last image made Shoshana smile. She missed her own father constantly, and something about happy father-daughter images always melted her heart because they made her remember him, which was a good thing.

She walked the three blocks over to Dunkin' Donuts to meet Nancy and begin exercising, which hopefully would culminate with a glass of wine. The crisp, sharp winter air felt fresh and full of promise against her cheeks. She saw Nancy in all her leopard-print spandex glory, and waved, happy to see her friend.

Alexis

March

NEW YORK

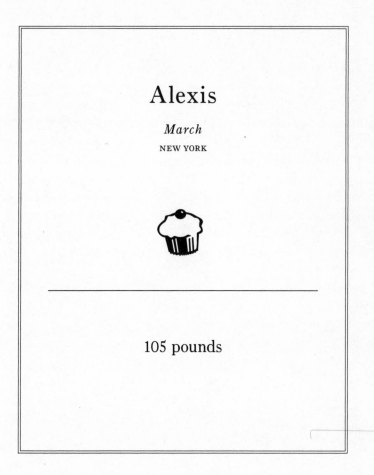

---

105 pounds

Skinny Chick

Beth Ditto was recently interviewed, and *The Frisky* ran her quote:

> "I'm not an unhealthy person and I feel like one of the most tiring parts of
> being fat and being proud of it is . . . you do a lot of proving yourself all
> the time. It's really interesting to me that people will look at a thin person
> and go, 'That's a healthy person.' I want to go, 'Come open my refrigerator
> and look and then let's talk about what you think is so bad.' To be thin and
> to stay really thin, sometimes . . . some people literally do coke all the
> time. Some people smoke cigarettes instead of eating. That's crazy. But
> that's 'okay' because you look healthier."

Of course, I just had to comment on this. Beth, I would love to take a
look inside your refrigerator. And your kitchen cabinets. And underneath your pillow. With 64 percent of American women overweight, I
find your comments ridiculous and I think you should stick to what you
do best: writing songs.

No, Beth, not every thin person snorts cocaine to maintain a healthy
body weight. Most of us simply believe making simple, smart choices
helps us feel better about ourselves.

If you're a multimillionaire pop star with a driver and stylist, and you
have business deals designing clothing for overweight women, you're
going to have higher self-esteem than the average American woman.
But Beth, most of us don't have those privileges. And trying to make
obesity somehow sound cool and righteous means you are digging
graves for your fans and promoting an unhealthy and unproductive life.
And that's more than gossip.

WHAT THE HELL DO PEOPLE *WEAR* TO A COOKING CLASS held within a chic gym? Alexis was not about to don an apron. She was knee-deep in the hallway closet she shared with Billy. In terms of a "walk-in closet," it was more like a "step-one-toe-into-closet." Each time she went downstairs she stared longingly through the window at the Container Store's organized shelving ideas, but she couldn't afford any of them. She and Billy and Vanya had barely scraped together enough money for rent last month, and Chelsea was getting more and more expensive. Soon they'd have to (gasp!) move to an outer borough, something she and Billy had once made a blood pact not to do.

Half the time she couldn't tell which clothing was hers and which belonged to Billy. She'd suggested she take the top bar and he the bottom, but when he hung up his clothes (which wasn't very often) he mixed his stuff in with hers, and as he wasn't that much larger than herself, she often ended up wearing his clothes. Seeing a flash of leopard print or having a soft fan of pink feathers brush against her cheek when she started rummaging around in there didn't tell her anything; it could belong to either one of them. She was glad skin-tight leggings were hot right now, as she'd throw on a pair in black and one of Billy's gray cashmere Ralph Lauren sweaters and leave several buttons open at the top, then loop a ton of thin gold necklaces around her neck, and pull on her knee-high black boots with the pointy heel that doubled as a weapon and could put someone's eye out if necessary. For tonight she chose skinny black jeans and a lacy black bra with a gray, loose-fitting tank top that was open on the sides and showed her ribs. She loved monochromatic, solid colors and stayed away from anything overly feminine. She was so thin she was almost androgynous, and she wore mainly gray or black. On her feet she slipped on her favorite pair of black suede Ferragamo knee-high boots with four-inch heels. She found one of Billy's sweaters scrunched and rolled up on the floor like a run-over animal on the road and put it over the tank for warmth.

She owned what she thought of as essential clothing; she'd get designer clothes at consignment stores, or she would save up her earnings from *Skinny Chick* until she could buy something rare and fabulous. She refused to shop at H&M or Target just to have a big wardrobe. She was careful, conscientious, and meticulous about her purchases. She might only collect one item of clothing a season, and would first stalk the store like a lion would a gazelle in the wild, stopping by Armani on Fifth Avenue to try on the same wrap dress five times, popping into Prada to measure a purse with a ruler, then practicing walking around the store with it, or heading on over to Saks (she loved the *smell* of the place, the little perfume sample wands, the rows of new clothing from every designer, even the dressing rooms!) and would slip on a pair of Michael Kors platform pumps and not buy them until a month later. Sometimes she had dreams about whatever piece she was contemplating buying.

She knew how best to dress her rail-thin frame and she didn't mind not having breasts. In fact, she was proud of her little mosquito bites. Billy even had bigger breasts than she did when he dressed in drag, which he would from time to time if the mood struck. His chest was sculpted and when he wore a push-up bra he had minor cleavage. He complained her size-A bras were too small to fit around his chest, so she told him to fuck off and buy his own bra, which he did, in a C cup so he could stuff it with a pair of wobbly chicken-cutlet-like fake breasts he had left over from a photo shoot and take up an hour in the bathroom affixing.

Hollywood had, in the last ten years, made thin very *in,* and clothes being made these days reflected that. Why else call regular old blue jeans "skinny jeans"? American culture had finally caught up with Alexis's shape and form, and she couldn't be more thrilled about it.

She fiddled with earrings on her dresser, finally settling on a pair of square-shaped gold ones bought from a street vendor in Chinatown. While she avoided the cheap stuff when it came to clothing, bags, and shoes, she wasn't snobbish about accessories and felt a surge of excitement when she found great, funky jewelry on the street. She wondered what kind of clothes the women that cute chef dated wore, and then was so surprised she cared that she paused in the hallway. She picked up men and discarded them like yesterday's newspaper. She couldn't remember the last time she'd dressed up for a boy. The thought bounced around her mind, shiny and exciting.

She locked the door to her apartment, passing the sound of her neighbor's guitar playing. His name was Jack and he was in a small indie rock band that traveled most of the year. Billy fed his goldfish for him when he was on tour and Billy and Alexis would snoop around in Jack's dresser, giggling about his leopard-print boxers. Jack worked out with hand weights and Billy would pump a few rounds of iron before getting bored and trying on all Jack's tight black jeans.

Alexis took the stairs, bypassing the elevator in favor of exercise. She'd gone slightly over her caloric intake at lunch, enjoying half of a chicken salad with mayonnaise that Billy had brought home from work.

Outside, a great gust of wind and wet hit her, throwing her hair across her face in one sticky move. She picked it off her forehead, wiped the water out of her eyes, combed her stick-straight white bob with her fingers, and set forth toward Soho Gym. Alexis had a strut, which she'd learned by watching Kate Moss walk the runway. She liked Kate because she was the most petite super-model, and therefore had a body similar to her own.

She turned on her iPod and strains of Woody Guthrie sounded in her ears. She loved folk music. It was a fact that always surprised people, though she didn't know why. She was very patriotic. She loved Pete Seeger, Taylor Swift, Joni Mitchell, Phil Ochs, James Taylor.

The night was balmy; spring wet and windy. She regretted the sweater and considered stripping it and only wearing the camisole underneath, but she would not stoop to winding it around her waist. People who did that looked like mountain hikers. It was absurd. Hopefully the kitchen was air-conditioned.

Approaching her gym, she marveled at its wide, etched glass front windows and oversized modern steel doors. It was so much a part of her life, she was surprised she never took advantage of one of its special cooking series. The idea of being around so many *people* had been a turnoff (Alexis hated crowds), yet this was the first time the instructor was so damn cute. Soho Gym had a huge state-of-the-art cooking facility and hosted several guest chef appearances a year. If nothing else, she could use healthy cooking tips for *Skinny Chick*, she mused.

Someone new was working the front desk, a woman in her late thirties with her black hair in a braid and a sculpted body. She smiled at Alexis and beeped in her membership card. This annoyed Alexis (she didn't like change) until she remembered Carlos said he was taking the cooking class tonight along with Sarah. Her usual routine was to enter the locker room and weigh herself, so it was odd to bypass it and instead walk in the opposite direction. It gave her pause. She still wasn't sure why she'd impulsively signed up for this cooking class. She sighed and fiddled with her earring.

Alexis passed the weight room, strutted by the little spa that was attached to the gym, breezed through the trainers' offices, until she finally came out into a high-ceilinged area that was spacious, with a modern design of bleached-blond wood countertops and shining steel stoves that took up a large portion of the room. On the wall were large black-and-white photos of various New York chefs such as David Chang and Mario Batali captured in stills while working at their craft.

She spotted Carlos and Sarah huddled in a corner talking with other gym members, some of whom she recognized. There was the chick who always did sit-ups with one of the medicine balls to conclude her workout. Talking to her was the Hispanic guy in his forties with gray sideburns who wore fingerless gloves to lift weights. Tonight he had on a suit, probably having come from work. There was the red-haired mother of three with the great legs whom Alexis always overheard complaining about her youngest son, who apparently was a troublemaker in the little day care at the gym. She looked relieved to be child-free. It was strange to see all the regulars in street clothes; like attending a costume party.

It was crowded, but the room was big enough that the twenty or so people taking the class were assembled in the front on white leather couches and matching chairs. Noah stood in front of a fireplace that gave the room a pleasant smoky aroma. Alexis found herself catching her breath. Noah was very, very tall and even more handsome in person; those coal eyes contrasting with the sleeves of his white cashmere sweater pushed back to showcase his rich, dark skin and sculpted forearms. He wore a pencil behind one ear. He was standing very close to two women who were waving cookbooks around and asking him questions. He appeared to be listening deeply, nodding his head as they spoke. Alexis could tell by their happy demeanor that they couldn't care less about the program. They were just happy to talk to Noah.

She walked over to Sarah and Carlos. She couldn't be sure, but it seemed like a flash of annoyance ran over Sarah's face as she approached but she quickly recovered and gave Alexis a broad smile. Alexis had known both of them for years, but never seen them socially. She felt absurdly shy. As a child she'd beaten people into submission until they were her "friend." Other than Billy, she didn't have any other friends. She sometimes wished she had better people skills and wasn't so neurotic. It was almost as if she couldn't ever relax enough to not care what other people thought, and she gave off tense vibes. She wasn't sure how to be perceived differently. Bitchiness was all she knew.

"Hi, Alexis! You look fabulous, as always. Those squats are paying off. Carlos and I were just talking about how we hope the cooking gets started soon. I'm starving!"

"Hi, Sarah, Carlos. I have some edamame in my purse," Alexis offered, pulling out a small plastic bag and opening it for Sarah. She made a mental note to adjust the calories on her phone app later.

"Thanks!" Sarah said, reaching her hand into the offered bag. "I guess I'm going to have to get used to eating all the time. I'm always either watching what I eat or stuffing a ton of protein down my throat for various triathlons. Eating more moderately is going to take some getting used to, so I think I'll learn a lot tonight."

"I was just hoping to be taught some good dishes to impress the girls," Carlos said, and Sarah punched him in the arm. He was wearing a hot pink netted tank top over a white wife-beater and jeans. Alexis could never tell if Carlos was gay or straight. He dressed pretty flamboyantly, but he was always flirting with her when she checked in at the front desk. He seemed to just simply like everyone.

"Do you ever not think with little Carlos?" Sarah asked. "You're just like my husband, with sex on the brain twenty-four/seven."

"Shhhhh, I think he's getting started, *mamacitas*. Pay attention." He put his arms around Sarah and Alexis, turning them both toward the front of the room.

A murmur went through the crowd as some of the women began taking their seats. Looking around, Alexis saw most had taken as much care as she had with choosing their outfits. She saw short skirts, high heels, expertly done makeup, tasteful jewelry. She crossed her arms. Noah might be hot, but she was here to learn recipes for *Skinny Chick*. Not to be suckered into drooling all over this guy, who probably had a big ego, what with all these women fawning over him.

"Hello, hello," he was saying, as people wrapped up their conversations. He had a warm baritone. He ran a hand through his curls, making some hair stand up on its own. He had two-day-old stubble, which bothered Alexis. If you're teaching a class, is it too much trouble for you to shave your face? She admitted it gave him a handsome kind of rustic outdoorsy look, but still. She didn't tolerate anyone who wasn't neat, like her—and a chef, no less!

"I'd just like to take a moment to thank everyone for coming to my cooking class tonight. I know a lot of you have families and it's difficult to get away."

"Not if you force your husband to watch the kids!" the red-haired, freckly woman who was sitting near Alexis shouted out.

"What is this, bingo night?" she whispered to Carlos, who choked on the iced coffee he was drinking. He loved Alexis. She was such a *diva*. Alexis got a pad of paper from her purse and started jotting down notes.

Noah laughed. He had a goofy laugh, a deep sound that was too dorky for a man so handsome. It sounded like the mating call of some exotic bird. Alexis found herself wondering if people teased him about it.

"Good for you," he was saying, nodding. "I know how important it is for some of you to have a night off from child care, and I promise you that I will be teaching the wonders and beauty of cooking low-fat, healthy chili. It's a recipe I perfected while hiking the Appalachian Trail. I ran out of food and had to borrow ingredients from other hikers. This recipe I hope to use someday when I open my own restaurant." He chuckled humbly. "*If* I ever open up my own restaurant. It's called Noah's Nasty Chili, and it's got a *major* spicy kick. So hold on to your seats, everyone! And be sure to drink lots of water!"

He gave a brief bio of his work, from helping in restaurants in Colorado where he was from, to his experience in various New York restaurants with names Alexis was impressed by.

A few oohs and aahs from the audience.

"Also, while we work we'll be sipping some of my organic beer, which I make in my apartment in Brooklyn. Trust me, it's worth the calories!"

Hmmm. Very few things were worth the calories. Alexis would skip the beer.

"He can come over to my place and cook for me anytime," a woman standing nearby whispered to her friend.

There were the sounds of shuffling feet as people formed groups around the gleaming stoves in the center of the room.

"Right! So I'll start passing out the ingredients, which I got at the Union Square farmers' market this morning," said Noah. He stood in the middle of his audience. Alexis was sitting on a low stool and he was so tall she had to crane her neck up to see him. He continued, "Always buy vegetables when they're in season, not when they have to be imported."

Alexis sighed loudly. So far she wasn't learning anything she didn't know. She'd blogged just recently about the importance of buying local and attending farmers' markets, and accompanied the entry with pictures of her wearing an adorable striped sailor dress she'd bought used at Tokio 7 and holding up squashes, zucchinis, and plums. She'd posted a picture of Billy with dark circles under his eyes. (He really did need to get more sleep.) She made a mental note to tell him. He held two coconuts as mock breasts on his skinny chest like a Hawaiian hula girl's bra. Alexis giggled every time she saw the picture.

Also, she didn't think making chili or drinking beer were very healthy, or appropriate for a gym cooking class. But she'd already paid the money, so she might as well learn something. If nothing else, it was fun to hang out socially with Sarah and Carlos.

Just before Noah went around the room passing out various foods, he flipped a large chalkboard over like a somersault in the front of the room. He'd drawn the ingredients in chalk, which included wasabi sauce and a few alarming-sounding hot peppers . . . and was that *scorpion sauce*? What the hell? At the bottom he wrote in all caps, = *NOAH'S NASTY CHILI*, like it was a math equation. That equal sign endeared him just a little to Alexis. It looked so determined up there. So complete, like Noah really cared about each person here adding up all the ingredients and ending up with piping hot chili. She cocked her head and peered at him closer. Her blunt, chic bob swayed forward. The lights on the ceiling glowed, a shimmery ring.

Noah had dropped off small silver bowls with colorful hand-fuls of ingredients. Carlos was fidgeting with the dials to turn on the stove. "This is about the only thing I can't turn on," he muttered, making Sarah and Alexis giggle.

Alexis picked up various shiny instruments that were lying on the table, like they were performing an operation. There seemed to be different-shaped knives, a few tools made from wood, and something that must be for pressing garlic. Or an egg. She wasn't very savvy in the kitchen, having never cooked before.

She leaned toward Sarah. "Can I help do something?" she asked.

"Sure!" Sarah's brow was furrowed. She clearly had no idea what she was doing, either. Yeesh. You'd think this Noah charac-ter would give a little more instruction. Right now he was standing with another nearby group of all women, laughing and touching one on the shoulder. Alexis rolled her eyes. She'd never learn how to make healthy chili at this rate.

Sarah handed her one of the shiny knives from the table. "Want to chop these onions here into small pieces? If the knife doesn't work you can bash them with this wooden mallet thingy. Just be careful, the knife is really sharp."

Carlos looked over from where he was now washing cilantro in the small sink attached to their island counter. "Hey, you can use the mallet on Aldo if he doesn't do diaper duty!"

"Totally!" Sarah responded, laughing and pushing her dark curls off her face.

"Hey, so what the hell do you think scorpion sauce is?" Alexis asked. "It sounds really weird. I can't imagine it makes for very good chili. What are we, living on top of a mountain or some-thing?" *I'm trying too hard*, she thought. She was trying to be funny, but she had a bit of a Valley girl voice and the joke came out sounding bitchy.

"Beats me," Sarah responded cheerfully. "Can't wait to find out, though. Maybe it will clear up my sinuses. I've had really bad allergies lately."

Alexis began chopping, wondering if Billy had recorded *The Real Housewives of New York City.* She hoped so. She'd shown him how to work the TV but half the time he came home from either a shoot or work tipsy and would press all the wrong buttons. Plus, he'd gotten red nail polish on the remote and she couldn't get it off, so the play button stuck. She was lost in thought.

The hum of chatter was all around her, women's laughter. Music was playing, something by Bob Marley that Alexis didn't know the title of. Just as she was starting to enjoy the class despite the unusual ingredients, she suddenly felt a sharp pain on her right hand, like someone had bitten her.

"Oh, honey, you're bleeding!" Carlos exclaimed, walking quickly to her side and taking her small hand in his own. Sarah looked down, and indeed, she'd cut herself pretty deeply.

"Oh!" she said, as though the screaming-red blood now coursing over her finger and wrist had surprised her somehow. Like the knife had betrayed her.

Suddenly a flock of women crowded around her, fussing over her finger, which Alexis realized with alarm was looking worse by the second.

"Here's some paper towels!"

"Put pressure on it!"

"Lay on your back and hold your legs up in the air!" Carlos shouted.

"That's when you're trying to get pregnant, dumbass!" Sarah shot back. "And I should know!"

Alexis found herself giggling, despite the situation. She probably should have eaten more than a few slices of turkey breast for dinner. Blood was seeping out of the paper towel Carlos had wrapped around her finger and dripping onto the floor. *So much for super absorbency*, she thought. Her finger pulsed in time with her heartbeat, a steady rhythm.

She felt a pair of strong hands wrap around her shoulders, and just as she realized how dizzy she was, she found herself staring into the warmest pair of chocolate-brown eyes she'd ever seen.

"Let me take you to the hospital," Noah said in a calm, steady voice.

"You'd make a good politician," Alexis told Noah, slightly giddy from the blood loss. She suddenly felt like being silly. "Like, okay, America, stay calm. Lock your doors. Go under your house into the bunker and lay on the floor." She giggled even more. Carlos and Sarah exchanged a worried look. Alexis never acted silly. She must be near death.

But Noah frowned. "My car's parked just out front. I think you're going to need stitches."

"You can't just leave your own class," Alexis said meekly. Sarah found a white towel and wrapped it around Alexis's finger.

"My class, my responsibility," he said firmly.

"We can hold the class next week instead," Carlos told Noah. "There's an opening during the week."

"Done," Noah said definitively.

And before she could protest any more she was being ushered up the aisle between stoves and felt hands clap her gently on the shoulder from all the women in the class as Noah led her gently by the elbow through the room and out the doors.

His rusty blue Subaru was parked in front of the gym, a small detail which Alexis was grateful for, as she really was beginning to feel quite dizzy. She'd bled a trail through the gym as they walked.

"Uh, what's that?" Alexis asked, gesturing to a yellow boot on Noah's right front wheel, which was quite deflated.

"Oh, I just put that on so I can park wherever I want," Noah said distractedly, as he removed it and threw it through the back window. There was an orange kayak strapped to the roof.

"So it's like a fake boot?" Alexis asked.

"Yeah." He quickly unlocked her door for her before running

around to his side and sliding behind the wheel. He was so tall his head touched the roof.

Alexis was amused. She liked people who beat the system.

Maps and water bottles were strewn everywhere, and the car smelled distinctly of *dog*.

"I figured I'd take you to NYU, it's close," he said. He drove quickly, never hesitating before turning or looking in the mirror. He drove *forcefully,* Alexis thought. She imagined him in bed, bossing her around. She had to look out the window at a wet New York evening to avoid smiling, despite the pain in her finger.

"What?" he asked, not taking his eyes off the road.

"Oh! Nothing," she said. "Just thinking about . . . chili."

He shot her an odd look.

"How's the finger?" he asked. He had an old-school CD system in his car, the kind one had in high school where the deck pops out so no one can steal it. He pressed play and strains of Phish rang out.

"Fine. It's really not a big deal, you know, I could have just taken a cab. I feel bad that you had to interrupt your cooking class. You won't get paid now."

"What, and let you never find out what scorpion sauce is?" he asked, raising an eyebrow at her.

Oh. She hadn't realized he'd been listening.

"So, what's your name?" he asked, pulling into NYU Medical Center's emergency entrance.

"Alexis. Alexis Allbright."

She realized she'd introduced herself the way her father had taught her to do when she was little, and inwardly cringed. *Always reach out and shake hands, Alexis. Then look the person right in the eye and state your full name, first and last.*

"I'm sorry to bleed all over your car. What year is it?" Her finger really hurt and it relaxed her to quiz him.

"I don't know, to tell you the truth." He grinned at her, and it was like the sun coming out. She was surprised by the effect it had on her. "I won it playing cards with a buddy back in Colorado, where I'm from."

What kind of guy didn't know what year his car was? Interesting. "So what else do you do, Noah, other than chauffeur girls around who cut themselves in cooking class?"

A taxi cut him off. "Big dummy!" Noah yelled out the window, shaking his fist.

Alexis raised a perfectly manicured eyebrow. "Is that the worst insult you can throw?" she asked. "Wow, you really are a country bumpkin."

"Sorry," Noah said sheepishly, pushing a stray curl off his forehead. "I can't stand the way people drive here."

Looking for a place to park near the emergency room entrance, Noah was squinting, which made him look even cuter, like a sailor. The wipers worked sporadically, and he had to manually roll down his window and stick his arm out to wipe off the windshield.

"Sorry," he said again, as they waited for someone to pull out of a spot. He reached over and put one of his large hands on her shoulder. "Just another minute and we'll get you right in there and fixed up. That must hurt."

She didn't say anything. His hand had brushed against hers a few times when he shifted gears, and it felt as warm as it did now, touching her sweater. It made her forget about the pain in her finger.

Alexis felt silly going through the big revolving doors with the loud red EMERGENCY sign above them. Surely there were people here much sicker than her. But she had bled all the way down the front of her sweater, which she attempted to wipe off as she strolled into the emergency room.

Noah walked very closely to her as she gave her name to a plump and cheerful Hispanic nurse named Inez who wore purple scrubs with Goofy on them. Noah had to help her get her wallet out of her purse to present her insurance card. She was led to a small, curtained-off area where she could see the shifting of shapes and colors through the flimsy white mesh meant to give patients the illusion of privacy.

"I'll wait right here for you," Noah said, taking a seat in a blue plastic chair at a low table meant for children in the waiting room. He looked oversized, like a giant. His legs were a mile long. On the table was a wooden game with different-colored balls you ran over a wire, and a stuffed bunny. Noah held up the bunny. "Just call us in if you need us. The bunny has a strong stomach."

Alexis giggled. "Um, you look really uncomfortable in that chair."

He shifted around. "What do you mean? It's great. Me and this chair are copacetic."

"Let your boyfriend hold your purse for you," Inez said, before she turned and said something about going to get the doctor.

"Oh, no, he's not—" but Inez was already gone in a flash of colorful scrubs.

"Just think, we can tell this story to our grandchildren," Noah said. He nonchalantly picked up a copy of the children's book *Leonardo, the Terrible Monster* and riffled through it.

"What story?" Alexis asked.

"The tragic tale, of how you hurt yourself in my chili-making class, and how I heroically whisked you over to the hospital for stitches. It will make a very romantic story, I assure you."

She rolled her eyes, but secretly felt a little spark of excitement. "You're crazy," she said.

"I remember being in the hospital when I was a kid, I was always breaking something and my mother would drive me, yelling and pinching my ear, she was so mad I'd hurt myself. I was more afraid of her than of the doctors. I broke the same arm three times in the third grade."

"Doing what?"

"Oh, you know. Rollerblading. Biking. Doing backflips."

"Backflips?"

"Of course. Off the roof of our garage. And one time I had to be brought in because I had one of those bugs in my ear, an earwig?"

Alexis sat in one of the little plastic chairs opposite him. It hurt her butt. "I thought that was a myth," she said.

"Oh, no. They crawl inside your ear and eat your brain. That's why I'm so crazy now." He crossed his eyes and stuck out his tongue.

Despite the pain, which was now creeping up her hand, Alexis laughed out loud.

Inez had come back. "Come, dear, the doctor's almost ready for you."

"Knock 'em dead," Noah said. "Rabbit and I are rooting for you." He held up the stuffed animal and made its paw wave to her.

Inez put her arm through Alexis's and steered her down a hallway with green footprints and a sign that read FOLLOW THE FEET TO ER. She sat her on a cot and drew a curtain around her in a circle so she was finally alone for the first time since she'd left her apartment what seemed like forever ago. Alexis reached for her phone to call Billy, only to see that she had no bars, and therefore no reception. A bright red splotch was coming through the paper towel on her finger, like a Rorschach test. She scooted on the cot, holding her finger in the air. The sheets felt scratchy beneath her.

The squeak of a gurney being pushed down the hallway filled her ears. Far off, someone was screaming, and the sound carried to her muted, like she was underwater.

A chart taped to the wall read WHAT IS YOUR PAIN LEVEL, ONE THROUGH TEN? The levels appeared to coincide with smiley faces, which ranged from very happy, to maybe you didn't get the Justin Bieber tickets you wanted, all the way to your boyfriend is screwing your best friend.

The screams faded out, and the sound of a heart monitor's beeping once again rushed into her ears. There was an elderly Indian woman lying inert behind the next curtain over. Someone, perhaps her son, slumped over the side of her bed, asleep. The woman stared at the ceiling, her chest rising and falling to the rhythm of the monitor. She seemed defeated, somehow. Like life had let her down. The red dot on the middle of her forehead matched the color seeping from Alexis's bandage.

Alexis knew how the woman felt—not alone, and yet very much so. She felt hungry and tired. Estranged from her parents, and making a living out of telling people a message they didn't want to hear ("You're overweight and it's killing you!"). Noah was in the waiting room and Alexis wished he'd leave. She was exhausted and felt awkward about him being there. Alexis was quite used to doing things on her own. Sometimes Billy accompanied her grocery shopping, or scouting for a bathing suit, or for a glass of wine at a new restaurant she'd read about in *New York* magazine, but most of the time it was just solo Alexis. She prided herself on walking around this great city without needing a gaggle of people with her.

Just last week she'd tried a new noodle bar in the East Village for dinner, sat on the counter with her elbows propped, and read *The Sun Also Rises* while enjoying ramen soup. All the while, as couples held hands on the sidewalk and she received a few glances while eating her dinner, inwardly she'd felt pride, a shameless pride, that she was able to enjoy herself, by herself. You can read all the articles in women's magazines that tell you to be independent, but actually living with very few people in your life can be hard to do. After dinner she went to the Sunshine Cinema to see a foreign film with subtitles, which she enjoyed. (She liked the big, over-done expressions and wild gesturing.)

Alexis lay there on top of stiff, starched sheets and people rushed past her curtained-off cot, and machines beeped, and wheelchair wheels squeaked past her, and all the while she hated this seedling of an emotion that had been growing inside her since she walked through the doors to the hospital. She took pride in fending off loneliness but as she lay on her back Alexis suddenly felt the overwhelming urge for Noah to come sit with her. It must have something to do with being in pain; her defenses were down, Alexis mused. She'd bounce right back to her old bitchy self in no time.

She startled when the curtain whisked back and a short, chubby man who had a pudgy baby face strode confidently over to her cot. White hair stuck up on either side of his head like waves. "I'm Dr. Whisk," he said. His smile lit up his whole face, relaxing Alexis immediately. "Like the tool you use to make a cake."

"You must have to say that a lot," she said dryly, shifting on the cot to sit up. Her finger throbbed.

"Never get tired of it," he said, still smiling and not missing a beat. He'd dealt with cranky gang members with multiple gun-shot wounds. Alexis with her attitude was nothing. "Now, what happened here?" he asked.

"I cut my finger during a cooking class," she said, gingerly holding it out to him.

He went to a gleaming white cabinet behind her cot and opened it. He reached inside and pulled out a kidney-shaped metal bin. "Well, what'd you do that for?" he joked cheerfully.

Alexis sighed. She didn't do banter. Not well, anyway.

"Sorry," Dr. Whisk said. "Started my day over in pediatrics. So I'm a little jazzed up and still have the happy face on."

Alexis decided to extend an olive branch. "How long have you been working here?"

He cheerily unwrapped her finger, whistled at the cut, and dumped the soaked bandages inside the basin. "I'm sixty-one," he answered. He winked at her. "I'm retiring to a small Rhode Island town soon, to deliver babies. I can't wait. The emergency room can wear a man down."

He gently took off the wrap she'd received when she first arrived (now soaked through with cherry-lollipop-red blood), then got down to the paper towels given to her in Noah's class.

"I have three sons. Two are doctors, and one is in clown school at Coney Island."

Alexis burst out laughing. "Well, it could be worse. He could have done what everyone else in his family did, and not follow his heart."

"You are a very wise woman," Dr. Whisk said.

Suddenly the sound of pulling back her curtain.

"Hey, is this where I can find New York's next top chef?" Noah peeked his head around. "Hey there, Doc," he said.

She felt a rush at seeing him. Suddenly the white of Dr. Whisk's coat looked brighter. She smiled, then hid it with her hand. The day tilted on its axis, seeming less sad, less dreary. She felt a shot of optimism course through her. If only he wasn't so damn *cute*.

"I told your boyfriend it was fine for him to sit with you, this will only take a minute," Dr. Whisk said, busying himself with rummaging around in the nearby cabinet.

"Oh, he's not my boyfriend," Alexis said, laughing nervously.

Noah angled his large frame in front of the curtain and sat down in a chair to Alexis's left. He crossed one long leg over the other and sat back. He looked too big for the small space, like that black-and-white Diane Arbus photograph of a giant with his parents in the Bronx. "I'm her knight in shining armor," he said.

"Hey, got you these," he continued, handing her a box of raisins. "Thought you might be hungry since you missed out on my chili."

"Oh! Thanks." She opened the lid with her good hand and dumped them into her mouth. She was starving. To hell with inputting their calories into her phone.

"You're not worried about missing the Yankees spring training coverage on the tube tonight?" Dr. Whisk said jokingly to Noah while rooting through a cupboard behind Alexis. His voice came out muffled.

"I DVR'd it, of course," Noah said.

Alexis rolled her eyes. Did men have to bring up sports any chance they got? Could they get back to her wound, please?

"Ow!" Alexis yelped. Dr. Whisk had walked back next to her and was examining her finger. The tip had gone nearly white, and light pink near the wound. It had stopped bleeding, but the cut was deep. She could see a shining sliver of bone.

"Sorry, sorry." He clapped his hands together. "What do you say we stitch you up and send you on your way?"

Alexis gulped, then squared her shoulders. She'd once broken her leg during cheerleading practice and not cried a single tear. She'd always had a high threshold for pain. She was her father's daughter. Tough.

"Sure," she said.

Noah scooted his chair around the table and nonchalantly reached out to take Alexis's other hand. He had keys in his pocket that jingled when his leg moved.

"Um. What are you doing?" she asked.

"Holding your hand," he said. "I got forty stitches on my back once. Fell rock-climbing on Flagstaff Mountain. Fucking killed."

"Er . . . thanks, I guess," Alexis said.

It didn't hurt as much as she'd thought it would. Whisk injected her with pain meds. It was more of a tugging sensation, with a prick of pain every time the needle dipped into her finger. The stitches looked like a line of shiny black ants. She blew air out of her mouth, which made her wispy hair go up and down, and tried to hold her finger out straight.

"Don't look at it," Noah said. "Look at me."

So she did. She stared into his eyes, which felt a little like swimming naked in the ocean at night. He had a tiny ring of gold inside his left iris.

Fifteen stitches and approximately one zillion forms to sign later, Alexis found herself sitting in a very uncomfortable green plastic chair in the hospital cafeteria across from Noah, doing something she never thought she would do: licking the sides of an ice-cream sandwich.

"What the hell is that?" she'd said, when Noah had come back with it to their little table.

"It's called an ice-cream sandwich. Ever seen one before?" he joked, putting it on the table and unwrapping it for her.

"I can do it myself with my other hand," she said crankily. "And what happened to getting me a salad?"

He didn't say anything, just looked at her with a bemused expression. "Some people might think the appropriate response in this situation is a simple thank-you."

Alexis sighed for what felt like the hundredth time tonight. It had started to rain in sheets that flung against the large windows in the cafeteria. She had to raise her voice to be heard over it. "I am on a strict-calorie diet. No more, no less. I don't change it, no matter what. So please, enjoy the ice cream yourself. Oh, and thank you. Sorry if I didn't say it right away."

Noah pushed back his sleeves. Alexis found herself staring at the soft brown fuzz that covered his muscular arms. She had the overwhelming urge to run her hands over him. She felt glad he wasn't very hairy. She liked her men neat.

"Hello, earth to Alexis," he said kindly. "Now listen. You happen to be sitting here with a professional chef. I know all there is to know about food. And I can tell you that this here ice-cream sandwich is known in some circles to be the epitome of fine dessert." He held it up, slowly taking off the white waxy paper like he was undressing a woman. "Notice the soft, spongy texture of the chocolate. The milky white vanilla ice-cream filling. Rome was not built in a day. And this sandwich didn't just one day formulate. It took years and years of experimenting to get it right. And you're going to turn it down?"

She was trying not to laugh.

"Listen." And he touched her arm, the gesture new and yet familiar at the same time. His voice was soft, soothing. She could listen to him talk all day. "You've had a shitty night. I just thought a little sugar couldn't hurt. I think our Dr. Whisk would approve."

So she took the treat from him, held it in her undamaged right hand, and took a small bite off one corner, putting her lips over her front teeth like a horse to keep from getting stung by the cold. It was delicious. She ate it quickly, like a prisoner who had been starved and just let out of her cell for a bite to eat. Noah sat back in his chair, crossed his long legs, and watched her, satisfied.

When she was finished, the unthinkable happened: Alexis Allbright, writer and founder of *Skinny Chick,* asked for another ice-cream sandwich. And ate it just as quickly as she had the first. And then . . . a third. At one point she took out her phone to input the calories and the number was so high she had to blink twice because her vision had blurred with shock.

They sat there for an hour, mostly in silence. But it was a comfortable silence between them, unusual in that they were two people who before this night had never met. Noah eventually went to the counter and got himself an ice cream. He ate his with the wrapper still attached, and he'd pull it down as he took bites, which Alexis found odd and charming. Her painkiller started to dissipate, which made her finger throb again, but she enjoyed his company and didn't want the night to end. Glancing at the clock above the checkout woman, she realized it was nearing midnight.

Somehow, by taking this class she'd signed up for as a lark, a way to have material to blog about, she'd cut her finger all the way to the bone and was now sitting in this gray cafeteria listening to the rain and eating an ice-cream sandwich with Noah. Life was funny, a day could shift its shape to reveal something else, something different. Life was like one of those Silly Bandz rubber bracelets that look round on your wrist, but when taken off spell LOVE.

He'd been watching her. "Can I give you a lift home?" he asked.

"Oh, I could just take a cab," she said. She felt pleased when his face fell.

"But you've just nearly cut your finger off. What if you have the sudden need for another ice cream? No, I think you'd better let me drive you home. You're not safe to wander around by yourself. You might hack off a leg or something."

"I barely know you. How do I know you're not a secret ax murderer?" she asked, using the back of her hand to open the swinging opening of the garbage can nearby to throw away all of their wrappers. When they stood up he towered over her, even in her heels.

"I'll save the axing for another day," he said. "I think you've been through enough tonight."

As they walked toward the front of the hospital Noah's shoes made sloshing sounds. Alexis realized he had no umbrella, and it was pouring outside. "Your shoes are soaked!" she told him.

"Nah," he said. "Nothing that a little heat on your feet in the car can't fix. Besides, I hate carrying umbrellas around. I like to just feel the rain on my face."

"Okay, whatever," Alexis said. She pushed him a little. She only came up to the middle of his back and she felt solid muscle under his shirt. "Hippie."

He looked back at her, surprised. Then he grinned. "I'd push you back, but I wouldn't want to hurt a cripple," he said. "Especially one who can't handle a knife."

She stuck out her tongue at him.

They passed a young girl sitting in a wheelchair and clutching a gigantic, rosy-cheeked baby boy with a huge wide face shaped like a cable satellite dish. He was very close to ten pounds and had Elvis hair, jet-black, which stuck straight up. His big face bunched and he started wailing when he saw Alexis.

"Babies always cry when they see me," she told Noah. She'd meant it as a joke, but it came out sounding awkward. They entered the large revolving door at the same time and she was pressed up against his back, which felt firm. She had the strange urge to hug him around his waist.

"Well, it's not surprising. Did you ever realize how much you frown?" he asked. "You look pretty scary."

She punched him in the arm. "What the hell? I do not."

"You do! You should see yourself. Frowning at everyone. What are you so mad about?" She felt her face go red.

What indeed? *Her father, fist smashing down on the dining room table, scattering bright green peas from his plate all over the floor after she'd told him she was quitting law school, her mother drunk at Mark's funeral, falling all over the casket and ripping off the American flag, the young Marines with their rifles and stiff posture who pretended they didn't see her.* Yeah. She was mad about a lot of things.

She stopped walking. "It's none of your business how often I frown. And I just didn't think your joke was funny. It was pretty lame, in fact. Kind of like you."

She turned on her heel and started walking down First Avenue, annoyed with Noah, but even more so with herself. What was she thinking, letting herself be rescued by the chef from her cooking class? Okay, yes. He was cute. And funny. And he made all the little blond hairs on her arms stand up when he came within five feet of her. But the man wore boots with mud caked around them, the car he drove her over in smelled of dog (Alexis was a cat person), he had no real job, her mother, with her old-fashioned views about marrying in to money, would have had a heart attack just knowing her daughter had gone out with this guy. Alexis squared her shoulders. If he called, she wouldn't answer. If he stopped by the gym, she'd . . .

Suddenly she felt an extraordinarily large hand wrap around her upper arm. She was whipped around, and found herself bumping right into Noah's chest, which was really a mistake because suddenly she breathed deeply and smelled cedar, like when you open an antique trunk, along with a mixture of clean sweat and laundry detergent.

"Where are you going?" Noah asked. He laughed. "God only knows how you walk so fast in those little torture devices you call boots. I'm six-three and I can barely keep up with you! You're like a cheetah when you take off. I had to run the whole block to catch you!"

She stared at him, her neck straining a little to look up into his eyes. She'd been outright rude to him and it didn't even seem to have registered. He was still looking at her with the same friendly expression, though a little bewildered.

"I was trying to get away from you," she said in a low voice that would have scared most men. A taxi honked on the street in front of them, making them both jump.

"What would you want to do that for, woman?" he asked. "It's obvious that you're madly in love with me. Let me drive you home, at least."

"Are you serious?" She opened her purse and took out a small mirror. She adjusted her thin hair roughly, pinching sections with her fingertips. "We are totally incompatible. All you do is eat. I hate food. You're like eight feet tall and I'm barely over five feet. You're a laid-back surfer type. I'm a bitch in heels." She closed the mirror with one hand, making a loud *snap* sound.

"You say tomato, I say tom*a*to, you say potato, I say pot*a*to. To-mato! Tom*a*to! Potato! Pot*a*to!" He was completely un-self-aware, as he danced a jig in the street.

She giggled, despite herself. He was an anomaly: a man who looked like a Calvin Klein model but who was so silly.

"See?" Noah said, laughing. "I'm already making you laugh. I'm good for you. My parents have been happily divorced thirty years and they always said they were too similar. Opposites attract."

"How can you be happily divorced?" Alexis asked. "That doesn't even make sense. It's an oxymoron. Anyway, I'm fine to catch a cab home. By myself." She held her arm out straight, trying to hail a cab. When she was by herself all she had to do was stick one skinny leg out into traffic and cars would come to a screeching halt. Noah was cramping her style.

Not taking the hint, he continued to cheerfully stroll alongside her, jumping in a puddle and sloshing rain down the side of her leg. He didn't seem to notice her sharp look. The bright red emergency room sign cast a shine on the pavement behind them. "My folks had me way too young," he continued. "They were both seniors at University of Colorado in Boulder. My mom had to finish up her spring semester the following year. I think they got married so they could live on campus with me; there was some kind of family housing. But they always said they were more like best friends than really attracted to one another, and the night they made me was meant to be more like a one-night stand. My parents both remarried and my dad has two awesome little boys, and I have a younger sister who lives in California."

She wondered which parent was black and which one was white, but of course asking that would be rude.

"You want to know what races my folks are, right?" he asked.

"What?" She stumbled on the sidewalk, and Noah grabbed her arm to steady her. "No! God, you are so self-centered," she said, rolling her eyes.

The man is like a damn Labrador retriever, Alexis thought wryly.

"So Dad's white and Mom is black. I know! It's usually the other way around."

"Um. I didn't say anything," Alexis mumbled.

Without pause, he continued: "Everyone is back home in Boulder. My parents are great. They meet for lunch once a month and catch up. I think the lunch probably consists of throwing their hands in the air and wishing I'd settle down and start my restaurant already. I've been tossing around that idea for so long now they've both been driven crazy by it."

"So why don't you, then?" Alexis asked. His story about his family had caught her attention. Despite wanting to be home, telling Billy what a disaster of a night she'd had, she loved hearing about people's lives.

"I don't know." He sighed, ran his hand through his thick curls, and leaned against a stop sign. "I guess I just haven't found the right space yet. Another chef buddy of mine wanted me to go in on a Meatpacking District upscale barbecue place with him but he couldn't snag a liquor license and the project got held up and then I pretty much lost interest . . ."

"Continue," Alexis said.

"The idea I have is kind of weird, too, but . . . okay. Picture this." He spread his arms wide, like he was a director setting up a scene. "A brewery!"

She stared at him.

"There are plenty in Brooklyn, like Kelso and Sixpoint, but not too many in Manhattan. I've got the ingredients written on the back of a napkin that I keep in my pocket." He reached inside his back pocket and showed her the napkin, which was crumpled and had lint clinging to it.

"It's just something I've been dreaming about for a long time. I've got a buddy, also from Boulder, who wants to go in on it with me, use all-local ingredients from the Tri-State Area. We could serve pub grub, and have a real relaxed, outdoorsy kind of vibe. Hamburgers. Fish and chips. Wings, ribs. Sawdust on the floor. Live acoustic on weekends. Thought I could call it Off the River Ale House, something like that. It's a joke, see? 'Cause it's way far from the Hudson. My buddy Peter that I rock-climb with at Chelsea Piers makes killer sliders, he said I could buy the recipe from him and use it. I could really use your advice, since you know New York and started your own business. I just need the right place to hang my shingle out front. Know of any cheap places for rent where I can do all that?"

"Actually . . . I can't believe I'm saying this, but I do," Alexis said. "There's a store that just went out of business across the street from where I live. I'll show it to you when you drop me off."

They walked close to one another over to his car. She felt bad, suddenly. Noah was a nice guy. And really, really hot. Why was she being so nasty to him? Could it be because she'd never actually *liked* a guy before? One-night stands got old after a while. But he was so . . . earnest. So easygoing. What did he see in her? She pictured him more with a big, tall, healthy-looking professional volleyball player. With tan legs and big white teeth. There was an empty storefront across the street from her apartment where the old fur shop had stood forever. It couldn't hurt to just show it to him, right?

He stopped in front of the blue Subaru he'd driven her over in.

"Well, here's Mister Blueberry. Might as well let me take you home since no cabs are stopping for you."

"Mister Blueberry?"

He looked sheepish. "I named the car that in college and it kind of stuck. I know, it's pretty silly."

"Hmph," Alexis responded.

Water bounced off the windshield of his Subaru. She did a little hop and skip to get off the pavement and into his car, soaking her feet and boots in a humongous hidden puddle on the way. She heard a clang as one of her earrings fell out of her ear and bounced off into a puddle with a splash.

Noah reached around, using the light from a nearby streetlamp to locate the earring. "Here ya go," he said. He wiped it on his pants leg. "Good as new."

"Er, thanks," Alexis said, gingerly taking it from him and putting it in her purse. Since it had fallen on the dirty street, she'd just as well have left it there.

She shivered inside the car and again was hit with overwhelming *eau de* doggie. She pinched shut her nose and tried to breathe through her mouth. Noah glanced at her and burst out laughing. "Are you getting ready to dive into a pool or something?"

She rolled her eyes. "Um, so do you have like ten dogs, or what? It *stinks* in here."

"Listen, beggars can't be choosers. And yes, I am the proud owner of a very large, breed-confused mutt named Oliver who likes to watch ESPN when I'm not home."

"Really?" She had an image of a big, shaggy dog sitting on a beat-up couch, watching television through a mop of hair.

"Yup. Sometimes he'll switch back and forth to CNN, but he mainly likes to watch football. He used to be a Broncos fan, but now he tells me he's rooting for the Giants more and more. It's a little disappointing."

She eyeballed him, then laughed out loud.

"So who else do you live with, besides Oliver?" she asked casually to prove how she was just asking to be polite, not out of any interest. She leaned forward and turned the heat on. Her thin gray tank was sticking to the tiny buds of her nipples. Noah politely averted his eyes as she reached into her shirt and adjusted her black bra, which was sticking uncomfortably to her ribs. Her sweater had gotten soaked with blood and it was scrunched up in her purse.

"Just Oliver," he said. "He's like my son. My furry son." He flicked on his right turn signal. It made a flashing red light in the dark velvet of the car. "You have any kids?"

She laughed unexpectedly, then choked. He had to slap her on the back.

"No. Definitely not."

"That little baby we saw when we left was pretty cute, though," he said.

Alexis wrinkled up her nose. "I don't want kids, but if I ever do have one it will be a beautiful, skinny baby. None of those elephant folds on *my* baby's thighs."

He laughed a big laugh, throwing back his head. Streetlights they drove past made the subtle gold streaks in his dark brown curls shine. "Did anyone ever tell you you're completely insane? You need to mellow out a little. Babies are supposed to be chubby, that's what makes them so cute."

She glared at him, watching his profile as he drove. "I don't think I need mellowing out. I think I just need a ride home, thank you." She fixed him with her scariest look, a cross between Anna Wintour and Naomi Campbell right before she chucks a cell phone at a maid, a look she'd practiced in the mirror many times, but Noah just laughed.

"Why are you squishing your face like that? Did you fart or something? Do you need a Tums?"

"No, I *do not* need a Tums. That's disgusting," she said, scooting farther away from him in the car toward the window.

"Okay, just asking. 'Cause if ya had a backblast I wouldn't judge you for it."

He was eyeing her, his dark eyebrows raised. She realized he was amused, and crossed her arms over her chest. "Can you just keep your eyes on the road, please?"

"Sure will. But bombs away in here, if you must. 'Cause me and Oliver, we don't care. That's how we roll in here."

She had turned her face to the window. She'd started to smile and didn't want him to see.

"Hey, remember that tune, about farts?" he asked. Without warning, he broke into song: "When you're sitting in your Chevy and you feel something heavy, its diarrhea. Diarrhea."

It must have been the early nineties, because her mother had that short haircut and she was smiling, looking back at Alexis in the silver Mercedes Alexis's parents had had for two years before trading it in for something newer. And Mark was next to her, they'd just picked him up from football practice because he still had his cleats on, and they were driving to the boat that would take them to Nantucket, where they had a house they went to every summer. Her mother looked radiant, her strawberry-blond hair tucked behind her ears, her long model legs and still-good figure stretched out in the seat. Alexis and Mark were trying to come up with more verses for the diarrhea song, and she'd won, even after their parents had threatened twice to turn the car around and head home if they con-

tinued to sing those dirty lyrics, but they'd known, of course, as all children do, that their parents were just bluffing.

"No, I don't," she said now jaggedly, still turned to the window. He seemed to not hear the anger and sadness in her voice, or was ignoring it.

"Oh, man, I used to know all the verses and everything," he said. He shifted from third gear to second to turn the corner, and she watched the muscles in his chest flex. "When you're sliding into first, and you feel something burst . . . Not even that one? Or the classic, when you're on the seat for hours and it doesn't smell like flowers, diarrhea."

"No!" she shouted. "I don't know that song and I don't want to sing it with you, okay?"

He looked sheepish. "Sorry," he said. "Sometimes I get carried away."

They were stopped at a red light. A motorcycle pulled up next to them, its engine idling. They passed an Irish bar, plants hanging from above its doorway, people huddled smoking around the entrance. He turned to look at her.

"Okay, change of subject. So what do you do with yourself when you're not acting as a weapon of self-destruction, Alexis Allbright? I'm down. So what's your job? Let me guess. You're a clothing designer."

"I wish. Guess again."

"Model?"

"Ha! Not nearly tall enough. My mom was, though. So you're getting warm."

"Well, I know you're not a chef. Not yet, anyway."

She glared at him.

"Okay, I give up."

She shifted around in her seat. Lowered the passenger-side mirror down. Took out a tube of bright red Chanel lipstick from her purse and swiped it over her lips. "I run a blog for women," she said, a note of pride creeping into her voice. "It's called *Skinny Chick*."

Noah laughed. "Blunt. I like it."

"Do you know anything about blogs?" she asked. Now they were on her turf. She loved talking about her work. She was damn good at it. Dogs, babies, ice-cream sandwiches—these all fell into the "No Interest" category. The Internet was home territory.

"Not a damn thing," he said. "And by the way, I should probably ask you where you live. As much as I enjoy driving around with you."

"Oh, right," Alexis said. "I live right above the Container Store."

"The *what* store?"

"Don't tell me you've never heard of it. Where are you from, a barn?"

"Close. I was doing the biking thing before going to the Culinary Institute."

"Biking as in . . . biking? Motorcycling?"

"No, the first one. The less cool, less-need-for-a-handlebar-mustache one. You know, two wheels, open road, the whole bit."

"Oh! So you were doing this professionally? Like getting paid to race?"

"Yes, ma'am." Every time he talked he took his eyes off the slick, gleaming road and glanced over at her, like he was somehow . . . absorbing her.

"Why'd you leave?" she asked.

"I was wanted for a bank murder and had to leave the state."

"Oh."

"I'm kidding!" he said, throwing his head back and laughing. "You should have seen your face. I *really* left to train to be a chef. I'll tell you all about it later. I want to hear more about this *Skinny Chick* blog. I want to know more about you, Alexis Allbright."

So she told him, and their voices ran parallel to the silence they'd shared inside the cafeteria. Their words felt tangible and filled the car and floated out the top of the roof and into the cloudy sky and upward, up and up, and she forgot about the pulsing pain in her finger from the stitches and the guilt over the ice-cream sandwiches she'd scarfed down.

She wasn't someone who naturally divulged aspects of her life, but in the darkness of Noah's car, surrounded by the smell of dog, the stories poured out of her mouth: how she'd worked her whole life, thinking she'd be a lawyer, how her father had pushed her into the law office where she interned and clerked every summer break in Greenwich, how she'd moved in with Billy and taken the LSATs and burned through night after night studying at the Forty-second Street library, then taking the bus home, staring out the window and wondering what the hell she was doing with her life, wondering why she was doing so well and yet felt so empty.

Noah quietly drove, one sure hand on the wheel as she described her reverent obsession with America's obesity epidemic, her fascination with diet and exercise stories in magazines and on the news, and how *Skinny Chick* was launched with a little help from a techie guy Billy was dating at the time. How she'd subsequently lost everything, her parents' respect and love, the five million dollars she was set to come into when she turned twenty-one. And how it had all been worth it, every last bit. She lived now with her best friend and ran her blog, got hundreds of endorsements, and got to be on *Oprah*. She wasn't rich, but she was able to support herself on her own dime, and she felt enormous pride in that.

She'd never talked so much in her whole life, and Noah just sat there listening. Alexis realized with a start that they were parked in front of her building. He turned the engine off and silence filled the car like a third passenger, a presence. Her light was still on in her room and its yellow beam lit a nearby tree. She'd left it on out of habit. Billy was always out working, and she didn't want to open her apartment door only to be greeted by darkness. Also she was kind of terrified to run into Vanya with the light off.

Alexis had never had a date inside her apartment before, but since this was certainly *not* a date, she didn't see the harm in inviting Noah in.

Other nights she stopped by Eastern Bloc after working on her blog all afternoon (she liked whiskey, neat) and would perch her perky tush on top of a stool and chat with Billy and the other bartender, Mike, who was short, was missing his left arm but wouldn't talk about it. Billy would be backlit by strobe lights, which reflected off her fake diamond hoops, splashes of red, green, yellow lights streaming across the faces of young, sweaty people in fabulous outfits swaying to the new indie band of the moment, the Fiery Furnaces, Florence and the Machine, Matt & Kim. Girls in sparkly silver tube tops, miniskirts, and jumpsuits would flirt with Billy in order to get served, then pout when he'd serve the handsome businessman in the gray and white pin-striped suit standing next to them first.

Even though Eastern Bloc was a gay bar, there were always a few straight men who wandered in for the trendy atmosphere and would come up to her all night. She never liked talking to guys who strolled in with a large group because it meant they were weak in character; they traveled in a pack for solidarity like a wolf. If someone shorter than her spoke to Alexis she pretended she didn't hear. The same protocol went for chubby men bold enough to saddle up to the barstool next to her. Alexis liked them successful, arrogant, handsome, and smart. Stockbrokers, doctors, business moguls. Married.

Most were pleased with this arrangement, at least at first. Later they'd start to get emotional about it, wanting more. Would she travel with them, would she ever want to meet their kids? The answer? No and no. What if he left his wife? as one Upper East Side record label president had asked her last year. No fucking way. She'd changed her phone number to be sure he couldn't contact her again.

She didn't feel guilty about these exchanges. If anything, she figured she was probably helping their marriages. Husband has a little fun on the side, goes back to his wife with a renewed sense of loyalty and dedication.

Noah was the kind of guy she would have completely ignored at Columbia. He belonged stuck to the side of a rocky mountain in a harness, not standing next to her in Chelsea in her fabulous leather boots. But there was something about the way he made her feel. She suspected that she amused him. She didn't think she'd ever amused anyone in her life, save maybe her brother.

"So what were you thinking for my restaurant?" he asked her, startling her out of her thoughts.

"It's the old fur store that closed," she said. "Just across the street."

They ran across the street, Noah strangely holding her hand as though he were her father. On a normal night she'd have shrugged him off. She wasn't big into the touchy-feely stuff. But her defenses were down. She was exhausted, and her finger really hurt. A group of loud teenage boys passed them on the sidewalk, and one threw what appeared to be a glass soda bottle onto the sidewalk. The other boys whooped at the sound of the smashing glass. She felt suddenly glad for Noah's huge presence next to her. Strange, that she'd made her way around the city for so many years on her own, and suddenly she felt appreciative of a male presence, as if she were some damsel in distress. Then again, what was wrong with easing off the tough New York attitude for one night? She pounded the streets with such armor. Even her favorite purse was silver with big metal studs adorning it like a shield.

Someone, maybe the landlord, had left a light on in the fur store. Alexis saw that the door was ajar. She cupped her hands around her eyes and peered inside. Racks lined both sides of the wall, and hangers still looped around them. The store's weathered white wooden sign—FANNY'S FURS: SINCE 1920—was broken in half on the ground. Splinters and nails showed. Two mannequins still stood in front of gold-etched mirrors. One had a fur collar on and nothing else. Alexis guessed the owners had forgotten to take it with them.

Suddenly Noah's arm shot out beside her and tried the knob. The door creaked, then opened.

"Noah!" Alexis hissed. "What are you doing?"

"Looking for opportunity," he whispered back, wiggling his thick eyebrows like some insanely tall Groucho Marx. She followed him, thinking she didn't have a choice, and prayed to the breaking-and-entering gods they wouldn't be found and arrested. The room smelled of mothballs.

"And there we have it, folks, the very first smile of the evening, and it's all due to my corny sense of humor."

He pulled Alexis into his arms and started twirling her around, humming a tune she didn't recognize. Dust kicked up around their feet. She caught a glimpse of herself in one of the smudged full-length mirrors in the store, and was surprised that the two of them didn't look as ridiculous as she'd imagined, given their difference in height. She put her bandaged hand up to her cheek. Her face flushed, and her twin in the mirror did the same.

"You know, when you're annoyed the tops of your ears turn pink," Noah said to her, bending down to whisper in her ear, even though they were the only people in the room. Traffic sounds congested outside the large window, but a heat rose inside Alexis as she realized that Noah wasn't stupid, or simple, or any of the things she'd assumed he was. It wasn't that he didn't get her sarcasm; he chose to ignore it. Alexis had been acting like a bitch for so long she wasn't sure where her true self and the famous blogger of all things skinny and mean ended. She was sure there had been a time, she *knew* there had been, before Mark was killed, when Alexis had been happy. When she'd enjoyed life more, not feeling so angry all the time.

Something about Noah's wide-eyed optimism was so anti–New York and anti-Alexis, and yet . . . and yet he was exactly like Mark, who could always wring a smile out of her, who laughed off her suggestions that he was the favored child, who signed up for the Marines and therefore ditched a football scholarship that would have eventually brought him millions. There was something of Mark in Noah's mischievous smile. His dimples. She was sure of it now as she allowed him to pull her into his arms and foxtrot around the store. She realized she was smiling.

"Oh! A second smile! Call the presses!" Noah yelled. He took the fur collar off the mannequin and wrapped it around the top of his head. It looked ridiculous, like a raccoon was sitting on his forehead. He kept dancing, and as the cars honked outside and the sky finally opened up and the rain rushed back in big, fat drops, Alexis felt a warmth spread all the way to her fingertips.

So when she found herself asking, "Do you want to come over for a drink?" she figured it must be the painkillers talking.

"Sure," he responded easily, shrugging his shoulders like it was the most natural procession in the world. When she began walking back to her building with Noah, she suddenly realized two things: how bone-tired she was, and the fact that there was a large green bicycle strapped to the back of his car next to the kayak that had been there all along and she hadn't noticed it.

"So you still bike?" she asked him. He had to take the key from her shaking, bandaged hand and open the door for them both. Noah had spent ten minutes folding up the bike and was now carrying it under his arm. Apparently it was worth a month's rent and he couldn't afford to have it stolen. She waited on the sidewalk as he unhooked straps and removed the kayak from the car's roof.

"Any other sports equipment coming in with you?" she asked sarcastically. She checked her mailbox, full of invitations to various fashion and PR events around the city and magazines and bills. Their mailbox had a black-and-white Johnny Cupcakes sticker on it that read MAKE CUPCAKES NOT WAR that Billy had affixed when they'd moved in together.

"Yeah, I live in Brooklyn, so when I need to come into the city for these cooking classes I usually bike over the bridge. Tonight I drove, though." She could picture his apartment: the essence of *male* everywhere, dog hair on his futon couch, sneakers scattered willy-nilly, a bike rack attached to the wall, a collection of jade plants on top of his refrigerator, a *Taxi Driver* poster as art above the couch, a brick wall facing his bed, soft gray sheets, a new stainless steel oven being the only extravagance, as surely a cook needed one.

"Do you think the bike and kayak will be safe down here?" he asked her, easily depositing both in the small entryway as if he were carrying feathers.

"No." Alexis responded. "Better bring them into my apartment."

She was aware of his eyes on her butt as she climbed the stairs, and was suddenly immensely grateful to Sarah and all her tough personal training sessions with squat after grueling squat.

Princess Pinkerton streaked out in front of the door as she opened it, and Noah had to do a little maneuvering to get inside her apartment door with the kayak, and after placing that in her tiny kitchen, the bike. The letters 3R were in brass and hanging crookedly by a nail.

"Is that your cat?" Noah asked, bending down.

"Yeah, but don't . . . Oh." Princess Pinkerton, who never let anyone but Billy pick her up without scratching them silly, was twisting and flipping onto her back to let Noah pet her fat stomach. *This man could charm anyone,* she thought. She said a silent prayer that Princess Pinkerton wouldn't choose this moment to show off her pooping-in-the-plant routine.

"I share her with my roommate, Billy," Alexis said.

They sat on the couch, an eggplant-purple cashmere throw making a soft pillow for her back. Alexis crossed her legs and held up her bandaged finger, examining it. It was still throbbing.

"Why don't you take one of those painkillers?" Noah asked. He got up, Princess Pinkerton jumping off his lap reluctantly, and walked over to her kitchen, which was a tiny letter-C-shaped alcove with tacky seventies brown and orange cupboards Billy had tried cheering up by lining their insides with poppy wallpaper. Maneuvering around the kayak and bike, he opened the fridge and poured her a glass of water from the Brita.

Alexis's stomach clenched as she heard a door open down the hallway. The apartment was a railroad, so she could just make out two coal-black eyes peering at them from Vanya's room, a trail of silver smoke drifting out from the bottom crack. Surely she wasn't casting spells in there? Alexis shivered, picturing some poor man who was being spiked with pins from her voodoo doll.

"Hey, there!" Noah called down the hallway.

"Shhhh!" Alexis hissed at him as he set down her glass, using one of the Playboy bunny coasters Billy had brought home from a photo-shoot set to be ironic.

But Noah wasn't listening and was, terrifyingly, strolling down the hallway to talk to Vanya, the witch. Alexis's breath caught in her throat; she was that scared. She watched his tall frame maneuver away from her, her heart thudding in her chest. "She will put a spell on you!" she stage-whispered, but he ignored her. She heard his deep, soothing voice but couldn't make out the words, and then he actually stepped across the threshold of Vanya's room and entered, the door seeming to *suck closed* behind him.

Alexis paced up and down in the living room for an eternity before Noah returned, tossing a "Talk to you soon" over his shoulder at Vanya, then came back to the couch and put his humongous feet on the coffee table. He put his muscular arms behind his head, the image of a man of leisure.

"What happened in there?" Alexis whispered. "I thought you were a goner for sure!"

"Oh, I was just chatting with your roommate Vanya. She's hilarious!" he said, grinning. His teeth were perfectly even and glowing white. She wondered if he'd had braces. "All that goth stuff is great, isn't it? I used to be really into Ozzy Osbourne in college."

She continued to stare at him.

He laughed his loud, goofy laugh. "He went a little far in his pigeon-head-biting-off days, but ya gotta admit the guy's got some killer tunes." He held his hands up in the universal rock-on symbol, his middle and ring fingers bent down with the others up like horns, and stuck out his tongue, which strangely turned her on.

Alexis scooted an inch closer to him. His hair smelled like coconuts and summer.

"Are you smelling me?" he asked.

Her eyes popped open. She realized she'd shut them for a moment. "Um . . ."

"'Cause if you are, I can't say I blame you. The ladies love the *eau de* Noah." He laughed.

She glared at him. "I was definitely *not* smelling you. Get over yourself."

"*Sure* you weren't." But he just kept grinning at her. "How's the hand?"

"Fine!" she sniffed.

"So what's that scale doing in the kitchen?" he asked. "Do you use it to cook?"

She blinked. "No, I use it to weigh food."

He raised his eyebrows. "You care that much? You're such a tiny little thing, I can't imagine you'd have to fight fat that hard. You're like a small bird."

She rolled her eyes. People were always telling her she didn't need to watch her weight. It got old after a while. How did they think she got such a great bod? Maintenance.

"The idea is to prevent getting fat in the first place, to get to your adult size and stay there," she responded. It was like reading from a script. "Mine is a two. Every girl I went to college with is now fat with three kids. That's not going to be me. That's the whole point of *Skinny Chick,* to promote healthy eating and smart food choices."

Noah smiled. "Yeah, but it sounds like you've gone a little coo-coo crazy about it. I mean, I practically had to put that ice-cream sandwich in an IV to get you to eat it."

She huffed out air. "Listen, I'm doing just fine without your opinions or help. I have my way of living and if you don't like it, maybe this should be good night." She stood up and teetered on her high heels for a second, before a wave of nausea hit her.

"Whoa." Noah stood and leaned her against him. She felt his hard chest beneath his jacket. "Let's get you off to bed." And before she could protest, Noah had picked her up like a knight in shining armor and was manhandling her down the hallway to her room. He slid her onto the bed, fully dressed.

"Why don't you stay on the couch?" she whispered to him in the dark, after she felt the coolness of her pillow against her cheek and moved onto her left side, the way she liked to sleep. "There's a blanket in the wooden chest."

"Oh, I don't want to trouble you," Noah said. "Besides, Oliver will be majorly bummed if I don't come home." He grabbed one of her boots and pulled. She wore her unicorn socks, which she'd had since high school. They'd been a Christmas gift from Bunny and there was a small crystal in the eye of the unicorn and pink pom-poms around the edge of each sock. They were hideous and Billy kept threatening to burn them, but they held sentimental value to her. She would have been mortified Noah was seeing this kooky side of her, if she wasn't so damn tired.

"Unicorns. Cute!" Noah said. "Well, you pull off a woman's shoe and there's a whole host of surprises underneath. Go figure." He pulled off her other boot and placed them carefully on the floor next to her bed. She felt like a child.

"So, Alexis." He spread his large hands. "I hope your finger heals really quickly."

She was seized with a sudden panic at the idea of him leaving. "Please?" she asked. Had she ever said that word, much less to a man? "Can you get someone to feed your dog, maybe?"

He seemed to be thinking, although she couldn't see his face in the darkness. "You know what? Sure. I have this neighbor across the hallway from me, Maria. She's a nurse, has five kids, and is always asking me if I got the flu shot. She has keys to my apartment and works nights, maybe I can catch her before she leaves for the hospital." He dialed her, his phone a spark of white light against the darkness. After speaking to her briefly, he flipped his phone closed. "She said no problem."

"Thank you," she said. Noah seemed to have some kind of effect on her. She felt safer with him around. Softer, happier. She felt like the Alexis she'd been before Mark had died and her mother had picked up the bottle, and the falling-out with her father over quitting the law. She'd still had her convictions about diet and exercise then, but hadn't she been a little less . . . strict? The private workout sessions, the scale, the constant weighing herself, the app on her phone that counted calories. That had all come . . . after.

"I'll see you in the morning," Noah said, and he surprised her by leaning down and kissing her on the cheek. Warm with the smell of him, Alexis fell asleep five minutes after Noah quietly eased the door closed. She could swear at some point she'd heard Vanya standing near her door whispering, "Great catch," but surely she'd imagined it.

In the morning, Alexis's alarm clock clicked on and Billy's voice screeched into her ears. "Aleeeexiiis, it's me, Billy. I know you're sleeping, but it's time to wakey-wakey. I know you want to lie around in bed for another two hours, but you know who lies in bed, don't you?"

"Fat girls," she whispered into her pillow.

Suddenly her door burst open and Noah came storming in, wearing only blue-and-white Yankees boxers with a rip in a suspicious place on the back. His body was even better than she could have dreamed. His nipples were a brown sienna, his six-pack prominent, his legs long, calves strong, probably from all that biking, Alexis mused. She raised her eyebrows at him and suddenly remembered she was wearing last night's clothing. Her one earring was tangled up in her frizzy mane of hair. She had cat-food breath. Her top was askew, which she quickly fixed.

"What the hell is that noise?" Noah asked, glaring at her alarm clock. "It's not even five o'clock!"

"I get up now and eat breakfast," Alexis said defensively. "And then I go work out."

"Now?" he gasped. "I didn't even get up this early when I was a professional athlete and trained every day. I mean, it's just freakishly early. The only person I knew up at this time was my grandfather, who was a lobster fisherman. And he only got up that early because he had to earn his bread that way."

"Well, this is me," Alexis said defensively, scooting out of bed. She realized that at some point in the night, Noah had put an extra blanket on her.

He followed her into the kitchen, then watched her slice her banana. She kept peering over her shoulder at him, feeling uncomfortable to be observed so closely. "Is that *it*?" he asked, after she'd finished her banana and milk.

She sighed. "Yes. I told you, I'm really careful about what I eat."

"Well, that just won't do," Noah said. "Stay here. I'm going out to get some groceries. I'll be right back."

As he turned, Billy, who had woken up to pee, shuffled down the hallway, still half asleep and rubbing his eyes. He wore blue silk pajamas, and Alexis saw he'd gotten his hair cut in a slight Mohawk. It looked very nonthreatening on Billy.

He glanced at the kayak, then the bike. Then shrugged.

When he saw Noah he stood still and stared. Alexis realized Noah was still half naked, and as Billy looked from her to him and back again it occurred to her it looked like they'd slept together. Billy gave Alexis a wink.

"Hello, delicious naked black man," Billy said, extending his hand.

Alexis closely watched Noah's reaction. If he didn't like Billy's flamboyancy, she'd drop him like a hot stone. She was very loyal to Billy. But Noah just did his deep, booming laugh and leaned across the breakfast bar to shake Billy's hand. "You must be Alexis's roommate Billy," he said. "I'm the random guy she met last night who was teaching a cooking class that she decided to commit suicide by knife in."

Billy, with great reluctance, tore his eyes off Noah's physique and truly saw Alexis for the first time. "Babe!" he said. "What the hell happened to your hand?" He gently cradled her hand in his own, examining it.

She waved him away. "It's nothing."

"She got fifteen stitches and a prescription for painkillers," Noah informed Billy.

"Well, hooray for the painkillers. I might take one myself for fun. Has she had one yet this morning?" Billy asked. "She seems to be sore. I can tell, she didn't even finish her banana."

"I'm standing right here, you know, guys," Alexis said drolly. They were discussing her like two surgeons standing over an open chest cavity, ready to begin surgery.

"He's right," Noah said. "You should probably pop one of those babies right after I make you some breakfast. With no food in your stomach they'd make you really nauseous."

He sauntered over to put on his clothes, which, as Alexis could have guessed, were strewn about in the living room. One sock was hanging from a lamp. She pictured his apartment again, and added dirty laundry hung about to her vision. Definitely not her type.

"I'll be right back, guys," he said, and after tucking his phone and scruffy brown leather wallet into his back pocket, he was gone, carrying his sports equipment downstairs on both shoulders. She felt the absence of him. The room was better with him in it, she decided.

"Wow!" Billy exclaimed, when the door shut behind Noah. "That guy is gorgeous. Chocolate that melts in your mouth. Yum."

Alexis laughed. "He's super . . . nice. He wants to open his own restaurant. He kind of reminds me of a Labrador."

"Well, woof!" Billy said, making them both giggle like schoolchildren. He plopped down next to her on the couch and put her feet in his lap, massaging her ankles. This was why he was her best friend. Billy just went with the flow. He didn't ask what Noah was doing here, or why Alexis broke her steadfast no-sleepovers rule. Billy was entirely nonjudgmental. At least of her. He made fun of other gay friends, for example: "Oh, you know those queens. *So* gay. Always having the same argument over what country to adopt a baby from. It's silly. They should just adopt me."

He also had zero tolerance for lesbians. "Terrible haircuts and oh, my god, when they fight they punch each other *in the face*! It's despicable." Alexis would try and point out that probably not every lesbian couple went around punching one another, certainly she couldn't imagine Ellen DeGeneres and Portia de Rossi DeGeneres socking each other in the eyeball on a daily basis, but when she brought up these points Billy would wave his hand at her or change the subject. And yet, he was nothing if not a walking contradiction. Alexis had *several* times caught him crying over gay or lesbian wedding announcements in the Style section of the newspaper. "We've come so far," he'd say, when she pressed him.

In addition to his various prejudices, Billy had steadfast opinions about which he never wavered: Asian women caused the most traffic accidents. If you see a blond person in Manhattan they're from Sweden. Going out drinking when you have a cold cures you faster than cold medicine and rest. If you play golf you are a Republican.

Alexis peered at Billy more closely. "You look tired."

He ran his hand over the frayed edges of his Mohawk. He had blue circles under his eyes. He put down her foot, looking distracted. "Yeah, I don't know what my deal is lately. I've been bartending nights for five years, and I never used to get tired."

"Did you go out after?" Sometimes Billy went what he called "gay dancing" after work. She'd gone with him a few times. They'd dress up like David Bowie, affix silver glitter lightning bolts to their cheeks, strap on platform shoes, and head out to Billy's favorite West Village bars, where they'd drink and dance themselves silly. Once Billy had talked her into wearing a skintight white bodysuit he'd taken home from the set of a future-themed movie that aired on the Sci-Fi Channel. "You look like a slutty Princess Leia!" he'd exclaimed, clapping his hands at the sight of her.

"No, that's just it," Billy said. He rummaged around in their cupboard for a few moments, and then pulled out a box of Raisin Bran. "I went straight home after work and I *still* feel like shit." His forehead had a light sheen of sweat on it.

"Maybe you should go to the doctor," she said, leaning against the kitchen doorframe. The room was so small that she could have reached out and touched his silk sleeve. "You might have mono."

His head was inside the refrigerator looking for the milk but she still heard his snort. "I don't have mono," he said. "Korean people are immune to it."

"Billy! Anyone can get mono."

He turned to her, his left hand perched on his hip, and gestured with the milk carton. "Seriously, babe. Have you ever fucking heard of a Korean person getting fucking *mono*?"

She shook her head. She walked toward him and put her hand on his forehead and gasped. "Billy! You are burning up. Let's go, I am putting you back to bed."

He poured his cereal and milk into the bowl, took a few bites, and sighed, putting his bowl in the sink. "Not hungry. But if I go back to bed I don't get to see more of Noah. And I want to see more of Noah. Nice, naked Noah."

She smiled. "You can after you take a nap. I'm serious. I only have one of you."

He let her lead him into his room, which he'd decorated with thick red-and-green-striped wallpaper, a Jonathan Adler headboard he'd been given as a gift from the set of *The Young and the Restless,* and the stuffed head of a deer they'd found at the Hell's Kitchen flea market two summers ago. He had a portable bar straight out of *Mad Men* in the corner, and six-hundred-thread-count sheets from Barneys. "Fabulous Prep" was how he'd described it over the phone to Alexis, as Billy had found the apartment and moved in first, when she was still living in Connecticut and applying to law school the summer after college.

He took off his pajama top and Alexis had to cover her mouth to stifle a scream.

"What? Oh, I know. Gross, right?"

Underneath Billy's left arm was a plum-sized lump.

"Why didn't you say anything?"

He slowly lifted his arm and inspected it casually, like it was a freckle or speck of dirt. "I don't know, it just seemed to materialize there a week ago. I was hoping if I ignored it, it would go away. You know how that sometimes happens," he said, laughing weakly.

He avoided looking at her.

She swallowed, not wanting Billy to see how scared she was. "Sarah from the gym is married to a doctor at NYU," she said. "I'll call her."

"Fine," Billy said. His voice didn't have an ounce of its usual attitude as he climbed into bed. "But come in here and get me if Noah takes his shirt off again."

"I will, I promise," Alexis said, smiling, and gently closed the door behind her.

The newness of Noah, and the throb of her finger, now were all forgotten as Alexis shakily dialed Sarah's 718-area-code number. She hoped she was home and not training today. Luckily, she reached her, and after Sarah promised she'd page her husband at work Alexis set down the phone, sitting on the couch and staring out the window. She'd felt a bolt of fear run through her body, and she didn't like it. Billy was her entire family, hook, line, and sinker. Her mother was a drunk, Mark was dead, and her father hated her. Those were the bare-bones facts. She had the sudden image of that fat girl's sister, what was her name, at *Oprah*, sticking her big, chubby finger in her face and shouting, *Obviously you don't have any family values or else you would never have said that just to win an argument!*

Emily, that had been her name. Shoshana's even fatter sister. "Family values," Alexis said now, aloud in her apartment, to the dust that settled into the floorboards, the sunlight streaming into the window, which had a crack running along the bottom.

Her head perked up at the sound of the buzzer, and she walked trancelike over to push her finger on the plastic button.

She could barely see Noah's face over the three stuffed-to-the-brim brown grocery bags. She decided not to mention Billy; after all, she wasn't sure what the lump meant, and she didn't want to spoil Noah's good mood. He was whistling.

"Now you just sit right there and relax," he said. She'd gone back to sit on the couch and his voice came out muffled from the kitchen as he stuck his head into bags, his large hands pawing over the food. "I am going to put some meat on those bones."

Alexis shuddered at the thought. But no one had ever cooked for her before, and she tried to look on the bright side; she might just get a blog post for *Skinny Chick* out of this. She was stuck on what to write about for tomorrow anyway.

Oh, but who cared? Who cared about Noah and his ears that stuck out adorably from the sides of his head and his big white smile that seemed to X-ray right through her clothes? What the fuck *was* that lump beneath Billy's arm? She got up and paced up and down, the floorboards creaking underneath her feet. She fiddled with her bandage. She checked her phone three times, hoping Sarah's husband Aldo would call.

He finally did, just as Noah was setting out two plates, searching around in the drawer for silverware. An amazing smell wafted over to her nose from the kitchen. Their plates, glasses, silverware were all mix-matched, nothing was part of a set. Some had been there when they moved into the apartment, and they eventually got over the initial grossness and used them, and then there were the odd-looking antique plates with horses and carriages on them that belonged to Billy. Vanya contributed some black plastic plates with a pink skull and crossbones on them, which Alexis and Billy were too scared to use, plus once your food was on there it was impossible to see what you were eating.

"Hello, Alexis, this is Dr. Aldo Martinez. Sarah said you wanted to speak with me about a friend of yours?" She heard someone being paged in the background, voices murmuring, telephones ringing.

"Yes, um, it's Billy. Billy is his name." Noah peered at her curiously, then sat down on one of the breakfast barstools. He clasped his hands in his lap and waited for her, which she liked. His manners seemed . . . antiquated somehow.

"And what seems to be the problem?" Aldo's voice was kind, but she could tell he was busy. Of course, he had other patients. Ones probably who were really sick. Billy probably had mono. Or the flu. She continued with more confidence, but kept her voice down so Billy wouldn't hear her discussing him.

"He has a lump . . . under his arm. About the size of a plum. And he says he's been tired, sluggish. He works nights, so he's tired a lot, but not like this. And he has blue circles under his eyes, I'm just . . . I'm worried about him."

"Yes, I see. Why don't you tell Billy to come see me in my uptown office today after nine? I'll be able to give a better diagnosis that way than over the phone."

She swallowed. She didn't like that word, "diagnosis." Did you get diagnosed for mono? She supposed one did. Just last night, she'd been diagnosed with a need for stitches, right? And that turned out to be no big deal.

"Okay, thank you so much, Aldo. I mean, Dr. Martinez. I really appreciate you taking the time to call me back."

Noah set down a plate of steaming-hot French toast in front of her. She pressed the off button on her phone, then set it slowly down next to her plate. She realized with a strange calmness that if her phone was off she couldn't input the calories into her app, but the thought swam in and out of her mind like a gentle tide. Absentmindedly, she took a bite. She stared at her fork, then cut off another piece, and ate that, too. Somewhere in the back of her mind alarm bells were going off about her caloric intake, but she was too worried to respond to them.

"Everything okay?" Noah asked, in that deep, calm voice of his. She felt she could listen to him talk all day, every day.

"Did you hear that?" Alexis asked.

"I think I have the gist," Noah answered. He put an arm around her. "Everything is going to be fine."

"It's just . . . Billy's my whole family and best friend wrapped into one, you know?" She instantly regretted saying it. Her voice had cracked. It sounded like she was asking him to pity her.

"I hear you," Noah said. "With my family so far away, it's pretty much me and Oliver in the bachelor pad. I think Billy is lucky to have you."

"Hmmm," Alexis said, unnerved by his praise. She stared out the window.

"Eat," Noah said gently. "Food helps ease the soul."

Alexis sighed. "I guess if I don't eat anything else for the rest of the day . . ." she said. The food was so good, so warm and sweet. As a child she'd devour French toast; their maid Elsa cooked it and put a whipped cream heart on top. She'd leave a square of butter on top and let them pour on as much maple syrup as they wanted. Mark called the butter "butter boats," and they would use their forks to race the yellow squares until they melted.

She ate slowly, relishing each bite. She spoke only once to ask for more syrup. Following the toast were homemade croissants, baked in her crappy little oven she'd been using to store extra shoes. Noah buttered hers, then ate four himself.

"I usually go to the gym now," she said reluctantly, when she'd finished everything on her plate, and then, when Noah wasn't looking, licked it.

"Aren't you exhausted?" he asked. "We didn't get home until pretty late." He glanced at the clock on the stove, and she realized he didn't wear a watch.

It was true. She ached everywhere, and longed to go back to her bed. "Want to come with me?" she asked. She smiled at him. Not her scary smile, the one she flashed right before telling guys off who approached her, but a tired one, a little-girl smile. She felt so full she could burst, but the food and the feeling it gave her was of being cared for. She understood suddenly how people ate to feel better, but she pushed away the thought. How horrible, if she were to turn into someone that weak. Today was an anomaly; she'd have to work twice as hard in the gym to work it off.

"I do," he said. He looked at her meaningfully, reading her.

"I can't believe you got me to eat all that starchy food," she exclaimed, as they walked down the hallway. She felt nervous, which was totally uncharacteristic of her. She was usually like a lioness before the kill when she went to bed with men. She enjoyed the buildup, the power. Now, she felt powerless. She didn't like it.

"Everybody needs a little comfort food now and again," he said. "Besides, I already told you: I'm gonna put some meat on those bones of yours. Otherwise people are going to think I'm starving you."

"You leave my bones alone," she said, bumping his shoulder with her own, as they walked to her room. But she'd liked what he'd said, as if these mythological "people" were surrounding them and their couplehood, watching them, that they were indeed to be a couple, or something along those lines.

Again, she got into bed fully clothed. Noah lay next to her, over the blankets. She leaned over and turned off the heater. She'd left it on last night when she left for the cooking class (*god, that seemed like ages ago!*) and her pillows were on fire.

"I'm going to kiss you now," he said, pulling her on top of him.

"Okay, then," she replied, and felt his hands wrap around her head, comb through her hair, gently turn her face to his, and then he did indeed kiss her, his large lips gentle but insistent. It wasn't until she felt the softness of his lips that she realized there was something so hard within herself, a boulder she'd thought was immovable. She'd closed herself off as rigidly as the smooth maple wood of Mark's casket she'd trailed her hands upon before he was lowered into the earth.

How strange, that she would think of her brother now, in this moment. When a boy kissed her. But it felt natural, as she thought of him so often. Every experience she had was tainted by her memory of him, and yet . . . and yet this one felt okay. Good, even. Like it was meant to be, and she was comforted that Noah somehow had caused her brother's lopsided grin to pop into her head.

She was glad Noah didn't use his tongue right away, at least not in her mouth. She wasn't into sloppy kissing, but Noah did everything right, and as he reached up in that way men do when they are so eager to cup your breasts, he whispered into her ear, "Are you on the pill?" and she whispered back, "No, it makes you fat. But I have condoms," and so that's what they used.

For the first time, Alexis Allbright had a man in her room other than Billy, and felt full of both homemade French toast and a tiny flicker of happiness. She allowed herself to unwind, to release into Noah. And he accepted her with such kindness, such gentle loving touches, she could barely entertain the notion that she'd only met him last night. It was only later, much later, that she realized she'd forgotten to input the calories of her breakfast into her phone app.

When she woke, the sun was hitting the wall opposite her bed, and the blinds left shadows of lines on her white duvet. Outside, a taxi horn beeped and two men yelled at one another in Spanish. The M3 bus squealed to a stop a block down. Two women discussed where to go for afternoon tea. She guessed it was midafternoon. It felt strange to not be at the gym. She missed her locker room suddenly, and her pink weights, running on the treadmill. But this was good, too.

Rolling over, she realized she was alone in the bed, and she nuzzled her face deeper into her pillow, smelling Noah everywhere. What he'd done to her, the places where he'd kissed and stroked her . . . he was so much more skilled and tender than the assholes she'd been seeing since she moved to New York. She felt she'd known him her whole life. She'd had an orgasm so strong she'd dug her fingers into his shoulders deeply enough that he'd have marks. She smiled, remembering. She didn't even care how many wrinkles smiling was causing her. Surely sex that scrumptious had been good for her body. She felt better than when Sarah put her through a grueling workout, or when she got a smorgasbord of positive comments on a *Skinny Chick* article or post. She felt the way one did after a cool shower on a hot day, after a full-body massage.

Billy and Noah were in the living room discussing their favorite microbreweries, she could hear their voices as she walked in. It turned out Noah had a vast net of knowledge when it came to beers Alexis had never heard of. "In Colorado every bar brews its own beer," he was saying. "It's awesome. I want to bring that laid-back vibe to New York."

"I've got to get out there," Billy said. "Alexis and I go to Blind Tiger a lot to sample new beers. You should totally come with!" As Noah nodded his head enthusiastically (the man was so damn *cheerful!*), Alexis studied Billy.

The dark circles underneath his eyes seemed less blue, and the sheen of sweat was gone from his face, but he still looked tired.

"Aldo called," Alexis said, leaning against the doorframe. Her hipbone jutted out and she rearranged her body so that the wood didn't poke her uncomfortably. Noah patted the seat beside him, but she pretended she didn't see. It was instinctual for her survival that she didn't let on how deeply he'd affected her. She was used to being the one in control, leaving the morning after in a cab. But here Noah was, still in her apartment. This made Alexis feel uneasy. She was in uncharted territory.

"Alexis, Noah has been baking up in here and you have to see the muffins he made. They are amazing! I don't even care if I add inches to my hips. He's like the black Julia Child, I swear to god!"

Noah laughed. Alexis was amazed by how comfortable he was around Billy, having just met him, even though Billy was pressuring Noah to take a cue from the Naked Chef and bake à la fresco when he opened up his restaurant. They usually didn't engage in conversation with outsiders, preferring to spend time with each other.

"I don't think that guy actually *is* naked, he just calls himself that," Noah was saying, amused.

She walked over to the kitchen. There, cooling, were rows and rows of plump tan muffins. They were beautiful and her stomach growled loudly. She quickly looked around for her bananas, took one off the microwave, and started cutting it.

"And he puts Guinness into them, too!" Billy exclaimed. "The man's a genius. Mr. Wu came by, and he's going to rent out the old fur store to Noah!"

"Wow, that's great," Alexis said. She wasn't sure how she felt about his brewpub being so close to her. She felt edgy again, closed in. It had all happened so fast, overnight. She felt a churning within her; something was changing. The worry passed, however, when Noah smiled across the countertop at her and she couldn't help but return it, shyly.

"Looks like we're in business," Noah said.

We?

Shoshana

April

HOBOKEN AND CHESTER, NEW JERSEY

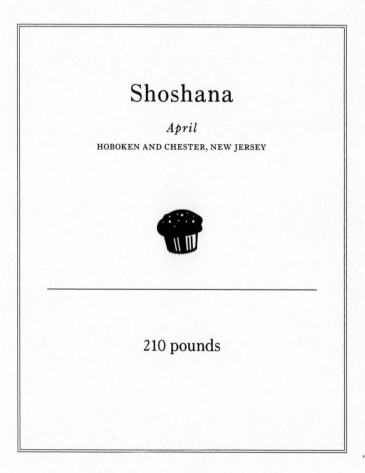

210 pounds

Fat and Fabulous

This is one of the strangest posts I've ever made. My great-aunt Mimi died last night. She was ninety, so I guess that means she lived a long life, but still: it's sad when anyone dies. I hadn't seen Mimi for a couple of years, since college, though I know my mother has visited her weekly. My father was raised by Aunt Mimi after his parents died in a car crash when he was eight.

Mimi loved the hell out of some wigs and makeup. Since she left me the farm I found a photo album at my mom's house and Mimi is shown equally blond, redheaded, and brunette throughout her life. She was married long ago, but my great-uncle Fred died in World War II. She never had children; I don't believe she could.

When I was thirteen and got my period, Mimi bought me maxi pads and showed me how to peel off the plastic liner and stick them into my underpants. I remember it felt like a torpedo. She was a Fattie, like me, and when she was young her job was to dress women to the nines for Universal Studios glamour shots. She even met Marilyn Monroe once. She knew how to dress a big body before the movement came along to do so, before one single fashion designer had nice clothing for curvy girls. She cut and sewed her own designs in all sorts of fabrics, silks, cashmeres, velvets . . . and they were gorgeous, exquisite, and classy.

Her farmhouse in Chester sits atop a stretch of fifteen acres that to me as a kid looked like the jungle in *Where the Wild Things Are* because Mimi never really had a green thumb. She let nature take over, which means all fifteen acres are forest, with thick brush intertwined with thorny rosebushes and hundreds of trees that are allowed to drop their seeds wherever they want when the wind blows. Letting the land remain overgrown was a metaphor for how Mimi lived her life; she didn't believe in forcing people to be one way or another. She thought wildflowers and woods were beautiful.

In the end, she'd gone a bit batty between the ears, but we still visited her from time to time. Once, a neighbor called my mom to tell her Mimi was sitting in a baby pool in her front yard, only she'd forgotten to put on a bathing suit and was drinking Manhattans all afternoon. When I lose my marbles, please let me be naked and drunk in a pool, not left to rot in an old-age home.

So, loyal readers, I'm sitting on a speeding train on good ol' New Jersey Transit to see my property. Yes, that's right: Mimi left her farm to me. Having been a city kid for so long here in Hoboken, I'm flabbergasted as to what to do with it, but Mimi was mysterious like that; you never knew when she was kidding, and I feel like somehow through me her legacy lives on. I just hope I'm worthy of the challenge!

Still, I can't imagine why she left a run-down house and land to someone who is used to living in a city with no backyard! I guess I'll find out. And all of you will, along with me. I love you, Mimi, always and forever. *Fat and Fabulous* will return after the trip to Chester. To be continued . . .

SHOSHANA LOVED WALKING FROM HER APARTMENT TO the Hoboken train station. She saw the same people every time, the characters that made up her neighborhood.

It had rained overnight and she kicked up wet leaves as she walked. One stuck to the side of her shoe but she didn't mind giving it a ride. FOR SALE signs were abundant, hanging from iron gates. Instead of front yards, or grass, buildings here had pavement and iron gates. Some had little bushes planted out front. She liked looking up and trying to guess whether the four- or five-story buildings were single-family or part of the many in Hoboken that were cut up and divided into several apartments. Some clues to determine a single-family were identical blinds or curtains in all windows, or pristine boxwood bushes and flower bed plantings in front. It was easiest to tell during the holidays, as often there would be a single candle lit and placed in all windows facing the street, but as it was spring she had a harder time playing the guessing game.

Shoshana passed a long line of people waiting for Carlos Bakery to open.

She arrived at the train station and took a moment standing on the cobblestones outside to crane her neck and view the vast building. Only half the train station was active. The other, abandoned years ago, had brilliant copper turrets turned bright lime-green from age that reminded Shoshana of the peaks in the Statue of Liberty's crown. Rumors had persisted for years the town would turn this half into a mall, as if there weren't enough malls in New Jersey already.

Walking into the station was like stepping back in time; conductors stood around in their dark blue uniforms, New Jersey Transit logo in gold on their breast pocket. They swung pocket watches, crossed their arms, and shot banter back and forth with coworkers, and wore 9/11 pins with the words NEVER FORGET. They often took off their stiff caps and peered at bright orange schedules tucked into the inside brim.

The flower salesman paced back and forth in front of his products, ever hopeful. Shoshana bought Gerber daisies, salmon-pink, canary-yellow, hothouse-orange, and she picked out the scratchy green filler leaves as she craned her neck searching for her track on the large board.

Her train was on track seventeen, which was only half covered with roof, and Shoshana caught a wet wind rushing over her from the direction of Jersey City. Spread out before her were the Gold Coast buildings, thrown up in a haste during the real estate boom of the early 2000s. Their glittering steel cast reflections into the Hudson River, as if someone were holding up a mirror and trying to burn ants.

On the train, she settled her large bag down next to her on the seat and reached her hand in to pet Sinatra, who had cheerfully come along for the ride. She produced a small bone from the pocket of her sweater, which he devoured with gusto, his crooked tongue touching her hand as she fed him.

Shoshana stuck her ticket inside the little loop on the stiff brown plastic chair in front of her and listened to Joss Stone on her iPod against the *click-clack* of the train's wheels. She opened her laptop and managed to pull a wireless signal out of the air and checked the recent message board comments on *Fat and Fabulous*. Yesterday she'd interviewed a gym teacher from Pennsylvania who devised a sports program curriculum for large girls who wanted to work out together after school but not enter traditional sports teams. So far she'd failed to get sponsorship from her town, but Shoshana hoped posting a story on it would shed enough light on her cause that the teacher would receive funding. She edited the interview for punctuation, cut some of its length, then hit the "go live" button and experienced that little thrill she got whenever she wrote a great entry that would generate a lot of feedback from her readers.

She checked her e-mail, and read a letter from a sixteen-year-old in Idaho who wanted to know why a major clothing label had canceled their plus-size line without an explanation. Shoshana wrote back: "Not sure re: cancellation. Will contact corporate HQ and post their reply on F.A.F."

She then read another e-mail from the social committee of her temple, the United Synagogue of Hoboken, asking if anyone was able to put together fruit baskets for their upcoming book club meeting. They were reading *The Help*. It was a departure from the usual zipper-ripper romance novels or silly beach reads she usually liked. The meeting was next week and she was only one chapter in. Her blog took up so much of her time, and now, with going to Mimi's house and getting things sorted, she wasn't sure if she'd ever finish the book.

She sighed. What was with the fruit basket idea, anyway? Had the whole world gone mad from lack of calories? What ever happened to book club wine-and-cheese parties? Or at least coffee, brownies, and chitchat?

Sometimes she felt like she had to be the one to "bring on the awesome," which was a phrase she used often on her blog. Hearing the women in her book club constantly moan about how they hate their bodies depressed Shoshana. She knew it was merely a ruse to get Shoshana's treatment of kind words and positivity (after all, she was famous for helping women end the cold war with their bods), but at times she felt like she was speaking to a brick wall;

her friends would just nod her to death and then go out and skip dessert and moan about the width of their thighs the second she turned her back.

She hit "reply all" and wrote: "Hey, everyone, I'll be there for the book club mtg. However, fruit baskets are not really my thing. A strawberry on a stick can only go so far. I'm just sayin'. Anyone up for mimosas and brownies? I am sure even Smaller Fats or Non Fats would enjoy them. If so, hit me back, I'd be happy to bring everything."

She logged back on to her blog and posted a picture from two weeks ago. Her roommates had thrown her a twenty-sixth birthday party in the back room of Onieals bar. Underneath the picture, she typed: "This is why they tell fatties not to wear stripes." She stared at herself, beefy arm thrown around Andrea and Greg, mouth a perfect, kissable pink from the new lipgloss Emily had bought for her that night. She was wearing a blue and white nautical dress and white flats that the weather had cooperated long enough for her to slip on. She'd thought the dress very trendy, and she smiled just looking at it. She knew she looked big and she didn't care. She loved her body. Eat your heart out, Victoria Beckham. Under the text, she added: "To those people, *Fat and Fabulous* says, 'Fongool!'"

On the train, watching Jersey flit by in colors muted into pastels by the condensation on the window, she fiddled with the tiny diamond stud in her right nostril.

Emily had pierced it with a sewing needle when Shoshana was sixteen. Her little sister held an extremely high tolerance for pain and therefore thought everyone should be pierced and tattooed. Only Emily was bossy about it, and after begging Shoshana to let her "experiment," she'd tilted back Shoshana's head on her mother's impractical purple velvet couch, which got so hot in the summer your thighs got a fever, and stuck an ice cube up her nose. Then, she'd walked into the kitchen to hold the needle over the stove's flame.

Shoshana watched Emily as she rotated the needle around and

around in the orange fire. Unfortunately, the glow cast upon her lit her face like a carnival monster and Shoshana began having second thoughts.

"At least put a towel under your neck to catch the blood," her father had said, stopping home from work for lunch and not appearing the least bit surprised by what his two daughters were up to. "You don't want to get any on your mother's couch." He was traipsing through the house, cakelike mud trailing off his boots and making tiny brown pancakes on the front hallway carpet. He wore a red and black flannel shirt that Kurt Cobain was out making hip at the time. His gut strained against the cloth, two missing buttons near his navel proof he wasn't sticking to the Weight Watchers diet his doctor had ordered for him. His jeans had rips in both knees, and green stains from kneeling in the grass.

The good thing about their dad owning his own landscaping business was that he often was hired by the wealthier neighbors in the large houses a few blocks away, and would come home on his lunch break, setting his saw or his lawn mower or his black plastic trays of bulbs on the front porch. He worked all week, taking only one day off in the year: for their mother's birthday, May first. Every year on that day he would buy new dress socks at ShopRite and put on a green and yellow plaid flannel tie and take Pam to dinner and a movie. Later that night, Emily and Shoshana would hear the mattress squeaking, and Emily would lean over the side of her bed (they slept in bunk beds from post-cradle until they were in their late teens) and stick her finger down her throat, rolling her eyes, and they'd both giggle uncontrollably, the thought of their parents naked and slick like baby seals and rolling around on white sheets totally grossing them out.

On the day Emily pierced Shoshana's nose, their father arranged a frayed white towel underneath Shoshana's chin and then sat down at the kitchen table and ate a roast beef sandwich Pam had made for him before she left for her afternoon shift at Overlook Hospital, where she was a nurse in the recovery room. She was the first person people saw when they woke up from surgery and realized they weren't dead, a white and gold halo surrounding her head if she were leaning too close to the windows, sunlight streaming in and lighting her like an angel.

"You're getting mud all over the house," Shoshana scolded him, only it came out as "Yumgettingmverdaouse" because the ice was inhibiting her breathing and shoved halfway up her nose to "numb it good," as Emily had told her.

Her father chewed his food slowly. "Does your mother know you two are up to this?" He wasn't mad. He was genuinely curious. His daughters were a constant source of amusement for him. He wanted to know what made them tick, why green was Shoshana's favorite color, why Emily collected buttons from flea markets. When they were small he taught himself to braid, and would set their hair in beautiful cornrows or plaits.

Pam was the disciplinarian, after he'd handed each girl twenty dollars, or bought them their second ice-cream cone. This sometimes left her exasperated with her husband. But she loved her big bear of a man, everybody did.

"Um . . . not exactly," Emily said, peering at the needle. "I think this is ready."

"You think or you know?" Shoshana called out from her position on the scratchy velvet couch. She was getting tired of counting flies in the ceiling light. They'd mashed into one big black speck now: a Jackson Pollock.

The pinch in her nose hurt more than she'd expected, but that was because Emily'd had to stab her three times before she got the needle through. "It always looks so easy when James does it," she said, mentioning the tattoo and piercing mentor she was working with after school.

"Maybe I should have had him do it, then," Shoshana said dryly, holding the towel over her nose. It felt like a yellowjacket was perched on her face, stinging her. Her eyes watered.

"Noooooo!" squealed Emily, throwing her arms around her big sister. "It's good for me to practice."

"Is that thing going to set off metal detectors at the airport?" Bill *asked, talking with his mouth full of sandwich. He'd come into the room and stood in the entryway, one muddy boot up against the doorframe. "'Cause if so, I'm not going to be seen with you," he joked.*

Now Shoshana turned the tiny diamond stud around in her nose, remembering the shadow her father's body had thrown on the sandy wood floor, the wild pink hair Emily had tied with orange yarn in two buns on the sides of her head, the sound of the percolator bubbling in the kitchen. Dad took his coffee black. "Anything else is just water," he'd say.

Sometimes, even though he died three years ago, it was almost as if he were still alive, his deep, booming voice calling out for their mother down the hallway when he couldn't find a clean pair of socks or chuckling over some idiot he read about in the paper.

He loved to peruse the crime section of the *Star-Ledger*. His favorite stories were when a thief was caught and arrested because of his own stupidity. "Look at this moron," he'd say, sitting in his leather chair and laughing so hard he'd turn an alarming shade of red. Shoshana would peer over his beefy shoulder, squinting at whatever story he was so amused by. It was always the bank robber who left his wallet at the bank, the thief who wore his mother's dress to rob a jewelry store, and then she'd seen it on television and called the cops to turn her own son in.

Sometimes, even now, Shoshana would buy the paper just to look for stories that would have made her dad laugh. She'd run her hand over the print, blackening the pads of her fingers.

The train's signboard lit up with NEXT STOP—CHESTER and Shoshana gathered up her purse (today's was the ever-popular I'm-not-a-plastic-bag one) and Frank Sinatra and headed for the front of the train by the doors, grabbing on to the back of a seat for balance as the train rocked into the station. The conductor did that series of mysterious conductor tasks, such as putting down the huge metal platform, throwing a few unlabeled metal switches, and jogging down the steps as the doors opened.

"Thank you," she said. She always thanked the conductors, even though no one else did. It made her feel good, being polite.

The tall, skinny conductor gave her an odd look. People in Jersey weren't usually so friendly. Usually it was a clear sign you were from somewhere midwestern—or Idaho.

She wore her favorite green wrap sweater. It had just begun to be warm enough not to need her winter coat anymore. She made a mental note to shop for a light spring jacket, but every year around this time she looked and never liked anything in the stores. The coats made for women her size always had ruffles sewn willy-nilly on them, as though being fat meant you also wanted to look six years old. She drew the wool collar of the wrap around her neck as she walked from the train to Mimi's house. A warm drizzle made her face wet.

The last time she'd been here was when their father was still alive, and Mimi was just starting to lose her marbles. She'd made Emily and Shoshana egg-salad sandwiches, but when Shoshana bit into hers she heard a distinct crunching sound; Mimi had left some of the shell. Shoshana saw her sister's pink mouth twist across the table with disgust as she took a bite.

"There's eggshell in here," Emily blurted out.

"I can feel it crunching on my back molars," Shoshana said.

"Shhh," her father had said, glancing up to make sure Mimi was still puttering around in the kitchen trying to roust the tea-kettle to boil. "Be polite."

"Does being polite mean having to have my stomach operated on?" Emily had asked. Shoshana had kicked her under the table.

She stepped off the train now in Chester and looked around. Small antique stores stood next door to quaint coffee shops, and a few people braved the wind and wet to sit outside, the steam from their mugs rising into the gray air. A toboggan sled was propped against the door to one store; a price tag written in black scroll on white paper dangling from it read $250. Whoa. Expensive.

The townspeople wore dark Hunter rain boots, North Face jackets, sensible yet expensive clothing. A woman in her sixties with white hair done up in a bun walked a brown Labrador through town, laughing as the dog strained against the leash. A man with muddy boots propped up on an iron chair outside the café petted the dog as he galloped by. The man looked so much like her father, his build, the mud on his shoes, that Shoshana had to slow down her pace to catch her breath. This happened to her several times a month, and the kickback from remembering he was dead always left her feeling empty.

But today she had a purpose. A destination. "Well, here we go, Sinatra," she said to the dog, who peeked his head out of the bag to sniff the air. His tongue stuck out crookedly from his mouth. As she walked, he tasted the air. She took out a crumpled map the lawyer had provided for her, with Mimi's house marked with a red X. She reached inside her jacket pocket and turned down the volume on her iPod and leaned into the sound like it was a warm wind. Strains of Rusted Root's "Ecstasy" were muted and she smiled, imagining Emily's face if she knew Shoshana's music choice: "You've been listening to the same hippie bands since high school!" Then Emily would force her to download Yeah Yeah Yeahs, Rancid, 7 Seconds, Lifetime, or Anti-Flag: loud, fast punk music Shoshana hated but her little sister loved.

As the town receded behind her and gave way to dirt roads and forest, the map folded in her hand, Shoshana realized she felt kind of shocked—still unable to process the fact that she'd just in-herited fifteen acres and a house. A tiny, run-down house. After living since college crammed into her little Hoboken apartment with four roommates, she wasn't sure she wanted to move to Ches-ter, where she'd be all alone, and a good hour from Manhattan's hustle and bustle. Her mother and sister were only about an hour away, but still . . . it seemed spooky, like she'd turn into a crazy cat lady who dies and then her cats eat her face.

She slid her finger over the map, passing streets with tree names: Hickory, Cherry, Oak . . . until she got to Apple. She wore several strands of colorful beaded necklaces and they clicked and clacked against one another as she walked uphill. She found the sign to Apple Road, which had been flattened by a large tree or struck by lightning—it was dangling from its metal post and its letters were so faded she had to brush off some dust and leaves to read it.

As she felt the muscles in her calves working away, and the ground retreating behind her up the hill, she came to two stone pillars and paused in front, a little out of breath. Different-shaped rocks were stacked from large to small, like a cairn that hikers leave along the trail. Thick ivy snaked through its foundation and up through the tops, where someone had mounted two metal, in-tertwined hearts, now rusty.

A squirrel sat perched on top of one pillar, his gray fur quiver-ing as he worked a nut from its shell, his small paws so much like hands. "Hello," Shoshana said to him. She was amazed how quiet it was here, how her ears seemed to somehow *expand*, to hear a bird tweeting in a bush behind her, or the slow drone of a prop plane buzzing overhead. She was so used to constant noise that the si-lence had a living, breathing presence. She put her finger to her neck and felt her pulse slow down after her walk.

She walked up the drive; it had probably once been filled with pebbles, as there were still a few white rocks scattered that crunched underneath her sneakers, but mainly the little road leading up to the house was distinct from the grass surrounding it only by the pillars and a slight indentation in the shoots of very green grass, like it had been trampled upon by many feet over the years.

She heard loud buzzing, and passed overgrown rosebushes, fat and busy bumblebees swarming around, their wings vibrating. Their life cycle was six weeks only. What would she do with her life if she only had six weeks to live it? Probably lie in bed and read. And eat chocolate, of course.

Sticks littered the ground. It had been raining often lately, and branches had been allowed to fall around the property without being collected. Small pools of water evaporated in the weak sun. Two giant willow trees covered most of the front of the farm-house, but Shoshana caught her breath as she rounded the drive and the house came into focus before her. It was more beautiful than she remembered, and it was all . . . hers.

The scene was from a fairy tale, a long stretch of ground inside a tunnel of lush trees. The structure was simple in its beauty: a white farmhouse with black shutters. All the sleepovers here with Emily when they were children, Shoshana terrifying her little sister with stories about a witch who lived in the attic and would visit them as soon as they fell asleep, whispering spells into their ears. She laughed now, remembering.

The house looked like it belonged in New England, with its black shutters, white wood detail, peaked roof, and small, falling-apart widow's walk off one of the top-floor bedrooms. The house was the shape of the letter *L*. The willow trees were in full bloom, their hunched branches reminding Shoshana of Aunt Mimi's curved spine. Shoshana felt a pang of pity for this kind woman who'd had no children and had felt Shoshana deserved her house.

On the ground were scattered hundreds of spindly pea-soup-green seed stalks. As the wind picked up, the willow trees gently swayed, caressing the front of the house. Surrounding the front door were bunches of snapdragons in an array of colors: purple, deep blues, and yellows. She trailed her hand through them, basking in their softness. Sinatra gave a little "Yep!" and she carefully lowered him to the ground and he sprang forth, sniffing and quivering with excitement, looking for a place to pee.

She inhaled deeply, and was suddenly struck with remorse that she had not asked her mother and Emily to come along with her. Shoshana dug around in her purse until she found the key Mimi's lawyer had mailed to her. It was in a beat-up envelope and its tape stuck to her fingers a little. It was old-fashioned, large, and heavy, and was made of a kind of metal she couldn't place. Its top was adorned with roses. Her hand trembled as she opened the front door, pushing on a rusty pineapple-shaped knocker.

She stepped into the front room of the house, which Mimi had made into a living room, and was hit with a not-unpleasant musky smell of wood chips. White sheets hung on the small oil paintings on the walls, as well as the couches and armchairs. She walked slowly into the room and placed her hand on the large, curved banister leading to the second floor. Through the arched doorway she could see the kitchen, with its fifties-style red and white tiles and once-bright white cupboards, now faded to pearl. The knobs were crystal and sparkled in the late afternoon light. Something about their smoothness made Shoshana want to cup her hand over them.

She saw her father leaning over the stove, stirring something (his famous spaghetti?) with a long wooden spoon, tomato sauce stuck in his beard, her mother wearing a peach-colored wrap dress and a sparkly butterfly clip in her hair, Shoshana playing hide-and-seek with Emily on the first floor, as the adults talked loudly in the kitchen, the sounds of Aunt Mimi's laughter filling the house and her mother asking when the sauce would be done. "You can't rush perfection, Pam," Bob said. Emily had been two, three, and Shoshana remembered the rough texture of the fabric under her fingers as she hid behind Aunt Mimi's robin's-egg-blue couch, Emily's legs crisscrossed on the Oriental rug as she counted to ten. That same rug was now faded from a deep red into a sort of sunset-orange, and it appeared to have gone into disrepair, with several little critter-made holes in it. Mimi had only been dead a month, but it looked like the place had been coming apart at the seams long before that. Shoshana felt another deep pang that she hadn't made more of an effort to come visit.

At her father's funeral, Mimi had bent over the grave crying. After the ceremony, Shoshana was collecting rocks to place next to the marker that would later become the gravestone and she saw Mimi and her mother standing close together. She overheard Mimi's gravelly voice: "I loved him like a son."

Birds twittering outside shook Shoshana out of her reverie. She ran her hands over the banister, the wood delightfully smooth and sandy, perhaps one of the few modern additions Mimi had made, and walked through the living room into the kitchen, where the image of her father stayed strong behind her eyelids. He was like a postcard she could take out and view any moment she wanted. She leaned over the deep white farm sink surrounded by a white porcelain counter to peer outside into the backyard, which stretched on in green splendor. It was hard to see past just a few feet, however, as large rosebushes spindled and twisted and grew against the house wildly. Shoshana wondered how Mimi had even gotten past them to walk around her property, then realized with sadness she might not have been feeling well enough to do so for quite some time. Spiderwebs covered part of the window and she made a mental note to buy cleaning products and paper towels. On the doorframe leading outside were markings. She stepped closer to peer at them. Drawn with silver pencil were indentations of her father's growth chart. She had to move closer to see the writing, which was faint and slightly smudged. She ran her finger over the dates, 1960, 1962, 1968. She thought of the love behind those numbers, how much Mimi had cared about her father, to keep track of his growth. She smiled. *Maybe that is all any of us can ask for out of life; to be deeply loved.*

Someone, perhaps the estate lawyer, had made a small attempt at tidying up, as the old-fashioned-looking refrigerator was clean and empty. Shoshana was grateful for that; dealing with rotting food would have been pretty gross at this point, and from what she could see of the house, she was going to have a lot of cleaning on her hands already.

She sighed, pushing a heavy lock of auburn hair out of her eyes. The question hummed in the air around her, filling the nooks and spaces, the breath she took in. Why had Aunt Mimi left her this house? It was beautiful, and the idea of owning the fifteen acres of land thrilled her to no end thanks to *The Secret Garden* being her favorite book growing up.

But she was only twenty-six. She had no children to fill these rooms, no husband to make the many repairs that needed doing. Part of her felt she should just sell the house and split the proceeds with Emily, but she kept coming back to the fact that Mimi had left it to her in a will, for goodness' sake. Pam said the will had been made out twenty years ago, when Shoshana was only *six years old*. What had Mimi seen in the child version of her? She and Emily had both loved Aunt Mimi, and Em had said she was fine with having been left a lump sum of money, not the house: "You visited her way more than I did." But the feeling persisted, the unknowing.

"You were just your sweet self at six," Pam had said a few nights ago, when Shoshana had called her with the startling news she'd received from the estate lawyer just that afternoon. "Aunt Mimi was quite smitten with you. I used to take you there for sleepovers and she'd let you try on all her wigs and dresses. Because she raised your father, she felt more like a grandmother to you girls than a great-aunt. Later, she started to slip and became more withdrawn, stopped having people living in the house with her, and I'd visit her on my own from time to time. But she always asked about you and Emily."

Suddenly a man's wrinkled and weathered face appeared in the window. Shoshana let out a bloodcurdling scream. He emitted a choked sound, jumping backward, startled. Shoshana heard a thump as he crumpled onto the front stoop.

"Oh!" she heard herself cry out, and before she could think it through she ran through the kitchen, back into the living room, and flung open the front door, the leaves and dust again filling the air and making her blink. A very tiny, skinny old man was sitting on her front stoop, shaking his head a little. A black-and-white sheepdog ran around him in circles, barking. Sinatra came over to see what the fuss was about and the two dogs sniffed each other's butts in a friendly way. The man, stooped with age, wore a full suit, gray with tiny white stripes, that looked Italian, or at least expensive. He had a mustard-yellow silk handkerchief in the pocket, which lent him old-fashioned charm.

"Are you okay?" she asked, bending down to grasp his elbow. His skin felt paper-thin, his bones razor-sharp. "I am so sorry. I didn't mean to scare you, I just was so lost in thought in there and I totally freaked and thought you were . . . well, never mind." She'd been about to say she thought he looked like the scarecrow from *The Wizard of Oz*, his face was so leathery.

To her surprise, he laughed. "Scared the 'ell out of me, that's fer sure," he said in a thick Irish brogue, standing and brushing off his suit. "Pipe down, Patrick O'Leary!" he shouted to the dog, who wagged his tail even harder, barking excitedly in circles. "Damn mutt," he said, patting him on the head. The man was ancient-looking and shorter than her. He had a full head of neat, snow-white hair that looked freshly combed, a pencil-thin mustache she ordinarily wouldn't have thought handsome but suited him, and the bluest eyes she'd ever seen. He had deep rivers of wrinkles at the corners of his eyes, as if he laughed hard and often, and she could see more tough skin where his neck met his crisp, sky-blue, expensive-looking button-down shirt. The back of his neck was a bright red.

Shoshana apologized once again for startling him. He was so thin, just a bag of bones, really.

"'Tis all right. Nothing my friend Jack Daniel here can't cure," he said jocularly, and somehow as if by magic produced from the depths of his jacket a silver flask with the initials JM etched across. She realized his voice was cheerfully slurred. He stood tilted to one side, like he had a wooden leg. The dog sat at his feet obediently and watched him. Shoshana could swear it looked like he was happy for his master and might want a sip himself. The man screwed off the top, threw his head back, and took a swig. It was an act that clashed with the posh look he was sporting. Not that the rich didn't imbibe, they certainly did their share, but somehow Shoshana got the feeling this man was an alcoholic, and yet his dress suggested that he'd once been very successful and hardworking, at *something*.

Shoshana realized with a start he had extended his arm and was offering her a drink.

"Just like me wife," he said, smiling that crinkly grin again. "Always lost in thought, daydreaming about the world."

"No, thank you," she said, putting her hand up as if to ward off the offered drink. "I'm kind of an after-the-sun-goes-down sort of girl."

"Suit yerself," he said jovially, sliding it back into the smooth dark silk lining of his inside pocket. "Hair of the dog, and all." He winked at Patrick O'Leary, who wagged his tail and let out a single bark.

"Joe Murphy," he said, sticking out his hand. When she grasped it she felt sandpaper slide across her palm.

"Shoshana Weiner."

"Well." His mouth hitched up on one side, a smile. "Tell yer the basics on me, sure. Born in Killarney and moved here to Chester back in ta fifties, my farm is just over those hills there."

She liked him immediately. There was something different about his reaction to her; usually when people encountered Shoshana for the first time their eyes did a sweep of her body, from head to toe, and then back up again, taking in her size. It was almost an unconscious thing, and they would smile at her after doing so, as she had such a warm, inviting face, but the body-sweep thing was so obvious that for someone *not* to care how big she was felt like a relief.

He bent suddenly and ripped a large dandelion weed out of the ground, the dirt falling from it like chunky chocolate chips. His gnarled fingers curled around the dark green stalks. "Been over 'ere ripping these things out for Mimi," he said. Shoshana looked around the front entrance to the house; there were thousands of dandelions, their yellow faces turned toward the sun, spread among the snapdragons.

Joe Murphy bent down and ripped another one out, holding it with a trembling hand and giving it a great big sniff.

Back among the trees lay many other types of growth, some snaking their way up trunks like gnarled fingers, others pushing through the dirt in a frenzy of knots. The brush was thick, and it would be a hell of a job for whoever cleared it. He startled her by talking. The day had such a hush to it; the woods were thick with muted beauty. "Your great-aunt was really a fine broad. Got a kick out of her. Could drink like a fish."

"I remember her just a little from when she was still healthy," Shoshana said. "Um, would you like to come in?" She didn't normally invite strange men inside, but she figured he looked a hundred and ten, so if he tried anything weird she could probably knock him over with one finger.

"Sure! Used ta come over here all the time for afternoon tea, before Mimi . . . well, you know. She wasn't all there in the end, damn near broke my 'art." He took out his flask, tipped it at the sky in homage to Mimi, and had a deep sip. He again offered Shoshana a swig. She shrugged. What the hell? This was turning into one of the strangest days of her life, and he seemed so comically pleased to share his whiskey with her that she giggled out loud and took the bottle from him as they walked inside. Joe Murphy and Patrick O'Leary followed her, the sound of the dog's nails on the dry wood floor sounding like tap-dancing.

"Now, you must be the older sister, right? The one who went off ta Princeton?" He pointed, and he was standing close enough to her that the smell of alcohol hit her like a slap. "Mimi always talked about ya girls," Joe said, leaning a little against the moth-eaten couch. He looked frail in the afternoon light. "She told me the older sister had auburn hair, like hers." It was true. Shoshana had seen pictures of Mimi when she was young, and she'd had the same long, fire-spun hair as her own. Emily's hair had been such a myriad of colors for so long she wasn't sure of its natural color anymore, but as a child it had been blond.

"Did you know my dad?" Shoshana asked.

"Course I knew Bob. Knew 'im since he was this high." He put a shaky arm out to demonstrate. "My wife and I used to watch ye girls running around here, chasing each other. Ye'd play hide-and-seek in my apple orchard, just like yer dad when he was a little boy," he said, smiling. "He ever tell you 'bout the time he fell out of one of your aunt's trees and broke three ribs?"

"No, he never said anything about that," Shoshana said, surprised. Her father had been a man of very few words, happy instead to listen to his wife and daughters chat. He was shy in many ways. He only spoke when he had something important to say.

"The poor chap. Must have been all of fourteen. Was trying to impress his mates, some boys who grew up down the road. Said he could pick an apple from one of Mimi's twenty-foot trees blind-folded."

"Really?" Shoshana exclaimed. She couldn't imagine her serious father *ever* showing off.

"Heard 'im screaming all the way from my house. Fockin' banjaxed. Mimi took him to the hospital, smacking him the whole way for being so reckless." He chuckled, then coughed, his face turning red. "Don't think he ever climbed 'em trees anymore, used a pick 'en pole rest of the time during harvesting season."

"What's a pick 'en pole?" Shoshana asked, walking back to the kitchen to hunt for a bowl to give the dogs some water. She also wanted to ask what "banjaxed" meant, but perhaps she didn't want to know. She found a large red ceramic bowl covered in dust that she rinsed under the faucet, using her finger to push out the cobwebs.

"Nifty little tool. It's a big long wooden stick, got a grabber for the high apples, little wee basket underneath to catch 'em, holds about five or six. Mimi's got some out in that shed, I believe." He indicated the white structure at the back of the house that was leaning to the right and had long strips of white paint peeling off it, with some flakes sprinkled on the ground like confetti.

"So you knew my dad most of his life, then?" Shoshana asked, leaning over to set the bowl on the floor. Patrick O'Leary gave her an enthusiastic lick on her hand, then began to drink. Sinatra was curled up on the couch, not sure how he felt about his new surroundings and visitors. Every once in a while he'd blow air out of his snout, sending the pouf of hair above his eyebrows straight up.

"When he was older, your old man would come over sometimes for a beer. Great guy. I was sad to hear he'd passed," Joe said, bowing his head respectfully.

His voice lulled her into memory: *Summer. Pressing her chubby little white hands against the smooth bark of an apple tree, she and Emily in matching white cotton dresses, the feel of tall grass swishing against her thighs as she ran, the feeling of roller-coaster excitement bubbling inside her as her father counted, "One, two, three, four, five, ready or not, here I come!" Pressing her small body as close to the tree as she possibly could to hide herself, the joy in her father finding her and throwing her onto his shoulders, going to look for Emily, who was always hidden in the long, seaweedlike grass, apples strewn around her body like red balls.*

"I remember!" Shoshana said now, delighted, her voice sounding loud to her own ears in the soft hush inside this house that was hers but not. "I remember running over that hill and into your fields. You have a huge mansion, right?"

He laughed. "Well, some folks might see it that way. I built it just like Georgina—that's my wife, see—just as she liked it. Fockin' saint, she was. She always saw herself living like the Queen of England, I think." By the way his eyes shone Shoshana could tell it was an inside joke, something he'd teased his wife about many times.

"I remember her," said Shoshana. "She used to bring us apple pies. Is she . . . is she still alive?"

"No, oh, no." He coughed a little, and took out a stiff white handkerchief to wipe his mouth. Shoshana fought the urge to clap him on the back. "Georgina died five years ago. She's buried right at the base of her favorite tree, ta first apple tree we ever planted," he said.

"Oh." Shoshana peered at him.

"Have you been through the house yet?" he asked her, shaking her out of her thoughts. "Mimi was real proud to be able to leave it to one of ye girls, you know. Meant a lot to her."

"Er, no, I haven't been through the house, not yet. I guess I should." She turned to sort through the cupboards, took out two chipped water glasses, and filled them from the tap. A small red beetle made its way lazily over the kitchen's blue floor tiles. The sun had come back out and it was hitting the green glass in the bottom half of the window, spilling the color onto the sink and counter. She handed a cool glass to Joe, and took a sip herself. The water felt wonderful rushing down her throat. She realized suddenly that she was starving.

"Can't beat good ol' Jar-sey tapwater," Joe said. "Best thing next to Jack, ain't that the lord's truth." Shoshana smiled; Joe Murphy seemed to ask questions and be perfectly content to respond to them himself.

"Cheers." And they clinked their glasses together.

"That's just the thing," she said tentatively. "I was kind of surprised that Aunt Mimi left the house to me. I mean . . . I loved her, we all did, but I hadn't been to see her in several years, when she started to . . . when the Alzheimer's . . . when she, um . . ." She wasn't sure how to phrase it. Here was a man Mimi's own age, who might very well be suffering from dementia himself, although she doubted it from the gleam of intelligence in his eyes when he threw back his head and laughed. It was a young man's laugh. Shoshana heard birds signaling to one another in the back of the house.

"When she was one card short of a full deck?" he asked. "It happens to the best of us. Fock! I've been batty for years. It's a damn shame, a woman as sharp as your aunt Mimi to lose her screws. Sad. The last few years, it's just been me and her. Thank god for that business, ye know, FreshDirect? Yer mom found out about them and had them deliver food to Mimi when she couldn't come by. Amazing little company. Crafty idea. Good for us old beans."

Shoshana sat down at the small wooden table in the kitchen. The top was made up of blue, white, and yellow tiles. She felt overwhelmed. She wished Mimi had never left her this house. What did she know about owning property? It was such a mess, too. She took off her sunglasses and took a deep breath, blowing it out of her mouth like a raspberry. Patrick O'Leary settled down at her feet, crossing one paw over the other. She felt his long, soft fur like a blanket over her ankles. She reached down to scratch him behind one ear, and then smiled when he rolled over, paws up, for her to rub his soft belly, which was spotted with light pink blots. Sinatra made a whining sound. "Oh, be quiet, you little jealous boy," Shoshana called over to him.

"Can I ask why you named him Patrick O'Leary?" she asked Joe, sitting down next to the dog cross-legged. She felt the floorboards shift beneath her weight. "Isn't it a mouthful for a dog's name?"

"Eh! My wife Georgina used to say the same thing. Patrick O'Leary was a skinny lad, lived down the lane from me back in the Aran Islands. Good lad he was, Patrick O'Leary. So skinny ye could see right through 'im. Then we became teenagers, and we would get into little bits of trouble 'ere and there. Patrick O'Leary was arrested, for trying to rob the gas station down the street. Wore his mother's dress and a wig, took his father's gun. Wouldn't ye know it, the lad never had used a gun before, and accidentally shot himself in a place that's not nice to talk about in front of a lady." He raised an eyebrow. "We called him 'Lefty' afta' that."

"And the dog?" Shoshana asked, cupping the animal's paw in her hand, feeling the roughness of the black pads beneath, dark like tar.

Then, looking down between the dog's legs, she got it. "Oh. I see. He's a 'lefty' as well."

"Pound had no idea how that happened, but he's just as much a man as he could be intact, ain't that the truth, Patrick O'Leary?"

The dog wagged his tail, his panting mouth open and showing his pink gums, as though he were smiling.

Shoshana burst out laughing. It felt good to laugh. The uncertainty of the day had been pressing at her. "My father would have liked your story," she said. "He loved dumb robber tales. He used to find them in the paper and cut them out."

Joe smiled, and took another swig from his flask. "Would ye like me ta help you go through the house? I can tell ye where everything is, I've been coming over here so long. And then, an early dinner? I don't know what ye like, but Greta can fix you anything ye want, she's our cook, although I've recently been informed she don't want ta be called that anymore."

Shoshana was struck by two things: One, that this man still referred to Greta as "our," as in his and his wife Georgina's, even though Georgina was dead. It was sweet. And two, that he could afford a private cook.

He rolled his eyes. "Women's lib, and all that. Bunch of cocka-mamie nonsense, if you ask me."

Shoshana laughed again. His misogyny was obvious, and thus harmless. "What does she want to be called, then?"

"Master chef, or some such nonsense. Can't get that woman off me back. Tried to fire her a hundred times over the years, but she wo't have it."

Shoshana got the distinct impression Joe was probably very reliant on Greta but didn't want to admit it. The name sounded familiar, like Shoshana had met her before, when she was young.

He kicked at some crispy leaves lining the floor. "We'll get some brooms and cleaning things, too. Place will be shinier than a baby's arse in no time."

"Um, sure. That sounds great," she said. She stood, and brought her glass over to the sink. Joe set his water down and she noticed he hadn't taken a sip.

"I don't want to bother you," she said as they walked toward the staircase. Patrick O'Leary, replenished, bounded up ahead of them. Sinatra reluctantly followed, eyeing the other dog and his master suspiciously.

Joe was struck with a sudden bout of coughing. Shoshana reached out and slapped him on the back. "Thanks, lass. Believe me, I ain't got much to do these days. You showing up is just about the highlight of my year. I'd much rather be around a young person than sit in my armchair and wait for death."

"Oh." She was touched, and she kind of liked his macabre sense of humor. She started up the stairs, glancing at the photographs lining the staircase, all black-and-white and tastefully framed. She saw Mimi young again. She was very curvaceous in a neat-looking swing coat, leaning over Marilyn Monroe on the set of *Gentlemen Prefer Blondes* to adjust a small pill hat atop Monroe's head.

In another photograph, taken in the forties, she was standing with her husband, Fred. He wore a fighter pilot uniform, the goggles resting around his neck, his arm thrown around Mimi, who wore a white polka-dot skirt. Her hair was pinned back in two

identical waves. Shoshana imagined he'd just whispered something naughty in Mimi's ear, as her head was thrown back in mid-
laugh, her arm pushing against his chest a little as if she were
admonishing him. Shoshana remembered Pam saying Mimi felt
sad her whole life about not having children.

In another picture Mimi stood with her arms around several
adults, and when Shoshana peered closer she could see both her
parents in the picture (god, they looked only a few years older than
she was now!) and Joe, standing with a woman who must have been
Georgina. Shoshana remembered her smile. Joe was younger but
instantly recognizable. Even then he wore a full suit, though everyone else was dressed casually.

Her father had on a checkered flannel shirt Shoshana knew
well, his beard surrounding his smiling face. He had one beefy
arm around Joe, who looked like a dwarf next to him. Georgina
was short, with large breasts her flowered dress couldn't hide, and
short, curly dark hair with streaks of white in it. Shoshana was
there, about ten, and Emily stood next to her, just around seven.
Emily was already chubby, and she was pouting at the photographer, her lower lip stuck out. Shoshana wore several beaded strands
around her neck and six or seven bracelets; costume jewelry that
must have belonged to Mimi.

Georgina looked like someone who smiled a lot, and Shoshana
turned to Joe, who had stopped beside her on the staircase to
view the photographs. He took some tobacco out of his pocket
and pushed it into his pipe. He stuck it in the corner of his mouth
and lit it before grinning at her. "We had some good times, all of
us. Your mother used to tell the filthiest dirty jokes."

"She did not!" Shoshana said, eyes wide.

"Oh, but she did! She liked to make your father laugh. The
dirtier the joke, the harder he laughed."

Shoshana peered at her parents. They'd been so happy. When
all her friends' folks were getting divorced, her mother lost her
soul mate. It simply wasn't *fair*. She had a flash of memory, calling
home from Princeton, in the winter of her junior year.

Her mother had answered the phone, breathless. "Hello?"

"Mom? You okay?"

"Oh, yes, my love. Your father and I were just out sledding! Can you believe that, in our old age?" *And she'd giggled, like a teenager.*

The farmhouse had two floors and a small crawl-space attic. The second floor held a large bedroom, bathroom, and two pint-sized guest rooms.

In one, Shoshana recognized her father's childhood toys. Mimi had kept it neat and clean, a fraying train quilt covering a single bed in the middle of the room. Sinatra leaped onto it, turning around several times before settling down with a soft, contented moan. Patrick O'Leary preferred to sniff around the room's corners, following some scent unnoticed by his human companions. On a bookshelf near the window were old comic books, carefully preserved in paper bags. She pulled some out, and was greeted by *Blue Beetle* and *Superman* covers.

Old records lined a milk crate, and she recognized the Beatles' *Sgt. Pepper's Lonely Hearts Club Band* with its cut-out people on it standing around, and Bob Dylan's *Blonde on Blonde,* where he wore that thick, striped scarf. She took *Blonde on Blonde* out of its sheath, ran her finger over it to clear the dust, and placed it on the record player atop the nightstand. She didn't have much experience with records, and she lifted the needle, carefully placing it down on a random spot. A warbly, scratchy Bob Dylan sang out "Just Like a Woman." The first few words of the song wafted over Shoshana: "You make love just like a woman, yes you do."

"Ah, Bobby," Joe said. "Everyone got so angry when he went electric. You'd have thought he killed the fockin' pope, or something."

They stood there for a little while, listening to the song, until it turned into "Most Likely You Go Your Way (And I'll Go Mine)," which they both agreed they didn't like nearly as much.

She spotted a cover with circus performers on it, a dwarf in a suit and top hat clicking his heels together, an overly tall man in a zebra-print skirt, a clown in black-and-white makeup juggling bright red balls on a cobblestone street. One man balanced another in midair.

"The Doors!" Shoshana exclaimed, turning the album over in her hands in disbelief.

Joe settled into a bentwood rocking chair near the door and puffed. His mouth was wrinkled around the lip of the pipe.

"Never did understand the craze myself," he said. "Thought the lad was a bit of a wanker, you ask me."

"I thought my dad didn't like him, either," Shoshana said softly, staring out the window.

She'd been in her dorm room at Princeton, and her parents had come to visit. It was the winter of her freshman year, and they'd driven down just before the storm hit, and decided to stay in a B&B in town that her father was grumbling over. Her mother tidied up the room, as Shoshana begged her to stop and relax. Dad was sifting through her CD collection, from time to time holding one up to ask about the musicians, like Indigo Girls, Sarah McLachlan, and Ani DiFranco.

"Strange Days, eh?" he'd said, holding it up. "I didn't know you were a Doors fan, Shosh."

"A guy in my Intro to Lit class gave that to me," she said shyly. It was a short-lived relationship, and he was about to go to visit his family in India that spring and never return.

"Didn't you used to listen to the Doors?" Pam asked her husband, while fluffing Shoshana's pillows. Even in college, Shoshana had had eight pillows on her bed.

"Nah," he'd said. "Not really my cup of tea."

And yet here was the album, solid, in her hands. Why hadn't he admitted to owning the record? Maybe that was what happened as you got older and forgot the fickle desires and passions of youth. She hugged the record to her chest, and a cloud of dust swirled around her head. It was a tiny clue about her father, like the height chart, and she cherished it. What more did this house have in store for her? What further history could she learn about the man she'd loved so much? Death brings an end to forming memories, and yet here she was, learning new things. Like opening up small gift after small gift, removing it from its box, holding it up to the light and watching it glitter.

Shoshana walked slowly out of the room and down the hallway, which held more pictures of Uncle Fred. In one photo taken on the front lawn, Shoshana could see the tangled mess of forest had once been a beautiful orchard. She walked further along, Joe Murphy and the dogs staying respectfully behind.

A small porch off the bedroom came with chairs and a Sue Grafton novel, turned facedown as if Mimi had just left to catch a ringing telephone. Pam was always checking mysteries out of the library for Mimi, arriving weekly with a new batch. Shoshana sighed. "I should have been here, with Mimi, reading mystery novels to her," she said aloud.

"She always knew you were thinking 'bout her, dear," Joe Murphy called out kindly. "And you spent a lot of your childhood running around these woods. Mimi loved you girls like her own. She knew you felt the same way."

Shoshana sighed again. She wondered when the guilt would ease.

She could start by sprucing up the place. Things were much neater upstairs; it looked as if Mimi had spent most of her time in her bedroom, and there were no leaves or covered sheets like on the first floor. Next to her bed were three leather photo albums, and Shoshana tucked them under her arm to look at later.

Mimi's bedroom had an assortment of beautiful textiles; during her brief time with Uncle Fred they'd traveled around and lived in Asia, India, Africa. Her bedspread was a faded purple and white quilt, with tiny yellow flowers spread around the hem that reminded Shoshana of the dandelions growing outside the front door. The light hanging from the ceiling was shaped like a lantern, its globe shape held up by several gold chains. A sewing machine sat abandoned in the corner and Shoshana knew many of the small quilts framed in light wood on the walls were Mimi's work. Light poured into the room from three large bay windows that gave a stunning view of the acres she'd inherited, now full of tangled bushes, dead leaves, mosses, and hundreds of trees. There were so many things growing, in fact, that Shoshana could barely make out the peaks of Joe's roof in the distance.

"It was once a fine apple orchard, you know." He had walked in to join her and was standing in the doorway. "Georgina and I got too old to maintain ours, so we cut it down, but most of your apple trees are still standing, just covered with other growth. We used to share the land, and Georgina and Mimi would make fine apple pies. That was a great time. Focking age." He packed more tobacco into his pipe and jabbed it into the corner of his weathered mouth, which sagged a little on the left side. "It sneaks up on ya."

"I remember the apple trees," Shoshana said. "Emily and I would help Mimi collect the fruit in wooden baskets. She called us apple fairies."

Spiderwebs would have to be swept in the windows of the bathroom, but it looked like Mimi had redone the floors recently, as they were sand-colored and smooth. "Bamboo," Joe said. "Mimi had them put in ten years ago, the floor was rotting. This farmhouse was built in the nineteenth century, so sometimes you have to do repairs, and Mimi liked the idea of sustainable wood. It was right before the old girl started to . . . well, slip."

The bathroom held a large white tub with brass claw feet. Shoshana smiled, remembering scaring Emily half to death with childhood tales that it would walk into their bedroom and bite them in the middle of the night. The sink was large and wide, with a white-framed mirror that took up most of the wall above it. The tiles on the floor were a bright cobalt blue. The window was open and one of the green willow trees' soft branches stuck through it, caressing the back of the tub. She pictured Mimi giving her father baths in it as a little boy, scrubbing behind his ears with a washcloth, easing out the dirt between his toes. A breeze lifted the soft hairs around Shoshana's face. A plane hummed in the sky outside. A shelf above the toilet held different-sized antique blue apothecary bottles, their glass twinkling in the sun as though they were reflecting the ocean.

"It's beautiful here," Shoshana said.

"'Tis," Joe replied. Then, "How 'bout some early supper? Can't think if ya can't eat."

"Sure!" Shoshana said. "Let me just get my sweater downstairs." Patrick O'Leary had some kind of doggie sense that they were talking about home, and he bounded off the bed in the other room and ran down the stairs, Sinatra barking at his heels, distrustful of his new friend's lack of reticence.

At the front door, she again fiddled with the strange skeleton key. "There's no need for locking up around here," Joe said. "Nobody around, really, but apple trees and crows. Jay-sus, Patrick O'Leary. That hot breath on my legs, now." His dog had the good sense to look guilty, tucking his tongue back into his snout and bounding ahead of his master.

"I know, but just in case," Shoshana said, finally hearing a satisfying click. She really was going to have to have regular locks put on these large doors. "I'm from Hoboken. You have to lock up in a city, so it's just become a habit."

They walked together, content not to talk. Patrick O'Leary had run over the hills and far ahead of them, until he was just a spot in the distance no bigger than the end of a pencil eraser. Sinatra stuck by Shoshana, sometimes just a speck of wriggly pink and gray in the tall grass, which caressed her legs. The sky was a bruise of colors, red fading into purple into yellow. It looked somehow . . . bigger here. The air was fresher, she could get more into her lungs with each breath. She felt like spreading out her arms like a child and running as fast as she could over the fields.

She was surprised when she heard the modern tones of her cell phone, ringing deep in the bottom of her purse. Since she'd just seen artifacts from her father's childhood, the cell phone felt out of place.

"Hi, Mom." She stopped walking. Joe dug around in his suit

pocket for more tobacco. He seemed to have an endless supply. "Guess who I am standing here with?"

"The wonderful Joe Murphy?" her mother asked.

"How did you know?"

"Well, honey, there's really no one else around there."

"Oh! I guess you're right," Shoshana said. "She knew it was you," she whispered to Joe, and he smiled crookedly around his pipe.

"Hello to your mam," he said.

"Joe says hello, Mom."

"Is he still drinking that whiskey?"

"Er . . . yeah."

"Guess you can't teach an old dog new tricks," Pam said. "Georgina tried all kinds of ways to get him off booze, nothing worked. But he was always such a *friendly* drunk; it didn't really seem to matter much. I remember him and your father got sloshed as skunks one night. I'd just baked a sheet of cookies and set them to cool on the back steps and they stomped all over them, squishing chocolate everywhere. I could have killed them both!"

It was another memory of her dad, and she filed it away somewhere inside herself. This place seemed full of them, a present she could keep on opening. The doubt started to subside within her. This was a magical place that held memories of her father. She wanted to collect and trap them like lightning bugs in jars. She started to understand a little better the gift Mimi had given her, the depth of it.

She ran her hand along the tops of white and brown reeds, a boat bumping along waves in the sea. She thought suddenly of Andrew Wyeth's *Christina's World,* the long grasses, the woman in the pink dress crawling. She'd seen the painting at a recent visit to the MoMA (Pam was always encouraging the arts to her daughters, and they did one cultural thing a week together, Broadway plays, art openings, book readings) and had a totally different viewpoint of the painting than her mother and sister, who pitied Christina, her twisted legs, her small form. But Shoshana had viewed Christina as someone who just wanted to be left alone, make her own choice to crawl instead of use a wheelchair, to feel the earth move beneath her body.

"That's funny, Mom." She was aware of Joe walking beside her, his shoulders slumped over with age. Small wisps of silver air puffed out of the end of his pipe and trailed into the sky, which was dotted with pink clouds like they were placed there by an artist's brush. The color was so vivid it shone against his white hair.

"Oh, Mom, guess what? I found some of Dad's old albums. Did you know he liked the Doors?"

Pam chuckled. "Bob always insisted he hated them, but he would hum along to 'L.A. Woman' on the radio when we were driving sometimes."

"I remember him saying they were crap when I was in college, but I found a Doors album! I feel close to him here. Like he's left us all these clues." She realized how corny she sounded and glanced quickly at Joe Murphy, but he'd stopped walking and was turning over a rock with a stick he'd found, gazing intently at whatever lay beneath.

"It was one of his favorite places," Pam said softly. "Are you going back there tomorrow?"

Was she? Since Mimi's lawyer had contacted her, she had been living in a kind of haze about the house. She had a hard time picturing herself as a homeowner. She'd always thought a husband would come first, and then she'd stick it out in the city atmosphere of Hoboken until moving to the burbs. But that had all seemed so far away, like buying a car and even the hubby. She'd worked her butt off to get into Princeton, but she didn't have that *drive drive drive* other people her age did, to make a lot of money and be outrageously successful beyond her wildest dreams. Her blog earned her a modest salary of thirty-five thousand a year, though she did hope to parlay it into a book deal, perhaps along the lines of feminist theory, or advice for Fellow Fatties, a hodge-podge of her posts on *Fat and Fabulous*.

But owning a house? Wasn't that something real adults did?

"Yes. I'll come back tomorrow with cleaning stuff. The farm needs a lot of work," she said. Crows pecked at the grass near her, huddled like football players. Their beaks were long and black.

"Your sister and I can meet you there in the afternoon. Em is working until two in the city."

"Okay, see you then. I guess just ring the doorbell?" In Hoboken, she was used to buzzer systems. The doorbell was so quaint. So suburban. She now owned something that had a *doorbell*. Far out.

"Love you."

"Love you, too, Mom."

"Lovely broad, yer ma," Joe said when she disconnected. He'd wandered back over to her, and now used the stick as a walking prop as they set forth again. "Never seen two people more in love than yer folks."

"They were married here, right?" Shoshana asked.

"That's right, summer of '76," he said. "Your mother was radiant as a dove, she was."

Shoshana smiled. Pam had been too heavy to fit into any traditional wedding gowns, so Mimi had hand-sewn her a white silk dress. A dove was the last thing Pam had looked like, but it was kind of Joe to say so.

They came to the rise of a small hill, when suddenly Joe's mansion rose like a mirage in the desert. A Tudor-style home, it showcased twelve bedrooms, six porches, and a horseshoe-shaped driveway with white pebble rocks. In front sat a blue Ford pickup truck that had left a little shiny brown oil stain in front of its left tire. It was an odd juxtaposition to the grandness of the house and she wondered if the truck was Joe's or maybe belonged to someone working on the property. Her first hunch was confirmed when he leaned into the glove compartment as they approached to grab a ziplock baggie full of tobacco. She was becoming used to its smell, like a wood-burning fireplace on an autumn night. In back of the mansion was a large red barn, leaning a little to the left.

"I remember this place," Shoshana said. She was whispering, a little in awe. "It still looks just as huge to me now as ever. When I was a kid Emily and I used to call it the Princess House. Your wife Georgina was always so nice to us. She let us come over and play with those antique dolls she collected. Do you still have them?"

"They're up in the attic, sure," he said. "Didn't want ta bother you with 'em when you were coming ta Mimi's as teenagers, though you're welcome to take them now. Thought you'd think I was a silly old man. And Emily had the spikes then. I was right scared."

Shoshana laughed. "That's right, I forgot about that. She did have a Mohawk for a while. One side was purple, the other blond."

"It's amazing to me what young people get up ta these days. How does Emily not set off metal detectors with all those piercings?"

"Sometimes she does!" Shoshana said as he leaned his bony shoulder on the front door and it swayed open.

She gasped. Potted palms the size of Christmas trees swayed in their colorful planters along the orange-tiled hallway, the kind that must feel cool under one's feet on a summer day. Their fronds turned up toward the sun streaming in from the end of the hallway. The room opened onto a spacious courtyard. Someone had strung white lights in boxwood bushes. The walls of the entryway were periwinkle, a blue so deep it touched purple.

She was distracted by a series of high-pitched barks she knew well, and she turned to find the source of Sinatra's anxiety. She heard a rush of feathers and an image swam into her vision that seemed impossible; a large peacock, its blue body waddling somehow with precision, its rainbow tail trailing behind it like a train, came strutting toward Joe, who immediately reached into his suit pocket and held out a box of raisins. The peacock walked in circles, emitting a loud screech, until Joe got the top open and scattered the snack onto the ground. Sinatra ran in circles, barking excitedly. The bird promptly ignored the dog, like an older sibling choosing maturity over bopping the younger one in the nose.

Its face was black and blue, with a yellow beard along the bottom. Shoshana swore it looked triumphant as its long neck stretched to gobble up the raisins. When it turned, Joe softly ran his hand down the feathers in back as they gathered and bunched, spread open and closed.

"This is P-Hen," Joe said, giving her one final affectionate pat. "Georgina and I used to keep a henhouse 'ere on the estate for fresh eggs. A man was transporting peacock eggs illegally—you're not allowed to cross state lines to sell exotic animals. Anyway, his truck broke down off ta highway and he walked 'ere. I always keep some gas in the toolshed, so I walked back with him to fill his tank. As a thank-you, he gave me P-Hen's egg. The old girl lived with our hens, when we still had a whole loud bunch of 'em."

"And P-Hen?" Shoshana reached down to scoop up Sinatra, who continued to bark like mad.

"A peahen 'tis a female peacock," he said by way of explanation, over the noise.

"Oh!"

"I wasn't very original in naming you, old girl," he said to the bird, who gathered up her feathers like a gown and strutted off down another long hallway, the walls lined with gold frames. A long green, yellow, and red Oriental carpet partially covered the tiles. Ceramic plates in a myriad of colors hung high gave the space a Mediterranean vibe.

An old woman so short she was almost dwarflike, with fluffy white hair and huge, luminous brown eyes, came bustling in, wearing a blue dress covered in little yellow poppy flowers. She had soft, pudgy skin that was very light, and tiny hands, which she wiped on the buttercup-yellow apron tied around her small waist and extended her arms, surprising Shoshana with a hug. Shoshana caught the sweet scent of vanilla.

"I remember you!" the woman exclaimed. "Shoshana, the older sister. I remember Emily, too, the naughty one." When she smiled, small wrinkles appeared all over her face, from the corners of her eyes to around her mouth. She had small gold earrings with green glass in them, causing her earlobes to droop slightly.

Shoshana laughed. "She's not so bad anymore." Emily had gone through a phase around puberty when she had a perpetual scowl on her face. She'd sit in her room listening to Nirvana for hours. Their father used to joke he was afraid she'd run off with a sword swallower and join the circus one day, with her multicolored tights, piercings, and rainbow hair.

"Hello, my dear." The woman reached out and held her arms wide for Sinatra, who leaped from the floor into her arms and immediately ceased barking. He laid across her bosom like it was his dog bed and licked the side of her face enthusiastically.

She closed her eyes and could almost feel soft hands guiding her small, plump ones as she mixed cake batter in an expansive white porcelain kitchen, somewhere in the depths of this house. A woman's pleasant voice telling her, "Now add the butter."

There are certain adults children innately love; they have patience with short, slow-walking legs, with dirt underneath fingernails. Shoshana remembered Greta's kindness toward her as a child and felt an invisible wave of warmth flow over her body when she hugged her.

"I remember you were very kind to us. And I remember saying your name in a funny way as a kid, I think I called you Get." P-Hen let out an ear-piercing shriek down the hallway, the sound filling the space around them, the afternoon sunlight streaming in from the open door.

Greta threw back her head with laughter. She had a wonderfully silly laugh, like someone being tickled. "Yes, you certainly did. My mother, she had high hopes. Named me for Greta Garbo. Then her daughter is born with a big nose and a mole on her chin. Go figure!" She made a gesture like pushing the thought away. She had an impish look in her eye that Shoshana liked. She bent down to gently stand Sinatra on the floor, and he sat with his legs crossed in front of him, looking up at Greta adoringly.

"Don't let her fool ya into thinking she's a nice old lady," Joe said. His pipe dangled from the corner of his mouth and his blue eyes sparkled. "Thirty years ago Greta had a man who was deeply in love with her. She near broke his 'art."

"Really?" Shoshana asked. She adored love stories. She was naturally curious when it came to stories of the heart. Maybe it had to do with the closeness she shared with her mother and sister. Or living with four drama queens.

"Don't listen to that old geezer," Greta said. "He's starting to lose his marbles."

"No more than you are, lass," Joe said. "Anyway, we once had a bloke named Guy who worked 'round here. We used to take in racehorses after they retired, let 'em graze on the grass on our estate, run through the woods if they wanted to." He took out his silver flask and raised it to his lips, his Adam's apple bobbing as he took a drink. Shoshana caught Greta glaring at him. She deduced Greta did not approve of Joe's drinking habit. "Guy fell in love with Greta over here, and when he decided to go back to Holland, where he was from, she wouldn't budge. Said she was a Jersey girl through and through, even though she's Ecuadorian, and the man left, broken."

"Look, you old goat, you would have been dead a long time ago from the drink if I hadn't stayed on," she said, gesturing to his flask. "Besides, there was no way I was leaving Ms. Georgina. Nicest woman on this green earth, god rest her soul. Now, would either of you like to join me? I was just about to say my afternoon prayers."

Shoshana looked over at Joe, who was rolling his eyes at her. She tried not to laugh. "Um . . . I'm Jewish," she said.

"Of course, sweetheart. But Jesus loves all his children."

Joe gestured with his flask. "Mother Teresa over 'ere decided she wanted ta get ordained as a minister, so she's been taking some online course this past year. Though if you ask me, I don't see how god transitions onto the Internet."

Greta swatted at his sleeve. "You are lucky I'm a minister, I'll be saving you from hell. And you forgot to take your vitamins this morning, I had them right next to your cereal bowl and you forgot. Getting senile, you are."

"Oh, go shit in your hat," Joe said.

Shoshana smiled. She could see it was an old routine, and she liked Joe more for being the kind of man who enjoyed being berated by his housekeeper, someone he employed.

There was a small gold-edged photograph on the wall, of an attractive middle-aged woman from the nineteenth century, sitting in a blue velvet chair with gold piping. Shoshana walked over to it. The subject had black curly hair piled on top of her head and held with a gold seashell clip. Her clothing was humble, a plain cotton dress with a high-collared shirt beneath.

A breeze from outside picked up and the palm fronds swayed in the hall.

"Beautiful, wasn't she?" Greta came and stood next to Shoshana.

Joe was again packing his pipe, his fingers working dexterously. "My ma," he said. "Back in Ireland. Been dead now fifty years, I can hardly believe it." Her cornflower-blue eyes, identical to Joe's, were forever fixed to stare at her own reflection in a large gold mirror across the hallway.

Shoshana remembered what the lawyer, Mr. Berkowitz, had told her: "Your new house is just a few acres down the road from Joe Murphy, whose family worked in the oil business. Huge tycoon, very old money." She looked at his mother's simple dress and wondered how he'd gone from immigrant to rich mogul.

"Come, my dear, let's get you fed," said Greta, holding her elbow. "I want to hear all about Ms. Mimi's house, and what you've been up to since I saw you as a little girl."

So Shoshana followed this tiny sparkplug of a woman down the hallway, in the direction from which P-Hen had waddled. Joe shuffled along behind them, walking slowly. Sinatra and Patrick O'Leary stayed in the entry hall, sniffing enthusiastically after some scent that led them to the windows. The rubber soles on Joe's dress shoes squeaked. Lining the hallway were black-and-white photographs of apple trees. There was one of Georgina and Mimi from sometime in the fifties, Georgina's arm slung casually around Mimi's round waist. Both women had their hair in tight curls, and they had matching dark lipstick on. Mimi was holding a wooden basket full of apples on her hip. They both squinted against the sun.

"That was taken in Mimi's orchard," Joe said. "It was such a beauty; I wish you could have seen it. She and Georgina grew Red Delicious, Cortland, Rome Winesaps, and Granny Smiths. People used to come from all around the Garden State ta buy Georgina and Mimi's special apple pies. It was quite a sight, all them trees. I'd get up on one and climb it right now, I wasn't so goddamn old."

"What did I tell you about cussing in this house?" Greta asked. "That'll be one dollar." She held out her hand. Shoshana noticed how pink her palms were. Perhaps from her years of labor in this house, the meals she'd cooked, the clothes she'd washed, and the apples she'd picked. Shoshana didn't think there'd been children. She wondered at the big house with no children in it, the loneliness of that. Joe, grumbling, reached into his pocket and pulled out a crumpled dollar bill.

"Thank you. This goes right to the needy children's fund for St. Jude's Children's Hospital."

"I told you, woman, I'll donate a million dollars ta them. You just name yer price!"

She made a *tsk* sound between her teeth. "It's much more fun to torture you."

He turned to Shoshana. "Do you see this abuse I put up with? One of these days she is going to poison my soup."

Shoshana giggled. "Seems to me she takes really good care of you."

"Like a pet," he said. "A dog she kicks." He had an impish way of talking out of the corner of his mouth, and his accent was so thick she had to strain her ears to decipher his language.

"A dog, I wish! A dog would be much easier to look after than you. A dog doesn't fall asleep in his armchair fully dressed with a lit pipe in his mouth."

"Hmph," Joe grumbled.

Shoshana realized Joe was getting somewhat cranky, and changed the subject. "So Mimi and you and your wife would harvest the apples?" she asked. "As a business?"

Joe smiled at her. "It was mainly your aunt Mimi, when she wasn't on a set, and Georgina. And Greta here, too. The Three Amigas, I'd call them. Unfortunately, I was always traveling ta the Middle East fer work. I thought I had to work in oil, be a big success. But looking back on all those years spent on airplanes and in boardrooms and carrying my briefcase . . . the happiest times were when I was right 'ere, picking apples with Georgina. I miss that woman so damn much."

A look of despair crossed his face, but it was gone almost instantly.

"One dollar, sir," Greta said, stretching out her hand again. Her smile was feisty. Shoshana realized she was trying to cheer him up.

"Oh, here, wretched woman. Take it. And don't dare hide my flask from me anymore." He dug around his pockets until he found a crumpled dollar bill and grumpily set it down on Greta's palm.

On the walk to the kitchen, they passed gold-edged mirrors that took up entire walls. She recognized a Lichtenstein, having taken Art History 101 at Princeton as a freshman. Was it real? She supposed it must be. Other smaller paintings were of rugged hillsides, bales of hay, and apple trees by the hundreds. They were all signed *BW* in a crooked script in the corners.

BW, BW. Bob Weiner?

"Did my father paint these?" she asked breathlessly, turning to Joe and Greta.

"Yes, dear, of course," Greta said. "He was very talented. Mimi had a local artist come and give him lessons when he was a boy."

"But he was a gardener," she said, feeling immediately foolish. "I never knew he painted." Tears filled her eyes unexpectedly.

"Oh, honey," Greta said, putting a soft arm around her. "Everyone has dreams when they're young. I'm sure providing a steady income for your family, supporting two beautiful girls, well, that was just more important to him."

Shoshana ran her finger over the bumps her father's brush had made. "He had some canvases and brushes up in the attic. I asked him about them once and he just said he tried painting but wasn't any good at it. But that's not true." She waved her arm around, gesturing to the paintings. "He was talented." A tear spilled onto her cheek and she brushed it away, willing the emotions of the day to stop washing over her.

"Can I bring Emily here to show her?" she asked, turning toward Joe. Greta squeezed her shoulder.

"Of course," Joe said. "Better yet . . ." He strode over to her and began lifting the canvases off the wall. "'Ere."

"Oh, no, that's not—"

"Don't be silly," Greta said. "He owns half the art they have on display at the MoMA and hundreds more in a warehouse in Chelsea. He can afford it."

"They all belong to you anyway, you should inherit 'em," Joe said gruffly.

"Oh, you just don't like to see a woman cry, you big sap," Greta said, jabbing him in the ribs with her elbow.

"Clam it, old broad. Now, where the hell's dinner?"

"Joe Murphy, that'll be another dollar. Anyway, you're older than me by ten years. I'll be burying you with these two hands under the tree out back, so you'd better be nice to me."

Did everyone who died around here get buried in the backyard?

Shoshana counted three more living rooms with fireplaces by the time they entered the bright white kitchen that Shoshana remembered. A farmer's sink was stained a dark copper, and the ceiling was tin. Pots and pans hung from hooks, and the last sip of the day's light poured in from two large spotlessly clean windows. A ruffle of white curtain brushed the bottom of the window. "You babysat us!" she exclaimed to Greta, who was setting out an array of meats and cheeses on a wooden platter with silver handles. She had a simmering pot of soup on the stove, and she used a long-handled ladle to spoon out the broth into small blue bowls. "I remember this kitchen, we used to bake cookies."

"You betcha," Greta said. "You two girls were cute as pie." She slapped Joe's hand as he reached for his flask.

Shoshana set the paintings down carefully on the counter. "After we eat I think I'll get started cleaning Mimi's house," she said. She corrected herself, the words feeling strange on her tongue. "I mean, my house. Greta, do you have paper towels and a mop?"

"Honey, I got everything. We'll do it as a team. Joe will probably take a nap—"

"I'm sitting right 'ere, woman, don't talk about me like I'm a child—"

"—so we can just head over there and get to work," she finished.

The food was delicious, and fresh. They sat in the dining room, along a table that was as long as a football field. Six giant candelabras lined the middle, along with baskets of wildflowers in brilliant blues and purples picked from the nearby fields. Joe Murphy sat at the head of the table in a red velvet armchair, mainly smoking and drinking from his flask and reluctantly sipping the delicious chicken soup with dill picked from the backyard.

And then it was time to leave. Shoshana longed to see the rest of the mansion but was eager to get the farmhouse in decent shape for her mother and Emily to visit tomorrow. The days were getting longer but it was still dark out by six, perhaps even more so here in the country.

After leaning over to give a sleeping Joe Murphy a kiss on the cheek (he had indeed fallen asleep in his armchair), Shoshana bade good-bye to P-Hen and Patrick O'Leary, and walked back over the hills with Greta and Sinatra. She turned around at one point and saw Patrick O'Leary watching them from the front window, his breath fogging up the glass.

Darkness fell over the rolling hills, like bluffs in an ocean of green, and she took in the rich smell of soil as the moon's light shone off a nearby field of wheat, the sounds of the crickets buzzing . . . she breathed deeply and Greta smiled at her, as if to say she understood the wonder of it all, and was glad someone else was there to appreciate it as well. Greta walked quietly at her side, observing the landscape as if seeing it for the first time. Shoshana had so many questions for her—this woman had watched Mimi raise her father, after all—but she wanted to get inside and put down the paintings first, as they were heavy.

"Your trees still produce apples, you know," Greta told her, her face open and friendly in the smudged navy blue dark.

"No, I didn't know." She felt a little out of breath from all the walking she'd done today. It was strange—in Hoboken with all its flat concrete she never tired in her walks with Nancy. It must be the fresh air out here. Her lungs were used to the pollution drifting over into Hoboken from all the factories and power plants near Newark Airport.

"You see?" Greta asked, pointing as they came over a hill and saw the lights Shoshana had left on spilling onto the orchard. "Right now there are apple buds on the trees the size of marbles. They are sleeping. Like a caterpillar, snug in its cocoon. Safe. Come summer, these trees are going to wake up. Depending on the variety, you'll start to have thousands of apples. I used to help Mimi pick them, so I remember. The McIntoshes will be ready in September, the Winesaps and Red Delicious making their debut in October."

Shoshana smiled. "It sounds like it's their debutante ball."

"Oh, honey, harvest season is so exciting. But this is trimming time. I did it for Mimi for years, until these hands got too arthritic." She held them up to Shoshana to observe, but Shoshana thought they looked just fine, with a few brown spots on them darker than her natural tawny skin color. They'd stopped walking and a butterfly flitted around their heads, its purple and black wings moving against the dark, expansive sky. She realized she never looked up in Hoboken; there was always a building blocking the moon, or the clouds.

"You mean trimming the trees? Like with pruners?"

"Exactly. You need to use shears for the little branches, I call 'em suckers. Then a small saw for the thicker ones. Mimi's trees are over fifteen feet high right now. You want to grow good apples, you got to space out the branches so they get an equal amount of sun. Around ten feet tall is perfect. Dwarf trees are the wave of the future, or so I hear when I go into town. You want a bright red Red Delicious? You got to give those babies some *sun*."

Shoshana felt overwhelmed. First the house would need cleaning, the leaves swept off the floor, cobwebs wiped from the windows and doorway frames, and the moth-eaten couch replaced. The idea of clearing the tangled *Where the Wild Things Are* forest in the back of the house was a whole different ball game, as her father used to say.

Back at her house, Shoshana struggled with the heavy brass key once more. When they entered, she was struck by how low the ceilings were, compared to Joe's mansion. What year was the farmhouse built? She made a mental note to look it up. A time when people were shorter than now. Certainly Mimi had been only about five feet, if that. The floor sloped, too.

"I'll tackle the second floor, you okay working down here?" Greta asked.

"Sure," Shoshana said. She swept her long, thick hair back into a ponytail; the brown rubber band she used had been around her wrist and left a red mark. She kicked off her shoes and found a bucket and a bottle of Murphy Oil Soap under the sink in the kitchen.

For the next two hours, Shoshana and Greta scrubbed, polished, swept, and wiped down the house. It was too late to make a train back to Hoboken. Her arms ached.

At last, Greta came into the kitchen, where Shoshana was just throwing out the last of the many sponges she'd used along the counters and cupboards. "Come, honey, let's have us a glass of wine," she said. So the two women walked back over the black ink hills to Joe's house, polished off a bottle of wine before the fireplace, watched the two dogs wrestle and bark at P-Hen, and chatted about the past.

Later, Shoshana walked back from the mansion and her eyes widened when she saw the farmhouse. It glowed, the full yellow moon behind it lighting it as if with a thousand bulbs. She breathed in the sweet air, watched the apple trees sway as the wind picked up. She let herself into the house (the key turned easily this time!), and climbed into her father's old bed fully dressed. Tomorrow she would wake, check *Fat and Fabulous,* then finish cleaning when her mother and sister arrived. After that she'd come up with a plan to tackle the vines and weeds that grew among the apple trees.

Just before sleep's tide pulled her in, Shoshana lay there, looking at the peaked ceiling and listening to Sinatra's soft snores, thinking this might just be it, this home, the fate she always knew she was searching for, that craving for a special destiny that had never subsided deep within her. Yes, this house, these hills, these beautiful trees . . . might just be part of a little something called fate.

Alexis

June

NEW YORK

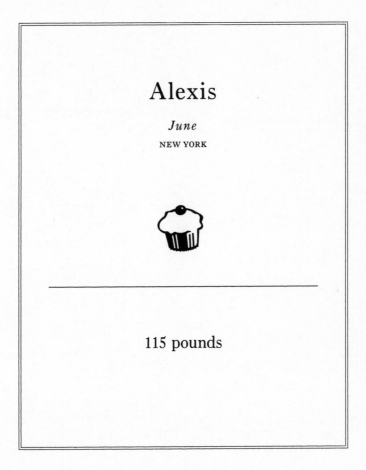

---

115 pounds

SUDDENLY, WITHOUT PREAMBLE OR FUSS, ALEXIS AND Noah were inseparable. How strange it felt, to glide so effortlessly from being a single entity on this planet to existing as one half of a couple. From food shopping for what Billy called her "single girl salad" to planning meals with another person in mind, Alexis felt she was going through a metamorphosis. She'd existed solely inside her own head, walking around Manhattan, answering her own thoughts. Her days used to revolve around her six tiny meals, her workouts, her blog. Now Noah took up so much space inside her it was like wearing a second skin.

It was Billy who changed her, of course. It wasn't falling in love with Noah, though the ways he made her feel certainly were the reasons behind pushing her daily workouts to afternoons so she could help him set up his resturant across the street in the old fur store they'd danced in months ago. She'd also stopped weighing both herself and her food at his insistence.

No, it was Billy and his diagnosis of cancer that set the course of the new Alexis, as spring bled into summer and the flocks of tourists in all their suitcase-dragging glory roamed the streets. The bicyclists came out of the woodwork, block parties lit the nights with color and fire, pedestrians were dripped on by air-conditioners humming along in high-rise apartments, and Alexis's life turned over on its belly and was suddenly, and most completely, changed forever.

Alexis got Billy squeezed in to a doctor's appointment right away, and Billy came home the afternoon of his meeting with Aldo (Alexis had a hard time calling him Dr. Martinez, since she saw him frequently at the gym wearing dorky, navy blue knee-high socks to play racquetball) looking distracted. Noah had long since gone home to care for Oliver, and Alexis was staring at the muffins on the counter as she tidied up the apartment, rebandaged her finger, and reminded herself of the ice-cream bars the night before. Fatness was a slippery slope. For all she knew, ice cream was a gateway . . . snack.

Vanya had showered and dressed in a black velvet cape over black jeans and gotten on her broomstick . . . well, not really. But she'd walked off to whatever job she worked at during the night. But not before talking to Alexis for the first time since she'd handed her a rent deposit in all silver dollars gathered together in a sparkly purple scarf that had littered pixie dust all over the floor when she opened it. Her voice was surprisingly feminine and little-girlish.

"Nice guy," she'd said, putting her hand high in the air to indicate she was talking about the very tall man who had the softest, most plump lips Alexis had ever kissed.

"Er, yes. Seems like it. Thanks," Alexis answered, hesitant to say anything else. Princess Pinkerton leaped onto her desk in a blur of gray fur and she shooed him off.

"He looks a little like Cernunnos."

"Who's that?"

"The horned god."

Alexis stared.

Vanya wasn't kidding.

"But he doesn't *have* horns," Alexis said, not really knowing whether to ask for more info.

Vanya drew her cape (*wasn't she roasting?*) around her in a huff. "It was meant to be a compliment. Cernunnos is the god of fertility. Wiccans, my people, worship him." And with that, she seemed to levitate down the hallway, until Alexis heard the front door slam. She rushed to the window to watch if Vanya actually flew away, knowing she was being silly, but Vanya simply turned left and disappeared into the crowd pushing and shoving their way home after a long and grueling day at work.

Out of the mass she saw a familiar lone figure, slight and stooped, and her breath caught in her throat as Billy walked home from the subway, the brown leather purse he sometimes carried ("My murse!") held away from his body. He walked stooped like someone much older. His head was down as though he were watching the sidewalk retreat behind his feet, his shoulders turned in like wings. She couldn't read the expression on his face from the distance of the window but something about his demeanor was different. It was as if someone had sucked out all the pizzazz, all the confident *Billyness*.

She hardly ever saw him alone, he usually insisted on at least Alexis plus a boyfriend or two to go everywhere with him, grocery shopping or manicures or a museum opening or to the movies . . . but for his meeting with Aldo he'd insisted she not come. She followed his slow shuffle up the street, and had the door to their apartment flung open before he could get out his key.

He'd arranged his expression to hide what came off him in waves, fear. But Alexis knew fear immediately; it was an emotion she was familiar with because it had painted the walls in her house after Mark was killed in Iraq. Her parents feared they'd never get over it, feared their own searing emotions, feared Alexis, their child who was still alive . . . It had been the catalyst to end their marriage, because although her parents still were legally married, in the months after the funeral Alexis almost never saw them speak to one another. Her father slept in the guest room, or in a hotel near his office. Fear was the secret ingredient sprinkled in with the vodka tonics her mother drank by the truckload each day. Having this knowledge, being able to sniff it out in people, was a skill Alexis learned from her father, who had a near-perfect success rate in the courtroom. Though she'd stepped off the path on her way to becoming a lawyer, this skill made Alexis win every argument. And now her Billy, the person she loved most in the world, was pretending nothing was wrong. Yet she knew *something* was definitely wrong. Everything about his posture read: scared. Whatever it was, it was bad.

"So?" she asked, trying to keep her tone neutral.

He was startled, lost in thought and not expecting Alexis to be waiting for him. He put down his bag and flopped onto the couch, placing his feet on the coffee table and draping his left arm over his eyes. His black hair shone under the lights.

"Ugh. Turn the light off," he said.

She rushed over and did so. He said nothing, so she followed his lead and sat back down next to him gingerly, hoping she was giving off a supportive vibe.

She listened to him breathe.

After a few minutes, a dark eye peered at her from beneath his blue cashmere Ralph Lauren sweater. "Where'd beefcake go?"

She smiled. "You mean Noah?"

"Yeah, Noah. I like him. I like him for you."

"But we don't like anybody," she said, putting her arm around him, the side of her forehead against his. She settled down onto the couch, tucking her feet underneath her.

"True," Billy said. He was eyeing the beer muffins, and after a moment got up to put three on a plate before sitting back down. Alexis rested her hand on his skinny thigh. He stuffed a large piece in his mouth.

After a couple moments of chewing, he returned to the conversation. "But the man is *something.*"

It was true. She had to admit, Noah certainly *was* something.

"Did he slip you the salami?" Billy asked, eating another beer muffin.

"Of course," she said. Alexis was no prude. She always told Billy about the guys she slept with. Sometimes with full details of sexual capability. They swapped stories and techniques. They were that close.

"And?" He wiggled his eyebrows at her.

She turned toward him. "And nothing. I don't know. I actually might keep it to myself." She glanced at him anxiously.

Billy was moody. He was known to turn in an instant from relaxed to bitchy. He was notorious for his stubbornness; once, he'd dumped a boyfriend over an argument while on a date at the Museum of Natural History. Wanting to wander off on his own, he'd asked the guy, a lawyer, to meet him at the Tyrannosaurus bones. After showing up at the designated time and not seeing him, Billy waited nearly two hours before locating his date on the third floor, wandering, confused. "There are Tyrannosaurus bones up here as well," he'd related to Billy.

"Everyone knows that one is made out of a mold, the real bones are in the lobby!" Billy had exclaimed. "How am I supposed to date such an airhead?"

Alexis had pointed out that it was an innocent mistake to make, she wasn't sure *she* knew which bones were real, but Billy had moved on.

To her surprise, now on the couch, he nodded, seeming to make up his mind about something. "That's how you know."

"Know what?"

"That he's The One. Because you don't want to ruin it by talking about it."

Crap, he was right.

"Just tell me one thing," Billy said, rising to place yet another muffin on his plate.

"Hmmm?" She took the bandage off her finger and peered at her stitches, which itched.

"Did he have a big one?"

"Huge."

They grinned at each other.

It was only later, much further into the night, after they'd split a bottle of wine and gotten Chinese takeout (from that shady place on Broadway they loved that always seemed to have stray cats hanging around), that he told her what had happened.

Dr. Martinez had sat in his office, listening closely to Billy explain his symptoms. He'd then furrowed his brow and examined Billy.

"That was when I first knew something was up, when he frowned like that," Billy said. "He didn't seem like a frowny kind of guy."

He'd then been brought to another sterile steel and tile room, where Dr. Martinez had taken a painful yet quick biopsy of the lump underneath his arm, now on a slide in transport to a lab. Did Billy feel swollen anywhere else? No, he'd responded. They'd have the lab results in a day or two.

Just to be sure, the doctor had felt around Billy's throat and groin, asking, "Are you sure you haven't had any other lumps? Does it hurt when you swallow?"

"That's when I *really* knew I was screwed," Billy said matter-of-factly now, putting his plate on the coffee table and resting his head back on Alexis's shoulder. She reached up and cupped his cheek awkwardly and they sat like that for a long time. Eventually the cat jumped between them and settled in for petting, her soft fur a white spray on Alexis's leg.

Two days later, Billy was called back in and this time let Alexis tag along. When told he had stage two Hodgkin's lymphoma, Billy had turned and said, "He's kidding, right? Korean people don't *get* Hodgkin's lymphoma." Alexis had immediately burst out crying, and then had the peculiar experience of being comforted by Dr. Martinez and Billy, as though *she* were the one with cancer. Billy had held a tissue up to her nose and ordered, "Blow, bitch."

She'd been emotional a lot since that appointment, so unlike her. Since her botched cooking class and meeting Noah, they had spent every day together. She'd gone to see the new Angelina Jolie flick with him just last week after Billy literally threw her out of the apartment because she'd been hovering over him, making sure he took his zillion pills and rested, and she'd cried during the movie. When sleeping over at Noah's Brooklyn apartment last week, she'd been struck with an odd and overwhelming love for his large, stinky dog Oliver, and even let the dog curl up next to her in the bed, letting go of the hatred for large pooches she'd harbored since childhood when a neighbor's German shepherd had eaten her Malibu Barbie. She'd petted him deep into the night, and had shed large, fat tears into his fur.

Somehow, Alexis had gone from not shedding one tear when Mark had died to crying nearly every day since Billy's diagnosis. She cried while lifting weights with Sarah at Soho Gym. She cried in Off the River Ale House when she knocked down a wall with a hammer while wearing a pair of four-inch pink Max Azria stilettos. She cried while she read the *Post*'s Page Six out loud to Billy during chemotherapy, where he now went three times a week.

Billy's grandmother Nana Kay visited him only once, as she was quite elderly and feeble now, though she still wore her bright red lipstick when she came to visit. Alexis called her weekly with updates on Billy's spirits. She spoke very little English, but Alexis made the effort anyway, as she was the only person from Billy's family he had a relationship with.

Nana Kay had stood over Billy where he lay on the couch and spoken to him in rapid Korean, between bouts of yelling. After a little while she hobbled away on her cane. Alexis ran after her to be sure she had money for cab fare.

"What was she yelling at you about?" Alexis asked after she returned, fascinated.

"She said I'm not eating enough," Billy muttered, staring blankly out the window. It was something they would have laughed about before (Alexis thought of everything as *before* and *after* Billy got sick), but Nana Kay's famous temper didn't seem funny now.

Alexis had secretly called Billy's parents and told them he was sick; had he found out he would have been furious, as they had disowned him when he came out of the closet. Surely, with him so sick they would relent, she thought.

"Call me if he needs money," his mother had said quietly. "Otherwise, do leave us alone." They lived in Philadelphia, easily close enough to drive up.

"He doesn't need money," Alexis had responded, fury a red-hot fire burning in her heart. "And shame on you. You have an amazing son and you're too stubborn to have a relationship with him when he needs you most."

The dial tone in her ear told her everything she needed to know.

And then, on an ordinary Tuesday morning, Alexis *really* cried when she went against Noah's wishes, stepped on a scale, and read with growing shock that she'd gained fifteen pounds. She cried at H&M when she had to buy a pair of size-four pants that looked suspiciously like mom jeans to Alexis, although they were just plain gray slacks, and *still* several sizes smaller than what the average woman in America wore. She had a moment of almost psychic connection with that fat girl Shoshana from *Oprah,* wondering what she would think of her, crying over buying size-four pants. She wouldn't understand, Alexis thought cattily as she handed over her debit card at the register. Shoshana probably surpassed a size four sometime around kindergarten.

Something was clearly up, and one day, after editing an article about refreshingly low-fat, cooling summer soups like cucumber or carrot, Alexis found herself sitting at her writing desk, deep in thought. *Something* was different and it was right on the tip of her tongue. It was a balmy Monday morning at the end of June, and she'd set up a fan on her desk, having decided they couldn't afford the electricity bill for air-conditioning this summer. Noah was across the street at his restaurant talking with the contractor, who would help install the kitchen equipment and countertops bought from a restaurant on the Lower East Side that went out of business; she could see his tall body and spring of curls from her window as he walked around. The sign, which read OFF THE RIVER ALE HOUSE in a strong Kelly-green, had just arrived that morning and hung in the window, which made everything feel more official and lent the day a certain fast-paced excitement.

Billy napped on the couch, as he often did these days. His boss at the bar loved him so much he had guaranteed Billy his job back after he beat the cancer, and Alexis was glad they'd both decided last year to pay the extra money and get health insurance, because it helped cover Billy's chemotherapy and checkups. Still, as things were, they were going to have to figure something out financially; he still had about two thousand a month in medical bills, even *with* insurance. They'd elected for the least expensive plan (which sadly came with the least amount of coverage), thinking that, at twenty-six years old, what could possibly happen?

Not a day went by that Alexis didn't think about how to pay Billy's bills.

Alexis sighed. It was her and Billy against the world, as it had been since college. If things got really bad she'd go to her parents, but after quitting law school and refusing her inheritance, she was reluctant to do so. Still . . . she would if it meant helping Billy. She'd do anything for him.

She heard Vanya rustling around in the kitchen cupboards and began mentally making a grocery list for when she went out later to do errands and hit the gym. Billy was craving cold things lately, which soothed him, so . . . Popsicles. Ice cream. Milk.

The sound of footsteps in the hallway, and then Vanya appeared. Her dark hair framed her face and Alexis saw . . . could it be? . . . light brown streaks tastefully woven with the black. Had she gotten *highlights*?

"Oh! Sorry to bother you while you're working," she said.

"No problem," Alexis said.

She was much less scared of Vanya now. Noah talked to her often, and discovered she worked in some hilarious vampire bar on the Lower East Side where the drinks had names like Vampire's Kiss, Whiskey of the Damned, Coffin and Coke, and, of course . . . Bloody Mary.

"She's just your typical goth chick," Noah said. "Why were you and Billy so afraid of her? She's nice."

Billy had asked Alexis not to mention the cancer, so she hadn't, but she was pretty sure Vanya knew; it's hard to hide a secret that large in such a small apartment. Alexis had found some strange powder in the bathroom one day, and thought it might be coke.

(Billy had been known to snort a line or two when they first moved in together, but the idea that he might be doing so now made her angry.)

"Were you doing coke in the bathroom?" she asked him one day, while he watched an episode of *Mad Men*.

"I wish!" he said without looking up.

She summoned up the nerve to ask Vanya about the substance, and was subsequently told it was something called "unicorn horn powder," which, apparently, was for healing. She was making it into a tea for Billy. So yes, Vanya knew. She was touched Vanya was trying to help him, in her own weird way.

Alexis chatted with her more and more lately, finding it easier to discover subjects in common with her when Noah was there. Billy called it the "Noah effect." People came into contact with Noah, and became instantly friendlier and more outgoing. She smiled, remembering Billy coining that phrase as the three of them sat in the cafeteria of the hospital after a particularly brutal chemo session. Billy hadn't eaten anything, claiming he just wanted to keep them company while they ate, which of course made Alexis so upset she had quietly gone to the bathroom and thrown up the pea soup she'd been so recently hungry for. Her stomach was in knots. Billy claimed the only thing he had an appetite for lately was Noah's cooking, and Noah continued to cook at their apartment, using their shitty 1970s yellow stove, claiming Billy was helping him get the ingredients for his chili or wings or Cajun chicken sandwich just right while he waited for the construction to be finished. Alexis suspected he was just cooking for Billy to try and heal him, like Vanya.

"Do you by chance have a tampon or pad? Just got my period," Vanya said now, in a shy, quiet voice.

Suddenly Alexis looked up from her papers and stared out the window, feeling startled. A nervous humming sounded in her ears. Something clicked, the thing that had been living in the back of her mind, vibrating in her nervous system these past few weeks. *When was the last time she'd bought tampons?* Or had a period, for that matter? It had been way over twenty-eight days ago. All the crying, the time she threw up the soup, the upset stomach, moving to a size *four,* her boobs being sore when Noah touched them, that could only mean one thing . . .

"*Oh, my god!*" Alexis screamed.

Vanya jumped back into the hallway, which Alexis would have found ironic two months ago, when she'd been the one terrified of this slight, sweet girl.

"*Oh, my god!*" She rushed past Vanya and grabbed her purse. Pushing past her, Alexis suddenly turned. "Wait. Did you get highlights?"

"Er . . . yeah." Vanya blushed and touched her hair. "Noah and Billy thought it might make me look less . . . freaky."

"Oh. Well, they look good."

She passed a sleepy Billy on the couch, grabbed her purse, and ran down the stairs to the bodega on the corner. She raced past the packaged nuts, the Lotto tickets, and cartons of cigarettes and cat food, until she found a dusty pink pregnancy test and plunked a twenty-dollar bill down on the counter. "Keep the change!" she screamed, the bells on the door clanging as it slammed shut behind her.

She streaked past Off the River Ale House just as Noah was shaking hands with the contractor on the sidewalk.

"Alexis?" he called out.

"No time!" she yelled, running like a marathoner across the street, dodging an MTA bus and two cabs, and finally getting out her keys before dropping them twice, her hands were shaking so hard.

Racing upstairs, she flung open the bathroom door, bit the plastic packaging open with her teeth, yanked down her pants, and peed on the stick.

"What's going on in there?" Billy asked, knocking on the door. "Is this some kind of new workout?" His voice sounded weak.

"No . . . just go away, Billy!" she said, a sob catching in her throat.

She knew he was still standing on the other side of the door, she could hear his breathing, but she didn't care.

Carefully, slowly, she placed it on the sink and stared, her new H&M pants around her ankles. When the first red line swam into vision she finally exhaled, until a smaller, fainter line met the first in a very unholy cross. She put her hand over her mouth to try and contain the alien and strange sound emitting from her throat. Then she bent over the sink and vomited. She had nothing in her stomach other than the eggs and bacon Noah had cooked for everyone this morning, and it came up, sweet and hot, burning her throat. Her eyes felt as though they'd pop out of her head when the feeling rushed over her and she vomited once more, making sad-sounding whimpers as she wiped her mouth with the back of her hand.

Alexis ran her slim hand over her flat stomach, feeling the familiar rush of pride over the thinness she'd worked so hard to achieve all her life. She may have slipped a little with eating high-calorie food as of late, but she'd still managed most of her workouts. Oh, it was all Noah's fault! This! The weight gain! Everything! She flipped the lid down and stood on the toilet in front of the large bathroom mirror and turned sideways, imagining herself pregnant, cheeks round, a stomach that stuck out like a shelf, bloated feet in slippers instead of her usual heels. The girl that was reflected back at her looked terrified. *I must be in shock,* she realized dazedly.

Noah picked that moment to come bursting into the apartment.

"Where is she?" he asked Billy.

"In here," he said. She could hear whispering, Billy and Noah discussing her.

She'd left the door unlocked and Noah threw it open.

"Babe!" His brown eyes were lit up. "Guess who I just met?" He'd let his hair grow long, and he ran his hand through it now, letting the soft curls stick up around his head like a crown. Alexis loved twirling bunches of it around her finger as they lay in bed.

The sun shone through two buildings across the street and made a vertical line of golden light across Alexis's face. He was struck as he always was by how beautiful she was to him. He was too excited to notice her stricken look, and, being Noah, didn't seem deterred that she was bottomless, her underwear and pants strewn about on the floor.

"Wh . . . who?" Alexis asked. Might as well delay telling him and ruining the rest of both their lives.

"Tony Andrews! He came by right after you went jogging past us. He reviews restaurants for *New York* magazine. He heard about my idea, you know, a laid-back kind of microbrewery normally found in Colorado but plunked down right in the middle of Manhattan? And he wants to write up Off the River Ale House as soon as it opens!"

"That's so great, Noah. I'm happy for you," she said flatly. She climbed down off the toilet and curled the test stick into her palm, dropping her arm behind her back.

He glanced at her face and frowned. When Noah frowned, he somehow had the ability to look even cuter. He'd taken off his shirt to help the contractor measure and install booths and his brown torso was sleek with sweat. "What's wrong? Billy said you were upset."

Not knowing what to say, she thrust the pregnancy test at his chest, as if she were jousting with a small plastic sword.

"Oh." He squinted at the small plus sign. "Never saw one of these in person before. Only in the movies."

"That's all you can *say*?" she shouted.

She heard Billy rustling on the couch, and tried to lower her voice. "What the fuck am I going to do?"

She hastily bent down to put on her pants, struggling with the button so hard it popped off, falling to the floor and bouncing twice before landing on the shower rug. Noah reached over to help her but she pushed him away. She sat back down on the toilet, head in hands, and sobbed quietly, hopelessly.

He was quiet for a moment, thinking. "Hey. Look at me, at least." He put his hand under her chin and raised her blotchy face gently up to his.

"It's not what you're going to do. It's what *we're* doing. We're in this together, you know."

"But how did this even happen?" Alexis cried, looking up at him. "We used condoms, every time."

"Well . . ." Noah said, chewing his lower lip, which in any other situation would have made Alexis want to kiss him. Instead, she stood and leaned over the toilet and vomited for a third time. She felt Noah's large, cool hands holding back her hair, and she had a sudden sense of déjà vu from the hospital, when he'd held her hand while she was stitched up. The stitches had since dissolved, but they'd left a slight white line.

She shook off Noah's hands and leaned over the sink to splash cold water on her face, shutting her eyes as she did so. She roughly wiped her face on the monogrammed hand towel Billy bought her for her nineteenth birthday to be ironic. *"Because we're like a married couple!"* he'd said gleefully.

"There was that one time, after we went to the movies in Union Square? I remember we were arguing about whether the butter they put on top of popcorn is real or not. Remember, we didn't have any condoms that night so we just . . . didn't use one?"

"Fuck, fuck fuck," Alexis wailed. "How could I be so irresponsible? This doesn't happen to people like us. It happens to stupid people."

"Alexis," he said softly. "This happens to all kinds of people. I must not have pulled out in time—"

"*Stop.* Just stop," she said, putting her hands over her ears. She sighed deeply. "So what now?"

"Now we go grocery shopping." Her list had fallen onto the shower mat and he bent down to retrieve it.

"Let's go buy . . ." He glanced down. "Popsicles."

"Are you on drugs? *Fuck* the Popsicles!" Alexis cried.

Noah crossed his arms and leaned against the wood doorframe. The muscles in his forearms bulged. "Alexis, it's not such a bad thing, you know. Some people might think this is actually . . . a happy day, really." He picked up steam as he spoke. His optimism, though usually a welcome shift in thinking for Alexis, served now only to annoy her.

"There are so many people who can't have kids," Noah continued. "And we're not spring chickens. I'll be thirty this fall. It's not like we're teenagers. I can support you and the baby. I've been saving money since college. I was going to put it toward the restaurant, but I can easily cut back there." He made up his mind as he spoke. The news had been shocking, of course, but Noah was nothing if not malleable, able to change direction, easygoing. And Alexis hated him for that. It wasn't practical.

"Are you fucking delusional?" she screamed. She was seriously reconsidering ever falling for Noah. "This is no time to be Mr. Optimist, okay? This is a disaster. This is worse than Hurricane Katrina. This is September Eleventh."

"This is not September Eleventh. Or Hurricane Katrina." He took a deep breath. She'd shaken off his hands from her shoulders, and they hung now at his sides like weights. "Don't be so dramatic. It's your body . . . but . . ."

"You're damn right it's my body. And I have the right to choose. And I choose getting rid of this . . . this *growth* as soon as possible. It's June. Bathing suit season. It's already making me fat."

Noah punched the wall, tearing a large-sized hole in the plasterboard. Alexis jumped. "You're not fat!" he shouted. Anger was so out of character for him that Alexis took a step back. "You are a size four! Do you know how many women would die to be a size four? My sister! My mother! Most of the women in America! And yes, you have the right to choose. And I will support that choice. But you're not making a choice here. You're basing your decision on what you'll look like in a stupid *swimsuit*. I'm so sick of this skinny shit. It's crazy!" He picked up her phone, which had fallen out of the pocket of her pants. "And this stupid button you press every time you eat something. It has to stop!" Before Alexis could stop him, he lifted the window behind him with a loud squeak, pushed up the screen, wound back his arm, and chucked her phone as far as he could.

Holy shit. She was so full of anger she literally saw red for a minute. Who was she, if she couldn't count her calories? It was part of what made Alexis, Alexis. Those tiny black numbers that adjusted throughout the day beneath her fingertip filled her with calm. She'd been in control and now she wasn't. The mood in the little room shifted into a scary calm, the eye of the storm. She set her shoulders back. The softer Alexis that had emerged recently, surprising her deeply, ran into a hole and hid. And the blackness she'd lived with since Mark died seeped back out. She realized it had never left. Her voice was a measured whisper.

"Thanks a lot, Noah. That phone cost a lot of money. So that's how you really feel, isn't it? You think what I do for a living is stupid. You think what I've done with my life, how I've earned a living since college with not a single dollar from my parents, is . . . what's the word you used? Crazy?"

"No, no, that's not what I meant." Noah looked pained. He wiped white plaster off his forearm. It tugged something within her, to see the big guy get upset, but she wasn't going to let sympathy back her down from the rage she hadn't tapped into since that evening in March when she'd sliced open her finger and fate had sprinkled that pixie dust over her and she'd met Noah, that rage she'd had bottled inside her for the three years since Mark had died and her parents had essentially disowned her.

"Alexis. Alexis, I—"

"Don't. Don't even say it." She didn't want to hear his I-love-you. She didn't want to hear anything else from him ever again.

"You don't respect me. All this time, all these months I've been helping you build your restaurant. I scrubbed that fur shop on my hands and knees, I held that chili-making contest for the neighborhood, I ate a million fattening *wings*."

She spit out the word.

"And for what? This is how you really feel. You think *Skinny Chick* is stupid. You think I'm stupid. Well, I don't need you. I was doing just fine on my own, before I met you."

"Alexis, whatever you decide, I want to help you."

"Stop," she said. "Just go." She pushed on his chest, which was solid, and she could feel his heart flutter beneath her hands. "I'll send you the bill for the abortion."

It was a horrible thing to say, cold and unfair, and she knew it the second the words left her lips. Noah looked shocked, like he'd been punched in the stomach. Resigned, he turned away and walked out of the bathroom. She kept thinking he'd turn around. She heard the apartment door open and close, and just like that, the man who had walked into their lives and made them all fall in love with him was walking down the stairs and out onto a very crowded New York street.

She wouldn't see him again for three months. And by then, everything had changed.

Shoshana

July

CHESTER, NEW JERSEY

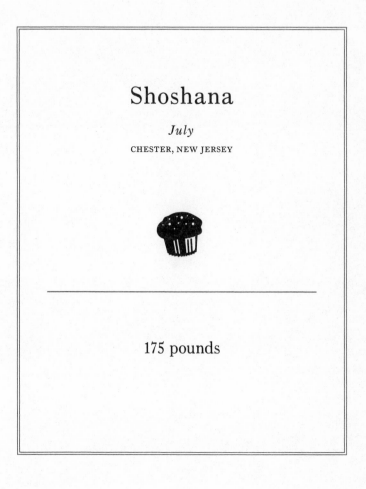

---

175 pounds

Fat and Fabulous

I was crossing the street between Washington and Bloomfield in Hobo-ken today, leaving my Vinyasa yoga class and feeling really good in my body after the workout, when out of nowhere a fire-red Ford pickup truck came screaming around the corner, its engine so hot and the car so close it left a scald mark on my calf.

As I gathered my bearings, having almost been killed in broad daylight, the driver leaned on the horn and shouted out the window, "Move your fat ass, lady!"

Now, it's been quite some time since I have encountered a FBA, or in layman's terms, a Fat Bigot Asshole. I was out of practice. I just about managed to flip him the state bird. It just brought me right back to why I started *Fat and Fabulous*. I've written (some may say even harped) about this many a time, but this blog is about healthy at any size, and ridding the word "diet" from your vocabulary (I always gained all the weight back, and statistically, so will you).

I wasted so many years hating my body, wearing XXL T-shirts over my bathing suit when I went swimming so I looked like a tent with tits, yo-yo dieting that put strain on my heart, trying to fit into the mold the media has set out for young women.

I have an e-mail folder where I put all of my "troll comments," or people with bad intentions who want to post mean comments on *Fat and Fabulous*. I think there is a special warm place somewhere in hell for troll people, like Mr. Ford.

But, I digress. When I heard Mr. Ford's slur it brought me right back to my roots. *Fat and Fabulous*'s goal is to force people to see Fatties in a whole new light, a pink, shimmery, luminescent one. I want FBAs to see not all of us are fat because we stuff our faces with junk food every night.

We once had a commenter on the message boards who posted stories about receiving nasty remarks because she uses a motorized scooter when she shops at Target. Really she uses the scooter because she has arthritis in her legs, but people automatically assume she is fat and lazy.

One of my favorite arguments (and you know I have many) is that everyone has one really skinny friend who eats like a linebacker and yet magically remains thin. Yes, of course we hate her, but we also can learn an important lesson there. Why is it that people believe it is possible to eat this much and stay skinny, but somehow they think it *impossible* to eat healthy food and yet still be fat? FBAs think we eat candy bars for breakfast, ice-cream sundaes for lunch, and donuts for dinner.

I launched *Fat and Fabulous* to start a conversation about Fat, and what it means to Americans. One of my bloggers, Jessica, wrote a story about a year ago (you might remember it) called "Thin for a Year," about when she went on Jenny Craig and lost two hundred pounds (which she has since gained back, but she says she feels okay with that). Jessica couldn't believe what a different world she was in—she felt like "Alice, when she falls down the rabbit hole." The cute barista at her local Starbucks grinned at her when he handed her a tall hot chocolate. Her parents told her how "proud" they were, apparently about the weight loss, though Amanda also happens to have a Ph.D. in biochemistry from Princeton and has published, twelve, yes, count 'em, twelve books. Aren't these accomplishments worthy of receiving flirtation and pride, more than the fact that you can fit into skinny jeans?

Another reason I started this blog was for my sister, Emily. This is the first time I have ever written about it, but Emily is a bigger Fattie than myself, and she's taken shit for it her whole life. I remember kids calling her "tub-o-lard" on the playground, and "Pillsbury Dough Girl" in ballet class. Emily is my favorite person and I won't stand to see someone I love so much get hurt.

I write this blog not only for my sister but for Angela White in Omaha, Nebraska, who wrote a beautiful post about her mother, who kept going to the same doctor for her entire life, even though that doctor told her, after only superficial exams, that her chronic shortness of breath was due to her being overweight.

Angela's mother passed away two months after gathering up the courage to seek a second opinion, whereupon she found out she had asthma. She suffered an immense asthma attack while out buying groceries and hadn't yet filled the prescription in her purse for an inhaler. Angela blames her mother's doctor—his prejudice against her weight blocked him from making an accurate diagnosis and his negligence was fatal.

But back to yesterday, back to Hoboken. After I caught my breath, and felt the anger with the FBA subside, I smiled. I smiled right there in the intersection, because he had done me a favor: he'd reminded me of all these reasons I mentioned above for why I started *Fat and Fabulous*. I smiled because I have a life, amazing friends, and I don't have time to worry about whether or not my ass jiggles as I walk across the street. I smiled because I love the hell out of lip gloss, face creams, Betty White, Italian festivals, and now apple orchards. I enjoy life, and this guy doesn't.

Because I eat what I want, which is sometimes asparagus and sometimes a frickin' cheeseburger. So what if I can't go braless, even at night? So what if I get glared at on planes, in the supermarket, in line to get my oil changed? I'm a person. With a mind, body, heart, and soul.

And I'm a good person who eats (mostly) healthy food. This redneck asshole brought it all back, and for that I can only say, Thank You. And I hope you someday get over having such a small penis you have to buy a large truck to compensate.

And on that classy note, loyal readers, I am taking a little mini-break from *Fat and Fabulous*. Before you start running for the hills, please note that this is only temporary, while I get the farm I inherited from Aunt Mimi in working order as a true apple orchard. As some of you know, for the last three months I have been splitting my time between my (very crowded) apartment in Hoboken and my little shabby chic farm in Chester. I have learned how to trim apple trees from twenty feet to ten, to hand-pull the weed vines that like to wrap themselves around the apple tree trunks, to hunt and destroy apple scab, a nasty disease that looks like the zits I got in middle school, and lastly, to bake the best apple pie on the East Coast. (I'm not kidding—I found Aunt Mimi's recipe, and let me tell you, it's awesome!)

Come September 1, I hope to be open for business as a real, live, working orchard! So if you live around Jersey, or even if you don't, *Fat and Fabulous* readers from far and wide will be able to come to Shoshana's Apple Orchard for meet-ups, book groups, and apple-pie-buying excursions! See you in three months. In the meantime, my friend Jane will be posting a great story about yo-yo dieting to fit into her wedding dress which almost led to disaster, and Andrea, who is a frequent contributor, is going to continue to write her column about healthy and yummy summer cocktails.

Dr. Amanda Weber will also be posting weekly about healthy eating, and also writing a riveting column on the language of anorexia—how to spot the hidden signs in your friends. See you all in the fall!

XO,

Shoshana

IT WAS A RARE FRIDAY NIGHT THAT SHOSHANA DIDN'T
have any guests sleeping over at the farm, and this weekend was no
exception. Her mom and Emily sat on the new couch given to her
by Joe Murphy and Greta, which Shoshana knew Greta had probably picked out and Joe had paid for. It was a dusky purple Crate &
Barrel microfiber wraparound in a much larger design than ever
would have fit in her Hoboken apartment. Shoshana was able to
balance living in both places, which felt worlds apart. She was a
city mouse *and* a country mouse. She recently learned that before
she died Mimi ingeniously had the property declared as a historic
landmark, and its land was also preserved. Therefore, Shoshana's
taxes would be low enough to allow her to keep the Hoboken
apartment.

In the past three months, she spent nearly every day here, and
with the assistance of Joe Murphy ("assistance" being a relative
word; he mostly sat in a lawn chair and sipped from his flask)
she'd cleared out the jungle behind the house and gotten started
on owning her own orchard, a notion that gave her the chills.
Greta brought her shoe boxes full of black-and-white pictures of
the farm in its heyday.

Joe taught her to recognize disease and treat it, how to cut the
branches and allow the optimum amount of sunlight through. He

provided a rich history of the farm, including more stories about her father as a child.

Every night, Shoshana walked over the hills with Sinatra to dine with him and Greta. Greta had patiently cleaned the farm with her, refusing all Shoshana's offers of pay. Shoshana often wondered what arrangement Greta and Joe Murphy had; Greta did all the cooking and cleaning, but the two bickered night and day, driving one another crazy.

Greta was fond of saying refrains like, "That man wouldn't remember to eat breakfast if it weren't for me." Or, "I doubt he even knows his own Social Security number. He'd be dead in a gutter if I didn't take care of him."

Joe Murphy put up a great show that Greta was the "beast on his back," but as she got to know them Shoshana could, even more than initially, see underneath how dependent on and grateful to Greta he was.

Her mother and sister had been visiting just about every weekend, and Emily had dropped a few comments about moving in, which then caused their mom to state that *she* might as well move in as well. Then Andrea asked if she could stay on the couch this weekend because Aggie had been driving her crazy with her kleptomania and weird sculptures: "If I have to smell that girl's patchouli one more day I'm going to strangle her with one of her dreadlocks!" The farm couldn't have come into her possession at a better time; Shoshana loved her roommates dearly, but with Jane's wedding tomorrow morning, everyone had been a little on edge at the apartment, especially Jane. She was glad she had a place to get away from the commotion.

Two days ago, Shoshana went back to Hoboken to power-walk with Nancy, her wealthy, cop-dating friend who lived uptown and helped Shoshana with her blog from time to time. Afterward, she and her roommates ironed out Jane's final preparations with her wedding favors. Jane declared if the four girls did not help her stuff three hundred high-heel-shaped cookie favors into cellophane she would never speak to any of them again.

"Have I been a Bridezilla?" she trilled, after Shoshana's fingers felt like they'd fall off any second. She glanced at the clock. It was three in the morning, and they'd finally finished the favors.

"Of course not," Andrea said, massaging her wrist.

"Don't be silly," Aggie said, rubbing her eyes.

"You've been like an angel sent from the heavens," Karen said, yawning.

The girls caught each other's eyes and burst out laughing.

"Liars!" Jane screamed, though the worry line that had been in her brow in recent months was slowly dissolving.

"Oh, you gave it away with that silly angel line," Shoshana said to Karen, throwing a shoe cookie at her.

"Just wait until you all get married," Jane yelled. "You'll see how crazy it makes you. I feel like I was kidnapped by aliens and now I'm just getting my brain back."

Needless to say, Shoshana hadn't gotten a lot of sleep last night, so when Greg asked if he could crash at the farm and the two would drive to Long Beach Island the following morning together, where the wedding was to be held, Shoshana agreed, as she'd have a ride. Greg had quit drinking alcohol recently to be healthy, so she loved forcing him to be the designated driver. Besides, she hadn't seen him in nearly three months, though they still talked on the phone every day.

Wanting to hear more about his latest conquest, Shoshana invited Greg out to see her new digs, and accompany her to Jane's wedding. He'd shown up around eight, when the fog was still a glistening blanket over the hills. She heard the crunch of the white gravel she'd had refilled by a local contractor, then the slam of his BMW door. She ran outside barefoot, excited to show him all the improvements she'd made on the farm.

She looked at Greg. He'd dressed his short and muscular frame with khakis, a polo shirt from a Montclair golf course, and brown boat shoes. She took in his thick eyebrows, full lips, and hazel eyes that twinkled mischievously. And above the top lip, could it be?

"Dude, what's with the 'stache?" she asked, giggling. "It's very hipster." Except it wasn't exactly manly, more like light brown fuzz.

Instead of answering, he'd just stared at her.

"Uh, who are you and what did you do with my best friend?" he asked finally.

Shoshana blushed. The crazy thing was, after years of wishing she were thinner, followed by years of accepting herself just as she was, she was feeling insecure about her weight loss. Over the last twelve weeks, after walking the mile back and forth to Joe Murphy's house, sometimes twice a day, clearing weeds and vines, chopping back apple tree branches, eating local food, and digging in the dirt to plant a vegetable garden beside the house, Shoshana had lost thirty pounds.

She started noticing her jeans slipping off her waist, and, not thinking anything of it, looped one of Mimi's old scarves through as a belt. It was also the lack of a damn ShopRite for miles that brought Shoshana to the farmers' market here on Saturdays. Also, Greta put Joe Murphy on a low-sodium diet for his heart (although Shoshana caught him sneaking all kinds of snacks when he was out walking in the fields with Patrick O'Leary), and as a result of eating dinner at their mansion nearly every night she grew to like the zucchini soup, ham sandwiches on wheat toast, and good, healthy cooking Greta served.

"I don't know what you mean," Shoshana said nonchalantly to Greg. A bird called out and received a hurried reply from a feathered friend inside a nearby willow tree as she turned and walked over the threshold into the house. She'd replaced Mimi's large, moth-eaten Oriental carpet with an oatmeal-colored sisal rug, and found a pretty, blue-colored glass light fixture for the entryway ceiling. Joe Murphy painted the walls a deep burnt orange, swaying frighteningly on the ladder while drinking from his flask. "This is fun!" he'd exclaimed. "Used to paint houses for a dollar a day back in Ireland. Haven't held a paintbrush in sixty fockin' years!"

She'd kept Mimi's photographs up around the house, enjoying

their black-and-white nostalgic vibe. Joining them on the wall were three of her father's paintings; she felt happy each time she walked by them. Her mom and Emily were sleeping over frequently, and, along with Greta, had helped her wash all the dust from the dishes in the kitchen, beat the rugs outside with a broomstick, wash the linens, and replace the old sixties refrigerator with a new one. She'd taken the silk handkerchiefs off the living room lamps and thrown out the living room curtains, flooding the small room with light. Shoshana was proud of the changes; she'd kept the heart of the place intact but contributed her own flair in the decorating. She surveyed the room with Greg as he stepped inside, and noticed he was still gazing intently at her.

"Okay, I may have lost some weight."

"Shoshana, you look fifty pounds lighter!"

"No. Not fifty pounds." She blushed. "Thirty." After posting many times about the importance of not weighing one's self, Shoshana had finally bit the bullet and found a rusty old-yet-functioning scale in the upstairs bathroom and tentatively climbed on. She'd bitten her lip in surprise when she saw the number read back to her, the needle hovering very closely to the 175 mark. She hadn't been under two hundred pounds since middle school.

Her eyes suddenly filled with tears. "Greg, I don't know what to do."

He smiled and put his arm around her. "Shosh, you should be proud of yourself."

"I didn't do this on purpose!" she wailed. "It was all that damn climbing up ladders and trimming apple trees and hauling branches to the road and walking Sinatra over these hills. I miss being fat."

He chuckled.

She stuck her tongue out at him. "It's not funny!"

"You're a babe both ways, but . . ."

He cocked an eyebrow at her.

"What? Just say it."

"Okay, don't hit me again. But isn't it a little easier to get around now? To fit into clothes? To *breathe*?"

"But I'm not Fat and Fabulous anymore," she moaned, sinking onto the new couch. Greg sat beside her, patting her knee. She wore her favorite brown cords she'd had since high school with her Birkenstocks, and a light, airy hippie blouse in a size ten she'd bought at a neighbor's yard sale down the road and which she still couldn't believe she fit into.

"Don't worry, you're still pretty fat," he said.

She punched him in the arm. "I'm serious," she said, but she was smiling now.

"Look, Shosh. Your whole blog . . . its purpose is to make chubby chicks feel good about themselves, right? Give them self-esteem, all that good stuff? Be yourself, healthy at any size, isn't that your motto?"

"Right," she said, picking up a circular pillow (a gift from Emily) that had the words I HEART APPLES sewn on it. She hugged it to her chest.

"So? Can't you continue to do that? You're not going to lose your audience if you're honest with them."

"Greg, you don't know my readers. Some of them get mad if I even mention that I like whole wheat bread. They think I'm going outside of the rules of *Fat and Fabulous* and dieting, or watching what I eat. If they find out I've lost weight, my career is over."

He wasn't going to be easily put off. "Since when are you someone who pays attention to rules? Besides, aren't there always extremists in the blogosphere? Didn't you tell me that once?"

"Shit." She blew hot air out through her mouth, pushing a thick lock of auburn hair from her forehead. "I did say that, didn't I?"

"From what I can tell from reading your blog, which I do once in a blue moon, is that a woman's main goal is to be true to herself. If you've dropped some pounds because you got this farm and you've turned it into a beautiful thing, a real working orchard, shouldn't you tell your readers about it? Your real fans will still respect you. They're not going to stop reading all of a sudden just because you've lost weight. You can still help them feel good about themselves through your positive attitude, Shosh. People just like talking to you, or reading your posts. Your job is to make them feel good, and you can do that at any weight."

Shoshana was taken aback.

"Wow. Who would have thought you'd give this, like, beautiful feminist speech? My Greggie, the biggest misogynist on the East Coast!"

She didn't say it, but it was also out of character for him not to talk about himself for so long. But she realized he was right. She'd been hiding from her readers. It was all too convenient to set up others to blog for her while she was fixing up the farm and shedding weight. It was time to reclaim *Fat and Fabulous*. And, as Greg had so eloquently pointed out, surely by America's standards she was still fat. The idea cheered her up. She closed her eyes and leaned forward to give him a hug.

Suddenly she felt a wet warmth on her mouth, followed by a tickling brush of lip hair.

"What the hell?" She jumped up from the couch.

"What? You wanted me to kiss you! You were totally moving toward me!" Greg had jumped back, and was cowering on the couch as she smacked him with a nearby copy of *Us Weekly* Andrea had left on the coffee table. "Stop hitting me! What is the big deal? I've, like, seen you naked a bazillion times before."

"That was in high school! Oh, my god. It was the mustache. The mustache is turning you into a crazy porn star! Besides, you only want to make out with me because I'm skinny now."

"Shosh, you're not exactly skinny."

"Well, whatever. Shut up, Greg. Besides, you know it's true."

He gave her a brooding look. "I really did think you wanted me to kiss you."

They looked at each other and burst out laughing. Then they fell off and rolled around on the new carpet.

"Porn . . .'stache . . ." was all she could get out.

"Thought you wanted . . . me to kiss you . . ." Greg said, hiccuping.

"Let's shake on never doing that again," Shoshana said, putting out her hand for him to take.

"Okay. Promise," Greg said.

"Pinkie swear, just to be safe."

"Shoshana, we're not five years old."

"Just do it!"

"Okay, okay." So they did, linking their smallest fingers, making the shape of the letter W with their pinkies.

She sat up on the floor. "Seriously, though, what's with that fuzz on your lip? It looks like the pubic hair of a twelve-year-old boy."

Greg bristled, picking up his brown leather overnight bag. "The new girl I'm seeing from my gym asked me to grow it. She likes men with facial hair."

Shoshana giggled. "Okay, whatever you say, David Hasselhoff."

"He's more famous for having a lot of chest hair."

This made Shoshana giggle even harder. "Thank you for educating me on the finer points of the Hoff. Want some lunch? Get you settled upstairs? Then I want to hear all about this new girlfriend. First of all, does she eat dessert?"

They spent the day eating fresh food from the local farmers' market, then strolling around the hills surrounding the farm with Sinatra in tow.

She'd saved the best part of the farm for last. Joe Murphy had paid to replace the rotting fence surrounding the orchard. She swung the gate closed behind her. Sunlight beamed across their faces, and Greg popped the collar of of his polo shirt, his eyes wide.

"This is . . . this is unbelievable."

She beamed. The apple trees were now just the right height, the branches perfectly horizontal. (She'd cut off all the "suckers" that grew the wrong way.) The apples were the size of golf balls now. Healthy, dark oval-shaped green leaves had formed on the branches. She'd gotten rid of all signs of apple scab, and as long as they didn't have too much rain this summer, she'd have a fully working orchard ready for picking in September. A small gray rabbit hopped behind one of the nearby trees. Greg reached his hand out to pull a branch close to his face, inspecting the tree as though it were one of his legal briefs.

"At one point in the fifties Mimi grew ten different varieties of apples," Shoshana said proudly.

"How many will you have?" Greg asked, picking up a leaf that had fallen, twirling it in his fingers like helicopter wings.

"Three!" she said, beaming, reaching out to rub one of the tree trunks like a proud mother patting her infant. "We were able to save almost all the trees for McIntosh, Winesaps, and Red Delicious. Some trees were too old, and the fruit they'd produce would be too small. So we cut them down, then removed their roots, and used the wood for firewood. We've got seventy-five trees here."

"We?" Greg asked.

Shoshana laughed. "Everyone's been so amazingly *involved*. Joe Murphy down the road, Greta, my mom, Emily, all four crazy girls I live with, you encouraging me on the phone . . . This isn't my orchard. It belongs to everyone. I think that's what Mimi had in mind when she gave it to me."

Having lived in her house for three months, Shoshana felt she was communicating with the essential *Miminess*. Even more important, with her father.

"I can't believe I didn't visit for years," Shoshana said, tearing up. "We were always playing here as kids, but in recent years Mimi had Alzheimer's so bad . . . just my mom came. I should have been here," she said, a tear spilling onto her cheek.

"Hey. Mimi knew you loved her. You always talked about her. Shosh, you're the kind of person everyone feels loved by." He hugged her, which was funny because she was an inch taller than him, so she was able to rest her head on his shoulder.

"You're not going to try and kiss me again, are you?" she asked, wiping her eyes.

"I don't want to get my ass beat, no." He smiled. "Hey, did you ever go on that date?"

"What date?"

"The guy with the funny name you told me about ages ago.

Lowcock, something like that? The nose, ear, and throat doctor from JDate?"

"I completely forgot about him," Shoshana said. She'd been so busy getting the orchard together, she'd forgotten about the e-mail she'd received months ago. He'd had a cute profile picture, too.

"Maybe I'll e-mail him back," she said finally.

"You should. He'd be lucky to go out with you," Greg said.

She smiled at him.

The rabbit peeked out from one of the apple trees, hopped around, then ducked beneath the white fence and took off, its body a blob of gray paint against the green hills.

"This sure ain't Hoboken," Greg said. They once again opened the latch for the fence, and walked back to the house through the tall grass. (She kept it on the long side. She couldn't get *Christina's World* out of her head, and didn't want short, suburbs-type grass. She didn't want a *lawn*. She wanted fields, and she ran her hand along the top of the grass as they walked. It tickled her palm.)

"No. It's the opposite. But I love it," Shoshana said. "I haven't figured out exactly what my plan is yet. I'm keeping my room in the 'Boken for now, and I'm back there once a week or so. Emily and my mom are threatening to move here."

"Do you have a business plan for the orchard yet?" A distant car's motor purred as it drove over the hills into town.

"Not really. I just figured I'd sell pies, and let people pick their own apples. I found all these cute wooden baskets in the shed out back that would be perfect."

They'd reached the doorway and he fingered the pineapple knocker. "You know, I do contracts for a living. I can set you up as a real business with a tax ID, like we did for the blog."

"That would be awesome! You'd really do that?"

"Of course. You should set things up properly if you're going to make any money."

"I know. I'm such a space cadet when it comes to business. But you're right. Thanks so much, Greggie!"

"After Jane's wedding we'll pick a date and I'll come out here with the forms."

"I love it when you speak lawyer to me, baby," she said in a deep, sexy voice that made them both laugh. They walked into the house and sat in the kitchen, talking the afternoon away. She'd baked a spinach quiche the day before and they each had a slice.

That evening they walked to the mansion for dinner with Joe Murphy and Greta. Joe had a chest cold. "A cold in the summer, ah, fockin' hell," he'd said when they rang the doorbell and Greta ushered them in. The hallway smelled like a combination of yummy cooking and . . . pee.

"P-Hen had a little accident on the rug," Greta said. Her white hair was tied back in a bun at the nape of her neck. "Why this crazy man insists on keeping a bird indoors is anyone's guess."

"She doesn't complain about my drinking!" Joe Murphy bellowed from his seat in the dining room.

Shoshana rolled her eyes. "They fight because they love," she whispered to Greg, who looked intrigued.

Dinner was a delicious combo of mussels in spicy broth, white bean and tomato soup, and an assortment of different kinds of meat and vegetable empanadas. "These were my mother's recipes," Greta said, her black eyes shining over the candlelight.

"I thought yer mother was wicked and beat you with a hickory stick," Joe Murphy said. He took sips from his silver flask whenever Greta went into the kitchen to bring out a dish.

"Yes, she did, but that was all she knew," Greta said. She ducked Shoshana under the chin gently. "She did the best she could with no money." She turned to Joe. "It would have done you some good."

"Greg, have you ever paid someone who yells at ya constantly?" Joe Murphy asked. He was feeding Patrick O'Leary scraps of food under the table.

Greg laughed and took a sip of his wine. "Yes, my assistant."

"Women!" He sat back in his chair and crossed his arms, exasperated.

"I'll toast to that," Greg said, tipping his wineglass to Joe.

Greta rolled her eyes, collecting their plates. "You can't live without us," she said. "You shriveled old prune." She placed one on top of the other, the sound of knives scraping against porcelain filling the great room. There were cherubs painted on the ceiling, and Shoshana spent time looking up at each one. P-Hen gave a great screech from the other room.

Joe was feeling tired, but he stayed up long enough to talk Greg into smoking a cigar with him (despite Greta's warnings about his blackened lungs). So the women sat on the back porch, watching night come over the fields.

"This sky is so different from Hoboken's," Shoshana said. They'd brought their wineglasses with them. They were big goblets, with red, blue, and green stones embedded in the silver stems. "You can see so many stars."

Greta smiled. "Your father said something exactly like that to me once. He missed the farm once he moved to Summit. He loved the house he bought with your mom because that was home, and then, well, you two gorgeous girls came along, but he enjoyed painting the sky out here."

"I love it that you remember so many things about my dad," Shoshana said.

Greta was quiet for a few minutes.

"Georgina, Bob, and Mimi were my family. Their souls still reside here, in this special place. I miss all three of them so dearly. I came here from Ecuador and didn't know a soul. They never treated me like a, what do you call it? Hired help? Even now, that crusty old man in there has set up a stipend with his bank for me after he goes. Though that won't be for a long time, if I have anything to do with it."

Shoshana smiled. Joe was pretty old. No matter how much Greta bugged him about his drinking and smoking, time was running out. But that didn't mean you didn't try to cheat death and take care of the people you loved, in the best way you knew how.

She tilted back her head, warm with wine and company, and

again looked up. She wished she knew how to tell planets from stars. Didn't one blink?

She wasn't sure what dress to wear to Jane's wedding tomorrow (though she'd recently bought a new cotton striped number from Target, not in the plus size section!), but it was okay to decide at the last minute. Life was led at a slower pace in the country. Splitting her time between Hoboken and here, her mother and sister and friends coming to live part-time with her, the anticipation of the harvest in the fall, informing her readers about her weight loss . . . It would all come together. The small apples that now lay sleeping on their boughs would soon become large and ripe. She didn't have to have life figured out to enjoy it.

Alexis

September

NEW YORK AND GREENWICH, CONNECTICUT

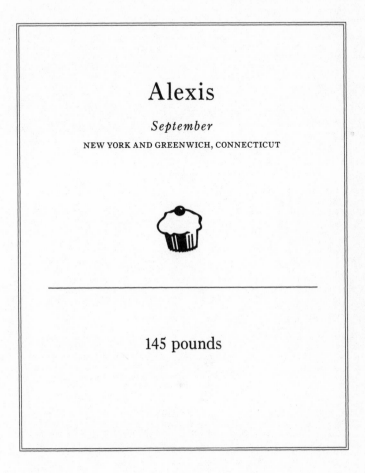

---

145 pounds

Skinny Chick

Dear *Skinny Chick* Readers:

I'm sorry I haven't written for so long, I've been dealing with a lot in my personal life. Not quite sure I'm ready to blog about it yet, but more on that to come soon.

The site has been getting a ton of comments about a certain women's fashion magazine editor. I don't even need to write her name because you all know whom I am talking about. She had a somewhat harsh viewpoint on obese people being allowed on television, and she wrote a column admitting she would be grossed out if she had to watch two fat characters on television kiss one another, like on *Mike & Molly.*

She then went on to claim she had many "plump friends," and was not a "fatist," or someone who was anti-fat. One *Skinny Chick* commenter said: "Right On! It's about time someone let the cat out of the bag. Watching fat people on TV grosses me out, too."

However, the main tone of comments on *Skinny Chick* were that the editor's comments took things a little too far. I have to say I agree. To be honest, I've come to the realization that I may have been a bit too judgmental in the past when it came to absolutes about weight.

I still think a person is generally happier and will live longer the better shape she is in, but there are always those scary extremes of anorexia and bulimia. Women have been cruel to one another forever, and comments like hers perpetuate that. *Skinny Chick* has never been about cruelty; rather, its core message is feeling your best, eating the right food, and getting the most out of your workouts.

Before you say I've sold out, I will always rally against obesity, but my posts going forward will be on a lighter note. A more uplifting one.

With that said, my heart goes out to the editor because, as you know, dear readers, my goal is to inspire, not bring down young women. I can be a bit of a bitch sometimes, too, but I'm working on it.

Warmly,

Alexis

ALEXIS HADN'T DRIVEN IN THE THREE YEARS SINCE she'd left Greenwich, so it felt strange to be behind the wheel of the rental car. The idea of visiting her parents sent shivers of nervousness down her spine as she steadied her hands on the wheel and 95 North sped by outside her windshield in a blur of asphalt and trees.

She had a small, raised ball of a belly that made the seat belt somewhat uncomfortable; she had to keep squirming around and changing position, something she imagined the baby inside her was doing in sync with her movements. When Billy was having a particularly hard day, they'd lie in bed together and she would read aloud to him from *What to Expect When You're Expecting.* This month, they learned the baby could begin to hear outside voices and low tones, so Billy would put his head on her stomach and hum Dolly Parton songs in a deep voice that made Alexis laugh. Last week after a round of "9 to 5," he'd looked up, his eyes tired, black fuzzy spots of hair coming in around his scalp, his cheekbones sharp like knives, and said:

"You have to call Noah, Alexis. You have to tell him you kept the baby. He asks about you every day and he has a right to know."

She hadn't responded. Instead, she walked to the living room window, and oh, how ironic, there was Noah pulling down the metal grate that covered the Off the River Ale House window at night. His silhouette, so familiar to her now with his wild curly hair, tall, strong build, and big hands . . . he always looked sad to Alexis, his shoulders slumped, and knowing she was the cause of his hurt only made things harder. Every day that went by, their fight loomed in the black velvet back part of her brain, seeping into every interaction, every inflection in her voice, every thought streaming through her brain. That moment when she'd flung angry words at Noah three months ago in the bathroom seemed ridiculous now, but she was too stubborn to admit it. She'd never fallen in love before and it terrified her. Billy told her he'd named a sandwich at the restaurant after her, "The Alexis," and the thought made her happy, like he'd been thinking about her, too.

Alexis blinked and gripped the wheel. She adjusted the strap of the seat belt again and sighed, remembering the horrible words she'd used, the anger she'd felt when Noah called *Skinny Chick* "crazy." Really, he was calling her crazy, right? She *was Skinny Chick*. Or at least she had been. She let out a bitter chuckle that sounded more like a bark as she flipped on her turn signal and entered her neighborhood. No one would call her skinny now. She'd gained forty-five pounds, and was nearly five months pregnant. The baby was due in January.

She had mixed feelings about keeping the baby. On the whole she was glad; she hadn't seen herself as a mother, at least not one who kissed skinned knees and packed school lunches, but in the last few weeks, seeing Billy so frail, she wanted to push death out of her house and welcome life with open arms.

She made an appointment a week after the argument with Noah for an abortion at a hospital on the Upper East Side. It was scheduled for nine a.m., and she was told not to eat anything the night before, which was hard because these days her appetite was so strong she often ate two dinners. She'd worn an absurd outfit, a raincoat with a large black hood she'd pulled over her face, and huge sunglasses, as if somehow she could crawl inside herself and hide. As if the paparazzi, or maybe her father, would be waiting outside her apartment building shouting, "Selfish bitch!"

Billy had been at a doctor's appointment, and didn't know she was going through with the abortion. She'd planned it that way, knowing he would try and talk her out of it, as he had been doing since she'd told him the news. Two blocks from the hospital she sat down on a street bench, hit with a wave of nausea. She'd looked up, and lo and behold, there was a coffee shop named Miracle Café, and she'd laughed out loud at the irony. Because wasn't her pregnancy a small miracle?

Placing her hand on her stomach as New Yorkers buzzed by her left and right, she realized either she had to eat something or else she would faint right here on this bench, so Alexis walked inside and ordered a whole wheat bagel with nonfat cream cheese, lox, and a large coffee. Then, she took a deep breath and changed her order with the waitress with amazing green eyes and a nose ring, to leave off the lox (uncooked fish) and change the large coffee to a small (too much caffeine, there were so many pregnancy rules!), and that was when Alexis let out a quiet gasp of surprise because she realized she was keeping the baby.

When posing for family pictures her mother always demanded, "Alexis, put one leg in front of the other! Now put one hand on your hip! There, now you look pretty." It was making the best of her pudgy, adolescent body, and couldn't she look at her pregnancy as a situation to make the best of? She wasn't quite sure yet how she would financially support the baby as a single mother and with Billy's medical bills streaming in, but that was why she was driving up to Connecticut today.

Since she had decided to keep "the littlest monster," as Billy referred to the baby (because he was convinced it was a Lady Gaga fan already), she'd begun speaking in her mind to it. Sometimes thinking about Noah and their fight made her feel overwhelmed, so she would try and think of other things like Billy getting better, or turning thirty. Her conversations with the littlest monster were shy; two strangers getting to know one another.

She took a lot of baths in their tiny tub, which Vanya scrubbed clean and into which she had put several bumpy octopus decals, so Alexis wouldn't slip. Her bump was tiny and hard, like a watermelon. It felt strange, like she was an actress and the baby was strapped to her body for a role. She had tiny purple lines on her hips which she put oil on every night. At first they had horrified her, but she'd grown used to them. Every day felt like a lesson in humility; it took her much longer to walk to the gym, which she went to only once a week now.

Alexis would stand in front of the mirror and run her hands over her breasts, which were still small but decidedly rounder, like puffed-up versions of themselves. She liked bathing at night, slapping the water with the flats of her palms, which made her feel oddly happy. She couldn't talk to it out loud, it felt too strange, so she would have private conversations with the baby in her head. *Hello,* she would think. *I'm your mother. Um . . . it's nice to meet you. I hope you are comfortable in there. I hope you will like me.*

At first, no matter how often Billy told her she looked fab, she still didn't believe him. She felt like everyone was staring at her on the street, thinking how fat she was. But as the weeks went on, after she heard the baby's heartbeat, felt it turn over (just once while she was folding laundry!), she stopped resenting the changes it was making on her body and secretly began feeling a tiny bit proud of her growing belly. Just a little. She found herself sticking her bump out farther than necessary while in line buying a newspaper, and catching the eye of another pregnant girl at the gym, putting her hand on her belly and rolling her eyes, earning a smile back from the other mother-to-be, as if, yes, she was going through the uncomfortable yet thrilling experience, too.

Billy also helped: "You're Posh Spice, baby. You're Heidi Klum with one of Seal's baby seals. You're Skinny Chick: the maternity version."

He had grown slightly obsessed with Heidi Klum and Seal's little family, hanging up large, colorful photographs of their three children around the apartment. "Stella will look just like their kids!" he'd say, clapping his hands together and smiling. Though she had yet to find out the gender, Billy had already decided it was a girl and named her Stella. "Stella is the queen bee of the class-room. Stella is the popular chick in high school," he would say, as if it were obvious.

The baby was the only topic that made Billy smile these days. He'd already had three rounds of chemotherapy that made his jet-black hair fall out.

Recently she found him in the shower, crouched and sobbing. At first she thought it was a cat meowing, the sound was so high-pitched and thin. "Oh, Billy!" she'd cried, opening the glass door and squatting next to him, fully clothed. The water rained down upon her face like a river current, blurring her vision. She felt her dress start to soak and tried to hold his frail body. Clumps of black hair were spread around the shower basin, looking like large black spiders.

"I was going to shave my head, to beat the cancer to it," he'd said, his voice low and wobbly against her neck. "Just last night I made a mental note to ask you to buy me a new razor, so I could do it today. But it just started fucking *falling out*."

She hadn't known what to say. All she could do was hold him. She was then three months pregnant, and felt like her whole world was caving in. Billy was getting sicker, and she missed Noah. Every week like clockwork a check would arrive. It was just a little at first, fifty or a hundred dollars. But as the lines for Off the River Ale House started stretching all the way around the block, the amounts greatly increased. Each one came with a note, pleading for her to take his calls. He'd continued to accompany Billy on half of his chemotherapy appointments. In fact, Noah and Alexis had arranged a schedule via e-mail, so that Billy never had to go alone.

"I feel like I'm the child of a joint-custody arrangement," Billy said sarcastically to Alexis one night, as they sat on the couch with each other's feet on their laps, watching *Heathers*. "Love those crazy bitches," he'd say, when she popped in the DVD.

After the first vomiting incident when she'd gotten the pregnancy test, Alexis had been virtually symptom-free. Well, symptom-free if you didn't include the weight gain, which had come on fast and furious.

"It's that little baby Seal in there, one-quarter Rastafarian," Billy would say. "He's easygoing, mon. No throwing up. No sore feet. No problems."

Alexis rolled her eyes as she watched Julia Roberts insult Cameron Diaz with: "Crème brûlée can never be Jell-O. *You* could never be Jell-O."

"Billy, just because Noah is half black doesn't mean he's Rastafarian. He's from Colorado."

He adjusted his scarf. Since losing his hair, he started wearing vintage Armani scarves tied on the side of his head like a pirate.

"Whatever you say. One love, baby. One love."

Alexis laughed, despite the fact that they were talking about Noah and talk of Noah always made her feel sad. Sad and very, very confused. Each time she opened an envelope with a check inside, accompanied by one of his stupid Post-its and boyishly messy handwriting, she felt a deep sense of confusion. She might have made a mistake, refusing to see him, turning him away. He'd been the only guy who had ever really *gotten* her. He made her laugh. He could cook. He loved her best friend. And he oozed sex appeal. What more could a woman ask for?

She was upset to the point of grinding her teeth at night. The sound was so loud she bought a mouth guard at Sports Authority, like some kind of ice-hockey player. She knew the root cause of the teeth-grinding was Noah, but she seemed unable to fix it. She'd always been stubborn; she just had to get used to the idea of being a single mom. How could she be with someone who kept pestering her to drop everything she stood for? Noah was relentless in the brief time they'd dated, hiding her scale so she couldn't find it; causing her to have to cancel workout sessions because she was lying around in bed with him into the late afternoon; cooking huge, fattening meals as he tried out different recipes for his restaurant . . . the man was clearly too different from her for it to work. Plus, even though he was working around the clock to set up the restaurant, he had a lazy, laid-back side that she didn't care for. He considered rock-climbing exercise, or walking uptown to Rollerblade in Central Park to be fun. Alexis had a very strict workout routine she'd stuck to for years, and Noah kept trying to get her out of her comfort zone. She had to admit she'd slightly enjoyed these new activities, especially when he'd taught her to yell out, "On belay!" and cupped her on the butt as she ascended the rock wall at Chelsea Piers, but she had a lot on her plate right now with Billy's illness, and she really shouldn't have been wasting time zigzagging around the city with Noah. One night in his apartment he actually got her to try smoking pot. Pot! Like those ridiculous skateboarders she'd so loathed in high school. And the awful part was she'd liked it! They'd watched *When Harry Met Sally* and giggled uncontrollably. Apparently, he would "partake in smoking the kind bud from time to time." Lying in his bed, with Oliver's warm body at her feet, smoke curling up to the ceiling, she'd felt really, truly happy. She'd relaxed. And she realized now what a mistake that was. Her columns had been slipping, the writing not as sharp. She'd been living like a child with Noah, and it was time to grow up. She'd gotten herself *pregnant,* for god's sake. Never before in her life had she acted so irresponsibly.

Billy would not leave her alone about making up with Noah. However, it was too late to repair things. Getting his friends back together was the only thing that gave Billy any of his old feistiness back; he was able to yell and coddle and charm and give Alexis the silent treatment as he made the case for why Noah was *the guy for her.* She let him badger her because it put a flush back into his cheeks.

It had been three months since the Bathroom Incident, as she thought of it. She ran her hand over her belly (it was so hard!), back and forth as she drove. Noah's restaurant had blown up into a colossal-sized success. She'd even heard rumors that TLC was courting him to do a cooking show. He didn't need Alexis Allbright and all the baggage that came with her in his life.

The lines outside the brewpub grew as summer strongly resisted fall's approach and the blacktop streets of Manhattan cooked like tar soup. The temperatures roared into the eighties. From her window she watched Noah arrive at the restaurant every morning. She was sleeping later these days, but she still set her alarm to see him pull up in his junky Subaru and hop out, Oliver leaping from the backseat and following Noah inside. He didn't know she could see him. Billy caught her watching him one day. "You really should talk to the guy, you know," he said.

The weekly checks from Noah couldn't have come at a better time. They were really hurting for money. Advertisements on *Skinny Chick* had slowed to a snail's pace. As Billy's medical bills, well . . .

The bills were what forced her back here today, right now, driving past hedges and BMWs, nannies and tennis courts, and everything else she hated most in the world that made up the town of Greenwich. Noah's checks had saved her from being thrown out of the apartment, but they were still swimming in debt. Those white envelopes with the plastic windows showing up every day in her mail made her fearful for their future.

Familiar sights swam into her vision as Alexis turned onto the street where she and Mark had grown up. Her street was named Happy Lane, which she found ironic, given the dispositions of her parents. She was wearing a black cotton maternity dress Vanya had brought home last week from Old Navy. "Of course it's black," Billy whispered when Alexis opened it. But she'd been touched.

"Thank you," she'd said to her roommate the next morning, passing her in the hallway.

"Well, I noticed you hadn't bought any maternity clothes," Vanya had answered shyly.

It was true. The idea of shopping for pants with a pouch or an Empire waist dress freaked her out, even though her little belly ball clearly hung out of her tank top at the gym, which was how Sarah had been the first person outside of home to point out her pregnancy. She was down to the last hook on her very expensive and very useless La Perla bra, and had felt shocked when she found her feet no longer fit in some of her favorite high heels.

"Holy shit!" Sarah said one day, eight months pregnant herself, her stomach sticking out like a shelf from her sculpted and toned body. "Alexis, you're knocked up!"

They were sitting on the mat, Alexis about to begin a series of military sit-ups. A woman sitting on a blue exercise ball nearby glanced at Alexis with surprise.

Tears immediately sprang to Alexis's eyes.

Seeing her friend distraught, Sarah grabbed Alexis by the arm and escorted her to the little office at the back of the gym the personal trainers shared. It was empty at the moment, and they sat down in black leather chairs facing one another.

"Alexis, honey, you can't do sit-ups when you're preggo. It's bad for the baby."

"This baby!" Alexis said, wiping her nose with the back of her hand. Staring at the glistening trail of snot, she couldn't believe how pathetic she'd become. "It is so demanding! I've gotten so . . . so fat! Sarah, I weigh a hundred and forty-five pounds, for god's sake! I'm a total heifer!"

Sarah hid her smile. "I'd noticed you gaining weight, but Alexis, you still look really great. Look on the bright side—now you have boobs! I just thought maybe you were eating differently. And besides, I don't see you as often anymore. I know you must be going through a lot with your friend so sick." She put her hand on Alexis's shoulder and squeezed.

It was true. Alexis had cut down on her private training sessions with Sarah in order to save money for Billy's medical expenses. She hadn't told him about it, and on former gym days she hid it by taking the bus to McNally Jackson Books and whittling away time curled up in a chair reading.

"Honey, it can't be that bad. The father . . . did he do bad by you? He, left?" Her pretty Latin skin flushed. "He didn't hurt you, did he? Because Aldo keeps a shotgun in the spare room, and I am not afraid to use it." Her voice turned to a whisper. "Did he hit you, Mama?"

Alexis was startled. "Oh, my god, Sarah! Nothing like that. No, we had a fight."

Sarah's eyes widened.

"No! A, um . . . verbal fight." She swiped her nose with the back of her hand again. She felt pathetic. "I got mad because he called *Skinny Chick* crazy, but I think he just meant . . . I think he just meant I was too hard on myself."

Once the words were out it was like the earth shifted underneath her feet, the clouds parted, and Alexis was able to view just how ridiculous she'd been when it came to Noah. No, he hadn't smacked her around. He hadn't walked out on her when he found out she was pregnant. In fact, it was the opposite: *she'd refused to see him.*

So yesterday, around the time she realized she and Billy were fifty thousand dollars in debt, she'd called and left Noah a message.

"Hi, Noah, it's me." Then, realizing he had probably moved on and could be dating someone new, and therefore not know who "me" was, she swallowed and took a deep breath. "It's Alexis. I want to talk. So, um, call me. If you want."

She'd checked her phone every five minutes since, but the screen had remained frustratingly blank.

Billy had two more weeks of this latest round of chemotherapy before Aldo would run tests to see if the cancer had finally run back to whatever hell it had sprung from. Billy had no idea of the extent of the costs (he thought insurance covered everything), as Alexis had intercepted the mail and hidden the bills in her pillowcase. He'd already lost his sarcastic smile, and his hair. She didn't want him to lose his soul as well.

So she was going home. Wasn't there an expression that you can never go home again? Yet here she was, turning into her parents' circular cobblestone driveway and gazing up at their ugly McMansion.

It hadn't changed much in three years. Still the same sandy

brick color with turrets everywhere, a manicured lawn that her father paid Mexican immigrants to care for, and a six-car garage that held three cars: her father's Jaguar, which he drove to his firm in town, a Mercedes her mother hadn't driven since she got her third DUI a year ago, and a beloved, beat-up Volvo that Mark had restored that golden summer he joined the Marines. It was ironic: a six-car garage for a fractured family in which only one person drove.

She pulled the car up to the front door, opting to leave it there as a visitor and not pull it into the garage. Her hands were restless birds in her lap. She wasn't planning on staying long, and she didn't like leaving Billy for more than a few hours, even though there were days when he would grow angry and shout for her to get out of the house and stop hovering over him. He seemed calmer when Noah took him to chemo; Alexis felt awkward and stilted in the waiting room, where several other cancer patients and their families also sat in tan leather chairs. When she closed her eyes the green tiles on the walls of the room were imprinted behind her lids, the smell of rubbing alcohol lingering in her nostrils.

"I know this freaks you out," Billy would say dryly. "Just go outside and grab lunch or something." Shamefaced, she'd retreat to the little diner around the corner with the words of the menu blurring under her tears.

She wished she were stronger, like Noah, who was a legend in the treatment center for bringing the staff his special beer every week. "He cracks me the fuck up," Billy would say after Noah dropped him off at the apartment after chemo. Alexis wanted to crack Billy the fuck up, but instead the place made her nauseous; she wanted to blame the pregnancy, but she knew it was more than that. Seeing Billy with no hair and an IV in his skinny arm depressed her.

Her mother answered the door, which was surprising. Alexis searched her memory and couldn't remember a single time her mother answered the door. It had usually been done by their maid.

"What happened to Elsa?" Alexis asked as she was drawn in for a big wet kiss on the cheek. *She's switched brands of vodka,* Alexis thought immediately. Her poison had always been Stoli, but this smelled . . . drier. Less sweet. The scent of alcohol was intense; ever since she got pregnant it was like she had Spider-Man sense. The smell of beer being brewed at Off the River Ale House drifting up into her window made her wistful. It was as if a part of Noah were extending itself, reaching up to her, caressing her each day. She thought about the message she'd left him, and squeezed the cell phone through her purse. He still hadn't called back. What did she expect? She'd given him the silent treatment for three months and lost her chance with him. He only sent money in case she'd kept their child, she guessed. She felt overwhelmingly tired.

Her mother waved a manicured hand around in the air. She'd been a real beauty once; her nickname in college had been "Steel Magnolia," since Bunny Allbright (formerly known as Bunny Montague) had been born and raised in Nashville, Tennessee. She had modeled to pay her way through college. Upon graduating, she landed the Cadillac of husbands at a polo match Alexis's father was playing in. He'd been captain of a national team that traveled throughout the country, and Bunny went with her girlfriends to watch the game.

Alexis never saw her parents' marriage as any great love story, but once, when she was ten and Mark thirteen, she learned that her father had once felt differently. It was during a Christmas Eve party, and Alexis and Mark were given the jobs of greeting guests at the door and bringing their coats and capes upstairs to be carefully placed in the master bedroom. Her arms laden with fur and leather, camel hair and silk, Alexis overheard the tail end of a conversation between her dad and one of the lawyers in his firm, a young up-and-comer named Steve Rubin, who'd recently become engaged to a woman he'd seen in a crowd at the Macy's Thanksgiving Day Parade.

"I met Bunny in a similar way," she'd heard her father say, followed by the deep inhalation as he took a puff of his cigar. It was a smell that still made her nostalgic—when her father had smoked cigars everything had been good at home. He'd quit with no explanation after Mark died.

Alexis paused in the doorway, her arms heavy.

"How's that, Mr. Allbright?"

"Please, call me John. Saw her at a polo match, back when I played. Down in Nashville." He said the name of the town in a faux-southern drawl, which both men laughed at. Listening, Alexis frowned.

"She was a beauty. I'll tell you what, Steve. Saw her in the stands, wearing this ridiculous hat, must have been a mile wide. In it were little plastic birds of different colors. She had curly blond hair down her back, and big blue eyes. A tiny nose, and long swan neck. The longest legs this side of the Mississippi. I took one look at her and thought, *I'm going to marry that woman.*"

"And you did, sir."

"Sure enough. But first I had to ask her daddy's permission, they do it very formally in the South, and wasn't he a hard-nosed prick . . ."

Their voices trailed off as they walked into another room, and Alexis scurried up the stairs, nearly bumping into Mark, who was on his way down. He'd winked at her; Mark was always up to some form of mischief himself, and encouraged that trait in others.

It was the tone in her father's voice when he'd called her mother a "beauty." She'd almost never seen them touch or act affectionate with one another, and things had grown worse (so much worse) when Mark died, but this was proof that once they'd been in love. Her mother had been so beautiful that she'd caught herself a husband just by wearing a big hat, her straw-blond hair softly blowing in the warm breeze on a hazy southern afternoon.

But now Bunny was speaking, her voice so crisp and clear anyone other than Alexis wouldn't know she'd been drinking steadily since rising from bed that morning:

"I fired Elsa yesterday. She was hiding my medicine from me.

Can you imagine that? Paying someone, and they are hiding your belongings."

Her blue eyes were wide and still startlingly beautiful, like looking into the Mediterranean and seeing clear through to the bottom, but Alexis could see the broken capillaries around her irises.

Alexis strode past her mother, setting her purse down on a bench in the hallway, which was white marble and cold like a mausoleum. The place needed carpets to warm the floor. Drapes to lend the large windows charm. Her mother's decorating style was bleak.

Her heart raced just entering the front hallway, seeing the familiar yet alien surroundings.

"Mom, Elsa was probably trying to help. And how could you fire her? I've known her my whole life."

"Well, you haven't exactly been around here making decisions lately, dearie. It's just me alone here running this household." She sighed dramatically, putting a hand up to her forehead.

Alexis sighed. She'd have to speak to her father about sending Elsa severance.

"How are you doing with the pills?" she asked her mother blandly.

Bunny let out air in a raspberry and laughed. "Alexis! You always had such an imagination. What pills?"

In addition to drinking, her mother popped a mixture of antidepressants and muscle relaxers like they were M&M's.

Alexis tried talking to her father about it a week after the funeral.

He'd been in his study, a manly cave at the back of the house Bunny once paid a decorator a hundred grand to furnish. The walls were a dark green topped with a banner of eagles and American flags. The desk was the size of a pool table. Two leather armchairs framed the front. After knocking to speak to her father, Alexis sank into one of them and leaned forward, putting her hands on her knee. The room had intimidated her since she was a child; she and Mark were restricted from entering. Once, while playing hide-and-seek, Mark hid under the desk and it had taken Alexis two hours to find him; she simply couldn't believe he'd had the nerve to choose the spot.

One silver-framed photograph sat on her father's desk, taken in the eighties, with his arm thrown around Ronald Reagan, who came to Greenwich for a charity golf tournament her father's law firm hosted annually. Mark's All-American football trophy stood to the right of the photograph.

Her father had worked the afternoon of the funeral. It was how he coped with things. Alexis knew this, and wished she could talk to him about it. *I understand you!* she'd say. *I get it. I know you throw yourself into work because it's the only way you can deal with Mark being . . . Mark being not here anymore. I'm the same way.*

But instead, there she had been, twenty-three and tongue-tied. He'd looked up after a few minutes, surprised she was there, and blinked a few times as though he'd forgotten he had a daughter.

"Yes, Alexis?" He removed his tortoise-shell glasses. Behind them, his eyes looked tired.

"I wanted to talk to you about Mom."

It was hard to get the words out. If she wasn't talking to her father about the law, he seemed uninterested in holding a conversation with her. She relished the tidbits of information she learned at the firm where her father had helped her gain an internship. "Dad, today I assisted in court!" Or, "I helped write a brief!" And they'd sit in his study and discuss her day. It was the only time in her life she had his full attention. He wasn't a cruel man; at least he hadn't been then. His own parents hadn't spoken much to him, they thought children should be seen and not heard; thus, he saw his children as separate entities from himself, who would maneuver through life independently.

"What about your mother?" he'd said, frowning at the distraction from his work.

It came out in a rush of garbled speech. "She's drinking too much. And why does she need to take Xanax?" She rushed ahead. "Also, she hasn't been going to her tennis lessons. I heard her on the phone canceling with the club."

Silence filled the room.

Her father sighed. He leaned back in his chair and crossed his legs. "Alexis, your mother is a grown woman who just lost her only son. It's not up to me to tell her how to live her life."

Alexis balled up her hands into fists. "I think she's depressed."

He swept all the papers off his desk in one quick move. "Of course she's depressed!" he bellowed.

Alexis watched the white documents fall like snow. She swallowed. "I just thought that maybe if you talked to her—"

"Alexis, I'm only going to say this once. Right now you need to be studying for your LSATs. Not skulking around the house following your mother's every move. She'll come around when she is ready. She'll . . . shake this thing once she's done mourning him." He was unable to say Mark's name.

Over the next few months, she'd watched Bunny slowly get worse. At first she preferred to not get out of bed until noon, and had Elsa leave a tray of food outside her door. Alexis would hear the door open and slam shut minutes later, a bagel with one bite taken, eggs barely touched. The gritty sound her shaker made as she mixed her first drink of the day would echo through the large house, the noise reverberating in the high ceilings. Even to this day, when Alexis visited Billy at work and someone fixed a cocktail, she'd cringe.

"You know what pills," she said to her mother now. "And what are you drinking these days, Mom, still a vodka tonic with a few Xanax thrown in as chasers?" The house had a morbid hush, like a funeral parlor entryway.

Bunny wore a pretty blue silk robe. *Did she even get dressed anymore?* She gathered the front sections together, trying on a mask of righteousness. The blue veins in her hands stood out against her pearly white skin. "You don't set foot in this house or call your mother for three years and now you've just come to insult me?"

Alexis sighed, walking into the kitchen, which had a ten-thousand-dollar fancy hooded stove that looked as though it hadn't been used since whenever Elsa left, and poured herself a glass of orange juice from the fridge.

"You're hurting yourself, Mom. Did you get the brochures I sent you?"

Alexis mailed her mother Alcoholics Anonymous pamphlets a few months ago. She had to attend a meeting at a church on the Lower East Side, and she'd felt embarrassed the entire time. She'd seen a sign on the subway that read DOES A LOVED ONE SUFFER FROM ALCOHOL ABUSE?

Bunny sniffed. She dug her big toe, painted fire hydrant red, against one of the kitchen tiles like a child. "Enough about me. I want to hear about your life, now." Her eyes filled with tears. "I miss you so much."

Alexis's heart turned over. She let her mother tentatively touch her arm, and then make small, rubbing circles. She felt a fluttering in the bottom of her stomach, and thought briefly, *I just felt the baby move.*

She turned toward Bunny. "Well, I didn't exactly feel welcome here, you know. Dad told me when I quit the law firm to leave and never come back."

"Oh, honey, he didn't mean it. You know how he gets." She ever so quickly glanced toward one of the cabinets, the one she'd always stored her bottles in, as if hiding them behind the spices were somehow keeping everyone from knowing she had a problem. It was the slightest of glances, just a flinch of her head, really, but Alexis caught it and sighed. Would even this moment be ruined by her drinking?

"Mom, I'm pretty sure Dad meant what he said." She took a sip of her juice and immediately regretted skipping lunch; the acidity of the fruit went right through her and she burped.

"Say excuse me," her mother said absentmindedly.

Alexis felt anger rising and tried to suppress it. "Excuse me," she said sarcastically, though Bunny didn't pick up on it.

Bunny clapped her hands together. "So, how are you, kitten? How's life in the Big Apple?"

Can she really not tell I'm pregnant? Alexis thought. *Don't mothers have a sixth sense about these things?*

"Well, I don't know if you got my e-mail, but I was on *Oprah* back in December." She stared out the window. The elementary school she and Mark had attended long ago had just let out, and a gaggle of pushing and shoving children flowed down the sidewalk like a river. One's backpack had a zebra's face on it, its mouth a zipper.

Bunny's eyes widened. "Noooooo, I didn't know. That's so wonderful, Lexa!"

Lexa was a nickname her mother had called her as a child. Alexis had been five, and declared she no longer wanted to go by Alexis. That she would only answer to the name Lexa. Bunny had been the single family member who agreed to call her by it, and hearing it now made Alexis afraid she might cry. She took a ragged breath.

"Right. Well, I left three messages with Elsa about it, with the date and times. I even called her when they showed a rerun."

"Oh, honey, she probably told me and I forgot. You know how bad I am about remembering things. And I've never watched much television."

Right, because it's every day that your only child is on Oprah.

"Where's Dad?"

"At work. He should be home soon."

"What are you guys having for dinner?" Her stomach rumbled.

Bunny peeked toward the cabinet again, the movement ever so slight. "Oh, we just grab any old thing these days." Her southern accent had sprung forth. "Thing" turned into "thang." She cupped her still-pretty face in her hands. "But I want to hear more about you, Lexa, darling. Have you got a young man?"

I did. He would have done anything for me and I asked him to leave. I had a man, and now I don't. Oh, and he's also the father of my child, but doesn't know I kept the baby.

"Sort of," Alexis said. She went to the refrigerator and found an old heel of bread, and, sitting down, began munching on it. Her parents had *millions* of dollars and never a scrap of food in the fridge. How ironic.

"Tell me about sort of. Sort of doesn't earn you a wedding ring on that lonely finger, honey."

Alexis rolled her eyes. It had always been like this with Bunny. It didn't matter when she was taking college-level classes while still in high school, or that she graduated in the top of her class at Columbia. Her mother had shown no interest when Alexis started *Skinny Chick,* and it *certainly* seemed to bore Bunny Allbright that her daughter had been on *Oprah.*

Alexis had an odd moment when she almost blurted out, *I'm pregnant!* but she knew Bunny's glee would soon be followed by concern that she wasn't married. When her father got home the scorn and contempt would be overwhelming, and she'd be right back where she started from three years ago, kicked out of the house, penniless, and alone. An image of Billy vomiting on the bus home after a particularly brutal round of chemo last week steeled her nerves. She was here for him, after all. For once, she had to focus on someone other than herself.

But her mother was waiting, her eyes bright and glassy. She lifted a hand, which was shaking with tremors, to push back a lock of Alexis's thin blond hair that had fallen into her eyes. Alexis flinched. A look of sorrow passed over Bunny's face, and Alexis regretted her impulse.

"I met this nice guy named Noah," she said, wanting to rectify the awkward moment. She looked around the room, her eyes fixing on a row of lamps of different colors and shades on the console.

"He owns a restaurant. It's a microbrewery as well. It's actually gotten pretty popular," she said with a note of pride in her voice. "I helped him find the space and fix up the inside. He's got these huge photographs on the walls . . ." She held her arms out to show how wide the pictures were and felt another nudge in her lower belly, as though the baby were reminding her it was here. "He went around the neighborhood and took pictures of some of the people that eat in the restaurant, and then had them blown up poster-sized and glossy. The space is gorgeous." She smiled for the first time since entering her house. "Naomi Watts had a beer in there the other day, with her family."

"Are you two pretty serious?" Bunny examined her already-perfect manicure.

"We were. We kind of had a falling-out."

Alexis's mother patted her arm. Again, the slight tremble. Bunny was holding out on pouring herself a drink in front of her daughter, and Alexis was strangely touched by this.

"Y'all will be making up in no time. Beautiful young girl like you? How could he stay angry for long?"

She wanted to say that she was the one who had been angry. That she'd ignored his calls, e-mails, love letters, and cards. Thrown away the most special thing that had ever happened to her because of her own stubbornness, which surely came from her father's gene pool. That she'd called him and left a message, but he hadn't returned it and probably never would. She wanted to tell her mother everything, and be held like she had been as a child, but Bunny was already getting up, gathering her robe around her large, still-pert breasts.

Suddenly it was as if she'd seen her daughter for the first time.

"You've put on some weight, darling." She said it as a fact, not an insult, but still the words burned through Alexis. She'd done a lot of thinking since Billy got sick, and there was Noah's encouragement that she put on weight and relax about religiously weighing herself and working out in such a harsh, exhausting way. Standing in her mother's kitchen and ruminating about food, Alexis suddenly realized how odd it was that Bunny had always eaten like a bird, and had such an aversion and outright hostility toward food.

Alexis couldn't have felt more different now.

Noah's cooking brought her house together; his spicy chili, oddly enough, was the only thing Billy felt like eating when his nausea was overwhelming. Noah coaxed Vanya out of the dark depths of her black room, he fed the homeless man who squatted in front of his restaurant, who in turn washed Noah's windows each morning. His arrival made a tornado of change in her rigidly structured life. Alexis grew up thinking food was the enemy, but something in the past few months had shifted. She had to eat to nourish the baby growing within her. That was a fact. She'd tried her old eating habits but Billy had called her OB/GYN and tattled on her, and Alexis was given a very strict and scary lecture for half an hour by her doctor. Besides, when she tried skipping meals or eating just half of what was on her plate, which was her tried and trusty rule for staying slim, she'd been hit with overwhelming sickness, almost as if the baby Noah had made inside her was echoing its father's thoughts that Alexis should eat more. So . . . she ate. And it surprised her how happy that act made her.

She blinked. Her mother was still looking at her. "Yeah—yes. I've put on some weight." She smiled thinly. "But the boy I was telling you about? He likes the extra curves."

"Oh," Bunny said, looking confused. Curves were not something valued around Greenwich, where all the wives had personal trainers, and skinny was always "in."

"Well, sugar, I'm going to run out and pick up something for dinner, since I assume you're staying and not running off on me again?"

"Sure. I'll stay and see Dad. Besides, I have to talk to him." Alexis walked over to the dishwasher and opened it, setting down her glass on one of the plastic rungs.

"That's settled, then." Bunny pushed her tall, thin frame away from the counter and stood. Her robe fell slightly open and Alexis could see her ribs, their ridges showing through her skin. *She's like a dying swan,* Alexis thought.

Suddenly her mother's arms were around her. Bunny hugged her daughter. "I'm so damn glad you're here. I get lonely, you know."

Alexis hugged her awkwardly, feeling the soft silk of the robe beneath her palm. "It's nice to see you, too, Mom." There was so much left unsaid, and the words hung in the air so heavily for

Alexis that she could almost see them, typewritten letters in a dark font.

While Bunny showered upstairs, and, Alexis suspected, took a few nips of booze, Alexis walked around the entryway and first floor, remembering.

She trailed her hand on the cool wall her mother painted a dark, muted silver, the color of a thunderstorm rolling over the ocean. Nearly all the walls were painted in this color, which gave a visitor the feeling of weightlessness.

Photographs of her and Mark were diagonally hung on the winding staircase off the entrance leading to the second floor. She walked up three steps and leaned her spine against the base of the banister, where it curved into a snail's shell. Mark never went through that traditional teenage ugly stage; he'd had twenty-twenty vision and the most metal he'd had to put in his mouth was a small retainer he'd worn at night for a year. There were many shots of him coming off the football field, his helmet (number 23) thrown up in the air triumphantly, his sandy blond hair sweaty and pushed off his forehead, his smile huge and infectious, his muscular body throbbing with life.

Alexis's pictures told a different story of adolescence. She'd been a gangly, slightly chubby, awkward teenager, not getting her period or (small!) breasts until three weeks before her sixteenth birthday. She knew this was often the story of famous supermodels and celebrities, that the very sleekness they were now famous for had once been unattractive to others. Tyra Banks often commented on how skinny and ugly people had thought she was.

She peered closer at a picture of herself in an unflattering J.Crew striped sweater that made her long neck look like a bird reaching for a worm from its mother. Her smile looked strained. The look in her eyes was, *Please like me!* She scoffed now, but stopped when she saw that all the pictures of Mark were shiny. She could see her own reflection, as if she were the ghost standing beside him instead of the other way around. When she straightened and surveyed the rest of *her* pictures—ten years old with buck teeth and pink Coke-bottle glasses, thirteen with a full set of braces (but at least wearing contact lenses now), midstride on the lawn at Columbia accepting her college diploma, sitting at a desk and looking serious at her law firm summer internship—the frames with pictures of her were dusty. The old familiar sick feeling rushed over her, and she had to literally put her hand on her lower stomach to catch her breath. It wasn't that her parents didn't love her; it was that they loved Mark more, always had, even with him dead.

He'd been the golden boy. It had been that way when they were kids; Mark the easygoing charmer who was always throwing a football in the backyard with their father, or willing to go to the mall and shop for a dress with Bunny. Alexis was the brooder, her bedroom door closed, her nose stuck in a book night and day.

He'd had dyslexia, which had forged the bond between him and Bunny, who had spent countless hours side-by-side with him playing books on tape, helping him write his papers all the way through middle school and even high school. If Alexis had one image from her childhood burned into her retinas it was Mark and her mother's butterscotch heads bent as Bunny helped him with homework, the warm golden glow of his desk lamp casting shadows over their bodies, the sounds of easy laughter as they worked through *Hamlet,* or the scratching sounds of pencil on paper while figuring out algebra.

She'd excelled on her own, earning straight A's without a lick of help, though both her parents had offered. She was in all honors classes, she was the head of the cheerleading squad, and she got into Columbia with a small scholarship. She'd done very well at the law firm internship, earning high praise, which, if it made its way up to her father, he'd never acknowledged.

Looking at another picture of Mark in uniform, taken when he'd completed boot camp, Alexis remembered before he'd died they'd spoken of taking a road trip together. He had been to Iraq earlier that year, and this second tour was going to be his last. She'd sat on his bed cross-legged, tired from studying for finals, and asked him what he planned on doing after he came back home. "Meet some nice woman and make her my wife," he'd said, grinning. What a a wicked smile he had! It could calm any tense situation. "I was actually thinking it might be nice to drive across the country, see the South, and the West Coast, then start classes, cause the Marines will pay tuition. Would you want to come with?"

She'd thought about it, playing with a twenty-five-pound weight he had resting on his dresser. They'd been eating bowls of chicken soup, slurping and talking. She could still remember the rich smell of the broth. "You know Dad would never let me," she'd said. "I'm supposed to be studying for the LSATs and then starting law school."

"You'll have the rest of your life to study for the LSATs," Mark had said. He chucked her on her chin. "I'll talk to Dad. Promise me when I get back you'll come cross-country with me. We'll rent some shitty motor home and eat beans for all three meals and just drive and fart all day, it will be awesome."

Alexis had laughed. Oh, the pleasure of Mark wanting to spend time with her! He always had been that way, even when they were teenagers. Never acting too cool to be with her, driving her to school each day, bringing her to parties his friends were throwing. He was proud of her.

"I promise," she'd said, eyes glittering with the promise of the trip, how much fun it would be to really have her brother back for good. When he came home from the first Iraq tour his light shone a little less brightly, he laughed just a tiny bit less easily. He had sand in his backpack and boots. She'd find it in the shower; it was as though Iraq had followed him home at the end of each tour. He'd been twenty-five when he died.

The last picture on the wall was one of his casket draped with an American flag. "So morbid, Mom," she imagined Mark would say, teasing Bunny. Alexis was the first to hear the news that he'd died. It had been the weekend, so when the doorbell rang Alexis was the only one home; Bunny was at a tennis lesson, and her father worked most Saturday mornings. She was supposed to be studying but she'd been hungry, and wandered downstairs to dig up a snack: celery and peanut butter. She was filling the celery stalks like small green canoes when the chimes of the doorbell rang. *Elsa will answer it,* she thought. It rang again. She suddenly remembered Elsa was away in El Salvador visiting her mother. Shit. She padded over to the door.

She was wearing Mark's blue striped pajama bottoms and a white tank top. The top was thin, but when the doorbell rang a third time she realized she didn't have time to grab a coat from the closet so she swung open the door.

There were three officers standing on the porch, their hats in their hands. *Mark can't be dead because in the movies it's always two guys,* Alexis thought, feeling a temporary relief at this inner proclamation.

"Hello," she said.

"Are you Bunny Allbright?" one asked. He couldn't be older than twenty and was short and muscular. *He must have been a wrestler.* She felt sorry for him immediately, to be her own age and be given this job. She wondered why he was in the States and not fighting overseas. He had red hair and freckles, and she wondered if he'd been teased about them in high school.

"That's my mom," she said.

The three men looked at one another. The oldest one, in his forties, seemed to be in charge. "May we come in and wait for her?" he asked respectfully.

She didn't say anything, but stepped aside and held the door. She gripped it so hard she later found a splinter shaped like a comma dug in her palm. The third serviceman was tall and well built, with chiseled features, messy brown hair, and full lips. Alexis felt him scan her body as he passed. It was lightning-quick, but she felt it nonetheless, as he kept his eyes averted from her the rest of the time he was in her house.

The three men sat on the white leather couch across from Alexis, their legs crossed, hats beside them. They didn't looked hurried or uncomfortable. They were trained for this. Their shoes shone, and their fingernails were clean. For some reason, focusing on their clean-cut appearances was the only thing that kept Alexis from screaming.

"Look. Just tell me," Alexis said. "Tell me what happened." Her voice wavered on "happened," and she squared her shoulders to fight it. She dug her fingers into the leather of the chair she was sitting on.

It was the older one who spoke. She appreciated this later, that he didn't treat her as a child, or tell her he had to wait until her parents got home, those were his orders. He looked Alexis right in the eye, and she thought what an unusual color they were, nearly purple, but they were kind.

Each word he spoke was like a tiny injury to her body: roadside IED, six others killed, three lives saved by Mark throwing himself on top of them, Mark a national hero to receive the Medal of Honor for gallantry at the risk of his life above and beyond the call of duty while engaged in an action against an enemy of the United States . . .

They stayed three hours. Alexis fixed them a plate of cheese and crackers, even though they said they were just fine, thank you. She also brought out three bottles of VitaminWater, which she placed on the table and then nearly collapsed, remembering Mark teasing her about purchasing it just a few months ago: "You know they don't really put all the vitamins in there that you need in a day," he'd said.

"They do, too! It says it right there on the label."

"Oh, Alexis, you are so gullible," and he'd put her in a headlock, mussing up her hair, and she'd punched him in the gut, which was like hitting a brick wall.

The red-haired one caught her, gently helping her sit back down. She'd finally put on *Wheel of Fortune* and the four of them watched it in silence, the men never trying to get comfortable, sitting rigidly and straight-backed. She felt like pulling out her hair the entire time, the feeling was so intense she finally sat on her hands.

When her father returned, it was Alexis who told him, an unintended affliction, which she would forever after regret. It was as if by this simple act she'd somehow made Mark's death her fault in John Allbright's eyes. She'd been the first person to deal the blow that would change everything. After she spoke to her father quietly she walked with him to the living room, where the three men had stood, saluting him. They spoke to him as they had to Alexis, matter-of-fact and quick. There was no beating around the bush. Her father nodded, thanked them for coming. "I will inform my wife, gentlemen," he said, as they turned and walked briskly out the door.

Her mother had needed to be sedated. Alexis sat on the stairs like she had as a child and listened to her being informed. Bunny screamed just once, "No!" and fainted. Their family doctor came to the house, administering the first dosage of sleeping medication she was still hooked on three years later. Alexis hadn't thought doctors still made house calls; it felt archaic and absurd. That it was her family that needed such an extravagance, or called for such an unwanted luxury.

Her father flew alone to Boston to collect Mark's body. The Marines held a ceremony at the airport. Alexis saw a photograph of it in the newspaper. There was an image of her father, standing stone-faced and grim among the fluttering flags on cars, the small white airplane landing behind him blurry. Alexis carefully cut the picture out and folded it inside one of her books.

Her father only cried at night. The sound was ragged, like a scuba diver coming up for air after a plunge into the ocean. Wet and ugly. It was more obscene to her than anything. Her father crying was such a strange phenomenon, a private and intimate sound. More intimate than sex. Her parents slept in separate bedrooms and his was directly above Alexis's, the sound filtering in through an air-conditioning vent in the wall. Alexis sat next to it and tried to read at night sometimes, her hand on the vent, an attempt to soothe.

Mark was buried during a snowstorm. The older, silver-haired officer and the short wrestler-type were there, holding the American flag that would be presented to Bunny. The governor of Connecticut attended, along with his pretty wife, who sobbed softly into her handkerchief the entire time, the sound like a baby bird chirping. *How odd,* Alexis thought at the time. *Here is this woman who never met Mark, and she is crying. And I cannot.* When the rifles went off in unison her mother pinched her arm.

The coldness had seeped into Alexis's bones, and the snow continued to fall. It was beautiful. Like confetti twinkling down on an empty stage. She'd thought of Mark teaching her how to snowboard on a trip to New Hampshire when she was nine, how he'd skied down the bunny slope with her again and again until she mastered it, their faces red and chapped.

Now she turned the door handle to his room. Bunny had turned it into a shrine. There were photographs of Mark in and out of uniform, condolence letters from former President George W. Bush, him and Alexis as kids, eating an ice-cream cone, a big splotch of green mint on his white Hanes T-shirt. He was missing a front tooth, his arm slung around Alexis. Her eyes welled up looking at it. He'd been so easy, even as a kid. In many ways Alexis was more like her dad than he was, so stiff, her emotions kept bottled inside. Mark was the opposite, like the sun had fallen in love with him and followed him wherever he went.

Alexis touched the gunmetal-gray weight that still resided on top of his dresser, the same weight she'd been playing with the day she'd promised him the cross-country trip. His deodorant had fallen off his nightstand and still lay on the floor, like a giant red bug. Football trophies spread across his dresser. Everything in here was silent and gleaming, as though someone (probably Elsa) dusted daily.

Alexis lay down on top of his red and blue plaid comforter, and stared at the ceiling. The bed felt soft beneath her. On the wall was his surfboard, long and off-white and sleek. Once after surfing in Rhode Island with friends, he'd come to dinner with seaweed in his hair and it had made her father laugh, changing the whole shape of his face.

Outside the window the wind picked up, and she noticed some of the leaves had orange tips. The seasons were shifting again, but Mark wouldn't be here to see it. The three years that had passed felt like three seconds. She felt a weight on her chest that made breathing unbearable. Just then she felt another nudge from within.

A tear streamed down Alexis's cheek. She wiped off the wetness, surprised still at the deep well of her emotions lately. It was as if she'd been saving up all her tears in a jar for quite some time, and it was now tipping over and pouring out.

"I feel you, baby," she whispered aloud in the empty room. The droning sound of a lawnmower started up outside. "I can feel you." She suddenly wished for a boy, and thought how much Mark would have loved him, carrying him around under his arm like a football. She would find out the gender in a week.

She heard the front door open and close, the sounds of heavy leather loafers treading across the marble floor in the front hall. She leaped off Mark's bed and smoothed down the blankets so there were no ripples. She'd slipped her boots off and quickly bent down to put them back on, zipping up the sides.

She leaned over the banister and called into the front hallway. "Dad?"

A few seconds of silence. Then he walked slowly out of his office, set down his briefcase, and stared up at Alexis. His hair had gone completely white since the last time she'd seen him. A former polo player and Marine, he was still thick in the chest and had strong forearms, one with an anchor tattoo that he kept covered with high-thread-count button-downs. Bunny picked out suits for him, and they were always excellently tailored. He was a handsome man, with a strong jaw like Mark's and the same Roman nose, but he had none of Mark's warmth or charm in his face.

"I thought we agreed you were going to not come back here," John Allbright said.

"Nice to see you, too, Dad."

She walked down the stairs, refusing to show how afraid she was. Her footsteps gave off an unpleasant clicking sound as she descended.

"Well?" he asked. The gold in his Marines ring glinted under the light.

"There's something I wanted to talk to you about."

He raised an eyebrow.

"It's about money," she said, reaching the bottom step and staying on it so that she would be at the same height as him, not giving him the upper hand.

He smirked. "Knew you'd run out of it eventually. It was inevitable. 'Send the girl a check,' your mother kept saying. As if you'd learn anything that way."

She burned with humiliation. *Billy,* she thought. *I'm doing this for Billy.* "Er, yes. You're right, Dad. I certainly have had some difficult times over the last few years, going at it on my own. But *Skinny Chick* is actually doing really well, I have three million subscribers and I was recently on *Oprah*—"

She stood up straighter. Squared her shoulders.

He held up a hand as though she were a small bug to swat away. "Enough. Get to the point. How much?"

Her mother came in the front door just then, a mix of Chanel No. 5 and vodka trailing behind her. She took off a long white camel-hair coat and flung it onto a chair dramatically as she strode to the kitchen. Alexis realized she must have had a car service take her grocery shopping, as a tall, thin man wearing a dark blue cap and a nervous expression followed her, carrying brown paper bags. She'd been so lost in thought in Mark's old room she hadn't heard the front door close.

"You two can talk business after dinner," Bunny trilled, her southern accent deeper when she was drunk. "We're having penne à la vodka with chicken!" She was wearing a deep orange silk dress, her long hair curled and pinned in a ballerina bun on the top of her head. *She is still so beautiful,* Alexis thought. As usual, she was overdressed.

Her father glanced at his Rolex. "How much time do I have, Bun? There are some papers I wanted to go through."

She made a *tsk* sound. "No time at all. The food's already been prepared. I just have to pop it onto plates! Isn't that wonderful?"

Alexis covered her smile with her hand. Her mother was famous for going to various restaurants in town and having them cook dinner, which she would then bring home and nonchalantly serve up as though every housewife did this. Her dad seemed to be trying not to smile as well, there was just a brief flicker of amusement on his stone face, and Alexis shared a moment with him in which she thought things might just be fine after all. Their eyes locked and a mutual frustration yet deep love for Bunny crossed between them. It was over before Alexis could be sure it had happened. John Allbright turned and strode into the kitchen.

Alexis followed him and sat down, glad to be off her feet again. They were starting to swell slightly from all the extra water weight. She reached down to rub her ankle under the boot.

"Up," Bunny said, shooing Alexis with a spatula.

"What?" Alexis asked. Oh, right. No one was allowed to sit in Mark's chair after he died. She'd forgotten about this rule.

"Mom, he's been dead three years. I'm sure Mark wouldn't mind."

Shocked silence hung in the air like a car wreck. Disappointment dripped down the walls. No one said a word. Her father picked up a section of *The Wall Street Journal* from the table and began perusing it. Befuddled, her mother grabbed the wrong plates, the crystal ones instead of the everyday ones they'd always used, and began serving up the pasta, using tongs to place small clumps of salad on each plate, her emotions tuned into a high key as the metal tongs scraped against the crystal plates.

"Apologize to your mother," her father said, his voice calm and low from behind his newspaper.

Alexis stared at the print. There was a story about a woman who was making a small fortune selling off her shoe collection. She had over five thousand shoes. The photograph was from above, with her surrounded by a plethora of pumps in different colors.

"Dad, I didn't say anything wrong. I knew Mark just as well as you did. He wouldn't mind me sitting in his chair. He wasn't some-one who cared about things like that."

John slammed his fist down on the table, making Alexis jump. "You've been god knows where doing god knows what. Your mother is allowed to mourn her only son any way she wants. Apologize."

Alexis's eyes filled with tears of anger. "I wasn't just twiddling my thumbs, Dad. I was in New York starting a blog that is loved by millions of girls! I was paying for my own rent, my own ex-penses. And I wasn't here, because you kicked me out, remember? You said if I didn't go to law school I should leave and never come back. Those were your exact words."

Her father's voice was cool, which was somehow scarier than if he'd shouted. "I said if you wanted to throw away your life, be my guest. I had your inheritance check ready for you when you turned twenty-one. Instead you made poor choices, Alexis."

She bit her lip to keep from crying. Bunny served dinner. Alexis started eating. She hated herself for doing so, wishing she could do something drastic and throw the plate down and storm out, but in reality she was starving and starting to feel light-headed. She had to eat. She had a baby to feed. Bunny made idle chitchat in that chirpy, mindless way she always did, something about a neighbor who had a groundhog problem in her front yard, a new mailman who gave her the creeps, a birdhouse she installed in the backyard, the cardinals and blue jays she'd seen.

Bunny stood and began clearing the plates, the sound violently loud in the silent kitchen.

"Thanks, Mom," Alexis said.

"You're welcome, dear," her mother said, fixing the comb in her hair. She proceeded to place the dirty dishes in the sink and then stare at them as if she were confused. "Oh, shucks. I think I'll have to ask Elsa back after all."

"I'm waiting for you to tell me why you're here," her father said finally, putting down his newspaper. "If you're in some kind of trouble . . ."

A hysterical giggle escaped Alexis's lips, which earned her a frown. She certainly *was* in some kind of trouble, wasn't she? Pregnant and not married, wasn't that, like, the definition of "trouble" since the dawn of time? But *that* particular trouble was not why she'd come here today.

She looked down at the table. "Billy is sick," she said quietly.

"Billy who, darling?" Bunny called out from the sink. She'd picked up a green sponge and was staring at it like it might bite her hand. "Is that one of your New York City friends?"

"What's he got, the virus?" John Allbright asked. Unbelievably, he chuckled, wiping his impeccably shaved chin with his cloth napkin. Her mother let out a twitter, though whether it was following along in the conversation and therefore contextual or was random, one couldn't know.

And then something cracked deep inside Alexis. It was like a volcano that had weakened over time and now the gash was quickly widening and the red-hot lava was starting to erupt through her veins, arteries, bones, and marrow. Her head felt like it was on fire.

"No, he doesn't have a virus." For one crazy moment, she had no clue what he was talking about. She hadn't lived through the height of the AIDS epidemic, and she had never discussed it with Billy. She knew it was still a very real and scary disease, but it wasn't part of their world, really. When it dawned on her that was what her father meant, and the malice behind his words, she thought she might throw up.

Alexis pushed her chair away from the table and stood. She felt light-headed, despite the meal. "That comment was pigheaded and stupid."

Bunny placed her hands over her ears.

"He has cancer. And we are really behind with hospital bills. I know Grandma Eleanor left me the five million dollars for a good reason. I'm here today to ask for some of it. Not for me. For Billy. He has Hodgkin's lymphoma. It's serious."

"Surely the young man has family resources . . ." Her mother tried to join the conversation. Her hand fluttered to her bun, pulling out the tortoiseshell clip somewhat awkwardly.

"He doesn't. His parents disowned him." She didn't want to mention Billy's mother had made a vague mention of helping if Alexis couldn't find the money elsewhere. The idea that a mother wouldn't visit her only child when he was dying made Alexis want to rob a bank, or speak to her father. Anything but go back to that woman and her somewhat pained voice, like Alexis was asking her to subscribe to a newspaper or switch phone plans.

"Understandably," John Allbright said sarcastically.

Alexis glared at him. "That's all you know, isn't it? Disowning your child. And why, Dad? Because I didn't want to be a lawyer? So fucking what?"

A gasp from Bunny. "Lexa!"

"Oh, have another vodka, Mom."

John Allbright smiled coldly. "I see you are still not able to keep your feelings in check. Perhaps it's better you didn't become a lawyer, after all. But my mother left you and Mark that money specifically stating that you would follow me into the family firm."

"Mark never would have been like you, and you know it," Alexis said. "When he got back from Iraq he was going to drive across the country in an RV, and take college classes. He wouldn't have ever become a lawyer."

Her father laughed bitterly. "Nonsense. He was going to complete that tour and apply to law school that spring. We had it all set up."

"Bullshit," Alexis said.

"Watch your mouth, young lady. I threw you out of this house once. I'm not afraid to do it again." He stood, his former polo-playing shoulders still powerful.

"Yeah, Dad? And how should I speak to you? You've never let me have a voice in this house. No woman is allowed to. You dope Mom up all day so she's like a fucking rag doll—"

"Alexis!"

But Alexis ignored him. Bunny started sobbing loudly into her hands like her heart was broken.

She stood up, meeting his eye. "You have a wife who is an alcoholic, and you do nothing about it. Both of you have been depressed for years. Mom solves it with booze, and you quiet your pain by working all the time. You sit there and judge other people and don't do *shit* when your own family needs you."

Bunny looked as though she'd been slapped. A red flush crept up her slim neck like ivy on a wall. Her father's fist came down on his plate, cracking it in half. Small pieces of glass lay on his suit leg. Her mother sobbed louder. Alexis jumped involuntarily, but stood her ground. A vein pulsed in her father's neck.

"I will not have this kind of talk in my house. Every time you come home it's something else. I didn't think you could upset your mother any more than dropping out of school, but this time you've really done it."

For a split second she wavered. His voice, the fury in his eyes . . . she felt five years old again, being reprimanded for some small crime. He was terrifying when angry, which was what made him such a good trial lawyer. He was still a big man at sixty, not having shrunk in that typical way men do as they age, and people cowered when he advanced on them in the witness stand. She felt the baby flutter its feet, and it gave her an inner strength.

"Billy does not have AIDS. Not every gay man who gets sick has AIDS. It's time you got over your homophobia, Dad, that's *so* outdated. He's my only friend in the world, my only family as far as I'm concerned, and I'm losing him. I will never come back here, and don't contact me in New York. I don't need your money. I'll figure something else out."

She picked up her purse by the front door. Then called out, "Mom?"

Bunny picked up her head, her once-beautiful blond hair showing streaks of gray, her tight face looking bleary and confused. Alexis wondered why she ever could have thought Bunny still looked young.

"Mom, if you ever stop drinking and want to get in touch with me, I won't change my phone number. That way you'll be able to find me. I hope someday you leave him. Just call me, okay? And I'll come and get you."

Her mother nodded, looked as if she wanted to say something, but instead gently eased herself off the kitchen chair, walked over to Alexis and touched her cheek. Alexis slowly closed the front door. She stood on the front walkway of her million-dollar house then glanced at the stupid heart-shaped boxwood bushes the gardener had clipped, the gleam off her father's Jaguar, Mark's bedroom window she used to raise for him when he'd sneak home after romancing some girl in the middle of the night. This hadn't been home for quite some time.

Her tiny apartment with Billy and Vanya. That rattrap was home, her *real* home. Not this McMansion with its ugly secrets.

She had one last thing to do before she left Greenwich forever. She got into her rental and drove over to the cemetery where Mark was buried. At one point, two deer walked into the road, but she had plenty of time to brake; her head turned and followed their soft brown leaps back into the woods.

Dusk fell as she pulled up to the cemetery. Two stone angels guarded the entrance, the light from the sky rendering them an inky blue. The grounds were pretty, if that was possible in a place of mourning, rolling green hills surrounded by oak trees big enough to wrap your arms around. Their leaves shone, glistening in yellows, greens, and oranges. She had not come here since the funeral. Alexis didn't believe in the afterlife and preferred to remember her brother as a living, breathing person. She had a crisp, perfect memory of him as a child. The family would drive up to Vermont on family vacations to a small rented cabin on a lake. When they arrived he'd run from the car, throw his T-shirt off onto the ground, and plunge off the dock, coming up sputtering, grinning, and shaking his head like a dog.

Someone had placed rocks on the top of his grave. Alexis had read somewhere this was a Jewish tradition, and she was touched that a stranger had visited his grave and cared.

On his tombshine sat a statue so large and hideous she knew he would have hated it. But when you die young, you don't get any say in your burial. Made of marble, it depicted a kneeling soldier, rifle in hand, tending to another wounded on the ground. The soldier's helmet was next to him.

MARK JONATHAN ALLBRIGHT
1983–2008
AMERICAN HERO
SAVED THREE MEN'S LIVES IN IRAQ BY PLACING HIMSELF IN
HARM'S WAY
GONE BUT NOT FORGOTTEN

Gone but not forgotten. No, he had not been. Not by Alexis, or her parents. She knew if Mark were alive he would have steered Bunny into rehab. He'd tell their father to get off his high horse about Alexis dropping out of law school. To give her the inheritance to help Billy. He would have said all of this in that fake Irish brogue he'd sometimes put on, which would make them all laugh, squinting one of his eyes closed like some drunken pirate.

"I'm pregnant!" Alexis whispered to the statue, the remains of her brother buried somewhere beneath. Then, "I'm pregnant!" she shouted the words and the wind picked them up, scattering leaves in a swirl around her, as though Mark were somewhere listening and nature was giving her a sign. She smiled through her tears. It felt so good to finally tell someone. She sat in a crouch in the grass and was wracked with sobs.

"Alexis?"

She turned, but had been crying so hard that Noah's figure was a blur. She wiped her nose on her sweater sleeve and blinked.

"Noah? What . . . what are you doing here?"

He touched the statue. "Is this Mark?"

"Yes. Noah, Mark. Mark, Noah." She stood up too quickly and leaned on Mark's grave until the dizziness passed. Something to do with her blood volume increasing, at least that's what the baby books said.

Noah approached her gingerly. He put his arms out, and she ran to him, keeping her round belly to the side so as to not squish the baby, but hugging him as hard as she could. His waist felt so narrow, the gray cashmere sweater he wore under a green Patagonia coat soft as fur beneath her hands.

"I'm so sorry," she said, still crying.

"No. I'm the one who is sorry," Noah said. His brown eyes were liquid chocolate. Warm, deep. He wiped away her tears with his big thumbs. "I never should have called *Skinny Chick* stupid. I didn't mean to hurt your feelings. I've been reading all the past blog posts, articles, and message boards. It's really a work of art. The writing is excellent."

"You know what?" Alexis said, laughing. "It is a little stupid, sometimes. A little shallow. *I* acted a little shallow. And I really am happy without that fancy phone."

Noah grinned widely, his teeth very white against the twilight, and placed his hands around the small ball of her belly. "You kept the baby," he said, pleased. Behind him, she saw a woman crouching down, placing flowers on the ground in the distance. The graves were muted, gray and silver half-moons in the dark green grass. She thought of the years she still had left with Noah. She didn't want to waste any more time.

"I did," Alexis breathed. "I thought about what you said. We're not kids. This baby is a surprise, not unwanted. We messed up, but it can turn into a *good* mess-up, can't it?"

God, the man had a sexy grin. "Definitely."

He touched her face tenderly. "I kept begging Billy for news, but he said it was up to you to tell me. He can be really fucking stubborn."

Alexis laughed. It felt good. "He can be," she said. "But I love him so much."

"Me, too," Noah said.

She reached up to where his famous 'fro had been. "Your hair—it's all gone." She'd seen his new haircut when she watched him from the window of her bedroom, but up close it was even more startling.

He ran his hand over his scalp. His head was beautifully shaped, round. "Shaved it when Billy lost his," he said. "Couldn't let a home-boy go through that alone, you know?"

Alexis stared at him. "Did he tell you I was here?"

"Yup. I bribed him with a Guinness beer muffin, you know those are his favorite. And I got your message. I'd been down in Philly, meeting this guy who is interested in canning my famous chili and distributing it, which would be insanely awesome. I drove here at, like, a million miles an hour." He looked around. "Pretty town. Preppy."

Alexis laughed. "Very." A look of sadness passed over her face. "I just remembered what a weird day I've had," she said.

Noah sat down cross-legged, pulling her onto his lap. He cradled her. "Tell me about it," he whispered.

So they sat there for over an hour, and Alexis talked and talked. Noah listened calmly, wrapping his jacket around her and putting his hands on her belly like it was a crystal ball that could reveal their future. The dirt and grass must have been wet and cold beneath Noah's legs, but he never budged.

She told him everything, every last ugly bit. The governor's wife with snow on her eyelashes who cried during Mark's funeral. His dust-free football medals standing silently on the shelf in his bedroom. Her mother's fading beauty and shaking hands. Her father's grief, and how it had manifested itself, making him hard as stone. The inheritance she'd once turned down. Billy's unpaid medical bills in her pillowcase, which crunched under her head as she slept at night. She sat near her beloved brother's body and talked until she was hoarse.

"What do you think? Am I screwed up or what?" she asked him when she was finished.

"Well, for starters, I think you're very brave," Noah said. Behind him, small birds flew from tree to tree, black against the sky.

Alexis laughed. People had called her a lot of things, Queen of All Media, Skinny Chick, shallow. A bitch. But no one had ever said she was brave.

"I think you've been shouldering a lot of things by yourself, and it's time for me to step up and be the man you need. Your best friend has been very sick. You're pregnant. Your parents are . . . difficult. You're not alone anymore, Alexis. You have me now. We're family."

She stared at him. And then a brand-new feeling swept over Alexis. Joy. Pure, undiluted joy. Their baby nudged again, and her stomach did a flip-flop.

"The baby just moved," she told him, laughing and crying at the same time.

Noah's eyes were bright. He squeezed her hand gently.

"I want to be with you, too, Noah. And I promise I won't look like this forever, someday I'll be my skinny self again."

He smiled. In it, she saw a warm, amused, indulgent expression—an appreciation of her transparent passions and insecurities.

"Not too skinny," he said. "I kind of like you with boobs."

She laughed, punching him on the shoulder. "Perv! But okay. Not too skinny."

"You look hotter to me right now with those curves than ever before, Alexis. I'm serious."

Since their fight, she'd imagined many different scenarios of running into Noah, but this was perfect. Mark, whom she had loved so much, was part of this special day. And as the wind picked up again, and the moon rose in the sky, she realized that she had a family again: Billy, Noah, and that cute little bump.

Shoshana

October

CHESTER, NEW JERSEY

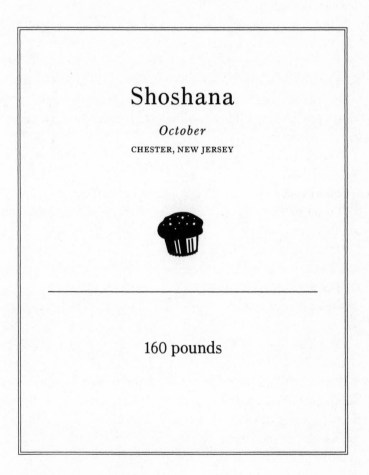

160 pounds

Fat and Fabulous

Dear Fellow Fats and Non-Fats Posse: I apologize for the lack of posts lately, but I think once I explain what the heck has been going on around here it will all start to make sense.

Okay, all you out there. Listen up. Put the chocolate bar down (I'm talking to you, Mom) and turn up the volume in your ears. Well, okay. You can pick up your chocolate again, who am I to say no? I'm just a girl wearing sweatpants with unwashed hair and a plate of cookies on my lap who writes her blog in bed. But I do have something completely crazy to tell you. Pinch shut your nose. Peel open your eyeballs. Shut the door, and close the curtains: I have been going braless here at the farm.

For someone who was forced to answer to the name "Blimp Boobs" in junior high, you can imagine what a triumph this is. Like carrying the torch in the Olympics. I think it's quite possible each of my boobs weighed something like thirty pounds, which, when put together, makes up one Jonas brother.

The *reason* I am able to go braless is the matter at hand here, the big enchilada in the room. Wait, now I'm just craving Mexican food. Yum.

The truth is, dear and loyal readers, I've lost some weight. *Please!* Before you tar, feather, and string me up in the town square, I did not go on a diet or watch what I ate. (That expression always calls to mind people with thick bifocals, holding a magnifying glass to each spoonful of food they place in their mouth, doesn't it?) Let me repeat what

I just wrote in a previous sentence. *I did not diet.* I will go to my grave protesting dieting and the ugly machine that is the weight-loss industry that follows it like a pale and sickly twin. No, I'm not counting food points. The only points a woman should be counting are her bowling league score or how many tubes of lip gloss fit into that tiny pocket on the inside of her purse.

No, dear readers, I lost weight because I inherited this old farm I've been blogging about, and I set out on a one-woman crusade to turn it into a real working apple orchard. Since spring I have been weeding, walking strange dogs with Irish names, trimming trees into half their former size, lugging bushels of brown apples across the orchard to make cider, and painting, sweeping, hanging shelves, and learning how to retile a bathroom.

I've also been buying my groceries at the local farmers' market, a habit I strongly recommend if it is available where you live. Walking into town and asking a farmer what vegetables are in season is education, exercise, and also you get to chat up farmers, who know their produce in and out. We've had posts about buying in season before, but I have to admit I never actually did it! The richness in flavor of a fresh zucchini or tomato is nothing to sneeze at.

This blog has grown exponentially in the last three and a half years. Without all of your pretty little fingers clicking and navigating onto my site, recommending it to friends and family, I'd be nowhere. I *know* I can give just as good advice chubby instead of Fattie, continue to post great nutritional and funny stories, and be your rock when this crap society we live in tries to make you feel unworthy due to your weight. I am here to accept all your comments and questions. That's what *Fat and Fabulous* is all about. Plus, when I gain back the weight (which is a very likely possibility) I know you'll have my back! Shoshana's Apple Orchard is opening. A lot of you who live in the Tri-State are coming. I can't wait to welcome you with open arms and free cider! More posts soon. Wish me luck, I'm more nervous than when I lost my virginity. Maybe because I was drunk when I lost my virginity. But, as always, I digress.

XO,

Shoshana

"OH, MY GOD, HAVE YOU SEEN THIS YET?" EMILY SANG out, throwing a *New York Post* onto the kitchen table with such unrestrained glee in her voice that Pam looked up from her position by the table where she'd just placed two steaming-hot plates of bacon and scrambled eggs. The table was handmade with a piece of driftwood Shoshana bought on eBay, and propped up with two crates. The eggs were laid that morning up the road at a farm where Shoshana donated a lot of firewood, and in return received free eggs. Things in Chester were done this way, an old-fashioned trading of amenities. There was a trust system here.

As Emily breezed into the kitchen from her trip to town and Andrea brewed a fresh batch of coffee, Greg and Shoshana went over the business plan for her orchard on an Excel sheet that made Shoshana slightly cross-eyed. They weren't getting much work done. Suddenly she got a pop-up message on her computer that there was a problem. Did she want to send an error message to Dell to report the issue?

"What are you doing?" Greg asked, looking over her shoulder.

"I'm sending an error message to the server so they fix the problem."

"What, you mean, like, that little message box that pops up when your computer can't load something on a Web site?"

"Yeah. That."

"Shoshana. No one actually looks at your error message, you know."

"Of course they do. I always click the button that says 'send error message,' and someone reads it and maybe fixes the problem for other browsers."

"And who is this person who does it, like, some little old guy with a white beard and silver wand who sits in a cardboard box all day with a laptop, wires running every which way, and he just solves all of the world's computer problems?"

"Perhaps . . ."

Greg laughed. "You are such an optimist. I love it."

"Would you two shut up for one second?" Emily shouted, pointing to the paper. "You gotta read this, Shosh."

Shoshana picked up the paper. As she skimmed the page, her eyes widened. Page Six held a photograph of Alexis Allbright, looking shocked as she exited a Whole Foods supermarket, a strikingly handsome and built black man carrying grocery bags beside her. They were both midstride, and it appeared her companion was shouting at the photographer, making a fist in the air with his free hand. Andrea, who sat across the table and read the article upside down, let out a gasp in the room, which had grown quiet.

MOO! HAS NEW YORK'S MEDIA QUEEN GONE TO THE COWS?

As this picture shows, blogger and socialite Alexis Allbright has put on weight. One Upper East Side doctor we queried estimates seventy-five pounds. Famous for lambasting in the press everyone and anyone whose BMI wasn't up to snuff, it's ironic that the queen of mean is now, well, fat as a cow herself.

"Isn't that the young woman from *Oprah*?" Pam asked, pouring coffee into several mugs. Then, "Gregory, get your feet off that chair."

Abashed, Greg said, "Sorry, Mrs. Weiner."

Shoshana giggled. Pam felt Greg was the son she'd never had, and was known to spit into her palm to fix his cowlick.

"That's the bitch who tried to show up Shoshana," Emily said. She smacked her fist down on Alexis's surprised face, causing the plates on the table to clatter. "And now she's a Fattie! I love it! Serves her right." Frank Sinatra, lying underneath the table in the hope of swallowing a bit of dropped food, let a bark in agreement. Andrea snuck him a slice of bacon.

Shoshana still was in Hoboken several times a week, but her pooch had quickly acclimated to country life, chasing rabbits in the orchard and getting spoiled on sleepovers at Greta and Joe's, where he had oddly enough fallen deeply in love with P-Hen, the peacock, and wouldn't be deterred, even when she pecked at him constantly. He was also best friends with Patrick O'Leary. Both dogs kept Joe Murphy company on his walks around the hills. Greta bought Sinatra a bed monogrammed with the words OL' BLUE EYES.

Shoshana frowned, holding the newspaper closer to her face. Alexis looked caught unawares, her eyes wide and confused, trying to shield her midsection with a shopping bag. Shoshana frowned.

"She might not be the nicest person, but I don't think she deserves being called a cow in the *Post*," she said finally, setting down the paper. "It's not exactly a win for feminism today. Besides, she definitely did not gain seventy-five pounds."

"She looks about fifty pounds heavier, at most," Andrea said. "The *Post* always exaggerates."

It was the weekend, so everyone was gathered at the farm. Emily had moved in three weeks ago, and took the train into the city every day. Andrea, Pam, and Greg slept at the farm Fridays and Saturdays only. They'd stayed up last night playing *The Sopranos* Trivia Game. Pam had shocked everyone by winning with the correct answer to: "Who helped Christopher bury his first victim in the start of season one?" Shoshana and Andrea guessed Paulie, but it was Big Pussy. Emily and Shoshana had collapsed in a fit of giggles at their mother saying, "Big Pussy," and even Greg kept asking Pam for the answer again, just to hear it.

Joe Murphy was often ill these days, but he and Greta came by for the game. Shoshana worried about his health from time to time, but she figured at his age he was not about to quit drinking whiskey or smoking cigars. Shoshana had never had this much fun, surrounded by the people she loved most. The farm was a magical place.

Emily was still stuck on the *Post* article. "Shosh, don't you see you've won? She might have had the last word on *Oprah,* but she looks like a fool in the paper! You deserve to gloat over this. Please gloat." Emily was wearing two slim silver rings in her nose, and she'd dyed her hair flamingo pink. Today it was in pigtails, and she wore black-and-white-striped tights and yellow overalls the color of a parakeet. She looked like a plus-size punk-rocker bee.

"I don't know." Shoshana glanced down at Alexis's picture once more. "It doesn't feel like a win. I just feel sorry for her, to be honest with you guys."

After breakfast she wandered upstairs to make her bed and get out the old junior high school yearbooks of her father's she'd found in the attic. He'd been on the basketball team, a surprise to all. The pictures were hilarious; he had long hair to his waist and a sweatband wrapped around his forehead. He'd been a big guy even then, the number 5 on his jersey stretched out across so it looked like an *s*. A Superman costume.

"Hello, honey." Pam wore scrubs with puppies on them; she was about to leave for work at her nursing job in the pediatric ward. Shoshana could hear her ragged breathing as she caught her breath after walking up the flight of stairs, and wished for the thousandth time there had been some way that instead of losing seventy-five pounds all herself, she could have taken the pounds from her mother and sister, with all three of them losing twenty-five each instead. Emily and Pam couldn't be happier for her, which made it somehow all worse. Or, as Emily put it, "Hell, you lost the weight through hard work fixing up this dump. You should be fucking proud."

"Hi, Mom. Driving to work?" She hugged her mother, inhaling her sweet smell of soap and cinnamon.

Pam looked around the room. Mimi's quilts still hung on the wall, and Shoshana had added some personal touches with Lilith Fair posters, her father's pretty paintings, and small, colorful blue and green vases of different sizes carefully placed on the fireplace mantel.

"Yes, just leaving, sweetie. Hey, I don't know if I've said it enough, but you know how proud I am of everything you've done with this farm. Your father would have loved to see it fixed up."

Shoshana rolled her eyes and smiled. "I know, Mom. You say it, like, a hundred times a day."

"Well, it's true. Your sister and I love spending time here with you." She sat down gingerly on the edge of the bed. Shoshana wished Pam didn't always look guilty about sitting down on beds, chairs, and people's living room couches. She seemed constantly aware of her weight, as if it were an evil twin who went around offending people.

"I wanted to tell you that I agree with what you said about that girl from *Oprah,* the one in the picture?"

"Alexis?"

"Right. Can you call the newspaper up, maybe give a counterquote?"

Shoshana stared at her mother. She fingered the patches on the quilt bedspread, and placed the yearbooks beside her. "Mom, she was horrid to me on TV. I feel badly that the press is slamming her, but I dealt with people judging me because of my size my entire life. And she's not even a Fattie! She probably weighs the same as me. I don't think it can hurt for her to walk a mile in my shoes for a little while."

Pam looked thoughtfully out the window, which had a stunning view of the orchard. A crow flew by, its wings spread widely.

Fall was her favorite season, always so beautiful in New Jersey. It had been Bob's busiest time for work, tending to people's lawns after summer droughts, planting new trees and bushes.

She paused before answering her daughter. "I understand what you're saying. But I disagree with Emily. I don't think people watching *Oprah* that day saw you on the losing side of the battle. I think they saw you as victorious, because you took the higher ground. You didn't get personal, the way she chose to do about Dad. You kept things professional, and even made everyone laugh."

"You're just saying that because you're my mom," Shoshana said, smiling slightly. But there was bitterness in her words. The *Oprah* experience had truly hurt her feelings—crushed them, really. She was fine with being questioned about the motivations behind *Fat and Fabulous*; it was a fight she was willing to take on, for all the fellow Fatties out there. But when Alexis brought up her father, and the way his weight had contributed to his death . . . it knocked all the air out of her chest, left her defenseless. It was like the scene in *Gladiator,* where Joaquin Phoenix stabs Russell Crowe in the chest quickly and stealthily, seconds before battle. Russell fights back, but he's been weakened by the wound. Alexis was a dirty fighter.

"Of course I'm saying that because I'm your mom," Pam said, throwing her arm around her daughter. "But I also mean it. I'm not alone in thinking you took the higher ground. All my girl-friends in my book club agree with me. I'm asking you to consider standing up for her."

"But isn't it enough if I just privately agree the article is mean?" Shoshana asked. "Calling up the paper and making a statement just continues this stupid rivalry the media has made between us. The press loves instigating fights, and this would add fuel to their fire."

"Just think it over, honey. That's all I'm asking."

"Will do, Mom." She pulled the yearbooks onto her lap. "Hey, guess what? I found these old yearbooks of Dad's. From junior high." She called loudly to her sister. The farmhouse was small enough that you could easily hear from one level to the other. "Emily!"

Her sister peeked her head in the room a few seconds later. "What?"

"Come see these crazy pictures of Dad with hippie hair!" The three Weiner women lay on the bed and pored over the yearbooks, another present from Mimi unearthed.

"He looks so young," Pam breathed. "I hadn't ever seen these."

"He must have forgotten Aunt Mimi'd had them all these years," Emily said. Then she hooted with laughter and jabbed her finger at a page. "Look at this one, from shop class! Who knew Dad hung out with all the stoners?"

Bob stood surrounded by a shaggy-looking group of lanky, long-haired adolescents and holding a boat he'd carved out of wood. He wore red bell-bottoms and a tight blue-and-white-striped boat shirt.

"I know that boat, I used to play with it when I was a kid!" Emily exclaimed.

"Yes," Pam said, smiling. "I just never knew he made it."

There was another photograph of their father dancing awkwardly at a school prom, his date so short she looked like a midget. He wore a plaid jacket and his long hair was tied back in a ponytail. His hands rested on her petite shoulders, and he looked so uncomfortable that Shoshana burst out laughing, her mother and sister following suit.

"Oh, my god, how freaked out does Dad look?" Emily said, pointing. Shoshana noticed she'd gotten a tattoo across her knuckles that spelled out LOVE.

"Bob was not much of a ladies' man," Pam said, chuckling. "That was one thing I never had to worry about, your father running around with other women."

She clipped her badge to the pocket of her scrubs and gave each girl a kiss before leaving for work.

Emily was still sifting through the yearbook, looking for more pictures. "It was just the two, believe me, I looked," Shoshana said, pushing herself farther back on the bed so she could rest against the bentwood frame. Emily shimmied over, placing her head on Shoshana's shoulder.

"Dad would have loved knowing we're living here," she said. "Remember he used to always bring us here when we were kids? It felt like an obligation, like going to temple. But now I've fallen in love with the place."

"It's cast its spell on all of us," Shoshana agreed. Then, "I feel badly I didn't come more after Dad died."

"Eh." Emily waved her arm in the air. "Get over it. She knew we loved her. Besides, she got crazy as a fox. Remember when she made us egg salad with the shells still in it?"

"Totally. That crunching sound was awful." They both giggled.

The sun moved in the sky, slanting in through the window, warming their legs.

"I feel closer to Dad here," Emily said softly. She shut the year-book and looked at Shoshana.

"Me, too," Shoshana said. "I think . . . I think that's why Aunt Mimi left the house to me, to us. It was like somehow she *knew* it would help us heal after he died, even though she made out her will years before."

"And I love it that you turned it back into an orchard. I can't wait for people to start showing up to pick their own! I asked at the tattoo shop, and I can work there mornings, so I'll be here after-noons to help you. I can woman the stand. I'll bring in lots of business. Everybody likes a woman with a big ass. "

Both sisters giggled.

"Awesome." It was perfect placing Emily in charge of collecting the five-dollar entrance fee, since she was open and friendly and would talk to anybody. "I was actually going to go out there and pick some of the less ripe apples to make cider, do you want to come?" Shoshana asked.

"Totally."

And so they spent the afternoon in the fresh air, collecting apples in wooden barrels found in the back shed. Joe Murphy had taught her to leave the ripe ones alone. (You could tell they wanted to be picked if they were yellow around the stem.) Frank Sinatra ran around the orchard, digging holes and chasing sticks. They had to use the pick 'en poles a few times for the higher apples, but the rest were reachable. Ripe apples twisted off easily, but since they were going for nonripe, they had to really struggle to get some off the branches. Bees and other insects hummed in the grass, and Shoshana worked up a sweat even with the cool breezy afternoon. Emily made for good company, telling funny stories about big, tough rock musicians who came into her tattoo shop, only to freak when she brought out her needles.

That night, Shoshana decided to host a wine-tasting. She had a full house, with all her Hoboken roommates plus Emily. When she'd moved into Mimi's house, so many neighbors had brought over bottles of wine (made at local vineyards) she felt like she'd stepped back in time and it was ancient Greece, with the wine flowing freely, women in white togas lounging and feeding their young lovers grapes by the bunch. So she made everyone wear white sheets, finding several extra ones in the linen closet outside her bedroom. She and Emily made headpieces out of vines plucked from the orchard. She dragged a wrought-iron table out from the shed and cleaned it off.

On the wine bottles, she put numbered pieces of paper over the labels. She put out pens, paper, and a basket of bread to cleanse the palate between tastings. Last, she neatly arranged blue and green glass goblets for the wine. She was glad Pam was at work, especially when things got a little wild and witching-hourlike, with some friends stripping and running through the fields, Sinatra barking at their heels.

Greg brought over his new girlfriend, Jessica, a hairdresser at a Hoboken salon. She was tall and blond with a Jersey spray-tan, and had a large nose that Shoshana found charming. Shoshana had always liked women with big noses; it gave their faces character. After several bottles of wine, Jessica came up behind Shoshana, who was sitting on a kitchen chair. Jane and her new husband, Andrew, were telling a story about their honeymoon in Venice. Apparently Jane had fallen into a canal, whereupon she was told by an old woman in the street that she'd never be able to bear children as a result of the contaminated water. Shoshana sat hugging her knees to her chest, something she'd never been able to do when she was heavier. She felt hands running through her hair. Jessica patted her shoulder. "You know, with your cheekbones you would look fabulous with a pixie cut," she said.

Shoshana reached over the table and poured herself another glass of Pinot Noir, then refilled a glass for Andrea, who winked at her.

Shoshana smiled. "Thanks, but females of the plump persuasion don't get short haircuts," she said.

Jessica looked around to see if perhaps she was missing something. "Yeah, but . . . you're not plump," she said. Shoshana blushed. It was so hard to remember this very obvious fact: that she was, indeed, no longer fat. She was the size of the average American woman. Smaller, even. There were so many ridiculous rules she'd cordoned off in her mind. Having short hair was on her list of things Fatties couldn't do, like wear miniskirts or cross-country ski. She knew it was ridiculous and the very sort of prejudice she rallied against; if any of her readers had stated such absolutes she would have asked them what they were afraid of.

There was a flip side to this mind-set. Before losing weight, she'd fantasized that life would be easy when she was thin. That she'd have no trouble finding a boyfriend. Never feel sad again. Become really outdoorsy, go backpacking with Outdoor Bound armed only with half a granola bar and a tarp. Wear four-inch fuck-me heels.

Thus far, she still hadn't found a hot guy who loved former fat girls who ran a blog and an orchard at the same time. (But she hadn't given up hope. She was cute and now an entrepreneur; who didn't think *that* was sexy?) She still felt sad from time to time, but no more than the average human being. The only outdoors traipsing she'd done was around her farm, and that had been in the beat-up sneakers she'd had since high school. As for the four-inch fuck-me heels . . . let's just say she was happy in either sneakers or the heavy plastic orange Mario-Batali-like gardening clogs Mimi left behind.

She forgot her weight loss constantly; but it was like a limb that had been sawed off, and she still felt tingling and itching sensations where it had once been attached to her body. She'd worn her plus-size bra until Emily had grabbed at the extra fabric through her dress a few weeks ago.

"Your tits are hanging loose, babe," she said, in her usual tactful way. "We need to take you bra-shopping."

So they'd driven to the Short Hills Mall, and Shoshana had nearly fainted when she was measured for a size 36C. "I haven't breezed past the letter *D* since the sixth grade," she'd said to the saleswoman, who hadn't looked in the least bit fazed by this proclamation. Pam came along, insisting on helping Shoshana shop, although she'd refused to buy something nice for herself in any of the stores, saying she preferred to "just order something from the catalogs."

Emily and Shoshana had exchanged a look while strolling through the mall, hordes of yuppies getting an insanely early start on holiday shopping. It broke Shoshana's heart that her mother never did anything nice for herself. It was as if by being heavy she felt she had to keep saying, "Excuse me," simply for *existing*. Buying clothing in a department store was a simple experience for most women; for Pam it was sheer torture. "Everyone stares at me," she said softly, when Emily pressed her.

So when Jessica stated the obvious, that Shoshana was no longer big (Jessica hadn't known Shoshana before, of course, and saw only the curvy yet fit young woman in front of her), Shoshana responded, "You know what? Fuck it. Let's do it. Cut away."

And that was how she found herself with an adorable bob. She had to run into the bathroom and stare at her reflection several times; it was her, and yet it wasn't. The haircut framed her face, light and whispery. All the years she'd had that long mane because she thought her face was simply too round to look good with a bob. Her long hair had been a curtain she'd hidden behind. She'd thought it was the only thing pretty about her, when in fact her deep brown eyes and clear, porcelain skin were there all along. And it took a complete stranger, a new friend, to show her the light.

The following morning, Shoshana woke around eight-thirty. Frank Sinatra lay snoring on the pillow next to her, and woke with a snort when she opened her eyes. She was waking earlier and earlier these days, juggling both the blog and the orchard. Just yesterday Emily had pointed out that the Red Delicious were ripe. Today she would have her first customers coming to pick their own. Last week she hung signs in town and placed an ad in the local paper beside sales of tractors and hens.

She scrolled through her e-mails. It was pretty much what she'd expected. Half her readers were shocked and horrified at her weight loss, accusing her of being a "sell-out" and "fraud." She wanted to scream, *I'm the one who freaking started this blog! I get to weigh whatever the hell I want to!* But she'd been heavy too long not to understand that their feelings and negative feedback were rooted in fear and confusion. They'd looked up to Shoshana. She was expected to be the most self-deprecating, the most fat, the funniest. Their idol had changed, and the fans were displeased.

However, the other half of the responses to yesterday's post were warm and positive. It was always that way with the Internet, wasn't it? Shoshana developed a thicker skin since starting *Fat and Fabulous*, although she still wanted to please everyone, though she knew that was impossible.

"You should be so proud that you lost weight through walking and eating fresh foods," Amy from Des Moines, Iowa, wrote. "Not dieting or running yourself into exhaustion, like most girls. I can't wait to see what your next blog posts are about. Keep up the great work!"

And from Mary Lenihan from Poughkeepsie, New York:

"Shoshana, I have followed your blog posts for three years. I've always known you to be nothing but genuine and funny. Your posts brighten up my day. I love you at any size. Three of my girlfriends who read your blog are going to make a trip in a few weeks to buy apples from your farm! Here's hoping there's an apple pie left for me. Hugs, Mary."

She edited tomorrow's post, a response by Dr. Amanda Weber to a report recently released from the American Heart Association that stated fatter patients were more likely to survive hospitalization and invasive treatments. The doctor's writing was getting better and better; Shoshana was proud she'd found her articles on positive messages for heavier women in a small newspaper and recruited her to write for *Fat and Fabulous*. Dr. Weber had become a gem. At first her writing and tone were stiff and doctorly, but after a few gentle edits she'd really figured out *F&F*'s breezy, girlfriends-chatting type of dialogue.

After checking all her messages, some which made her cry (in a good way), others that made her laugh out loud, and still more that made her cry yet again (in a bad way), Shoshana shut down her computer and sat on her bed, thinking. The house was silent, everyone tucked into their beds, sleeping off hangovers. She ran her fingers through her hair, enjoying the way it swept across her neck.

She walked to the bathroom and discovered there was a note sticking to her bathroom mirror, along with a photo. She reached up and slowly peeled off the tape that held up the photo, studying the image. It was a picture of Shoshana at five years old, her cheeks round and red. Her auburn hair was in pigtails, tied with two red bows. Two giant hands held her up, and by his slim gold wedding band she recognized them as her father's. A Post-it was stuck to the picture: *You have always been our sweetie pie. Please consider calling the newspaper.* Shoshana sighed. She'd be fifty and her mother's guilt trips would still resonate.

She dug around in her bedroom until she found the unflattering picture of Alexis from the *Post*. The section was edited by someone named Judy Price. Shoshana pictured her: English major, sleek hair, glasses on top of her head, lives in Brooklyn. She Googled the *Post*'s main phone number and asked for Judy Price, who miraculously was in.

"This is Price."

She had a smoker's deep, throaty voice.

"Hi . . . Price. This is Shoshana Weiner, I run a blog called *Fat and Fabulous*."

Pause.

"I'm aware."

This wasn't going to be as easy as Shoshana had thought. "I don't really know how to say it . . ."

"Is this about the Alexis Allbright story?"

"Uh . . . you mean the picture?"

"No. Story. Girl made everyone feel shitty about not being skinny, then gets fat herself. Makes for great print. I saw what she did to you on *Oprah*. Ouch."

"Yeah, well, that's kind of why I'm calling."

"Shoshana, my father used to have a saying. If you have a mouthful of shit, spit it out."

Shoshana stared at the phone.

"Right. Well, the thing is . . ." She glanced down at the clipping on her lap. At Alexis's startled eyes, her protective hand over her midsection, unsuccessfully hiding her weight gain from the camera. Shoshana sat up straighter. "I want to make a statement about the picture you ran."

"Yeah? What kind of statement?" Shoshana could hear typing in the background. She pictured Judy Price as a multitasker: pencil behind her ear, jabbing at keys, drinking a mug of coffee, and talking to Alexis, the phone glued to her shoulder.

So Shoshana told her, and when she was finished, Judy Price had a humdinger of a quote for tomorrow's paper.

Shoshana went downstairs to wake up her lot; each person had a special role for the orchard's grand opening. After jumping up and down on Emily a few times and ducking her sister's threats to "punch you in the vag," she rapped on Greg and Jessica's door, likewise with Jane and Andrew (in case either couple was having some early morning loving, she didn't want to disturb them by opening their doors), and snuggled Andrea spoonlike until she finally agreed to get out of bed due to Frank Sinatra licking her face with his doggie breath. Next, she woke up Karen and Aggie, who had gone out late last night to the Black Horse Tavern, a bar in Mendham. Shoshana heard them come in sometime around two, Aggie's dreadlock bells jingling as she walked up the driveway.

"Wow, your haircut looks really pretty," Karen said now, stretching her long legs and yawning.

"Thanks. Now get your butt in the shower."

Shoshana was opening the gates at ten o'clock, so she put out cereal and milk for everyone. Fuel. As her friends padded downstairs barefoot and ate, chatting away, Shoshana looked around and realized she had fallen in love after all: with the farm. It brought all the people she cared about under one roof, and gave her a passion she'd never known she had: to grow and tenderly take care of apple trees. The scent of their trunks, the shine in their leaves, the smell of fresh cider . . . she was indeed in love. There was work to be done each season, and she was excited to take it on.

Joe Murphy and Greta arrived after most of the breakfast bowls had been put into the sink and washed by Aggie. Everyone got a kick out of Joe, who recently invited her whole crew over for dinner, plying them with whiskey and his stories of overseas travel when he worked in the oil industry.

Shoshana divided the work to be done: Joe and Greta would educate people on the history of the orchard and help them choose the type of apple they desired. Aggie, Andrea, and Jane were put in charge of commanding the apple pie booth. The pies were all made with Red Delicious; after a taste test with Greta, they agreed it was the best type of apple to make pies from. Andrew and Greg would serve free apple cider to guests milling about the grounds, and Jessica would woman the gate in case anyone needed directions up the driveway.

Shoshana offered a percentage of sales to all her friends, yet they'd politely refused. "It's your orchard!" they'd exclaimed. "Besides, it's fun to come out here to the sticks and mooch off you." No one would accept any percentage of profits, not even Greg, who'd helped her trademark the orchard's name and drew up the business plan, which they finally went over together late last night.

Shoshana walked outside to put the final touches on the orchard, hanging a wooden sign at the foot of her driveway road so people knew where to turn when coming from town. Aggie had painted SHOSHANA'S APPLE ORCHARD in cheery red and green lettering. Aggie had also donated a four-foot-tall penis sculpture to bless the farm, which Shoshana had quietly whisked away and hidden inside the back shed.

Pam returned from her shift at the hospital just as Shoshana was about to open the gates. She stood with her arms around both her daughters' waists, surveying the property from the driveway. She saw the fresh coat of white paint Greg had put on the house. The yellow and violet mums Mimi planted so long ago had come up, dotting the landscape. She saw the pretty white rocks that now filled the driveway, the apple orchard that had once been a tangled jungle, now with seventy-five apple trees, cut short and thinned out, their beautiful branches hanging sideways like arms reaching for a hug.

"I am so proud of both of you," Pam said, her eyes welling with tears. "Mimi would have been thrilled."

Shoshana smiled. It had been more work than she'd ever imagined, but with the help of friends both old and new, it all came together. Holy shit, she was a frickin' *farmer*! A reporter from *New Jersey Monthly* was coming out next week to interview her and take pictures of the house and orchard for a profile. She suspected Pam of calling the magazine, but she had no proof.

"I love it here," Emily said. "It's so *you*, Shoshana."

"Will you keep the Hoboken apartment?" Pam asked.

"As long as I can afford to, sure," Shoshana said. "It's not that much for rent, and I like being able to live in the city and country at the same time. I can hang out here taking care of my apple trees, but hop on the train and be in Hoboken in an hour, go out in the city, see Broadway shows, and visit Em at work. I feel really lucky."

"I just can't believe how little there is of you to put my arm around!" Pam said, giving her oldest daughter a squeeze.

Both girls laughed. Shoshana had been unsure how Emily would react to her weight loss, but she'd been nothing but happy for her sister. "Being fat ain't fun," Emily said one night as they lay on the grass outside the house, looking up at the stars, looking for the Milky Way. "Let's be honest."

There had to be a balance, which was the direction Shoshana was struggling with when it came to *Fat and Fabulous*. She wanted to exist somewhere in the middle of fat and skinny, and she was going to figure it out, no matter how long it took. She might not have all the kinks worked out just yet but she would. Her weight, her body . . . it was all an adventure we call life.

Around eleven, when Shoshana started to fear no one would show up, a few families started walking up the driveway, looking curious.

"That's my cue!" Emily said, walking over to her little table where she had a PICK ALL YOU WANT FOR FIVE BUCKS! sign.

Soon after, cars started pulling up the driveway, and folks from Chester and many surrounding towns streamed into Shoshana's Apple Orchard. She recognized several farmers whose products she'd bought in past months, and walked over to greet them. The seeds Mimi, Georgina, Joe, and Bob had planted so long ago gave Shoshana some of the juiciest apples around, everyone agreed.

The day sped by in a blur. The opening was a smashing success. She sold every pie, chatted with neighbors, loaded barrel after barrel full of red apples into pickup trucks, and finished the last of the apple cider. As the sun shot dark red and purple rays into the expansive sky, Shoshana and her friends packed up the tables and shared the very last apple pie, which Shoshana had saved, heating it up in the oven. Greta made an assembly line in the kitchen, plopping a scoop of vanilla ice cream on each plate. Joe Murphy had snuck nips from his whiskey flask throughout the day, and now slept sitting up on the living room couch, Frank Sinatra and Patrick O'Leary cuddling at his feet and his pipe still stuck in the corner of his mouth. "Yer fa-tha would have been real proud," he'd said to her earlier in the day.

He grunted a few times in his sleep, and then seemed to rouse himself. He was wearing the three-piece suit he'd worn the day she met him, the vest and jacket perfectly pressed and neat even though he'd been napping in it. Shoshana sat on a purple velvet armchair across from him, finishing her pie. Sinatra woke and came to jump up on her lap, helping himself to a taste of the food on her plate, lapping it with his crooked tongue.

Greta came into the room with Pam. She wiped her hands on her apron and walked over to Joe, pinching him hard on the nose.

"Christ, woman!" he howled.

"Oh. Sorry. I thought you were still asleep," she said.

"Bloody hell. No. Just a little drunk," he muttered. "And I haven't forgotten about our announcement, neitha'."

"What announcement?" Emily asked. She'd walked into the room and sat down on Shoshana's lap. Shoshana grunted and then tried to cover her mouth so as not to let the sound escape.

"My mother used to say don't call it a trout till it's in the bank," Joe said, standing and lighting his pipe.

"Eh, shut up, old man. You're in the bank, and you know it."

"Wait, I'm confused. Who is the trout?" Greg called out from the kitchen, where he was playing cards with Andrew and Aggie and drinking a beer.

"Seems I'm to get married," Joe said. And he blushed, which was so out of character Shoshana let out a huge laugh.

Pam ran to Greta and hugged her. "Greta! I have goose bumps. After all these years."

Greta shrugged. "Everyone we loved is dead. We figured, what the hell?"

It wasn't exactly the most romantic of wedding announcements, but it would do.

"I t'ink this calls for some celebrating," Joe said.

"Fuck, yeah," Emily said. She shook her head. "Picture that, you two old buzzers, falling in love."

"Well, don't get ahead of yerself, now, woman," Joe said. "It's more like I finally realized this beast on my back wasn't getting off."

"Pshaw," Greta said, laughing. "You just didn't want to die alone, you old fart. You need someone to change your diapers."

"Oh, hell, if I'm gonna marry you, the least ya can do is take me in the back of the house and shoot me like a lame horse," Joe said, sipping from his flask.

"You two," Pam said, smiling. She clasped her hands to her ample bosom. "I know Mimi would be so happy about it if she were here. I'll get the cups." She rushed into the kitchen and produced several mason jars, which Joe filled with whiskey. Everyone had some, even Pam.

While Greta and Pam prepared dinner in the kitchen, Shoshana's friends stood around on the screened-in back porch, laughing and teasing one another. Someone found an old transistor radio in a drawer, and Creedence Clearwater Revival's "Proud Mary" played. Shoshana leaned into the music like it was a warm wind. It had been a day she would remember for the rest of her life.

The next morning, Shoshana stared at the bright glaring light on her laptop. She couldn't believe what she was reading in her in-box:

Hi Shoshana, this is Alexis Allbright. You can totally say no if you want, but I was wondering if you'd meet me for a cup of coffee to-morrow. I know from your blog you live above a coffee shop, I could come meet you there in Hoboken? I would understand why you

would say no, but I just wanted to thank you for what you said in
the Post. *Coffee is on me, of course!*

It was the exclamation point at the end that got to her. It was so
darn cheerful. For so long, Alexis Allbright had stood for every
pretty, skinny girl who laughed at Shoshana in high school, glared
at her as she tried to ease her bulk into a crowded train seat, giggled as she jogged past them. She'd been the dark to Shoshana's
light, the enemy lying in wait for her in the Fat-O-Sphere. The
media pitted them against each other in article after article. Whenever a new story about obesity hit the press, they'd both get interviewed. She was so used to hating Alexis that she had no idea what
she would say to her when they were face-to-face. Besides, what did
Alexis want that she couldn't just say in an e-mail? This wasn't the
Alexis she knew. It was like Darth Vader lifting his mask and suddenly singing out hits from *The Sound of Music.*

She hit reply and sat staring at the blinking cursor. It was Sunday. Her friends would be going back to Hoboken anyway. She
could hitch a ride and not have to take the train. (As much as she
dearly loved New Jersey Transit, it made a lot of stops from Chester
to Hoboken and that made the trip agonizingly slow.) She thought
about her mom's advice. Alexis's frown line between her eyebrows
and cruel, black heart. She didn't trust her. Surely Emily would
agree the only reason to meet in person again would be to tell her
to go to hell. But telling people off wasn't Shoshana's style. She
sighed, looking around her bedroom at the soft salmon-pink of
the walls, the pretty lace curtains she'd found in an antique store
in town, Mimi's black-and-white stills from movie sets, her beaded
lampshade, the vase of blue hydrangea flowers Pam left on her
bedside table. She was happy, happier than she'd ever been before.
So what could Alexis do or say that would take that away?

It was that exclamation point that finally won Shoshana over. It
was cute and girly, written in the style *she'd* type to friends, or to
her readers. Shoshana sometimes put so many exclamation points
in her blog posts she was teased about it.

She typed quickly, before she could change her mind. "Hi Alexis, got your e-mail. Coffee tomorrow sounds fine."

She shook her head and erased the word "fine."

"Coffee sounds nice. How about Empire at two o'clock?"

She had barely hit send before Alexis's name popped right back up on her in-box.

Shoshana paused. She moved her mouse over Alexis's name and clicked.

"Great! See you there."

She looked out the window and the stirring of people walking around below washed over her in muted sound. Dishes clattering, voices murmuring, toilets flushing. There was an unused paintbrush from a watercolor Pam was working on left on the windowsill, and Shoshana reached to pick it up, running the soft bristles over her palm. She liked the feeling.

Driving back to Hoboken that afternoon in Greg's car with Jessica in front, squished between Andrea and Aggie, and Frank Sinatra asleep on her lap, Shoshana watched the scenery, her cheek pressed against the window, as they drove over the Pulaski Bridge. Planes landing at Newark Airport flew directly overhead; she imagined if she reached her arm out, she could touch one. Traffic was snarled, the bridge looking as though it were made of cardboard, lit against the sky with unnatural shades of orange and purple. Exhaust and steam merged on the street below, creating a heat mirage that made the buildings of Bayonne and Union City seem as though they were melting.

"Did someone fart?" Andrea asked.

A chorus of "Nope"s.

"Just New Jersey, then," Andrea said, satisfied. It was a conversation most people had on the expanse of travel between Newark Airport and the Holland Tunnel. Even natives felt a certain satisfaction in asking a rhetorical question. A simple checking-in of olfactory wellness, if you will.

Shoshana smiled. She felt at home in both places: Hoboken and Chester. And yet they were so different. Perhaps it was symbolic, of both *Fat and Fabulous* and *Skinny Chick*. The two blogs had separate agendas, but did they have to be pitted against each other as enemies? If Shoshana found beauty and love in both towns, couldn't she find peace and a middle ground with Alexis?

The following day, Shoshana woke up in her bed to find Frank Sinatra licking his pink and black paws on the pillow next to her head. "Who needs a man when I've got you?" she crooned at him, and he licked her face in agreement. She stared into his bug-eyes and scratched him behind his ears the way he liked.

She could already smell the coffee beans roasting downstairs as she put on jogging shorts and laced up her sneakers. It was a nice day outside and she felt like exercising. She still marveled at her own agility; she could bend down over her leg and tie her shoe-laces. When she was heavy, she would have to put her leg up on a chair to reach over her stomach. Another thing about weighing only 150 pounds: she wore shorts. Shorts were not her friend before, the material getting stuck between her thighs and chafing her, the shape of them cutting off her body at mid-leg and making her legs look like two sausages. She'd walked over to a jogging store on Washington yesterday and picked up a pair of cute pink mesh shorts. Peering outside now, she didn't see much sun, so she threw on a long bright orange scarf with red flowers and a sweatshirt that read FAT AND FABULOUS at the last minute.

She walked the mile through town, dodging beer delivery trucks, mailmen, dog walkers with their packs, and stroller moms. A street-sweeping truck beeped near her as it collected the leaves that had already given in to the season. It was warm for October, still in the low seventies, but gray and cloudy, making the skyline of Manhattan on her left seem that much grander, the lights in the buildings shining across the Hudson, a dark blue barge making its way lazily up the river. The town's maintenance crew chased a flock of geese off the lawn of the shipyard pier, and the birds took off in unison, flying for a destination where they'd hopefully be more wanted.

A woman with a child yelled, "Leave the birds alone!"

One of the men responded with, "It's these guys that took down that plane into the Hudson!"

"Jeez," Shoshana said to Frank Sinatra. "No love for geese these days."

He growled.

"Hmmm, maybe you agree with the men," Shoshana said, wagging a finger at him. She could see the Empire State Building's radio signal flashing red from its roof, the Chrysler's fish-scale design, and all of downtown's low settlements stretching to the Financial District. Her favorite parts of the skyline were downtown and uptown. She could just as soon skip the middle part; Times Square and Penn Station were a zoo. The NEW YORKER sign lit up bloodred against the stark sky.

She did her loop around Hoboken, and then sat outside at Onieals for an iced tea. Sinatra sat in her lap, his pink tongue protruding from the corner of his mouth. A football game was on the television inside, and although it was early in the day there were a few people eating lunch outside.

After promising the friendly bartender to come back for the following day's wine-tasting event (she'd bring her roommates), Shoshana walked home. The day had soft edges. She'd almost forgotten about meeting Alexis for a cup of coffee. Remembering this immediately twisted her stomach into knots.

Last night she couldn't sleep, stressing about what she would say to Alexis. She even practiced telling her off, trying out what she would say on Frank Sinatra, who had jumped and hidden underneath the bed. Now things no longer seemed so finite or troublesome. Her feelings were murky, and she wasn't sure what Alexis would say to her. However, she had started her own apple orchard; she could deal with a rude skinny girl from Connecticut, for god's sake.

She could make out Alexis's profile in the window of Empire Coffee. Shoshana glanced quickly at her watch; she was fifteen minutes late. "Shit!" She'd been relaxing at Onieals and the time had escaped her. She tied up Sinatra outside.

"Sorry, sorry," she said, sitting down across from Alexis, unwrapping the long scarf from her neck and fanning herself. "I totally lost track of the time, and here you are coming all the way from the city and all."

Alexis blinked.

And just like that, both girls seemed to notice each other for the first time. "You're preggo!" Shoshana shouted, just as Alexis exclaimed, "You lost so much weight!"

They laughed.

"Yeah. I guess I did," Shoshana said. She still felt insecure about becoming so much *less*. About losing the weight. And seeing the admiring look in Alexis's eyes (was there even a green flash of jealousy?) made Shoshana angry, insane as that may be. She did not lose the weight to make people like Alexis admire her. She wished for her old body back, suddenly. She straightened her shoulders. She knew she was damn good at running *Fat and Fabulous*. It didn't matter what size she was.

"I caught hell about it from my readers," Shoshana said.

"I hear you on that one," Alexis said. She frowned. "I didn't lose too many advertisers, but I definitely feel like I need to go in a new direction. A lot of my longtime fans stuck by me, but others moved on. They said they didn't really think I could give advice about keeping weight off when I was putting on weight like a champ, no matter the reason. Sometimes I feel like I want to write about something else, I'm just not sure what. Your readers can box you in. Try to control you. I just don't know what else I'm good at. Except getting knocked up." She winked at Shoshana.

"Wow, I didn't know you did self-deprecating," Shoshana said, still feeling a bit wary toward Alexis.

Surprisingly, Alexis laughed, causing Shoshana to jump in her chair an inch. "You know what? I've been doing a lot of things I never thought I would."

"Oh. Well, who's the lucky guy?" Shoshana asked. Okay . . . if Alexis wanted to talk about boys, she could sit here all day. She loved talking about boys. But she suspected there was another reason for Alexis's visit, and part of her just wanted to get it over with.

Alexis blushed. "His name is Noah. He's wonderful."

Shoshana smiled. "Well, good for you. I'm happy for you."

"Thanks. It's been a crazy fucking year, that's for sure."

She had a potty mouth! Which didn't show up on her blog or any public appearances. Shoshana loved people with potty mouths. Mostly because she had one herself.

"So . . . what is it with your family anyway?" Shoshana asked tentatively. "I mean, I remember you hinted that you hadn't seen them in a long time, when we did *Oprah*. Have things gotten better?"

So Alexis told Shoshana everything, about Billy's cancer, her mother's drinking, losing her inheritance when she quit the law. And as she spoke, Shoshana found herself understanding more and more the bitterness and caustic attitude she'd seen in Alexis that had been such a turn-off. Whenever she'd peeked at Alexis's blog throughout the years, she'd been struck by her coldness, her bitchy attitude. Most of that seemed to have dissipated, if she was judging her character correctly. Her mother always said it was one of her talents, figuring a person out.

"That's a lot to deal with while you're preggo," Shoshana said.

Alexis blew out a deep breath, as though she'd been holding it since she'd walked into the café. "Things are improving, though. After I left Connecticut last month, after the huge fight with my dad, I got a letter from Bunny, who checked herself into an expensive rehabilitation facility in Arizona. I don't know how that came about, especially since I'd been begging my dad to admit her since she started drinking, but however it happened I'm thrilled and we've started up a tentative relationship again."

"That's great!" Shoshana couldn't imagine being lucky enough to have two parents and yet not feeling close to either one of them.

"Yeah. Well, the important thing is that when I told Mom about Billy, she sent me a check. And every week since, she's been sending the inheritance that my grandparents left me, and I've been using it to pay off Billy's medical bills. I don't think my father knows about it."

"Wow!"

"I know. It sounds like we should be on *All My Children,* right? We're a pretty fucked-up family, but I have to admit, I really love these letters from my mom. My dad still says I'm dead to him, but I don't think anything I can do would change his mind. He's an asshole, always has been. The fact that my mom is helping me and Billy, and is interested in her grandchild . . . I don't know. She mentioned visiting me when she gets out of rehab, so I think I'm going to let that happen. I'm a little freaked out by it, but I love my mom, you know?"

"I think this is great. Whether you ever make up with your dad or not, at least you'll have more family in your life. The more family, the better!" Shoshana said.

Alexis chuckled, and Shoshana was again struck by how different her demeanor was.

"Can I get you a cup of coffee?" Alexis asked.

"Sure! I'll have a medium hazelnut with extra cream and extra sugar."

Alexis paused. She'd been about to stand. "So I guess you're not watching your calories, then."

Something came to a halt inside Shoshana. The bitch! She was about to say something snappy right back, but something in Alexis's face stopped her. The thing was, the tone was off. If Alexis was saying it to be hurtful, surely her face wouldn't look so open and relaxed. Shoshana almost felt sorry for her. It was as if Alexis had said it without thinking, that her old mind-set of counting calories hadn't quite caught up with her current rounder self.

And wasn't that a little bit like Shoshana and her weight loss?

Why else was she purposefully eating two dinners a night, and sometimes even two desserts, in some silly effort to gain a little of her weight back, for fear her readers would think she was a fraud? She didn't think she'd ever be besties with Alexis; the girl was still too caustic. But wasn't there perhaps some similarity to be found in their experiences over the last year?

So instead of starting another war, Shoshana simply relaxed. She crossed one sole of her sneaker over her leg and smiled. "You know what? I lost this weight by starting up a farm, out in Chester. I didn't change my diet too much, and I still heart calories!"

Alexis smiled back, though the expression still seemed foreign on her face. Like she was trying it out. "Well, isn't *Fat and Fabulous* always talking about listening to your body? Your body wanted to change, and you listened. You should be proud of yourself."

Shoshana was surprised Alexis had read her blog. "Thanks. You should see the farm sometime. You can come pick your own apples on the weekends."

"I can't wait to hear all about it."

"How's your best friend doing now?" Shoshana asked.

"Billy's in remission, actually. I just found out this morning. His latest tests showed him as cancer-free. But I almost lost him." Tears sprang to Alexis's eyes. "Sorry. I seem to cry all the time now. It's the hormones. They really fuck you up."

"That's okay!" Shoshana said, digging in her purse and coming up with a crumpled napkin for Alexis. "I'm a really emotional person, and I'm not even pregnant!"

Alexis laughed, sniffling and reaching for the napkin. "Let me go get our coffees, then we can talk."

As Alexis stood up and awkwardly eased her bump around the table, Shoshana silently observed how much better she looked. She was still wearing four-inch heels (didn't those make her back hurt?), but the tank top was fitted to her stomach, and she wore maternity skinny jeans and a pretty, knee-length brown sweater with ruffles running down it. Her face, always so angular with high cheekbones, had softened with the additional weight and rounded slightly. She'd grown out her trademark stick-straight blond bob to mid-shoulder-length. Shoshana always thought girls looked better with some shape, and she admired Alexis's butt in an off-hand way in her jeans as she walked up to the counter. In all, she looked curvier. Shoshana approved.

Alexis brought the coffees over, along with a banana nut muffin she cut in half to share with Shoshana, who thought inwardly that maybe Alexis hadn't changed *that* much, as who wanted to eat only half a muffin? But she was surprised when Alexis suddenly spread her hands on the table and looked earnestly at Shoshana.

"I wanted to thank you for sticking up for me in the *Post*," she said.

Shoshana chewed her half a muffin, listening.

"You had the opportunity to get me back and you didn't take it. That takes guts. I . . . I know this is going to sound crazy, but I really admire you. I always have. I was, well, I was jealous of you, really."

Shoshana opened her eyes wide. *This is hard for her*, Shoshana realized. *Much harder for her than it is for me. My mom was right.* "Jealous? Of me? What for?"

"You just always seemed so happy. Blogging about your mom, sister, and that wild pack of roommates. Before Noah came along I had no family that was speaking to me. It was just me and Billy. He was the only friend I had in the world. I guess I've softened up a bit. I used to see the world in black-and-white terms: skinny or fat. It seemed so clear to me that excess weight meant a lack of self-control. Now I see there are a million reasons for it."

Shoshana smiled and tentatively put her hand on Alexis's arm. "Including happiness," she said.

Alexis blushed. Shoshana realized how pretty she was, the rose in her cheeks spreading all the way to her straw-colored hair. She looked so much better at a normal weight, but it wasn't just the weight gain that had her looking better, it was something that radiated from within, a shift in thinking.

"Right. Including happiness," Alexis said softly.

They ended up talking for two hours, as the golden light outside turned to dusk and customers walked in and out in bright, colorful streaks. She eventually felt sorry for Sinatra and smuggled him underneath the table. The hum of grinding beans drowned out their voices. Muted conversations took place around them, and Shoshana came to a place of relaxation finally, within this conversation with a woman who had once been her enemy. A deep calm spread across her chest; her shoulders dropped from around her ears.

It fascinated Shoshana to learn that Alexis had experienced a similar backlash of hate mail from readers because of her change in weight. Alexis had been too afraid to blog about her weight change, but the *Post* story had seen to it that everyone knew. Both girls agreed they couldn't please everyone, and their core readers, the loyal ones who had stuck by their blogs, were the ones giving support and who would stay on. She wasn't sure she and Alexis would ever be super close, but she knew she'd just collected another friend, as Pam would say. She was over the *Oprah* fight; she was through with worrying about whether her readers would drop her because of the weight loss. She was just herself, Shoshana. Her father would be proud.

Alexis and Shoshana

October

CHICAGO

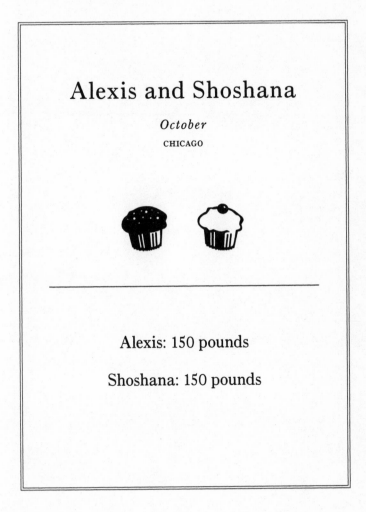

Alexis: 150 pounds

Shoshana: 150 pounds

WHEN THEY GOT TO THE DRESSING ROOM, SHOSHANA and Emily found Alexis struggling with a pair of Spanx.

"You know that's totally insane, right?" Shoshana told her new friend.

Emily eyed Alexis warily. It had taken the entire flight from New Jersey to Chicago to convince Emily she shouldn't kick Alexis's ass.

"Let me get this straight," Emily said to her sister, as they flew over Pennsylvania. "We like her now?" The hum of the motor from the belly of the plane made it hard to hear Emily, who was sitting on Shoshana's left, her mom on her right. Oprah had flown out her immediate family again, much to the delight of Pam and Emily, whose tattooing had slowed. (Her business was highest in the summer months, when New Yorkers showed more flesh.) At the hospital, many of the younger nurses had been let go due to cutbacks, and Pam was working four shifts a week instead of three. She needed the diversion from work.

In recent weeks, Shoshana experienced an overwhelming response to her orchard; after the *New Jersey Monthly* profile came out with glossy spreads of Shoshana surrounded by Greta, Joe, and all her friends with the trees in the background, she'd had an influx of customers and was baking apple pies around the clock. Greta took over the orchard while she was away.

Now, on the plane, while popping peanuts into her mouth, maneuvering them around her lip ring, Emily said dryly, "I still can't pop blondie one?"

"Right," Shoshana said, taking a sip of her free Coca-Cola, which the cheerful stewardess brought over a few moments ago.

"And you two are going on *Oprah* to make a big announcement that you won't even tell your only sibling in the world, who adores you."

"Or her mother!" Pam chimed in, folding her colorful *Food Network* magazine in half. She'd become a huge Paula Deen fan lately, cooking up big batches of comfort food like lasagna and various casseroles for everyone at the farm.

"Correct," Shoshana said. An announcement came on the loudspeaker from the pilot, informing them to begin preparation for landing. Shoshana always found this ridiculous; what was she supposed to do to prepare, ease up on the throttle? The crew came by with a trash bag, and Shoshana leaned over Emily to throw her plastic cup inside.

"But Shosh!" Emily cried. "I can't stand the suspense."

"Well, you'll just have to," Shoshana said, cackling like Dracula at her sister.

When they'd boarded, a painfully thin redheaded woman wearing a gray St. John suit had leaned over and whispered something in the ear of her husband. Shoshana was the closest and overheard:

"I thought they had weight restrictions on airplanes now."

Then, unbelievably, she'd pointed to Pam, who, luckily for the woman, hadn't heard her, and nor had Emily. Shoshana could just picture their trip starting out with bailing Emily out of jail.

"They also have restrictions against assholes," Shoshana had said, leaning over and whispering to the woman. "But I see you slipped right past security."

Ignoring the woman's shocked face, she'd sat down. Having always been heavy, she was hyperaware of the way people viewed her mother and sister these days. She sometimes felt as though she were wearing a fat suit like Gwyneth Paltrow in *Shallow Hal*. An invisible line of energy, about two inches from her body, which pulsated invisibly to everyone else. Some days, her new body felt like a costume she'd tried on. But she was getting used to it. Her roommates took her shopping recently, after tiring of seeing Shoshana wearing ridiculously baggy pants, held up by belts and even string. She grudgingly admitted it was fun shopping at J. Crew and H&M, with all their pretty displays and attractive clothing; before, their sizes had not run high enough to fit her body.

So when she came into the dressing room backstage at *Oprah* and found Alexis struggling with a tan-colored Spanx bodysuit, she grabbed it out of her hands. They'd talked on the phone twice since meeting at Empire. "These are not a friend of the pregnant lady," she told Alexis wryly.

A deep baritone resonated behind Alexis. "Thank you. I tried to do the same, but she wouldn't let me. She seems determined to squash our baby into a pancake."

"I keep telling her bumps are chic, baby," said a slight Asian man with a short buzz of hair growing on his scalp. He had a wary look on his face, like he'd been beaten up recently, but a bright spark of mischief lay just beneath the surface.

"Hi. You guys must be Noah and Billy. I'm Shoshana, and this is my mom, Pam, and sister, Emily."

Introductions were made all around.

Pam walked over to Alexis and put a plump arm around her shoulders. Emily looked at Shoshana and raised one eyebrow.

"Everything okay, dear?" Pam asked Alexis, who had tears in her eyes.

"I refuse to go out there looking like this. Everyone is going to compare me with how I looked the last time I was on the show, when I was skinny."

Pam looked taken aback. "But you're pregnant, love. The baby needs you to put on weight. You look wonderful."

Noah took a sip of his coffee. "I agree. And besides, you were *too* skinny before," he said gently. Then he impishly reached out and pinched her on the behind. "You know I love that booty."

Shoshana was surprised when Alexis laughed. She was able to see why the two were such a perfect pair: Noah extinguished Alexis's neuroses. It happened like that sometimes, she mused, as the soundman fitted her for a microphone, his cool hands on her lower back snaring a wire up through her shirt. This time she didn't flinch; she was an old hand at this. It was someone different, this time.

A person wanders the planet lost, split in half. Then she finds the right person, and wham! She's whole, the anxieties and twitches slow down and dissolve, and the brightness that had always shone within her somewhere is allowed to emerge. Shoshana felt she'd always been a bright spirit and didn't think the man she'd someday end up with would be the one to bring it out of her. Whoever Shoshana would meet and fall in love with would be getting almost two persons: the 150-pound woman, and the Fattie who still lived inside of her. Both versions loved dirty jokes, pillows with weird statements on them, and chick flicks. The boy she chose someday would have to love both versions of her.

Emily was begrudgingly admiring Alexis's high heels, which were quirky and had a taxicab pattern, the toes being yellow, the rest black-and-white-checkered. "They're very punk," she said, which made Shoshana and Pam exchange a look because that was Em's highest compliment to pay someone.

"Five minutes until set," a short woman with red hair and freckles who was wearing a headset said, spreading her fingers like a starfish to show how much time was left. Shoshana glanced at the monitor. The show had not begun yet, and she saw Oprah, which gave her a rush of excitement. Oprah was already sitting on the stage and going over notes with an assistant while simultaneously getting her makeup retouched.

"Okay, I'll give up the Spanx," Alexis said, sighing and, after some struggle, ripping the hosiery down the middle with her bare hands. Everyone cheered. Alexis plopped down on the brown leather couch and poured herself a sip of water into a tumbler glass. "The baby was protesting it, anyway." She rubbed her stomach, which was a perfect beach ball.

"Yeah. If I can't wear a fat suit to try and be who I used to be, you definitely can't try and squish into Spanx," Shoshana said, sitting down next to her.

As their friends and family mingled, snatches of their conversation reached Shoshana's ears as she leaned close to Alexis. "Are you ready to do this?" she asked, wiggling her eyebrows.

Alexis smiled. "I was born ready. Let's show the world what we're made of."

"Two minutes," the stagehand called.

Shoshana and Alexis stood, and Shoshana found herself watching Alexis maneuver in her heels down the same hallway with the large black-and-white photos of celebrity guests she'd eyed last time she was here.

"Knock them dead!" Noah shouted.

"Make sure you mention our clothing line!" Billy called out.

"We love you!" Pam and Emily called. Shoshana watched their figures get shadowy and small as she turned and walked down the hallway, butterflies in her stomach but a steely resolve in her heart.

"What clothing line?" Shoshana whispered to Alexis as they walked.

"Oh! I totally forgot to tell you. Billy and I designed these chill robes for cancer patients who are undergoing chemo. We have leopard-print and zebra and there's even a cartoonist in the Village drawing prints for us. They're going to be awesome!"

"Wow," Shoshana said. "I never would have pictured you doing something like that when I first met you."

Alexis sniggered. "Why, because I was a total selfish bitch?"

"Well, yeah."

"Well, I bet you never thought you'd open up an apple orchard, either," Alexis said, her eyes bright.

"You're right about that." They giggled, as they heard Oprah announcing their names to the audience.

The two women entered the stage holding hands, a show of unity that came naturally and spontaneously to them. They sat on the couch to thunderous applause.

"Hello, hello," Oprah said, turning her warm gaze on them. She wore a brown wrap dress that matched her eyes, and large teardrop diamond earrings that shone under the lights. Shoshana admired her blue eye shadow and wondered if she herself could pull it off. There was no way to find out but try!

"We are so lucky to have two special guests back on today's show, Alexis Allbright, founder of *Skinny Chick,* and Shoshana Weiner, who writes *Fat and Fabulous.*"

Another round of cheers. Shoshana could make out the faces of Noah, Billy, Emily, and her mother. They were sitting in the second row. She winked at Emily, who gave her the rock 'n' roll devil horns. Shoshana ran her hands through her short, wavy bob.

"Now, before we begin talking to these fascinating guests, I'm going to show a brief clip."

Alexis and Shoshana exchanged an oh-shit glance, as the screen behind them rose and the scene between Shoshana and Alexis from last year played out before their eyes. The light bounced in such a way that dark blues ran across Alexis's face, giving her the appearance of having two black eyes.

What Shoshana couldn't believe from the video was how *tense* she herself looked. Her hands balled into fists, a frown on her face as she countered Alexis's accusations. A stranger. It was also strange to see herself fat again. Like looking at one's baby pictures. How could she have morphed and shifted and become someone else in just a year?

Alexis was so upset by how aggressive and nasty she'd been that she kept her eyes on Shoshana's face. She knew if she watched the video she would only feel worse, which would ruin the fun of making their joint announcement. She heard herself shouting statistics about obesity at Shoshana, and cringed. She literally slunk down in her seat when she heard her old self say, *"Her father died of a heart attack. Four years ago. He was only forty-nine. He was mowing the front yard of his quiet suburban home in New Jersey, and he simply dropped dead right there."*

"I'm so sorry," she whispered to Shoshana.

"I know you are," Shoshana whispered back. "I am, too."

Some of the audience hadn't seen this particular episode, and gasped at some of the segments, clapped at others. The clip seemed to go on forever, though it was probably only a minute at most. The girls suffered through it, trying not to wiggle around awkwardly on the sofa.

The lights went back up to full tilt. "I saw the two of you come in here holding hands," Oprah said. She smiled her thousand-watt smile. "After everyone at home watched that video, I have to ask: Y'all worked things out, didn't you?"

Scattered laughter.

"We did, indeed," Shoshana said confidently. "And we're here to tell the audience about it."

"Wonderful. But first, I think the question on a lot of people's minds is, tell us about the baby bump and the weight loss! Is it true you both weigh the same now, a hundred and fifty pounds?"

Thunderous applause.

Alexis blushed. "Well, yes. But also, a lot of things have changed for myself and Shoshana over this past year. My best friend was diagnosed with cancer but he's now in remission, thank god. Hi, Billy!" She waved, and Billy stood, doing a little twirl as the cameras zoomed in on him.

The audience clapped for Billy.

"I met a man who . . . put things in perspective for me, to put it mildly," Alexis said.

"Yes, and I've been to his restaurant, Off the River Ale House in New York," Oprah said. "It is worth the calories, people." She turned on the couch to Shoshana. "Now, Shoshana, you've lost a good deal of weight."

Clapping thundered off the walls, the sound bouncing up, up, up to the ceiling like bright, shiny bubbles. The cameras panned the audience; the lights moved and changed direction on the floor of the stage to illuminate Shoshana's face.

"Yes, that's right," Shoshana said.

"But aren't you the face of *Fat and Fabulous*?" Oprah asked. "How do your readers feel about you no longer being, well . . . fat?"

"This brings us to the main point of today," Alexis said, wanting to rescue Shoshana. "We are here to unveil a brand-new blog."

Behind them on the screen, the words WORTH THE WEIGHT flashed in hot pink.

"Wow!" Oprah said, crossing her bright yellow leather heels at the ankle. "Tell us a little bit about this new venture."

"The idea is to combine *Fat and Fabulous* and *Skinny Chick*," Shoshana said. She felt nervous, but as she spoke she gained confidence. She could see her mother giving the thumbs-up from her seat, and seeing this took the wobble out of her voice. She was her father's daughter. He had loved her so much she had a store of it inside her, giving her strength. It was a wide, silver river, and she could dip into it whenever she wanted.

"Now, I know a lot of readers will feel shocked by this, since Alexis and I had such opposing viewpoints. But lately we've come to realize we have more in common than we thought. We both want what's best for women—to eat healthily, exercise at least twice a week, and have good self-esteem. We are bringing the doctors and nutritionists from both our blogs to *Worth the Weight,* as well as all our contributing writers. We will have a search-engine feature for news articles about nutrition and body image, and continue to fight the war against negativity for women's body issues that the media perpetuates. We'll also include posts that pertain to us personally, such as healthy eating during pregnancy, and ways to feel good about your weight, no matter what size you are."

"I have to admit, I am shocked," Oprah said. She turned to another camera for a close-up. "After watching that video of the two of you arguing, it's wonderful that you were able to find common ground."

She turned to someone working backstage.

"Now, I want to tell you all, I was horrified when I picked up my *New York Post* and saw the photograph printed of Alexis. Steve, can we bring up that picture?" It materialized like a wave of the Good Witch Glinda's wand: the picture of Alexis coming out of Whole Foods, her hand protectively covering her stomach.

Alexis turned away. Shoshana smiled reassuringly at her.

"Alexis, you're wearing a cute little black shapeless dress, so it might be kind of hard for the audience to see you, but do you want to tell us why you were covering your belly in this shot? I don't think it's because you gained weight, right?"

Alexis let out the breath she'd been holding. "I'm pregnant, actually," she said proudly.

The audience cheered. Shoshana clapped so hard her hands hurt.

Oprah shook her head. "It's really a shame that the media seems to only like to print negative stories sometimes. I know the paparazzi have caught me unawares before, and it ain't pretty. They also seem to have totally missed that you gained weight be-cause you were pregnant, which is necessary and healthy for the baby. Most women gain an average of thirty to fifty pounds during pregnancy."

She looked down at her notes. "Now, Shoshana, you followed this up with a comment in the same paper. You said, 'I think Alexis looks much healthier with the additional weight. It's a sad day for feminism when we start criticizing other women's bodies.' Honey, I completely agree with you."

So did the audience, from the sound of it.

"Now I'd like to invite questions. Don't be shy!" Oprah smiled widely.

A tall woman with blond curly hair wearing a black pencil skirt and pink silk blouse stood. "Hi, Alexis; hi, Shoshana. I've been a reader of *Skinny Chick* for a while now. I lost eighty pounds two years ago, and your recipes and advice really helped me through the process."

Alexis nodded. "First of all, congratulations. You look wonderful. And yes. I promise that kind of help and support will remain true with *Worth the Weight.*"

"My question is for Shoshana. Shoshana, as someone who was formerly heavy . . . how do you think you'll be able to continue making girls feel positive and good about themselves at higher numbers than your own weight? Won't it be hypocritical to tell them to be happy being fat?"

Alexis squeezed Shoshana's hand.

"That's a great question," Shoshana began. "The fact is, women often go up and down in their weight throughout their lives."

"I can attest to that," Oprah said wryly, eliciting a big laugh from her loyal audience.

"As a woman who has weighed nearly three hundred pounds at one point in my life, to someone who now weighs a hundred and fifty, the truth of the matter is that my hopes and fears have not changed because I can fit into Juicy sweatpants. I still have insecurities. Alexis and I agree that both of our blogs were too extreme. Just blogging about being heavy or being skinny is boring. Most women are somewhere in between. I lost this weight through changing where I bought my food, and getting a ton of cardio setting up my apple orchard. I didn't starve myself or diet, because dieting is not listening to your body. I feel confident I can continue to counsel and understand women. 'Healthy at any size' is still my motto. That's why *Worth the Weight* is so important; Alexis and I are starting a blog for every woman, not just skinny or fat. Weight is a gray line, not so black and white. I think America is ready for a Web site that doesn't care what number your scale reads back to you."

Thunderous applause.

Oprah scanned the audience. "It seems we have one more question, folks."

Really? Alexis had to pee and hoped they could wrap things up quickly. What else could they possibly say on the subject?

"Yes, I have a question for one of your guests, Alexis Allbright."

Alexis looked up. She knew that voice. She turned her head, and Shoshana was grinning at her like a loon. So was Oprah. What was this all about? Suddenly she saw Noah standing in the aisle with a microphone. Her heart flipped in her chest.

"Alexis Allbright, mother of my child to be. Would you marry me?"

Shoshana let out a little squeal of glee.

Someone in the audience let out a loud whoop.

Alexis swallowed.

"Well, dear, what do you say?" Oprah asked.

Noah made his way down the aisle, getting clapped on the back by a few people, but he ignored everyone and kept his eyes locked on Alexis's.

Her voice trembled, then grew stronger: "Yes. Yes, of course I will."

"She said yes!" Oprah said, beaming. The audience gave them a standing ovation, and the cheering was deafening.

Noah climbed the three steps onto the stage and got down on one knee. Shoshana clapped until her hands hurt. She loved proposals. And weddings. And anything romantic, for that matter. Noah slipped a very small, humble ring on Alexis's hand. Shoshana loved the diamond; it was small, pear-shaped, and not at all the kind she would have associated with Alexis. She would have figured her for a Tiffany girl. However, the ring was beautiful and Alexis was clearly thrilled.

Noah kissed Alexis, to even more cheering. Alexis's cheeks were a bright rosy red.

"Well, I love a happy ending," Oprah said. "And I greatly look forward to reading *Worth the Weight* posts, and having you two back on the show in the near future. I wish you nothing but success," Oprah said, and she stood up to hug both of her guests before they made an exit off the stage.

Oprah turned to the camera closest to her. "When we get back from break, we have a very special guest returning to the show, my friend and yours, Dr. Oz, here on a break from his own show to talk to us about the importance of eating heart-healthy foods."

The ceiling camera panned over the audience as they clapped for Alexis and Shoshana, who exited just as they'd come on the show, holding hands. Once they were out of view they grabbed each other tightly and hugged.

"We did it!" Shoshana shouted.

"We really pulled it off!" Alexis screamed.

"You're getting married!"

"Holy shit, I know! You better be a bridesmaid!"

"I will! I'd wear taffeta for you, I swear!"

They jumped up and down.

Last year felt like a lifetime ago—Shoshana and Alexis couldn't wait to start pooling their resources of advertisers and contributors. They'd rented a studio above Noah's restaurant, where they would share a writing space. Neither could have afforded such an extravagance before. Interest from sponsors was already high, and they had plenty of money for the start-up from a combination of Alexis's inheritance and the money Shoshana had saved from *Fat and Fabulous* advertisements.

Pam watched Shoshana gracefully leave the set, head held high, shoulders back. Grabbing the brand-new soft, pretty pearl-gray coat she'd bought herself that morning in a size XXXL, she couldn't help but beam with pride as she went to congratulate her daughter backstage. She found her holding a glass of champagne.

Gathered together were Billy, Emily, Alexis, and Noah. "To *Worth the Weight*," Alexis said, taking a very small sip, then leaning over to give Noah a soft kiss. The tiny diamond glinted on her finger. Shoshana winked at her, and felt the sweet taste of the bubbly slide down her throat. She looked around the room and felt extremely lucky. It didn't matter if she weighed 150 pounds or 215. What mattered was that she found happiness. And she had. They both had.

Acknowledgments

I'm not sure that anyone ever bothers to read the acknowledgments page, but when I was young and developing a love for reading books it always struck me as a secret passageway into the author's mind; after the reader lives with fictional characters for many pages, when the book is done they are suddenly thrust into a cold bath of reality, and reminded that the world they'd just inhabited has come to an end. Because of this, I hope the warmth behind my words shines through, spreads cheer, and that the gratefulness I feel is evident.

Thank you to Ryan Fischer-Harbage, my agent, who almost a decade ago allowed a kid just out of college to bombard him with a manuscript and a dream, and made that dream a reality.

This book would have never happened if it weren't for my amazing editor, Katie Gilligan, who totally *gets* funny, quirky women. Katie, you are not only a smart and talented person, but you run marathons! You are my hero.

Thank you to the entire Thomas Dunne Books team, the art department for creating such a fun cover, and Dave Cole for copyediting *150 Pounds*. Without his dedicated work I would have dates out of order, characters spouting nonsensical sentences, and Shoshana's bra size wrong.

Thanks also to Kate Harding, author of *Lessons From the Fat-O-Sphere,* which I picked up one day and could not put back down. Thanks for letting me call you up and interview you all the way in Chicago! *Shapely Prose*, though closed down, was a blog that had a huge impact on me.

Thank you to my friend Kevin O'Donnell for helping me come up with a very important expression that Billy uses, and to Dana Spencer for giving birth to the real Noah.

Thank you to my loyal readers, who have not only provided support on Facebook as I wrote *150 Pounds*, but actually bought my first book and therefore made me a writer.

Thank you to my parents, Michael Rockland and Patricia Ard, and my brother, Joshua Rockland, for listening to me talk about this book for two years.